She and Allan by H. Rider Haggard

Sir Henry Rider Haggard, KBE was born on June 22nd, 1856 at Bradenham in Norfolk, England.

After his education he was pushed towards an Army career but failed the entrance exam. Next Haggard was positioned to work for the British Foreign Office but he seems not to have sat that exam. Using family connections, he was sent to Southern Africa by his father in search of a further opportunity of a career.

Haggard spent six years there before a return to England and marriage. He had begun to write and publish some non-fiction in Africa but it was only after studying Law in the hope it might prove to be the proper career his father wanted for him that Haggard began to write fiction, using his African experiences as the basis.

His first fiction was published in 1885 and the following year King Solomon's Mines was published. It was a phenomenal success. His career was set.

Haggard wrote well and wrote often. He managed to sympathise with the local populations even though they were exploited and manipulated by Europeans intent on amassing fortunes in money, people and resources. His writing career covered the great sprint to Empire of several European powers and both reflects and criticizes these events through his well-loved characters including Allan Quatermain and Ayesha.

In his later years Haggard pursued much in the way social reform as well as standing for Parliament and writing a great many letters to The Times.

Henry Rider Haggard died on May 14th, 1925 at the age of 68. His ashes were buried at Ditchingham Church.

Index of Contents

NOTE BY THE LATE MR. ALLAN QUATERMAIN

My friend, into whose hands I hope that all these manuscripts of mine will pass one day, of this one I have something to say to you.

A long while ago I jotted down in it the history of the events that it details with more or less completeness. This I did for my own satisfaction. You will have noted how memory fails us as we advance in years; we recollect, with an almost painful exactitude, what we experienced and saw in our youth, but the happenings of our middle life slip away from us or become blurred, like a stretch of low-lying landscape overflowed by grey and nebulous mist. Far off the sun still seems to shine upon the plains and hills of adolescence and early manhood, as yet it shines about us in the fleeting hours of our age, that ground on which we stand to-day, but the valley between is filled with fog. Yes, even its prominences, which symbolise the more startling events of that past, often are lost in this confusing fog.

It was an appreciation of these truths which led me to set down the following details (though of course much is omitted) of my brief intercourse with the strange and splendid creature whom I knew under the names of Ayesha, or Híya, or She-who-commands; not indeed with any view to their publication, but before I forgot them that, if I wished to do so, I might re-peruse them in the evening of old age to which I hope to attain.

Indeed, at the time the last thing I intended was that they should be given to the world even after my own death, because they, or many of them, are so unusual that I feared lest they should cause smiles and in a way cast a slur upon my memory and truthfulness. Also, as you will read, as to this matter I made a promise and I have always tried to keep my promises and to guard the secrets of others. For these reasons I proposed, in case I neglected or forgot to destroy them myself, to leave a direction that this should be done by my executors. Further, I have been careful to make no allusion whatever to them either in casual conversation or in anything else that I may have written, my desire being that this page of my life should be kept quite private, something known only to myself. Therefore, too, I never so much as hinted of them to anyone, not even to yourself to whom I have told so much.

Well, I recorded the main facts concerning this expedition and its issues, simply and with as much exactness as I could, and laid them aside. I do not say that I never thought of them again, since amongst them were some which, together with the problems they suggested, proved to be of an unforgettable nature.

Also, whenever any of Ayesha's sayings or stories which are not preserved in these pages came back to me, as has happened from time to time, I jotted them down and put them away with this manuscript. Thus among these notes you will find a history of the city of Kôr as she told it to me, which I have omitted here. Still, many of these remarkable events did more or less fade from my mind, as the image does from an unfixed photograph, till only their outlines remained, faint if distinguishable.

To tell the truth, I was rather ashamed of the whole story in which I cut so poor a figure. On reflection it was obvious to me, although honesty had compelled me to set out all that is essential exactly as it occurred, adding nothing and taking nothing away, that I had been the victim of very gross deceit. This strange woman, whom I had met in the ruins of a place called Kôr, without any doubt had thrown a glamour over my senses and at the moment almost caused me to believe much that is quite unbelievable.

For instance, she had told me ridiculous stories as to interviews between herself and certain heathen goddesses, though it is true that, almost with her next breath, these she qualified or contradicted. Also, she had suggested that her life had been prolonged far beyond our mortal span, for hundreds and hundreds of years, indeed; which, as Euclid says, is absurd, and had pretended to supernatural powers, which is still more absurd. Moreover, by a clever use of some hypnotic or mesmeric power, she had feigned to transport me to some place beyond the earth and in the Halls of Hades to show me what is veiled from the eyes of man, and not only me, but the savage warrior Umhlopekazi, commonly called Umslopogaas of the Axe, who, with Hans, a Hottentot, was my companion upon that adventure. There were like things equally incredible, such as her appearance, when all seemed lost, in the battle with the troll-like Rezu. To omit these, the sum of it was that I had been shamefully duped, and if anyone finds himself in that position, as most people have at one time or another in their lives, Wisdom suggests that he had better keep the circumstances to himself.

Well, so the matter stood, or rather lay in the recesses of my mind—and in the cupboard where I hide my papers—when one evening someone, as a matter of fact it was Captain Good, an individual of romantic tendencies who is fond, sometimes I think too fond, of fiction, brought a book to this house which he insisted over and over again really I must peruse.

Ascertaining that it was a novel I declined, for to tell the truth I am not fond of romance in any shape, being a person who has found the hard facts of life of sufficient interest as they stand.

Reading I admit I like, but in this matter, as in everything else, my range is limited. I study the Bible, especially the Old Testament, both because of its sacred lessons and of the majesty of the language of its inspired translators; whereof that of Ayesha, which I render so poorly from her flowing and melodious Arabic, reminded me. For poetry I turn to Shakespeare, and, at the other end of the scale, to the Ingoldsby Legends, many of which I know almost by heart, while for current affairs I content myself with the newspapers.

For the rest I peruse anything to do with ancient Egypt that I happen to come across, because this land and its history have a queer fascination for me, that perhaps has its roots in occurrences or dreams of which this is not the place to speak. Lastly now and again I read one of the Latin or Greek authors in a translation, since I regret to say that my lack of education does not enable me to do so in the original.

But for modern fiction I have no taste, although from time to time I sample it in a railway train and occasionally am amused by such excursions into the poetic and unreal.

So it came about that the more Good bothered me to read this particular romance, the more I determined that I would do nothing of the sort. Being a persistent person, however, when he went away about ten o'clock at night, he deposited it by my side, under my nose indeed, so that it might not be overlooked. Thus it came about that I could not help seeing some Egyptian hieroglyphics in an oval on the cover, also the title, and underneath it your own name, my friend, all of which excited my curiosity, especially the title, which was brief and enigmatic, consisting indeed of one word, "She."

I took up the work and on opening it the first thing my eye fell upon was a picture of a veiled woman, the sight of which made my heart stand still, so painfully did it remind me of a certain veiled woman whom once it had been my fortune to meet. Glancing from it to the printed page one word seemed to leap at me. It was Kôr! Now of veiled women there are plenty in the world, but were there also two Kôrs?

Then I turned to the beginning and began to read. This happened in the autumn when the sun does not rise till about six, but it was broad daylight before I ceased from reading, or rather rushing through that book.

Oh! what was I to make of it? For here in its pages (to say nothing of old Billali, who, by the way lied, probably to order, when he told Mr. Holly that no white man had visited his country for many generations, and those gloomy, man-eating Amahagger scoundrels) once again I found myself face to face with She-who-commands, now rendered as She-who-must-be-obeyed, which means much the same thing—in her case at least; yes, with Ayesha the lovely, the mystic, the changeful and the imperious.

Moreover the history filled up many gaps in my own limited experiences of that enigmatical being who was half divine (though, I think, rather wicked or at any rate unmoral in her way) and yet all woman. It is true that it showed her in lights very different from and higher than those in which she had presented herself to me. Yet the substratum of her character was the same, or rather of her characters, for of these she seemed to have several in a single body, being, as she said of herself to me, "not One but Many and not Here but Everywhere."

Further, I found the story of Kallikrates, which I had set down as a mere falsehood invented for my bewilderment, expanded and explained. Or rather not explained, since, perhaps that she might deceive, to me she had spoken of this murdered Kallikrates without enthusiasm, as a handsome person to whom, because of an indiscretion of her youth, she was bound by destiny and whose return—somewhat to her sorrow—she must wait. At least she did so at first, though in the end when she bared her heart at the moment of our farewell, she vowed she loved him only and was "appointed" to him "by a divine decree."

Also I found other things of which I knew nothing, such as the Fire of Life with its fatal gift of indefinite existence, although I remember that like the giant Rezu whom Umslopogaas defeated, she did talk of a "Cup of Life" of which she had drunk, that might have been offered to my lips, had I been politic, bowed the knee and shown more faith in her and her supernatural pretensions.

Lastly I saw the story of her end, and as I read it I wept, yes, I confess I wept, although I feel sure that she will return again. Now I understood why she had quailed and even seemed to shrivel when, in my last interview with her, stung beyond endurance by her witcheries and sarcasms, I had suggested that even for her with all her powers, Fate might reserve one of its shrewdest blows. Some prescience had told her that if the words seemed random, Truth spoke through my lips, although, and this was the worst of it, she did not know what weapon would deal the stroke or when and where it was doomed to fall.

I was amazed, I was overcome, but as I closed that book I made up my mind, first that I would continue to preserve absolute silence as to Ayesha and my dealings with her, as, during my life, I was bound by oath to do, and secondly that I would not cause my manuscript to be destroyed. I did not feel that I had any right to do so in view of what already had been published to the world. There let it lie to appear one day, or not to appear, as might be fated. Meanwhile my lips were sealed. I would give Good back his book without comment and—buy another copy!

One more word. It is clear that I did not touch more than the fringe of the real Ayesha. In a thousand ways she bewitched and deceived me so that I never plumbed her nature's depths. Perhaps this was my own fault because from the first I shewed a lack of faith in her and she wished to pay me back in her own fashion, or perhaps she had other private reasons for her secrecy. Certainly the character she discovered to me differed in many ways from that which she revealed to Mr. Holly and to Leo Vincey, or Kallikrates, whom, it seems, once she slew in her jealousy and rage.

She told me as much as she thought it fit that I should know, and no more!

Allan Quatermain.
The Grange, Yorkshire.

CHAPTER I

THE TALISMAN

I believe it was the old Egyptians, a very wise people, probably indeed much wiser than we know, for in the leisure of their ample centuries they had time to think out things, who declared that each individual personality is made up of six or seven different elements, although the Bible only allows us three, namely, body, soul, and spirit. The body that the man or woman wore, if I understand their theory aright which perhaps I, an ignorant person, do not, was but a kind of sack or fleshly covering containing these different principles. Or mayhap it did not contain them all, but was simply a house as it were, in which they lived from time to time and seldom all together, although one or more of them was present continually, as though to keep the place warmed and aired.

This is but a casual illustrative suggestion, for what right have I, Allan Quatermain, out of my little reading and probably erroneous deductions, to form any judgment as to the theories of the old Egyptians? Still these, as I understand them, suffice to furnish me with the text that man is not one, but many, in which connection it may be remembered that often in Scripture he is spoken of as being the home of many demons, seven, I think. Also, to come to another far-off example, the Zulus talk of their witch-doctors as being inhabited by "a multitude of spirits."

Anyhow of one thing I am quite sure, we are not always the same. Different personalities actuate us at different times. In one hour passion of this sort or the other is our lord; in another we are reason itself. In one hour we follow the basest appetites; in another we hate them and the spirit arising through our mortal murk shines within or above us like a star. In one hour our desire is to kill and spare not; in another we are filled with the holiest compassion even towards an insect or a snake, and are ready to forgive like a god. Everything rules us in turn, to such an extent indeed, that sometimes one begins to wonder whether we really rule anything.

Now the reason of all this homily is that I, Allan, the most practical and unimaginative of persons, just a homely, half-educated hunter and trader who chances to have seen a good deal of the particular little world in which his lot was cast, at one period of my life became the victim of spiritual longings.

I am a man who has suffered great bereavements in my time such as have seared my soul, since, perhaps because of my rather primitive and simple nature, my affections are very strong. By day or night I can never forget those whom I have loved and whom I believe to have loved me.

For you know, in our vanity some of us are apt to hold that certain people with whom we have been intimate upon the earth, really did care for us and, in our still greater vanity—or should it be called madness?—to imagine that they still care for us after they have left the earth and entered on some new state of society and surroundings which, if they exist, inferentially are much more congenial than any they can have experienced here. At times, however, cold doubts strike us as to this matter, of which we long to know the truth. Also behind looms a still blacker doubt, namely whether they live at all.

For some years of my lonely existence these problems haunted me day by day, till at length I desired above everything on earth to lay them at rest in one way or another. Once, at Durban, I met a man who was a spiritualist to whom I confided a little of my perplexities. He laughed at me and said that they could be settled with the greatest ease. All I had to do was to visit a certain local medium who for a fee of one guinea would tell me everything I wanted to know. Although I rather grudged the guinea, being more than usually hard up at the time, I called upon this person, but over the results of that visit, or rather the lack of them, I draw a veil.

My queer and perhaps unwholesome longing, however, remained with me and would not be abated. I consulted a clergyman of my acquaintance, a good and spiritually-minded man, but he could only shrug his shoulders and refer me to the Bible, saying, quite rightly I doubt not, that with what it reveals I ought to be contented. Then I read certain mystical books which were recommended to me. These were full of fine words, undiscoverable in a pocket dictionary, but really took me no forwarder, since in them I found nothing that I could not have invented myself, although while I was actually studying them, they seemed to convince me. I even tackled Swedenborg, or rather samples of him, for he is very copious, but without satisfactory results. [Ha!—JB]

Then I gave up the business.

Some months later I was in Zululand and being near the Black Kloof where he dwelt, I paid a visit to my acquaintance of whom I have written elsewhere, the wonderful and ancient dwarf, Zikali, known as "The-Thing-that-should-never-have-been-born," also more universally among the Zulus as "Opener-of-Roads." When we had talked of many things connected with the state of Zululand and its politics, I rose to leave for my waggon, since I never cared for sleeping in the Black Kloof if it could be avoided.

"Is there nothing else that you want to ask me, Macumazahn?" asked the old dwarf, tossing back his long hair and looking at—I had almost written through—me.

I shook my head.

"That is strange, Macumazahn, for I seem to see something written on your mind—something to do with spirits."

Then I remembered all the problems that had been troubling me, although in truth I had never thought of propounding them to Zikali.

"Ah! it comes back, does it?" he exclaimed, reading my thought. "Out with it, then, Macumazahn, while I am in a mood to answer, and before I grow tired, for you are an old friend of mine and will so remain till the end, many years hence, and if I can serve you, I will."

I filled my pipe and sat down again upon the stool of carved red-wood which had been brought for me.

"You are named 'Opener-of-Roads,' are you not, Zikali?" I said.

"Yes, the Zulus have always called me that, since before the days of Chaka. But what of names, which often enough mean nothing at all?"

"Only that I want to open a road, Zikali, that which runs across the River of Death."

"Oho!" he laughed, "it is very easy," and snatching up a little assegai that lay beside him, he proffered it to me, adding, "Be brave now and fall on that. Then before I have counted sixty the road will be wide open, but whether you will see anything on it I cannot tell you."

Again I shook my head and answered,

"It is against our law. Also while I still live I desire to know whether I shall meet certain others on that road after my time has come to cross the River. Perhaps you who deal with spirits, can prove the matter to me, which no one else seems able to do."

"Oho!" laughed Zikali again. "What do my ears hear? Am I, the poor Zulu cheat, as you will remember once you called me, Macumazahn, asked to show that which is hidden from all the wisdom of the great White People?"

"The question is," I answered with irritation, "not what you are asked to do, but what you can do."

"That I do not know yet, Macumazahn. Whose spirits do you desire to see? If that of a woman called Mameena is one of them, I think that perhaps I whom she loved—"[*]

[*] For the history of Mameena see the book called "Child of Storm."—Editor.

"She is not one of them, Zikali. Moreover, if she loved you, you paid back her love with death."

"Which perhaps was the kindest thing I could do, Macumazahn, for reasons that you may be able to guess, and others with which I will not trouble you. But if not hers, whose? Let me look, let me look! Why, there seems to be two of them, head-wives, I mean, and I thought that white men only took one wife. Also a multitude of others; their faces float up in the water of your mind. An old man with grey hair, little children, perhaps they were brothers and sisters, and some who may be friends. Also very clear indeed that Mameena whom you do not wish to see. Well, Macumazahn, this is unfortunate, since she is the only one whom I can show you, or rather put you in the way of finding. Unless indeed there are other Kaffir women—"

"What do you mean?" I asked.

"I mean, Macumazahn, that only black feet travel on the road which I can open; over those in which ran white blood I have no power."

"Then it is finished," I said, rising again and taking a step or two towards the gate.

"Come back and sit down, Macumazahn. I did not say so. Am I the only ruler of magic in Africa, which I am told is a big country?"

I came back and sat down, for my curiosity, a great failing with me, was excited.

"Thank you, Zikali," I said, "but I will have no dealings with more of your witch-doctors."

"No, no, because you are afraid of them; quite without reason, Macumazahn, seeing that they are all cheats except myself. I am the last child of wisdom, the rest are stuffed with lies, as Chaka found out when he killed every one of them whom he could catch. But perhaps there might be a white doctor who would have rule over white spirits."

"If you mean missionaries—" I began hastily.

"No, Macumazahn, I do not mean your praying men who are cast in one mould and measured with one rule, and say what they are taught to say, not thinking for themselves."

"Some of them think, Zikali."

"Yes, and then the others fall on them with big sticks. The real priest is he to whom the Spirit comes, not he who feeds upon its wrappings, and speaks through a mask carved by his father's fathers. I am a priest like that, which is why all my fellowship have hated me."

"If so, you have paid back their hate, Zikali, but cease to cast round the lion, like a timid hound, and tell me what you mean. Of whom do you speak?"

"That is the trouble, Macumazahn. I do not know. This lion, or rather lioness, lies hid in the caves of a very distant mountain and I have never seen her—in the flesh."

"Then how can you talk of what you have never seen?"

"In the same way, Macumazahn, that your priests talk of what they have never seen, because they, or a few of them, have knowledge of it. I will tell you a secret. All seers who live at the same time, if they are great, commune with each other because they are akin and their spirits meet in sleep or dreams. Therefore I know of a mistress of our craft, a very lioness among jackals, who for thousands of years has lain sleeping in the northern caves and, humble though I am, she knows of me."

"Quite so," I said, yawning, "but perhaps, Zikali, you will come to the point of the spear. What of her? How is she named, and if she exists will she help me?"

"I will answer your question backwards, Macumazahn. I think that she will help you if you help her, in what way I do not know, because although witch-doctors sometimes work without pay, as I am doing now, Macumazahn, witch-doctoresses never do. As for her name, the only one that she has among our company is 'Queen,' because she is the first of all of them and the most beauteous among women. For the rest I can tell you nothing, except that she has always been and I suppose, in this shape or in that, will always be while the world lasts, because she has found the secret of life unending."

"You mean that she is immortal, Zikali," I answered with a smile.

"I do not say that, Macumazahn, because my little mind cannot shape the thought of immortality. But when I was a babe, which is far ago, she had lived so long that scarce would she knew the difference between then and now, and already in her breast was all wisdom gathered. I know it, because although, as I have said, we have never seen each other, at times we walk together in our sleep, for thus she shares her loneliness, and I think, though this may be but a dream, that last night she told me to send you on to her to seek an answer to certain questions which you would put to me to-day. Also to me she seemed to desire that you should do her a service; I know not what service."

Now I grew angry and asked,

"Why does it please you to fool me, Zikali, with such talk as this? If there is any truth in it, show me where the woman called Queen lives and how I am to come to her."

The old wizard took up the little assegai which he had offered to me and with its blade raked our ashes from the fire that always burnt in front of him. While he did so, he talked to me, as I thought in a random fashion, perhaps to distract my attention, of a certain white man whom he said I should meet upon my journey and of his affairs, also of other matters, none of which interested me much at the time. These ashes he patted down flat and then on them drew a map with the point of his spear, making grooves for streams, certain marks for bush and forest, wavy lines for water and swamps and little heaps for hills.

When he had finished it all he bade me come round the fire and study the picture across which by an after-thought he drew a wandering furrow with the edge of the assegai to represent a river, and gathered the ashes in a lump at the northern end to signify a large mountain.

"Look at it well, Macumazahn," he said, "and forget nothing, since if you make this journey and forget, you die. Nay, no need to copy it in that book of yours, for see, I will stamp it on your mind."

Then suddenly he gathered up the warm ashes in a double handful and threw them into my face, muttering something as he did so and adding aloud,

"There, now you will remember."

"Certainly I shall," I answered, coughing, "and I beg that you will not play such a joke upon me again."

As a matter of fact, whatever may have been the reason, I never forgot any detail of that extremely intricate map.

"That big river must be the Zambesi," I stuttered, "and even then the mountain of your Queen, if it be her mountain, is far away, and how can I come there alone?"

"I don't know, Macumazahn, though perhaps you might do so in company. At least I believe that in the old days people used to travel to the place, since I have heard a great city stood there once which was the heart of a mighty empire."

Now I pricked up my ears, for though I believed nothing of Zikali's story of a wonderful Queen, I was always intensely interested in past civilisations and their relics. Also I knew that the old wizard's knowledge was extensive and peculiar, however he came by it, and I did not think that he would lie to me in this matter. Indeed to tell the truth, then and there I made up my mind that if it were in any way possible, I would attempt this journey.

"How did people travel to the city, Zikali?"

"By sea, I suppose, Macumazahn, but I think that you will be wise not to try that road, since I believe that on the sea side the marshes are now impassable and you will be safer on your feet."

"You want me to go on this adventure, Zikali. Why? I know you never do anything without motive."

"Oho! Macumazahn, you are clever and see deeper into the trunk of a tree than most. Yes, I want you to go for three reasons. First, that you may satisfy your soul on certain matters and I would help you to do so. Secondly, because I want to satisfy mine, and thirdly, because I know that you will come back safe to be a prop to me in things that will happen in days unborn. Otherwise I would have told you nothing of this story, since it is necessary to me that you should remain living beneath the sun."

"Have done, Zikali. What is it that you desire?"

"Oh! a great deal that I shall get, but chiefly two things, so with the rest I will not trouble you. First I desire to know to know whether these dreams of mine of a wonderful white witch-doctoress, or witch, and of my converse with her are indeed more than dreams. Next I would learn whether certain plots of mine at which I have worked for years, will succeed."

"What plots, Zikali, and how can my taking a distant journey tell you anything about them?"

"You know them well enough, Macumazahn; they have to do with the overthrow of a Royal House that has worked me bitter wrong. As to how your journey can help me, why, thus. You shall promise to me to ask of this Queen whether Zikali, Opener-of-Roads, shall triumph or be overthrown in that on which he has set his heart."

"As you seem to know this witch so well, why do you not ask her yourself, Zikali?"

"To ask is one thing, Macumazahn. To get an answer is another. I have asked in the watches of the night, and the reply was, 'Come hither and perchance I will tell you.' 'Queen,' I said, 'how can I come save in the spirit, who am an ancient and a crippled dwarf scarcely able to stand upon my feet?'

"'Then send a messenger, Wizard, and be sure that he is white, for of black savages I have seen more than enough. Let him bear a token also that he comes from you and tell me of it in your sleep. Moreover let that token be something of power which will protect him on the journey.'

"Such is the answer that comes to me in my dreams, Macumazahn."

"Well, what token will you give me, Zikali?"

He groped about in his robe and produced a piece of ivory of the size of a large chessman, that had a hole in it, through which ran a plaited cord of the stiff hairs from an elephant's tail. On this article, which was of a rusty brown colour, he breathed, then having whispered to it for a while, handed it to me.

I took the talisman, for such I guessed it to be, idly enough, held it to the light to examine it, and started back so violently that almost I let it fall. I do not quite know why I started, but I think it was because some influence seemed to leap from it to me. Zikali started also and cried out,

"Have a care, Macumazahn. Am I young that I can bear bring dashed to the ground?"

"What do you mean?" I asked, still staring at the thing which I perceived to be a most wonderfully fashioned likeness of the old dwarf himself as he appeared before me crouched upon the ground. There were the deepset eyes, the great head, the toad-like shape, the long hair, all.

"It is a clever carving, is it not, Macumazahn? I am skilled in that art, you know, and therefore can judge of carving."

"Yes, I know," I answered, bethinking me of another statuette of his which he had given to me on the morrow of the death of her from whom it was modelled. "But what of the thing?"

"Macumazahn, it has come down to me through the ages. As you may have heard, all great doctors when they die pass on their wisdom and something of their knowledge to another doctor of spirits who is still living on the earth, that nothing may be lost, or as little as possible. Also I have learned that to such likenesses as these may be given the strength of him or her from whom they were shaped."

Now I bethought me of the old Egyptians and their Ka statues of which I had read, and that these statues, magically charmed and set in the tombs of the departed, were supposed to be inhabited everlastingly by the Doubles of the dead endued with more power even than ever these possessed in life. But of this I said nothing to Zikali, thinking that it would take too much explanation, though I wondered very much how he had come by the same idea.

"When that ivory is hung over your heart, Macumazahn, where you must always wear it, learn that with it goes the strength of Zikali; the thought that would have been his thought and the wisdom that is his wisdom, will be your companions, as much as though he walked at your side and could instruct you in every peril. Moreover north and south and east and west this image is known to men who, when they see it, will bow down and obey, opening a road to him who wears the medicine of the Opener-of-Roads."

"Indeed," I said, smiling, "and what is this colour on the ivory?"

"I forget, Macumazahn, who have had it a great number of years, ever since it descended to me from a forefather of mine, who was fashioned in the same mould as I am. It looks like blood, does it not? It is a pity that Mameena is not still alive, since she whose memory was so excellent might have been able to tell you," and as he spoke, with a motion that was at once sure and swift, he threw the loop of elephant hair over my head.

Hastily I changed the subject, feeling that after his wont this old wizard, the most terrible man whom ever I knew, who had been so much concerned with the tragic death of Mameena, was stabbing at me in some hidden fashion.

"You tell me to go on this journey," I said, "and not alone. Yet for companion you give me only an ugly piece of ivory shaped as no man ever was," here I got one back at Zikali, "and from the look of it, steeped in blood, which ivory, if I had my way, I would throw into the camp fire. Who, then, am I to take with me?"

"Don't do that, Macumazahn—I mean throw the ivory into the fire—since I have no wish to burn before my time, and if you do, you who have worn it might burn with me. At least certainly you would die with the magic thing and go to acquire knowledge more quickly than you desire. No, no, and do not try to take it off your neck, or rather try if you will."

I did try, but something seemed to prevent me from accomplishing my purpose of giving the carving back to Zikali as I wished to do. First my pipe got in the way of my hand, then the elephant hairs caught in the collar of my coat; then a pang of rheumatism to which I was accustomed from an old lion-bite, developed of a sudden in my arm, and lastly I grew tired of bothering about the thing.

Zikali, who had been watching my movements, burst out into one of his terrible laughs that seemed to fill the whole kloof and to re-echo from its rocky walls. It died away and he went on, without further reference to the talisman or image.

"You asked whom you were to take with you, Macumazahn. Well, as to this I must make inquiry of those who know. Man, my medicines!"

From the shadows in the hut behind darted out a tall figure carrying a great spear in one hand and in the other a catskin bag which with a salute he laid down at the feet of his master. This salute, by the way, was that of a Zulu word which means "Lord" or "Home" of Ghosts.

Zikali groped in the bag and produced from it certain knuckle-bones.

"A common method," he muttered, "such as every vulgar wizard uses, but one that is quick and, as the matter concerned is small, will serve my turn. Let us see now, whom you shall take with you, Macumazahn."

Then he breathed upon the bones, shook them up in his thin hands and with a quick turn of the wrist, threw them into the air. After this he studied them carefully, where they lay among the ashes which he had raked out of the fire, those that he had used for the making of his map.

"Do you know a man named Umslopogaas, Macumazahn, the chief of a tribe that is called The People of the Axe, whose titles of praise are Bulalio or the Slaughterer, and Woodpecker, the latter from the way he handles his ancient axe? He is a savage fellow, but one of high blood and higher courage, a great captain in his way, though he will never come to anything, save a glorious death—in your company, I think, Macumazahn." (Here he studied the bones again for a while.) "Yes, I am sure, in your company, though not upon this journey."

"I have heard of him," I answered cautiously. "It is said in the land that he is a son of Chaka, the great king of the Zulus."

"Is it, Macumazahn? And is it said also that he was the slayer of Chaka's brother, Dingaan, also the lover of the fairest woman that the Zulus have ever seen, who was called Nada the Lily? Unless indeed a certain Mameena, who, I seem to remember, was a friend of yours, may have been even more beautiful?"

"I know nothing of Nada the Lily," I answered.

"No, no, Mameena, 'the Waiting Wind,' has blown over her fame, so why should you know of one who has been dead a long while? Why also, Macumazahn, do you always bring women into every business? I begin to believe that although you are so strict in a white man's fashion, you must be too fond of them, a weakness which makes for ruin to any man. Well, now, I think that this wolf-man, this axe-man, this warrior, Umslopogaas should be a good fellow to you on your journey to visit the white witch, Queen—another woman by the way, Macumazahn, and therefore one of whom you should be careful. Oh! yes, he will come with you—because of a man called Lousta and a woman named Monazi, a wife of his who hates him and does—not hate Lousta. I am almost sure that he will come with you, so do not stop to ask questions about him."

"Is there anyone else?" I inquired.

Zikali glanced at the bones again, poking them about in the ashes with his toe, then replied with a yawn,

"You seem to have a little yellow man in your service, a clever snake who knows how to creep through grass, and when to strike and when to lie hidden. I should take him too, if I were you."

"You know well that I have such a man, Zikali, a Hottentot named Hans, clever in his way but drunken, very faithful too, since he loved my father before me. He is cooking my supper in the waggon now. Are there to be any others?"

"No, I think you three will be enough, with a guard of soldiers from the People of the Axe, for you will meet with fighting and a ghost or two. Umslopogaas has always one at his elbow named Nada, and perhaps you have several. For instance, there was a certain Mameena whom I always seem to feel about me when you are near, Macumazahn.

"Why, the wind is rising again, which is odd on so still an evening. Listen to how it wails, yes, and stirs your hair, though mine hangs straight enough. But why do I talk of ghosts, seeing that you travel to seek other ghosts, white ghosts, beyond my ken, who can only deal with those who were black?

"Good-night, Macumazahn, good-night. When you return from visiting the white Queen, that Great One beneath those feet I, Zikali, who am also great in my way, am but a grain of dust, come and tell me her answer to my question.

"Meanwhile, be careful always to wear that pretty little image which I have given you, as a young lover sometimes wears a lock of hair cut from the head of some fool-girl that he thinks is fond of him. It will bring you safety and luck, Macumazahn, which, for the most part, is more than the lock of hair does to the lover. Oh! it is a strange world, full of jest to those who can see the strings that work it. I am one of them, and perhaps, Macumazahn, you are another, or will be before all is done—or begun.

"Good-night, and good fortune to you on your journeyings, and, Macumazahn, although you are so fond of women, be careful not to fall in love with that white Queen, because it would make others jealous; I mean some who you have lost sight of for a while, also I think that being under a curse of her own, she is not one whom you can put into your sack. Oho! Oho-ho! Slave, bring me my blanket, it grows cold, and my medicine also, that which protects me from the ghosts, who are thick to-night. Macumazahn brings them, I think. Oho-ho!"

I turned to depart but when I had gone a little way Zikali called me back again and said, speaking very low,

"When you meet this Umslopogaas, as you will meet him, he who is called the Woodpecker and the Slaughterer, say these words to him,

"'A bat has been twittering round the hut of the Opener-of-Roads, and to his ears it squeaked the name of a certain Lousta and the name of a woman called Monazi. Also it twittered another greater name that may not be uttered, that of an elephant who shakes the earth, and said that this elephant sniffs the air with his trunk and grows angry, and sharpens his tusks to dig a certain Woodpecker out of his hole in a tree that grows near the Witch Mountain. Say, too, that the Opener-of-Roads thinks that this Woodpecker would be wise to fly north for a while in the company of one who watches by night, lest harm should come to a bird that pecks at the feet of the great and chatters of it in his nest.'"

Then Zikali waved his hand and I went, wondering into what plot I had stumbled.

CHAPTER II

THE MESSENGERS

I did not rest as I should that night who somehow was never able to sleep well in the neighbourhood of the Black Kloof. I suppose that Zikali's constant talk about ghosts, with his hints and innuendoes concerning those who were dead, always affected my nerves till, in a subconscious way, I began to believe that such things existed and were hanging about me. Many people are open to the power of suggestion, and I am afraid that I am one of them.

However, the sun which has such strength to kill noxious things, puts an end to ghosts more quickly even than it does to other evil vapours and emanations, and when I woke up to find it shining brilliantly in a pure heaven, I laughed with much heartiness over the whole affair.

Going to the spring near which we were outspanned, I took off my shirt to have a good wash, still chuckling at the memory of all the hocus-pocus of my old friend, the Opener-of-Roads.

While engaged in this matutinal operation I struck my hand against something and looking, observed that it was the hideous little ivory image of Zikali, which he had set about my neck. The sight of the thing and the memory of his ridiculous talk about it, especially of its assertion that it had come down to him through the ages, which it could not have done, seeing that it was a likeness of himself, irritated me so much that I proceeded to take it off with the full intention of throwing it into the spring.

As I was in the act of doing this, from a clump of reeds mixed with bushes, quite close to me, there came a sound of hissing, and suddenly above them appeared the head of a great black immamba, perhaps the deadliest of all our African snakes, and the only one I know which will attack man without provocation.

Leaving go of the image, I sprang back in a great hurry towards where my gun lay. Then the snake vanished and making sure that it had departed to its hole, which was probably at a distance, I returned to the pool, and once more began to take off the talisman in order to consign it to the bottom of the pool.

After all, I reflected, it was a hideous and probably a blood-stained thing which I did not in the least wish to wear about my neck like a lady's love-token.

Just as it was coming over my head, suddenly from the other side of the bush that infernal snake popped up again, this time, it was clear, really intent on business. It began to move towards me in the lightning-like way immambas have, hissing and flicking its tongue.

I was too quick for my friend, however, for snatching up the gun that I had lain down beside me, I let it have a charge of buckshot in the neck which nearly cut it in two, so that it fell down and expired with hideous convulsive writhings.

Hearing the shot Hans came running from the waggon to see what was the matter. Hans, I should say, was that same Hottentot who had been the companion of most of my journeyings since my father's day. He was with me when as a young fellow I accompanied Retief to Dingaan's kraal, and like myself, escaped the massacre.[*] Also we shared many other adventures, including the great one in the Land of the Ivory Child where he slew the huge elephant-god, Jana, and himself was slain. But of this journey we did not dream in those days.

[*] See the book called "Marie."—Editor.

For the rest Hans was a most entirely unprincipled person, but as the Boers say, "as clever as a waggonload of monkeys." Also he drank when he got the chance. One good quality he had, however; no man was ever more faithful, and perhaps it would be true to say that neither man nor woman ever loved me, unworthy, quite so well.

In appearance he rather resembled an antique and dilapidated baboon; his face was wrinkled like a dried nut and his quick little eyes were bloodshot. I never knew what his age was, any more than he did himself, but the years had left him tough as whipcord and absolutely untiring. Lastly he was perhaps the best hand at following a spoor that ever I knew and up to a hundred and fifty yards or so, a very deadly shot with a rifle especially when he used a little single-barrelled, muzzle-loading gun of mine made by Purdey which he named Intombi or Maiden. Of that gun, however, I have written in "The Holy Flower" and elsewhere.

"What is it, Baas?" he asked. "Here there are no lions, nor any game."

"Look the other side of the bush, Hans."

He slipped round it, making a wide circle with his usual caution, then, seeing the snake which was, by the way, I think, the biggest immamba I ever killed, suddenly froze, as it were, in a stiff attitude that reminded me of a pointer when it scents game. Having made sure that it was dead, he nodded and said,

"Black 'mamba, or so you would call it, though I know it for something else."

"What else, Hans?"

"One of the old witch-doctor Zikali's spirits which he sets at the mouth of this kloof to warn him of who comes or goes. I know it well, and so do others. I saw it listening behind a stone when you were up the kloof last evening talking with the Opener-of-Roads."

"Then Zikali will lack a spirit," I answered, laughing, "which perhaps he will not miss amongst so many. It serves him right for setting the brute on me."

"Quite so, Baas. He will be angry. I wonder why he did it?" he added suspiciously, "seeing that he is such a friend of yours."

"He didn't do it, Hans. These snakes are very fierce and give battle, that is all."

Hans paid no attention to my remark, which probably he thought only worthy of a white man who does not understand, but rolled his yellow, bloodshot eyes about, as though in search of explanations. Presently they fell upon the ivory that hung about my neck, and he started.

"Why do you wear that pretty likeness of the Great One yonder over your heart, as I have known you do with things that belonged to women in past days, Baas? Do you know that it is Zikali's Great Medicine, nothing less, as everyone does throughout the land? When Zikali sends an order far away, he always sends that image with it, for then he who receives the order knows that he must obey or die. Also the messenger knows that he will come to no harm if he does not take it off, because, Baas, the image is Zikali himself, and Zikali is the image. They are one and the same. Also it is the image of his father's father's father—or so he says."

"That is an odd story," I said.

Then I told Hans as much as I thought advisable of how this horrid little talisman came into my possession.

Hans nodded without showing any surprise.

"So we are going on a long journey," he said. "Well, I thought it was time that we did something more than wander about these tame countries selling blankets to stinking old women and so forth, Baas. Moreover, Zikali does not wish that you should come to harm, doubtless because he does wish to make use of you afterwards—oh! it's safe to talk now when that spirit is away looking for another snake. What were you doing with the Great Medicine, Baas, when the 'mamba attacked you?"

"Taking it off to throw it into the pool, Hans, as I do not like the thing. I tried twice and each time the immamba appeared."

"Of course it appeared, Baas, and what is more, if you had taken that Medicine off and thrown it away you would have disappeared, since the 'mamba would have killed you. Zikali wanted to show you that, Baas, and that is why he set the snake at you."

"You are a superstitious old fool, Hans."

"Yes, Baas, but my father knew all about that Great Medicine before me, for he was a bit of a doctor, and so does every wizard and witch for a thousand miles or more. I tell you, Baas, it is known by all though no one ever talks about it, no, not even the king himself. Baas, speaking to you, not with the voice of Hans the old drunkard, but with that of the Predikant, your reverend father, who made so good a Christian of me and who tells me to do so from up in Heaven where the hot fires are which the wood feeds of itself, I beg you not to try to throw away the Medicine again, or if you wish to do so, to leave me behind on this journey. For you see, Baas, although I am now so good, almost like one of those angels with the pretty goose's wings in the pictures, I feel that I should like to grow a little better before I go to the Place of Fires to make report to your reverend father, the Predikant."

Thinking of how horrified my dear father would be if he could hear all this string of ridiculous nonsense and learn the result of his moral and religious lessons on raw Hottentot material, I burst out laughing. But Hans went on as gravely as a judge,

"Wear the Great Medicine, Baas, wear it; part with the liver inside you before you part with that, Baas. It may not be as pretty or smell as sweet as a woman's hair in a little gold bottle, but it is much more useful. The sight of the woman's hair will only make you sick in your stomach and cause you to remember a lot of things which you had much better forget, but the Great Medicine, or rather Zikali who is in it, will keep the assegais and sickness out of you and turn back bad magic on to the heads of those who sent it, and always bring us plenty to eat and perhaps, if we are lucky, a little to drink too sometimes."

"Go away," I said, "I want to wash."

"Yes, Baas, but with the Baas's leave I will sit on the other side of that bush with the gun—not to look at the Baas without his clothes, because white people are always so ugly that it makes me feel ill to see them undressed, also because—the Baas will forgive me—but because they smell. No, not for that, but just to see that no other snake comes."

"Get out of the road, you dirty little scoundrel, and stop your impudence," I said, lifting my foot suggestively.

Thereon he scooted with a subdued grin round the other side of the bush, whence as I knew well he kept his eye fixed on me to be sure that I made no further attempt to take off the Great Medicine.

Now of this talisman I may as well say at once that I am no believer in it or its precious influences. Therefore, although it was useful sometimes, notably twice when Umslopogaas was concerned, I do not know whether personally I should have done better or worse upon that journey if I had thrown it into the pool.

It is true, however, that until quite the end of this history when it became needful to do so to save another, I never made any further attempt to remove it from my neck, not even when it rubbed a sore in my skin, because I did not wish to offend the prejudices of Hans.

It is true, moreover, that this hideous ivory had a reputation which stretched very far from the place where it was made and was regarded with great reverence by all kinds of queer people, even by the Amahagger themselves, of whom presently, as they say in pedigrees, a fact of which I found sundry proofs. Indeed, I saw a first example of it when a little while later I met that great warrior, Umslopogaas, Chief of the People of the Axe.

For, after determining firmly, for reasons which I will set out, that I would not visit this man, in the end I did so, although by then I had given up any idea of journeying across the Zambesi to look for a mysterious and non-existent witch-woman, as Zikali had suggested that I should do. To begin with I knew that his talk was all rubbish and, even if it were not, that at the bottom of it was some desire of the Opener-of-Roads that I should make a path for him to travel towards an indefinite but doubtless evil object of his own. Further, by this time I had worn through that mood of mine which had caused me to yearn for correspondence with the departed and a certain knowledge of their existence.

I wonder whether many people understand, as I do, how entirely distinct and how variable are these moods which sway us, or at any rate some of us, at sundry periods of our lives. As I think I have already suggested, at one time we are all spiritual; at another all physical; at one time we are sure that our lives here are as a dream and a shadow and that the real existence lies elsewhere; at another that these brief days of ours are the only business with which we have to do and that of it we must make the best. At one time we think our loves much more immortal than the stars; at another that they are mere shadows cast by the baleful sun of desire upon the shallow and fleeting water we call Life which seems to flow out of nowhere into nowhere. At one time we are full of faith, at another all such hopes are blotted out by a black wall of Nothingness, and so on ad infinitum. Only very stupid people, or humbugs, are or pretend to be, always consistent and unchanging.

To return, I determined not only that I would not travel north to seek that which no living man will ever find, certainty as to the future, but also, to show my independence of Zikali, that I would not visit this chief, Umslopogaas. So, having traded all my goods and made a fair profit (on paper), I set myself to return to Natal, proposing to rest awhile in my little house at Durban, and told Hans my mind.

"Very good, Baas," he said. "I, too, should like to go to Durban. There are lots of things there that we cannot get here," and he fixed his roving eye upon a square-faced gin bottle, which as it happened was filled with nothing stronger than water, because all the gin was drunk. "Yet, Baas, we shall not see the Berea for a long while."

"Why do you say that?" I asked sharply.

"Oh! Baas, I don't know, but you went to visit the Opener-of-Roads, did you not, and he told you to go north and lent you a certain Great Medicine, did he not?"

Here Hands proceeded to light his corncob pipe with an ash from the fire, all the time keeping his beady eyes fixed upon that part of me where he knew the talisman was hung.

"Quite true, Hans, but now I mean to show Zikali that I am not his messenger, for south or north or east or west. So to-morrow morning we cross the river and trek for Natal."

"Yes, Baas, but then why not cross it this evening? There is still light."

"I have said that we will cross it to-morrow morning," I answered with that firmness which I have read always indicates a man of character, "and I do not change my word."

"No, Baas, but sometimes other things change besides words. Will the Baas have that buck's leg for supper, or the stuff out of a tin with a dint in it, which we bought at a store two years ago? The flies have got at the buck's leg, but I cut out the bits with the maggots on it and ate them myself."

Hans was right, things do change, especially the weather. That night, unexpectedly, for when I turned in the sky seemed quite serene, there came a terrible rain long before it was due, which lasted off and on for three whole days and continued intermittently for an indefinite period. Needless to say the river, which it would have been so easy to cross on this particular evening, by the morning was a raging torrent, and so remained for several weeks.

In despair at length I trekked south to where a ford was reported, which, when reached, proved impracticable.

I tried another, a dozen miles further on, which was very hard to come to over boggy land. It looked all right and we were getting across finely, when suddenly one of the wheels sank in an unsuspected hole and there we stuck. Indeed, I believe the waggon, or bits of it, would have remained in the neighbourhood of that ford to this day, had I not managed to borrow some extra oxen belonging to a Christian Kaffir, and with their help to drag it back to the bank whence we had started.

As it happened I was only just in time, since a new storm which had burst further up the river, brought it down in flood again, a very heavy flood.

In this country, England, where I write, there are bridges everywhere and no one seems to appreciate them. If they think of them at all it is to grumble about the cost of their upkeep. I wish they could have experienced what a lack of them means in a wild country during times of excessive rain, and the same remark applied to roads. You should think more of your blessings, my friends, as the old woman said to her complaining daughter who had twins two years running, adding that they might have been triplets.

To return—after this I confessed myself beaten and gave up until such time as it should please Providence to turn off the water-tap. Trekking out of sight of that infernal river which annoyed me with its constant gurgling, I camped on a comparatively dry spot that overlooked a beautiful stretch of rolling veld. Towards sunset the clouds lifted and I saw a mile or two away a most extraordinary mountain on the lower slopes of which grew a dense forest. Its upper part, which was of bare rock, looked exactly like the seated figure of a grotesque person with the chin resting on the breast. There was the head, there were the arms, there were the knees. Indeed, the whole mass of it reminded me strongly of the effigy of Zikali which was tied about my neck, or rather of Zikali himself.

"What is that called?" I said to Hans, pointing to this strange hill, now blazing in the angry fire of the setting sun that had burst out between the storm clouds, which made it appear more ominous even than before.

"That is the Witch Mountain, Baas, where the Chief Umslopogaas and a blood brother of his who carried a great club used to hunt with the wolves. It is haunted and in a cave at the top of it lie the bones of Nada the Lily, the fair woman whose name is a song, she who was the love of Umslopogaas."[*]

[*] For the story of Umslopogaas and Nada see the book called "Nada the Lily."—Editor.

"Rubbish," I said, though I had heard something of all that story and remembered that Zikali had mentioned this Nada, comparing her beauty to that of another whom once I knew.

"Where then lives the Chief Umslopogaas?"

"They say that his town is yonder on the plain, Baas. It is called the Place of the Axe and is strongly fortified with a river round most of it, and his people are the People of the Axe. They are a fierce people, and all the country round here is uninhabited because Umslopogaas has cleaned out the tribes who used to live in it, first with his wolves and afterwards in war. He is so strong a chief and so terrible in battle that even Chaka himself was afraid of him, and they say that he brought Dingaan the King to his end because of a quarrel about this Nada. Cetywayo, the present king, too leaves him alone and to him he pays no tribute."

Whilst I was about to ask Hans from whom he had collected all this information, suddenly I heard sounds, and looking up, saw three tall men clad in full herald's dress rushing towards us at great speed.

"Here come some chips from the Axe," said Hans, and promptly bolted into the waggon.

I did not bolt because there was no time to do so without loss of dignity, but, although I wished I had my rifle with me, just sat still upon my stool and with great deliberation lighted my pipe, taking not the slightest notice of the three savage-looking fellows.

These, who I noted carried axes instead of assegais, rushed straight at me with the axes raised in such a fashion that anyone unacquainted with the habits of Zulu warriors of the old school, might have thought that they intended nothing short of murder.

As I expected, however, within about six feet of me they halted suddenly and stood there still as statues. For my part I went on lighting my pipe as though I did not see them and when at length I was obliged to lift my head, surveyed them with an air of mild interest.

Then I took a little book out of my pocket, it was my favourite copy of the Ingoldsby Legends—and began to read.

The passage which caught my eye, if "axe" be substituted for "knife" was not inappropriate. It was from "The Nurse's Story," and runs,

"But, oh! what a thing 'tis to see and to know That the bare knife is raised in the hand of the foe, Without hope to repel or to ward off the blow!"

This proceeding of mine astonished them a good deal who felt that they had, so to speak, missed fire. At last the soldier in the middle said,

"Are you blind, White Man?"

"No, Black Fellow," I answered, "but I am short-sighted. Would you be so good as to stand out of my light?" a remark which puzzled them so much that all three drew back a few paces.

When I had read a little further I came to the following lines,

"'Tis plain, As anatomists tell us, that never again, Shall life revisit the foully slain When once they've been cut through the jugular vein."

In my circumstances at that moment this statement seemed altogether too suggestive, so I shut up the book and remarked,

"If you are wanderers who want food, as I judge by your being so thin, I am sorry that I have little meat, but my servants will give you what they can."

"Ow!" said the spokesman, "he calls us wanderers! Either he must be a very great man or he is mad."

"You are right. I am a great man," I answered, yawning, "and if you trouble me too much you will see that I can be mad also. Now what do you want?"

"We are messengers from the great Chief Umslopogaas, Captain of the People of the Axe, and we want tribute," answered the man in a somewhat changed tone.

"Do you? Then you won't get it. I thought that only the King of Zululand had a right to tribute, and your Captain's name is not Cetywayo, is it?"

"Our Captain is King here," said the man still more uncertainly.

"Is he indeed? Then away with you back to him and tell this King of whom I have never heard, though I have a message for a certain Umslopogaas, that Macumazahn, Watcher-by-Night, intends to visit him to-morrow, if he will send a guide at the first light to show the best path for the waggon."

"Hearken," said the man to his companions, "this is Macumazahn himself and no other. Well, we thought it, for who else would have dared—"

Then they saluted with their axes, calling me "Chief" and other fine names, and departed as they had come, at a run, calling out that my message should be delivered and that doubtless Umslopogaas would send the guide.

So it came about that, quite contrary to my intention, after all circumstances brought me to the Town of the Axe. Even to the last moment I had not meant to go there, but when the tribute was demanded I saw that it was best to do so, and having once passed my word it could not be altered. Indeed, I felt sure that in this event there would be trouble and that my oxen would be stolen, or worse.

So Fate having issued its decree, of which Hans's version was that Zikali, or his Great Medicine, had so arranged things, I shrugged my shoulders and waited.

CHAPTER III

UMSLOPOGAAS OF THE AXE

Next morning at the dawn guides arrived from the Town of the Axe, bringing with them a yoke of spare oxen, which showed that its Chief was really anxious to see me. So, in due course we inspanned and started, the guides leading us by a rough but practicable road down the steep hillside to the saucer-like plain beneath, where I saw many cattle grazing. Travelling some miles across this plain, we came at last to a river of no great breadth that encircled a considerable Kaffir town on three sides, the fourth being protected by a little line of koppies which were joined together with walls. Also the place was strongly fortified with fences and in every other way known to the native mind.

With the help of the spare oxen we crossed the river safely at the ford, although it was very full, and on the further side were received by a guard of men, tall, soldierlike fellows, all of them armed with axes as the messengers had been. They led us up to the cattle enclosure in the centre of the town, which although it could be used to protect beasts in case of emergency, also served the practical purpose of a public square.

Here some ceremony was in progress, for soldiers stood round the kraal while heralds pranced and shouted. At the head of the place in front of the chief's big hut was a little group of people, among whom a big, gaunt man sat upon a stool clad in a warrior's dress with a great and very long axe hafted with wire-lashed rhinoceros horn, laid across his knees.

Our guides led me, with Hans sneaking after me like a dejected and low-bred dog (for the waggon had stopped outside the gate), across the kraal to where the heralds shouted and the big man sat yawning. At once I noted that he was a very remarkable person, broad and tall and spare of frame, with long, tough-looking arms and a fierce face which reminded me of that of the late King Dingaan. Also he had a great hole in his head above the temple where the skull had been driven in by some blow, and keen, royal-looking eyes.

He looked up and seeing me, cried out,

"What! Has a white man come to fight me for the chieftainship of the People of the Axe? Well, he is a small one."

"No," I answered quietly, "but Macumazahn, Watcher-by-Night, has come to visit you in answer to your request, O Umslopogaas; Macumazahn whose name was known in this land before yours was told of, O Umslopogaas."

The Chief heard and rising from his seat, lifted the big axe in salute.

"I greet you, O Macumazahn," he said, "who although you are small in stature, are very great indeed in fame. Have I not heard how you conquered Bangu, although Saduko slew him, and of how you gave up the six hundred head of cattle to Tshoza and the men of the Amangwane who fought with you, the cattle that were your own? Have I not heard how you led the Tulwana against the Usutu and stamped flat three of Cetywayo's regiments in the days of Panda, although, alas! because of an oath of mine I lifted no steel in that battle, I who will have nothing to do with those that spring from the blood of Senzangacona—perhaps because I smell too strongly of it, Macumazahn. Oh! yes, I have heard these and many other things concerning you, though until now it has never been my fortune to look upon your face, O Watcher-by-Night, and therefore I greet you well, Bold one, Cunning one, Upright one, Friend of us Black People."

"Thank you," I answered, "but you said something about fighting. If there is to be anything of the sort, let us get it over. If you want to fight, I am quite ready," and I tapped the rifle which I carried.

The grim Chief broke into a laugh and said,

"Listen. By an ancient law any man on this day in each year may fight me for this Chieftainship, as I fought and conquered him who held it before me, and take it from me with my life and the axe, though of late none seems to like the business. But that law was made before there were guns, or men like Macumazahn who, it is said, can hit a lizard on a wall at fifty paces. Therefore I tell you that if you wish to fight me with a rifle, O Macumazahn, I give in and you may have the chieftainship," and he laughed again in his fierce fashion.

"I think it is too hot for fighting either with guns or axes, and Chieftainships are honey that is full of stinging bees," I answered.

Then I took my seat on a stool that had been brought for me and placed by the side of Umslopogaas, after which the ceremony went on.

The heralds cried out the challenge to all and sundry to come and fight the Holder of the Axe for the chieftainship of the Axe without the slightest result, since nobody seemed to desire to do anything of the sort. Then, after a pause, Umslopogaas rose, swinging his formidable weapon round his head and declared that by right of conquest he was Chief of the Tribe for the ensuing year, an announcement that everybody accepted without surprise.

Again the heralds summoned all and sundry who had grievances, to come forward and to state them and receive redress.

After a little pause there appeared a very handsome woman with large eyes, particularly brilliant eyes that rolled as though they were in search of someone. She was finely dressed and I saw by the ornaments she wore that she held the rank of a chief's wife.

"I, Monazi, have a complaint to make," she said, "as it is the right of the humblest to do on this day. In succession to Zinita whom Dingaan slew with her children, I am your Inkosikaas, your head-wife, O Umslopogaas."

"That I know well enough," said Umslopogaas, "what of it?"

"This, that you neglect me for other women, as you neglected Zinita for Nada the Beautiful, Nada the witch. I am childless, as are all your wives because of the curse that this Nada left behind her. I demand that this curse should be lifted from me. For your sake I abandoned Lousta the Chief, to whom I was betrothed, and this is the end of it, that I am neglected and childless."

"Am I the Heavens Above that I can cause you to bear children, woman?" asked Umslopogaas angrily. "Would that you had clung to Lousta, my blood-brother and my friend, whom you lament, and left me alone."

"That still may chance, if I am not better treated," answered Monazi with a flash of her eyes. "Will you dismiss yonder new wife of yours and give me back my place, and will you lift the curse of Nada off me, or will you not?"

"As to the first," answered Umslopogaas, "learn, Monazi, that I will not dismiss my new wife, who at least is gentler-tongued and truer-hearted than you are. As to the second, you ask that which it is not in my power to give, since children are the gift of Heaven, and barrenness is its bane. Moreover, you have done ill to bring into this matter the name of one who is dead, who of all women was the sweetest and most innocent. Lastly, I warn you before the people to cease from your plottings or traffic with Lousta, lest ill come of them to you, or him, even though he be my blood-brother, or to both."

"Plottings!" cried Monazi in a shrill and furious voice. "Does Umslopogaas talk of plottings? Well, I have heard that Chaka the Lion left a son, and that this son has set a trap for the feet of him who sits on Chaka's throne. Perchance that king has heard it also; perchance the People of the Axe will soon have another Chief."

"Is it thus?" said Umslopogaas quietly. "And if so, will he be named Lousta?"

Then his smouldering wrath broke out and in a kind of roaring voice he went on,

"What have I done that the wives of my bosom should be my betrayers, those who would give me to death? Zinita betrayed me to Dingaan and in reward was slain, and my children with her. Now would you, Monazi, betray me to Cetywayo—though in truth there is naught to betray? Well, if so, bethink you and let Lousta bethink him of what chanced to Zinita, and of what chances to those who stand before the axe of Umslopogaas. What have I done, I say, that women should thus strive to work me ill?"

"This," answered Monazi with a mocking laugh, "that you have loved one of them too well. If he would live in peace, he who has wives should favour all alike. Least of anything should he moan continually over one who is dead, a witch who has left a curse behind her and thus insulted and do wrong to the living. Also he would be wise to attend to the matters of his own tribe and household and to cease from ambitions that may bring him to the assegai, and them with him."

"I have heard your counsel, Wife, so now begone!" said Umslopogaas, looking at her very strangely, and it seemed to me not without fear.

"Have you wives, Macumazahn?" he asked of me in a low voice when she was out of hearing.

"Only among the spirits," I answered.

"Well for you then; moreover, it is a bond between us, for I too have but one true wife and she also is among the spirits. But go rest a while, and later we will talk."

So I went, leaving the Chief to his business, thinking as I walked away of a certain message with which I was charged for him and of how into that message came names that I had just heard, namely that of a man called Lousta and of a woman called Monazi. Also I thought of the hints which in her jealous anger and disappointment at her lack of children, this woman had dropped about a plot against him who sat on the throne of Chaka, which of course must mean King Cetywayo himself.

I came to the guest-hut, which proved to be a very good place and clean; also in it I found plenty of food made ready for me and for my servants. After eating I slept for a time as it is always my fashion to do when I have nothing else on hand, since who knows for how long he may be kept awake at night? Indeed, it was not until the sun had begun to sink that a messenger came, saying that the Chief desired to see me if I had rested. So I went to his big hut which stood alone with a strong fence set round it at a distance, so that none could come within hearing of what was said, even at the door of the hut. I observed also that a man armed with an axe kept guard at the gateway in this fence round which he walked from time to time.

The Chief Umslopogaas was seated on a stool by the door of his hut with his rhinoceros-horn-handled axe which was fastened to his right wrist by a thong, leaning against his thigh, and a wolfskin hanging from his broad shoulders. Very grim and fierce he looked thus, with the red light of the sunset playing on him. He greeted me and pointed to another stool on which I sat myself down. Apparently he had been watching my eyes, for he said,

"I see that like other creatures which move at night, such as leopards and hyenas, you take note of all, O Watcher-by-Night, even of the soldier who guards this place and of where the fence is set and of how its gate is fashioned."

"Had I not done so I should have been dead long ago, O Chief."

"Yes, and because it is not my nature to do so as I should, perchance I shall soon be dead. It is not enough to be fierce and foremost in the battle, Macumazahn. He who would sleep safe and of whom, when he dies, folk will say 'He has eaten' (i.e., he has lived out his life), must do more than this. He must guard his tongue and even his thoughts! he must listen to the stirring of rats in the thatch and look for snakes in the grass; he must trust few, and least of all those who sleep upon his bosom. But those who have the Lion's blood in them or who are prone to charge like a buffalo, often neglect these matters and therefore in the end they fall into a pit."

"Yes," I answered, "especially those who have the lion's blood in them, whether that lion be man or beast."

This I said because of the rumours I had heard that this Slaughterer was in truth the son of Chaka. Therefore not knowing whether or no he were playing on the word "lion," which was Chaka's title, I wished to draw him, especially as I saw in his face a great likeness to Chaka's brother Dingaan, whom, it was whispered, this same Umslopogaas had slain. As it happened I failed, for after a pause he said,

"Why do you come to visit me, Macumazahn, who have never done so before?"

"I do not come to visit you, Umslopogaas. That was not my intention. You brought me, or rather the flooded rivers and you together brought me, for I was on my way to Natal and could not cross the drifts."

"Yet I think you have a message for me, White Man, for not long ago a certain wandering witch-doctor who came here told me to expect you and that you had words to say to me."

"Did he, Umslopogaas? Well, it is true that I have a message, though it is one that I did not mean to deliver."

"Yet being here, perchance you will deliver it, Macumazahn, for those who have messages and will not speak them, sometimes come to trouble."

"Yes, being here, I will deliver it, seeing that so it seems to be fated. Tell me, do you chance to know a certain Small One who is great, a certain Old One whose brain is young, a doctor who is called Opener-of-Roads?"

"I have heard of him, as have my forefathers for generations."

"Indeed, and if it pleases you to tell me, Umslopogaas, what might be the names of those forefathers of yours, who have heard of this doctor for generations? They must have been short-lived men and as such I should like to know of them."

"That you cannot," replied Umslopogaas shortly, "since they are hlonipa (i.e. not to be spoken) in this land."

"Indeed," I said again. "I thought that rule applied only to the names of kings, but of course I am but an ignorant white man who may well be mistaken on such matters of your Zulu customs."

"Yes, O Macumazahn, you may be mistaken or—you may not. It matters nothing. But what of this message of yours?"

"It came at the end of a long story, O Bulalio. But since you seek to know, these were the words of it, so nearly as I can remember them."

Then sentence by sentence I repeated to him all that Zikali had said to me when he called me back after bidding me farewell, which doubtless he did because he wished to cut his message more deeply into the tablets of my mind.

Umslopogaas listened to every syllable with a curious intentness, and then asked me to repeat it all again, which I did.

"Lousta! Monazi!" he said slowly. "Well, you heard those names to-day, did you not, White Man? And you heard certain things from the lips of this Monazi who was angry, that give colour to that talk of the Opener-of-Roads. It seems to me," he added, glancing about him and speaking in a low voice, "that what I suspected is true and that without doubt I am betrayed."

"I do not understand," I replied indifferently. "All this talk is dark to me, as is the message of the Opener-of-Roads, or rather its meaning. By whom and about what are you betrayed?"

"Let that snake sleep. Do not kick it with your foot. Suffice it you to know that my head hangs upon this matter; that I am a rat in a forked stick, and if the stick is pressed on by a heavy hand, then where is the rat?"

"Where all rats go, I suppose, that is, unless they are wise rats that bite the hand which holds the stick before it is pressed down."

"What is the rest of this story of yours, Macumazahn, which was told before the Opener-of-Roads gave you that message? Does it please you to repeat it to me that I may judge of it with my ears?"

"Certainly," I answered, "on one condition, that what the ears hear, the heart shall keep to itself alone."

Umslopogaas stooped and laid his hand upon the broad blade of the weapon beside him, saying,

"By the Axe I swear it. If I break the oath be the Axe my doom."

Then I told him the tale, as I have set it down already, thinking to myself that of it he would understand little, being but a wild warrior-man. As it chanced, however, I was mistaken, for he seemed to understand a great deal, perchance because such primitive natures are in closer touch with high and secret things than we imagine; perchance for other reasons with which I became acquainted later.

"It stands thus," he said when I had finished, "or so I think. You, Macumazahn, seek certain women who are dead to learn whether they still live, or are really dead, but so far have failed to find them. Still seeking, you asked the counsel of Zikali, Opener-of-Roads, he who among other titles is also called 'Home of Spirits.' He answered that he could not satisfy your heart because this tree was too tall for him to climb, but that far to the north there lives a certain white witch who has powers greater than his, being able to fly to the top of any tree, and to this white witch he bade you go. Have I the story right thus far?"

I answered that he had.

"Good! Then Zikali went on to choose you companions for your journey, but two, leaving out the guards or servants. I, Umhlopekazi, called Bulalio the Slaughterer, called the Woodpecker also, was one of these, and that little yellow monkey of a man whom I saw with you to-day, called Hansi, was the other. Then you made a mock of Zikali by determining not to visit me, Umhlopekazi, and not to go north to find the great white Queen of whom he had told you, but to return to Natal. Is that so?"

I said it was.

"Then the rain fell and the winds blew and the rivers rose in wrath so that you could not return to Natal, and after all by chance, or by fate, or by the will of Zikali, the wizard of wizards, you drifted here to the kraal of me, Umhlopekazi, and told me this story."

"Just so," I answered.

"Well, White Man, how am I to know that all this is not but a trap for my feet which already seem to feel cords between the toes of both of them? What token do you bring, O Watcher-by-Night? How am I to know that the Opener-of-Roads really sent me this message which has been delivered so strangely by one who wished to travel on another path? The wandering witch-doctor told me that he who came would bear some sign."

"I can't say," I answered, "at least in words. But," I added after reflection, "as you ask for a token, perhaps I might be able to show you something that would bring proof to your heart, if there were any secret place—"

Umslopogaas walked to the gateway of the fence and saw that the sentry was at his post. Then he walked round the hut casting an eye upon its roof, and muttered to me as he returned.

"Once I was caught thus. There lived a certain wife of mine who set her ear to the smoke-hole and so brought about the death of many, and among them of herself and of our children. Enter. All is safe. Yet if you talk, speak low."

So we went into the hut taking the stools with us, and seated ourselves by the fire that burned there on to which Umslopogaas threw chips of resinous wood.

"Now," he said.

I opened my shirt and by the clear light of the flame showed him the image of Zikali which hung about my neck. He stared at it, though touch it he would not. Then he stood up and lifting his great axe, he saluted the image with the word "Makosi!" the salute that is given to great wizards because they are supposed to be the home of many spirits.

"It is the big Medicine, the Medicine itself," he said, "that which has been known in the land since the time of Senzangacona, the father of the Zulu Royal House, and as it is said, before him."

"How can that be?" I asked, "seeing that this image represents Zikali, Opener-of-Roads, as an old man, and Senzangacona died many years ago?"

"I do not know," he answered, "but it is so. Listen. There was a certain Mopo, or as some called him, Umbopo, who was Chaka's body-servant and my foster-father, and he told me that twice this Medicine," and he pointed to the image, "was sent to Chaka, and that each time the Lion obeyed the message that came with it. A third time it was sent, but he did not obey the message and then—where was Chaka?"

Here Umslopogaas passed his hand across his mouth, a significant gesture amongst the Zulus.

"Mopo," I said, "yes, I have heard the story of Mopo, also that Chaka's body became his servant in the end, since Mopo killed him with the help of the princes Dingaan and Umhlangana. Also I have heard that this Mopo still lives, though not in Zululand."

"Does he, Macumazahn?" said Umslopogaas, taking snuff from a spoon and looking at me keenly over the spoon. "You seem to know a great deal, Macumazahn; too much as some might think."

"Yes," I answered, "perhaps I do know too much, or at any rate more than I want to know. For instance, O fosterling of Mopo and son of—was the lady named Baleka?—I know a good deal about you."

Umslopogaas stared at me and laying his hand upon the great axe, half rose. Then he sat down again.

"I think that this," and I touched the image of Zikali upon my breast, "would turn even the blade of the axe named Groan-maker," I said and paused. As nothing happened, I went on, "For instance, again I think I know—or have I dreamed it?—that a certain chief, whose mother's name I believe was Baleka— by the way, was she not one of Chaka's 'sisters'?—has been plotting against that son of Panda who sits upon the throne, and that his plots have been betrayed, so that he is in some danger of his life."

"Macumazahn," said Umslopogaas hoarsely, "I tell you that did you not wear the Great Medicine on your breast, I would kill you where you sit and bury you beneath the floor of the hut, as one who knows—too much."

"It would be a mistake, Umslopogaas, one of the many that you have made. But as I do wear the Medicine, the question does not arise, does it?"

Again he made no answer and I went on, "And now, what about this journey to the north? If indeed I must make it, would you wish to accompany me?"

Umslopogaas rose from the stool and crawled out of the hut, apparently to make some inspection. Presently he returned and remarked that the night was clear although there were heavy storm clouds on the horizon, by which I understood him to convey in Zulu metaphor that it was safe for us to talk, but that danger threatened from afar.

"Macumazahn," he said, "we speak under the blanket of the Opener-of-Roads who sits upon your heart, and whose sign you bring to me, as he sent me word that you would, do we not?"

"I suppose so," I answered. "At any rate we speak as man to man, and hitherto the honour of Macumazahn has not been doubted in Zululand. So if you have anything to say, Chief Bulalio, say it at once, for I am tired and should like to eat and rest."

"Good, Macumazahn. I have this to say. I who am the son of one who was greater than he, have plotted to seize the throne of Zululand from him who sits upon that throne. It is true, for I grew weary of my idleness as a petty chief. Moreover, I should have succeeded with the help of Zikali, who hates the House of Senzangacona, though me, who am of its blood, he does not hate, because ever I have striven against that House. But it seems from his message and those words spoken by an angry woman, that I have been betrayed, and that to-night or to-morrow night, or by the next moon, the slayers will be upon me, smiting me before I can smite, at which I cannot grumble."

"By whom have you been betrayed, Umslopogaas?"

"By that wife of mine, as I think, Macumazahn. Also by Lousta, my blood-brother, over whom she has cast her net and made false to me, so that he hopes to win her whom he has always loved and with her the Chieftainship of the Axe. Now what shall I do?—Tell me, you whose eyes can see in the dark."

I thought a moment and answered, "I think that if I were you, I would leave this Lousta to sit in my place for a while as Chief of the People of the Axe, and take a journey north, Umslopogaas. Then if trouble comes from the Great House where a king sits, it will come to Lousta who can show that the People of the Axe are innocent and that you are far away."

"That is cunning, Macumazahn. There speaks the Great Medicine. If I go north, who can say that I have plotted, and if I leave my betrayer in my place, who can say that I was a traitor, who have set him where I used to sit and left the land upon a private matter? And now tell me of this journey of yours."

So I told him everything, although until that moment I had not made up my mind to go upon this journey, I who had come here to his kraal by accident, or so it seemed, and by accident had delivered to him a certain message.

"You wish to consult a white witch-doctoress, Macumazahn, who according to Zikali lives far to the north, as to the dead. Now I too, though perchance you will not think it of a black man, desire to learn of the dead; yes, of a certain wife of my youth who was sister and friend as well as wife, whom too I loved better than all the world. Also I desire to learn of a brother of mine whose name I never speak, who ruled the wolves with me and who died at my side on yonder Witch-Mountain, having made him a mat of men to lie on in a great and glorious fight. For of him as of the woman I think all day and dream all night, and I would know if they still live anywhere and I may look to see them again when I have died as a warrior should and as I hope to do. Do you understand, Watcher-by-Night?"

I answered that I understood very well, as his case seemed to be like my own.

"It may happen," went on Umslopogaas, "that all this talk of the dead who are supposed to live after they are dead, is but as the sound of wind whispering in the reeds at night, that comes from nowhere and goes nowhere and means nothing. But at least ours will be a great journey in which we shall find adventure and fighting, since it is well known in the land that wherever Macumazahn goes there is plenty of both. Also it seems well for reasons that have been spoken of between us, as Zikali says, that I should leave the country of the Zulus for a while, who desire to die a man's death at the last and not to be trapped like a jackal in a pit. Lastly I think that we shall agree well together though my temper is rough at times, and that neither of us will desert the other in trouble, though of that little yellow dog of yours I am not so sure."

"I answer for him," I replied. "Hans is a true man, cunning also when once he is away from drink."

Then we spoke of plans for our journey, and of when and where we should meet to make it, talking till it was late, after which I went to sleep in the guest-hut.

CHAPTER IV

THE LION AND THE AXE

Next day early I left the town of the People of the Axe, having bid a formal farewell to Umslopogaas, saying in a voice that all could hear that as the rivers were still flooded, I proposed to trek to the northern parts of Zululand and trade there until the weather was better. Our private arrangement, however, was that on the night of the next full moon, which happened about four weeks later, we should meet at the eastern foot of a certain great, flat-topped mountain known to both of us, which stands to the north of Zululand but well beyond its borders.

So northward I trekked, slowly to spare my oxen, trading as I went. The details do not matter, but as it happened I met with more luck upon that journey than had come my way for many a long year. Although I worked on credit since nearly all my goods were sold, as owing to my repute I could always do in Zululand, I made some excellent bargains in cattle, and to top up with, bought a large lot of ivory so cheap that really I think it must have been stolen.

All of this, cattle, and ivory together, I sent to Natal in charge of a white friend of mine whom I could trust, where the stuff was sold very well indeed, and the proceeds paid to my account, the "trade" equivalents being duly remitted to the native vendors.

In fact, my good fortune was such that if I had been superstitious like Hans, I should have been inclined to attribute it to the influence of Zikali's "Great Medicine." As it was I knew it to be one of the chances of a trader's life and accepted it with a shrug as often as I had been accustomed to do in the alternative of losses.

Only one untoward incident happened to me. Of a sudden a party of the King's soldiers under the command of a well-known Induna or Councillor, arrived and insisted upon searching my waggon, as I thought at first in connection with that cheap lot of ivory which had already departed to Natal. However, never a word did they say of ivory, nor indeed was a single thing belonging to me taken by them.

I was very indignant and expressed my feelings to the Induna in no measured terms. He on his part was most apologetic, and explained that what he did he was obliged to do "by the King's orders." Also he let it slip that he was seeking for a certain "evil-doer" who, it was thought, might be with me without my knowing his real character, and as this "evil-doer," whose name he would not mention, was a very fierce man, it had been necessary to bring a strong guard with him.

Now I bethought me of Umslopogaas, but merely looked blank and shrugged my shoulders, saying that I was not in the habit of consorting with evil-doers.

Still unsatisfied, the Induna questioned me as to the places where I had been during this journey of mine in the Zulu country. I told him with the utmost frankness, mentioning among others—because I was sure that already he knew all my movements well—the town of the People of the Axe.

Then he asked me if I had seen its Chief, a certain Umslopogaas or Bulalio. I answered, Yes, that I had met him there for the first time and thought him a very remarkable man.

With this the Induna agreed emphatically, saying that perhaps I did not know how remarkable. Next he asked me where he was now, to which I replied that I had not the faintest idea, but I presumed in his kraal where I had left him. The Induna explained that he was not in his kraal; that he had gone away leaving one Lousta and his own head wife Monazi to administer the chieftainship for a while, because, as he stated, he wished to make a journey.

I yawned as if weary of the subject of this chief, and indeed of the whole business. Then the Induna said that I must come to the King and repeat to him all the words that I had spoken. I replied that I could not possibly do so as, having finished my trading, I had arranged to go north to shoot elephants. He answered that elephants lived a long while and would not die while I was visiting the King.

Then followed an argument which grew heated and ended in his declaring that to the King I must come, even if he had to take me there by force.

I sat silent, wondering what to say or do and leant forward to pick a piece of wood out of the fire wherewith to light my pipe. Now my shirt was not buttoned and as it chanced this action caused the ivory image of Zikali that hung about my neck to appear between its edges. The Induna saw it and his eyes grew big with fear.

"Hide that!" he whispered, "hide that, lest it should bewitch me. Indeed, already I feel as though I were being bewitched. It is the Great Medicine itself."

"That will certainly happen to you," I said, yawning again, "if you insist upon my taking a week's trek to visit the Black One, or interfere with me in any way now or afterwards," and I lifted my hand towards the talisman, looking him steadily in the face.

"Perhaps after all, Macumazahn, it is not necessary for you to visit the King," he said in an uncertain voice. "I will go and make report to him that you know nothing of this evil-doer."

And he went in such a hurry that he never waited to say good-bye. Next morning before the dawn I went also and trekked steadily until I was clear of Zululand.

In due course and without accident, for the weather, which had been so wet, had now turned beautifully fine and dry, we came to the great, flat-topped hill that I have mentioned, trekking thither over high, sparsely-timbered veld that offered few difficulties to the waggon. This peculiar hill, known to such natives as lived in those parts by a long word that means "Hut-with-a-flat-roof," is surrounded by forest, for here trees grow wonderfully well, perhaps because of the water that flows from its slopes. Forcing our way through this forest, which was full of game, I reached its eastern foot and there camped, five days before that night of full moon on which I had arranged to meet Umslopogaas.

That I should meet him I did not in the least believe, firstly because I thought it very probable that he would have changed his mind about coming, and secondly for the excellent reason that I expected he had gone to call upon the King against his will, as I had been asked to do. It was evident to me that he was up to his eyes in some serious plot against Cetywayo, in which he was the old dwarf Zikali's partner, or rather, tool; also that his plot had been betrayed, with the result that he was "wanted" and would have little chance of passing safely through Zululand. So taking one thing with another I imagined that I had seen his grim face and his peculiar, ancient-looking axe for the last time.

To tell the truth I was glad. Although at first the idea had appealed to me a little, I did not want to make this wild-goose, or wild-witch chase through unknown lands to seek for a totally fabulous person who dwelt far across the Zambesi. I had, as it were, been forced into the thing, but if Umslopogaas did not appear, my obligations would be at an end and I should return to Natal at my leisure. First, however, I would do a little shooting since I found that a large herd of elephants haunted this forest. Indeed I was tempted to attack them at once, but did not do so since, as Hans pointed out, if we were going north it would be difficult to carry the ivory, especially if we had to leave the waggon, and I was too old a hunter to desire to kill the great beasts for the fun of the thing.

So I just sat down and rested, letting the oxen feed throughout the hours of light on the rich grasses which grew upon the bottom-most slopes of the big mountain where we were camped by a stream, not more than a hundred yards above the timber line.

At some time or other there had been a native village at this spot; probably the Zulus had cleaned it out in long past years, for I found human bones black with age lying in the long grass. Indeed, the cattle-kraal still remained and in such good condition that by piling up a few stones here and there on the walls and closing the narrow entrances with thorn bushes, we could still use it to enclose our oxen at night. This I did for fear lest there should be lions about, though I had neither seen nor heard them.

So the days went by pleasantly enough with lots to eat, since whenever we wanted meat I had only to go a few yards to shoot a fat buck at a spot whither they trekked to drink in the evening, till at last came the time of full moon. Of this I was also glad, since, to tell the truth, I had begun to be bored. Rest is good, but for a man who has always led an active life too much of it is very bad, for then he begins to think and thought in large doses is depressing.

Of the fire-eating Umslopogaas there was no sign, so I made up my mind that on the morrow I would start after those elephants and when I had shot—or failed to shoot—some of them, return to Natal. I felt unable to remain idle any more; it never was my gift to do so, which is perhaps why I employ my ample leisure here in England in jotting down such reminiscences as these.

Well, the full moon came up in silver glory and after I had taken a good look at her for luck, also at all the veld within sight, I turned in. An hour or two later some noise from the direction of the cattle-kraal woke me up. As it did not recur, I thought that I would go to sleep again. Then an uneasy thought came to me that I could not remember having looked to see whether the entrance was properly closed, as it was my habit to do. It was the same sort of troublesome doubt which in a civilised house makes a man get out of bed and go along the cold passages to the sitting-room to see whether he has put out the lamp. It always proves that he has put it out, but that does not prevent a repetition of the performance next time the perplexity arises.

I reflected that perhaps the noise was caused by the oxen pushing their way through the carelessly-closed entrance, and at any rate that I had better go to see. So I slipped on my boots and a coat and went without waking Hans or the boys, only taking with me a loaded, single-barrelled rifle which I used for shooting small buck, but no spare cartridges.

Now in front of the gateway of the cattle-kraal, shading it, grew a single big tree of the wild fig order. Passing under this tree I looked and saw that the gateway was quite securely closed, as now I remembered I had noted at sunset. Then I started to go back but had not stepped more than two or three paces when, in the bright moonlight, I saw the head of my smallest ox, a beast of the Zulu breed, suddenly appear over the top of the wall. About this there would have been nothing particularly astonishing, had it not been for the fact that this head belonged to a dead animal, as I could tell from the closed eyes and the hanging tongue.

"What in the name of goodness—" I began to myself, when my reflections were cut short by the appearance of another head, that of one of the biggest lions I ever saw, which had the ox by the throat, and with the enormous strength that is given to these creatures, by getting its back beneath the body, was deliberately hoisting it over the wall, to drag it away to devour at its leisure.

There was the brute within twelve feet of me, and what is more, it saw me as I saw it, and stopped, still holding the ox by the throat.

"What a chance for Allan Quatermain! Of course he shot it dead," one can fancy anyone saying who knows me by repute, also that by the gift of God I am handy with a rifle. Well, indeed, it should have been, for even with the small-bore piece that I carried, a bullet ought to have pierced through the soft parts of its throat to the brain and to have killed that lion as dead as Julius Cæsar. Theoretically the thing was easy enough; indeed, although I was startled for a moment, by the time that I had the rifle to my shoulder I had little fear of the issue, unless there was a miss-fire, especially as the beast seemed so astonished that it remained quite still.

Then the unexpected happened as generally it does in life, particularly in hunting, which, in my case, is a part of life. I fired, but by misfortune the bullet struck the tip of the horn of that confounded ox, which tip either was or at that moment fell in front of the spot on the lion's throat whereat half-unconsciously I had aimed. Result: the ball was turned and, departing at an angle, just cut the skin of the lion's neck deeply enough to hurt it very much and to make it madder than all the hatters in the world.

Dropping the ox, with a most terrific roar it came over the wall at me—I remember that there seemed to be yards of it—I mean of the lion—in front of which appeared a cavernous mouth full of gleaming teeth.

I skipped back with much agility, also a little to one side, because there was nothing else to do, reflecting in a kind of inconsequent way, that after all Zikali's Great Medicine was not worth a curse. The lion landed on my side of the wall and reared itself upon its hind legs before getting to business, towering high above me but slightly to my left.

Then I saw a strange thing. A shadow thrown by the moon flitted past me—all I noted of it was the distorted shape of a great, lifted axe, probably because the axe came first. The shadow fell and with it another shadow, that of a lion's paw dropping to the ground. Next there was a most awful noise of roaring, and wheeling round I saw such a fray as never I shall see again. A tall, grim, black man was fighting the great lion, that now lacked one paw, but still stood upon its hind legs, striking at him with the other.

The man, who was absolutely silent, dodged the blow and hit back with the axe, catching the beast upon the breast with such weight that it came to the ground in a lopsided fashion, since now it had only one fore-foot on which to light.

The axe flashed up again and before the lion could recover itself, or do anything else, fell with a crash upon its skull, sinking deep into the head. After this all was over, for the beast's brain was cut in two.

"I am here at the appointed time, Macumazahn," said Umslopogaas, for it was he, as with difficulty he dragged his axe from the lion's severed skull, "to find you watching by night as it is reported that you always do."

"No," I retorted, for his tone irritated me, "you are late, Bulalio, the moon has been up some hours."

"I said, O Macumazahn, that I would meet you on the night of the full moon, not at the rising of the moon."

"That is true," I replied, mollified, "and at any rate you came at a good moment."

"Yes," he answered, "though as it happens in this clear light the thing was easy to anyone who can handle an axe. Had it been darker the end might have been different. But, Macumazahn, you are not so clever as I thought, since otherwise you would not have come out against a lion with a toy like that," and he pointed to the little rifle in my hand.

"I did not know that there was a lion, Umslopogaas."

"That is why you are not so clever as I thought, since of one sort or another there is always a lion which wise men should be prepared to meet, Macumazahn."

"You are right again," I replied.

At that moment Hans arrived upon the scene, followed at a discreet distance by the waggon boys, and took in the situation at a glance.

"The Great Medicine of the Opener-of-Roads has worked well," was all he said.

"The great medicine of the Opener-of-Heads has worked better," remarked Umslopogaas with a little laugh and pointing to his red axe. "Never before since she came into my keeping has Inkosikaas (i.e. 'Chieftainess,' for so was this famous weapon named) sunk so low as to drink the blood of beasts. Still, the stroke was a good one so she need not be ashamed. But, Yellow Man, how comes it that you who, I have been told, are cunning, watch your master so ill?"

"I was asleep," stuttered Hans indignantly.

"Those who serve should never sleep," replied Umslopogaas sternly. Then he turned and whistled, and behold! out of the long grass that grew at a little distance, emerged twelve great men, all of them bearing axes and wearing cloaks of hyena skins, who saluted me by raising their axes.

"Set a watch and skin me this beast by dawn. It will make us a mat," said Umslopogaas, whereon again they saluted silently and melted away.

"Who are these?" I asked.

"A few picked warriors whom I brought with me, Macumazahn. There were one or two more, but they got lost on the way."

Then we went to the waggon and spoke no more that night.

Next morning I told Umslopogaas of the visit I had received from the Induna of the King who wished me to come to the royal kraal. He nodded and said,

"As it chances certain thieves attacked me on my journey, which is why one or two of my people remain behind who will never travel again. We made good play with those thieves; not one of them escaped," he added grimly, "and their bodies we threw into a river where are many crocodiles. But their spears I brought away and I think that they are such as the King's guard use. If so, his search for them will be long, since the fight took place where no man lives and we burned the shields and trappings. Oho! he will think that the ghosts have taken them."

That morning we trekked on fast, fearing lest a regiment searching for these "thieves" should strike and follow our spoor. Luckily the ox that the lion had killed was one of some spare cattle which I was driving with me, so its loss did not inconvenience us. As we went Umslopogaas told me that he had duly appointed Lousta and his wife Monazi to rule the tribe during his absence, an office which they accepted doubtfully, Monazi acting as Chieftainess and Lousta as her head Induna or Councillor.

I asked him whether he thought this wise under all the circumstances, seeing that it had occurred to me since I made the suggestion, that they might be unwilling to surrender power on his return, also that other domestic complications might ensue.

"It matters little, Macumazahn," he said with a shrug of his great shoulders, "for of this I am sure, that I have played my part with the People of the Axe and to stop among them would have meant my death, who am a man betrayed. What do I care who love none and now have no children? Still, it is true that I might have fled to Natal with the cattle and there have led a fat and easy life. But ease and plenty I do not desire who would live and fall as a warrior should.

"Never again, mayhap, shall I see the Ghost-Mountain where the wolves ravened and the old Witch sits in stone waiting for the world to die, or sleep in the town of the People of the Axe. What do I want with wives and oxen while I have Inkosikaas the Groan-maker and she is true to me?" he added, shaking the ancient axe above his head so that the sun gleamed upon the curved blade and the hollow gouge or point at the back beyond the shaft socket. "Where the Axe goes, there go the strength and virtue of the Axe, O Macumazahn."

"It is a strange weapon," I said.

"Aye, a strange and an old, forged far away, says Zikali, by a warrior-wizard hundreds of years ago, a great fighter who was also the first of smiths and who sits in the Under-world waiting for it to return to his hand when its work is finished beneath the sun. That will be soon, Macumazahn, since Zikali told me that I am the last Holder of the Axe."

"Did you then see the Opener-of-Roads?" I asked.

"Aye, I saw him. He it was who told me which way to go to escape from Zululand. Also he laughed when he heard how the flooded rivers brought you to my kraal, and sent you a message in which he said that the spirit of a snake had told him that you tried to throw the Great Medicine into a pool, but were stopped by that snake, whilst it was still alive. This, he said, you must do no more, lest he should send another snake to stop you."

"Did he?" I replied indignantly, for Zikali's power of seeing or learning about things that happened at a distance puzzled and annoyed me.

Only Hans grinned and said,

"I told you so, Baas."

On we travelled from day to day, meeting with such difficulties and dangers as are common on roadless veld in Africa, but no more, for the grass was good and there was plenty of game, of which we shot what we wanted for meat. Indeed, here in the back regions of what is known as Portuguese South East Africa, every sort of wild animal was so numerous that personally I wished we could turn our journey into a shooting expedition.

But of this Umslopogaas, whom hunting bored, would not hear. In fact, he was much more anxious than myself to carry out our original purpose. When I asked him why, he answered because of something Zikali had told him. What this was he would not say, except that in the country whither we wandered he would fight a great fight and win much honour.

Now Umslopogaas was by nature a fighting man, one who took a positive joy in battle, and like an old Norseman, seemed to think that thus only could a man decorously die. This amazed me, a peaceful person who loves quiet and a home. Still, I gave way, partly to please him, partly because I hoped that we might discover something of interest, and still more because, having once undertaken an enterprise, my pride prompted me to see it through.

Now while he was preparing to draw his map in the ashes, or afterwards, I forget which, Zikali had told me that when we drew near to the great river we should come to a place on the edge of bush-veld that ran down to the river, where a white man lived, adding, after casting his bones and reading from them, that he thought this white man was a "trek-Boer." This, I should explain, means a Dutchman who has travelled away from wherever he lived and made a home for himself in the wilderness, as some wandering spirit and the desire to be free of authority often prompt these people to do. Also, after another inspection of his enchanted knuckle-bones, he had declared that something remarkable would happen to this man or his family, while I was visiting him. Lastly in that map he drew in the ashes, the details of which were impressed so indelibly upon my memory, he had shown me where I should find the dwelling of this white man, of whom and of whose habitation doubtless he knew through the many spies who seemed to be at the service of all witch-doctors, and more especially of Zikali, the greatest among them.

Travelling by the sun and the compress I had trekked steadily in the exact direction which he indicated, to find that in this useful particular he was well named the "Opener-of-Roads," since always before me I found a practicable path, although to the right or to the left there would have been none. Thus when we came to mountains, it was at a spot where we discovered a pass; when we came to swamps it was where a ridge of high ground ran between, and so forth. Also such tribes as we met upon our journey always proved of a friendly character, although perhaps the aspect of Umslopogaas and his fierce band whom, rather irreverently, I named his twelve Apostles, had a share in inducing this peaceful attitude.

So smooth was our progress and so well marked by water at certain intervals, that at last I came to the conclusion that we must be following some ancient road which at a forgotten period of history, had run from south to north, or vice versâ. Or rather, to be honest, it was the observant Hans who made this discovery from various indications which had escaped my notice. I need not stop to detail them, but one of these was that at certain places the water-holes on a high, rather barren land had been dug out, and in one or more instances, lined with stones after the fashion of an ancient well. Evidently we were following an old trade route made, perhaps, in forgotten ages when Africa was more civilised than it is now.

Passing over certain high, misty lands during the third week of our trek, where frequently at this season of the year the sun never showed itself before ten o'clock and disappeared at three or four in the afternoon, and where twice we were held up for two whole days by dense fog, we came across a queer nomadic people who seemed to live in movable grass huts and to keep great herds of goats and long-tailed sheep.

These folk ran away from us at first, but when they found that we did them no harm, became friendly and brought us offerings of milk, also of a kind of slug or caterpillar which they seemed to eat. Hans, who was a great master of different native dialects, discovered a tongue, or a mixture of tongues, in which he could make himself understood to some of them.

They told him that in their day they had never seen a white man, although their fathers' fathers (an expression by which they meant their remote ancestors) had known many of them. They added, however, that if we went on steadily towards the north for another seven days' journey, we should come to a place where a white man lived, one, they had heard, who had a long beard and killed animals with guns, as we did.

Encouraged by this intelligence we pushed forward, now travelling down hill out of the mists into a more genial country. Indeed, the veld here was beautiful, high, rolling plains like those of the East African plateau, covered with a deep and fertile chocolate-coloured soil, as we could see where the rains had washed out dongas. The climate, too, seemed to be cool and very healthful. Altogether it was a pity to see such lands lying idle and tenanted only by countless herds of game, for there were not any native inhabitants, or at least we met none.

On we trekked, our road still sloping slightly down hill, till at length we saw far away a vast sea of bush-veld which, as I guessed correctly, must fringe the great Zambesi River. Moreover we, or rather Hans, whose eyes were those of a hawk, saw something else, namely buildings of a more or less civilised kind, which stood among trees by the side of a stream several miles on this side of the great belt of bush.

"Look, Baas," said Hans, "those wanderers did not lie; there is the house of the white man. I wonder if he drinks anything stronger than water," he added with a sigh and a kind of reminiscent contraction of his yellow throat.

As it happened, he did.

CHAPTER V

We had sighted the house from far away shortly after sunrise and by midday we were there. As we approached I saw that it stood almost immediately beneath two great baobab trees, babyan trees we call them in South Africa, perhaps because monkeys eat their fruit. It was a thatched house with whitewashed walls and a stoep or veranda round it, apparently of the ordinary Dutch type. Moreover, beyond it, at a little distance were other houses or rather shanties with waggon sheds, etc., and beyond and mixed up with these a number of native huts. Further on were considerable fields green with springing corn; also we saw herds of cattle grazing on the slopes. Evidently our white man was rich.

Umslopogaas surveyed the place with a soldier's eye and said to me,

"This must be a peaceful country, Macumazahn, where no attack is feared, since of defences I see none."

"Yes," I answered, "why not, with a wilderness behind it and bush-veld and a great river in front?"

"Men can cross rivers and travel through bush-veld," he answered, and was silent.

Up to this time we had seen no one, although it might have been presumed that a waggon trekking towards the house was a sufficiently unusual sight to have attracted attention.

"Where can they be?" I asked.

"Asleep, Baas, I think," said Hans, and as a matter of fact he was right. The whole population of the place was indulging in a noonday siesta.

At last we came so near to the house that I halted the waggon and descended from the driving-box in order to investigate. At this moment someone did appear, the sight of whom astonished me not a little, namely, a very striking-looking young woman. She was tall, handsome, with large dark eyes, good features, a rather pale complexion, and I think the saddest face that I ever saw. Evidently she had heard the noise of the waggon and had come out to see what caused it, for she had nothing on her head, which was covered with thick hair of a raven blackness. Catching sight of the great Umslopogaas with his gleaming axe and of his savage-looking bodyguard, she uttered an exclamation and not unnaturally turned to fly.

"It's all right," I sang out, emerging from behind the oxen, and in English, though before the words had left my lips I reflected that there was not the slightest reason to suppose that she would understand them. Probably she was Dutch, or Portuguese, although by some instinct I had addressed her in English.

To my surprise she answered me in the same tongue, spoken, it is true, with a peculiar accent which I could not place, as it was neither Scotch nor Irish.

"Thank you," she said. "I, sir, was frightened. Your friends look—" Here she stumbled for a word, then added, "terrocious."

I laughed at this composite adjective and answered,

"Well, so they are in a way, though they will not harm you or me. But, young lady, tell me, can we outspan here? Perhaps your husband—"

"I have no husband, I have only a father, sir," and she sighed.

"Well, then, could I speak to your father? My name is Allan Quatermain and I am making a journey of exploration, to find out about the country beyond, you know."

"Yes, I will go to wake him. He is asleep. Everyone sleeps here at midday—except me," she said with another sigh.

"Why do you not follow their example?" I asked jocosely, for this young woman puzzled me and I wanted to find out about her.

"Because I sleep little, sir, who think too much. There will be plenty of time to sleep soon for all of us, will there not?"

I stared at her and inquired her name, because I did not know what else to say.

"My name is Inez Robertson," she answered. "I will go to wake my father. Meanwhile please unyoke your oxen. They can feed with the others; they look as though they wanted rest, poor things." Then she turned and went into the house.

"Inez Robertson," I said to myself, "that's a queer combination. English father and Portuguese mother, I suppose. But what can an Englishman be doing in a place like this? If it had been a trek-Boer I should not have been surprised." Then I began to give directions about out-spanning.

We had just got the oxen out of the yokes, when a big, raw-boned, red-bearded, blue-eyed, roughly-clad man of about fifty years of age appeared from the house, yawning. I threw my eye over him as he advanced with a peculiar rolling gait, and formed certain conclusions. A drunkard who has once been a gentleman, I reflected to myself, for there was something peculiarly dissolute in his appearance, also one who has had to do with the sea, a diagnosis which proved very accurate.

"How do you do, Mr. Allan Quatermain, which I think my daughter said is your name, unless I dreamed it, for it is one that I seem to have heard before," he exclaimed with a broad Scotch accent which I do not attempt to reproduce. "What in the name of blazes brings you here where no real white man has been for years? Well, I am glad enough to see you any way, for I am sick of half-breed Portuguese and niggers, and snuff-and-butter girls, and gin and bad whisky. Leave your people to attend to those oxen and come in and have a drink."

"Thank you, Mr. Robertson—"

"Captain Robertson," he interrupted. "Man, don't look astonished. You mightn't guess it, but I commanded a mail-steamer once and should like to hear myself called rightly again before I die."

"I beg your pardon—Captain Robertson, but myself, I don't drink anything before sundown. However, if you have something to eat—?"

"Oh yes, Inez—she's my daughter—will find you a bite. Those men of yours," and he also looked doubtfully at Umslopogaas and his savage company, "will want food as well. I'll have a beast killed for them; they look as if they could eat it, horns and all. Where are my people? All asleep, I suppose, the lazy lubbers. Wait a bit, I'll wake them up."

Going to the house he snatched a great sjambok cut from hippopotamus hide, from where it hung on a nail in the wall, and ran towards the group of huts which I have mentioned, roaring out the name Thomaso, also a string of oaths such as seamen use, mixed with others of a Portuguese variety. What happened there I could not see because boughs were in the way, but presently I heard blows and screams, and caught sight of people, all dark-skinned, flying from the huts.

A little later a fat, half-breed man—I should say from his curling hair that his mother was a negress and his father a Portuguese—appeared with some other nondescript fellows and began to give directions in a competent fashion about our oxen, also as to the killing of a calf. He spoke in bastard Portuguese, which I could understand, and I heard him talk of Umslopogaas to whom he pointed, as "that nigger," after the fashion of such cross-bred people who choose to consider themselves white men. Also he made uncomplimentary remarks about Hans, who of course understood every word he said. Evidently Thomaso's temper had been ruffled by this sudden and violent disturbance of his nap.

Just then our host appeared puffing with his exertions and declaring that he had stirred up the swine with a vengeance, in proof of which he pointed to the sjambok that was reddened with blood.

"Captain Robertson," I said, "I wish to give you a hint to be passed on to Mr. Thomaso, if that is he. He spoke of the Zulu soldier there as a nigger, etc. Well, he is a chief of a high rank and rather a terrible fellow if roused. Therefore I recommend Mr. Thomaso not to let him understand that he is insulting him."

"Oh! that's the way of these 'snuff-and-butters' one of whose grandmothers once met a white man," replied the Captain, laughing, "but I'll tell him," and he did in Portuguese.

His retainer listened in silence, looking at Umslopogaas rather sulkily. Then we walked into the house. As we went the Captain said,

"Señor Thomaso—he calls himself Señor—is my manager here and a clever man, honest too in his way and attached to me, perhaps because I saved his life once. But he has a nasty temper, as have all these cross-breeds, so I hope he won't get wrong with that native who carries a big axe."

"I hope so too, for his own sake," I replied emphatically.

The Captain led the way into the sitting-room; there was but one in the house. It proved a queer kind of place with rude furniture seated with strips of hide after the Boer fashion, and yet bearing a certain air of refinement which was doubtless due to Inez, who, with the assistance of a stout native girl, was already engaged in setting the table. Thus there was a shelf with books, Shakespeare was one of these, I noticed—over which hung an ivory crucifix, which suggested that Inez was a Catholic. On the walls, too, were some good portraits, and on the window-ledge a jar full of flowers. Also the forks and spoons were of silver, as were the mugs, and engraved with a tremendous coat-of-arms and a Portuguese motto.

Presently the food appeared, which was excellent and plentiful, and the Captain, his daughter and I sat down and ate. I noted that he drank gin and water, an innocent-looking beverage but strong as he took it. It was offered to me, but like Miss Inez, I preferred coffee.

During the meal and afterwards while we smoked upon the veranda, I told them as much as I thought desirable of my plans. I said that I was engaged upon a journey of exploration of the country beyond the Zambesi, and that having heard of this settlement, which, by the way, was called Strathmuir, as I gathered after a place in far away Scotland where the Captain had been born and passed his childhood, I had come here to inquire as to how to cross the great river, and about other things.

The Captain was interested, especially when I informed him that I was that same "Hunter Quatermain" of whom he had heard in past years, but he told me that it would be impossible to take the waggon down into the low bush-veld which we could see beneath us, as there all the oxen would die of the bite of the tsetse fly. I answered that I was aware of this and proposed to try to make an arrangement to leave it in his charge till I returned.

"That might be managed, Mr. Quatermain," he answered. "But, man, will you ever return? They say there are queer folk living on the other side of the Zambesi, savage men who are cannibals, Amahagger I think they call them. It was they who in past years cleaned out all this country, except a few river tribes who live in floating huts or on islands among the reeds, and that's why it is so empty. But this happened long ago, much before my time, and I don't suppose they will ever cross the river again."

"If I might ask, what brought you here, Captain?" I said, for the point was one on which I felt curious.

"That which brings most men to wild places, Mr. Quatermain—trouble. If you want to know, I had a misfortune and piled up my ship. There were some lives lost and, rightly or wrongly, I got the sack. Then I started as a trader in a God-forsaken hole named Chinde, one of the Zambesi mouths, you know, and did very well, as we Scotchmen have a way of doing.

"There I married a Portuguese lady, a real lady of high blood, one of the old sort. When my girl, Inez, was about twelve years old I got into more trouble, for my wife died and it pleased a certain relative of hers to say that it was because I had neglected her. This ended in a row and the truth is that I killed him—in fair fight, mind you. Still, kill him I did though I scarcely knew that I had done it at the time, after which the place grew too hot to hold me. So I sold up and swore that I would have no more to do with what they are pleased to call civilisation on the East Coast.

"During my trading I had heard that there was fine country up this way, and here I came and settled years ago, bringing my girl and Thomaso, who was one of my managers, also a few other people with me. And here I have been ever since, doing very well as before, for I trade a lot of ivory and other things and grow stuff and cattle, which I sell to the River natives. Yes, I am a rich man now and could go to live on my means in Scotland, or anywhere."

"Why don't you?" I asked.

"Oh! for many reasons. I have lost touch with all that and become half wild and I like this life and the sunshine and being my own master. Also, if I did, things might be raked up against me, about that man's death. Also, though I daresay it will make you think badly of me for it, Mr. Quatermain, I have ties down there," and he waved is hand towards the village, if so it could be called, "which it wouldn't be easy for me to break. A man may be fond of his children, Mr. Quatermain, even if their skins ain't so white as they ought to be. Lastly I have habits—you see, I am speaking out to you as man to man—which might get me into trouble again if I went back to the world," and he nodded his fine, capable-looking head in the direction of the bottle on the table.

"I see," I said hastily, for this kind of confession bursting out of the man's lonely heart when what he had drunk took a hold of him, was painful to hear. "But how about your daughter, Miss Inez?"

"Ah!" he said, with a quiver in his voice, "there you touch it. She ought to go away. There is no one for her to marry here, where we haven't seen a white man for years, and she's a lady right enough, like her mother. But who is she to go to, being a Roman Catholic whom my own dour Presbyterian folk in Scotland, if any of them are left, would turn their backs on? Moreover, she loves me in her own fashion, as I love her, and she wouldn't leave me because she thinks it her duty to stay and knows that if she did, I should go to the devil altogether. Still—perhaps you might help me about her, Mr. Quatermain, that is if you live to come back from your journey," he added doubtfully.

I felt inclined to ask how I could possibly help in such a matter, but thought it wisest to say nothing. This, however, he did not notice, for he went on,

"Now I think I will have a nap, as I do my work in the early morning, and sometimes late at night when my brain seems to clear up again, for you see I was a sailor for many years and accustomed to keeping watches. You'll look after yourself, won't you, and treat the place as your own?" Then he vanished into the house to lie down.

When I had finished my pipe I went for a walk. First I visited the waggon where I found Umslopogaas and his company engaged in cooking the beast that had been given them, Zulu fashion; Hans with his usual cunning had already secured a meal, probably from the servants, or from Inez herself; at least he left them and followed me. First we went down to the huts, where we saw a number of good-looking young women of mixed blood, all decently dressed and engaged about their household duties. Also we saw four or five boys and girls, to say nothing of a baby in arms, fine young people, one or two of whom were more white than coloured.

"Those children are very like the Baas with the red beard," remarked Hans reflectively.

"Yes," I said, and shivered, for now I understood the awfulness of this poor man's case. He was the father of a number of half-breeds who tied him to this spot as anchors tie a ship. I went on rather hastily past some sheds to a long, low building which proved to be a store. Here the quarter-blood called Thomaso, and some assistants were engaged in trading with natives from the Zambesi swamps, men of a kind that I had never seen, but in a way more civilised than many further south. What they were selling or buying, I did not stop to see, but I noticed that the store was full of goods of one sort or another, including a great deal of ivory, which, as I supposed, had come down the river from inland.

Then we walked on to the cultivated fields where we saw corn growing very well, also tobacco and other crops. Beyond this were cattle kraals and in the distance we perceived a great number of cattle and goats feeding on the slopes.

"This red-bearded Baas must be very rich in all things," remarked the observant Hans when we had completed our investigations.

"Yes," I answered, "rich and yet poor."

"How can a man be both rich and yet poor, Baas?" asked Hans.

Just at that moment some of the half-breed children whom I have mentioned, ran past us more naked than dressed and whooping like little savages. Hans contemplated them gravely, then said,

"I think I understand now, Baas. A man may be rich in things he loves and yet does not want, which makes him poor in other ways."

"Yes," I answered, "as you are, Hans, when you take too much to drink."

Just then we met the stately Miss Inez returning from the store, carrying some articles in a basket, soap, I think, and tea in a packet, amongst them. I told Hans to take the basket and bear it to the house for her. He went off with it and, walking slowly, we fell into conversation.

"Your father must do very well here," I said, nodding at the store with the crowd of natives round it.

"Yes," she answered, "he makes much money which he puts in a bank at the coast, for living costs us nothing and there is great profit in what he buys and sells, also in the crops he grows and in the cattle. But," she added pathetically, "what is the use of money in a place like this?"

"You can get things with it," I answered vaguely.

"That is what my father says, but what does he get? Strong stuff to drink; dresses for those women down there, and sometimes pearls, jewels and other things for me which I do not want. I have a box full of them set in ugly gold, or loose which I cannot use, and if I put them on, who is there to see them? That clever half-breed, Thomaso—for he is clever in his way, faithful too—or the women down there— no one else."

"You do not seem to be happy, Miss Inez."

"No. I cannot tell how unhappy others are, who have met none, but sometimes I think that I must be the most miserable woman in the world."

"Oh! no," I replied cheerfully, "plenty are worse off."

"Then, Mr. Quatermain, it must be because they cannot feel. Did you ever have a father whom you loved?"

"Yes, Miss Inez. He is dead, but he was a very good man, a kind of saint. Ask my servant, the little Hottentot Hans; he will tell you about him."

"Ah! a very good man. Well, as you may have guessed, mine is not, though there is much good in him, for he has a kind heart, and a big brain. But the drink and those women down there, they ruin him," and she wrung her hands.

"Why don't you go away?" I blurted out.

"Because it is my duty to stop. That is what my religion teaches me, although of it I know little except through books, who have seen no priest for years except one who was a missionary, a Baptist, I think, who told me that my faith was false and would lead me to hell. Yes, not understanding how I lived, he said that, who did not know that hell is here. No, I cannot go, who hopes always that still God and the Saints will show me how to save my father, even though it be with my blood. And now I have said too much to you who are quite a stranger. Yet, I do not know why, I feel that you will not betray me, and what is more, that you will help me if you can, since you are not one of those who drink, or—" and she waved her hand towards the huts.

"I have my faults, Miss Inez," I answered.

"Yes, no doubt, else you would be a saint, not a man, and even the saints had their faults, or so I seem to remember, and became saints by repentance and conquering them. Still, I am sure that you will help me if you can."

Then with a sudden flash of her dark eyes that said more than all her words, she turned and left me.

Here's a pretty kettle of fish, thought I to myself as I strolled back to the waggon to see how things were going on there, and how to get the live fish out of the kettle before they boil or spoil is more than I know. I wonder why fate is always finding me such jobs to do.

Even as I thought thus a voice in my heart seemed to echo that poor girl's words—because it is your duty—and to add others to them—woe betide him who neglects his duty. I was appointed to try to hook a few fish out of the vast kettle of human woe, and therefore I must go on hooking. Meanwhile this particular problem seemed beyond me. Perhaps Fate would help, I reflected. As a matter of fact, in the end Fate did, if Fate is the right word to use in this connection.

CHAPTER VI

THE SEA-COW HUNT

Now it had been my intention to push forward across the river at once, but here luck, or our old friend, Fate, was against me. To begin with several of Umslopogaas' men fell sick with a kind of stomach trouble, arising no doubt from something they had eaten. This, however, was not their view, or that of Umslopogaas himself. It happened that one of these men, Goroko by name, who practised as a witch-doctor in his lighter moments, naturally suspected that a spell had been cast upon them, for such people see magic in everything.

Therefore he organised a "smelling-out" at which Umslopogaas, who was as superstitious as the rest, assisted. So did Hans, although he called himself a Christian, partly out of curiosity, for he was as curious as a magpie, and partly from fear lest some implication should be brought against him in his absence. I saw the business going on from a little distance, and, unseen myself, thought it well to keep an eye upon the proceedings in case anything untoward should occur. This I did with Miss Inez, who had never witnessed anything of the sort, as a companion.

The circle, a small one, was formed in the usual fashion; Goroko rigged up in the best witch-doctor's costume that he could improvise, duly came under the influence of his "Spirit" and skipped about, waving a wildebeeste's tail, and so forth.

Finally to my horror he broke out of the ring, and running to a group of spectators from the village, switched Thomaso, who was standing among them with a lordly and contemptuous air, across the face with the gnu's tail, shouting out that he was the wizard who had poisoned the bowels of the sick men. Thereon Thomaso, who although he could be insolent, like most crossbreeds was not remarkable for courage, seeing the stir that this announcement created amongst the fierce-faced Zulus and fearing developments, promptly bolted, none attempting to follow him.

After this, just as I thought that everything was over and that the time had come for me to speak a few earnest words to Umslopogaas, pointing out that matters must go no further as regards Thomaso, whom I knew that he and his people hated, Goroko went back to the circle and was seized with a new burst of inspiration.

Throwing down his whisk, he lifted his arms above his head and stared at the heavens. Then he began to shout out something in a loud voice which I was too far off to catch. Whatever it may have been, evidently it frightened his hearers, as I could see from the expressions on their faces. Even Umslopogaas was alarmed, for he let his axe fall for a moment, rose as though to speak, then sat down again and covered his eyes with his hands.

In a minute it was over; Goroko seemed to become normal, took some snuff and as I guessed, after the usual fashion of these doctors, began to ask what he had been saying while the "Spirit" possessed him, which he either had, or affected to have, forgotten. The circle, too, broke up and its members began to talk to each other in a subdued way, while Umslopogaas remained seated on the ground, brooding, and Hans slipped away in his snake-like fashion, doubtless in search of me.

"What was it all about, Mr. Quatermain?" asked Inez.

"Oh! a lot of nonsense," I said. "I fancy that witch-doctor declared that your friend Thomaso put something into those men's food to make them sick."

"I daresay that he did; it would be just like him, Mr. Quatermain, as I know that he hates them, especially Umslopogaas, of whom I am very fond. He brought me some beautiful flowers this morning which he had found somewhere, and made a long speech which I could not understand."

The idea of Umslopogaas, that man of blood and iron, bringing flowers to a young lady, was so absurd that I broke out laughing and even the sad-faced Inez smiled. Then she left me to see about something and I went to speak to Hans and asked him what had happened.

"Something rather queer, I think, Baas," he answered vacuously, "though I did not quite understand the last part. The doctor, Goroko, smelt out Thomaso as the man who had made them sick, and though they will not kill him because we are guests here, those Zulus are very angry with Thomaso and I think will beat him if they get a chance. But that is only the small half of the stick," and he paused.

"What is the big half, then?" I asked with irritation.

"Baas, the Spirit in Goroko—"

"The jackass in Goroko, you mean," I interrupted. "How can you, who are a Christian, talk such rubbish about spirits? I only wish that my father could hear you."

"Oh! Baas, your reverend father, the Predikant, is now wise enough to know all about Spirits and that there are some who come into black witch-doctors though they turn up their noses at white men and leave them alone. However, whatever it is that makes Goroko speak, got hold of him so that his lips said, though he remembered nothing of it afterwards, that soon this place would be red with blood—that there would be a great killing here, Baas. That is all."

"Red with blood! Whose blood? What did the fool mean?"

"I don't know, Baas, but what you call the jackass in Goroko, declared that those who are 'with the Great Medicine'—meaning what you wear, Baas—will be quite safe. So I hope that it will not be our blood; also that you will get out of this place as soon as you can."

Well, I scolded Hans because he believed in what this doctor said, for I could see that he did believe it, then went to question Umslopogaas, whom I found looking quite pleased, which annoyed me still more.

"What is it that Goroko has been saying and why do you smile, Bulalio?" I asked.

"Nothing much, Macumazahn, except that the man who looks like tallow that has gone bad, put something in our food which made us sick, for which I would kill him were he not Red-beard's servant and that it would frighten the lady his daughter. Also he said that soon there will be fighting, which is why I smiled, who grow weary of peace. We came out to fight, did we not?"

"Certainly not," I answered. "We came out to make a quiet journey in strange lands, which is what I mean to do."

"Ah! well, Macumazahn, in strange lands one meets strange men with whom one does not always agree, and then Inkosikaas begins to talk," and he whirled the great axe round his head, making the air whistle as it was forced through the gouge at its back.

I could get no more out of him, so having extracted a promise from him that nothing should happen to Thomaso who, I pointed out, was probably quite unjustly accused, I went away.

Still, the whole incident left a disagreeable impression on my mind, and I began to wish that we were safe across the Zambesi without more trouble. But we could not start at once because two of the Zulus were still not well enough to travel and there were many preparations to be made about the loads, and so forth, since the waggon must be left behind. Also, and this was another complication—Hans had a sore upon his foot, resulting from the prick of a poisonous thorn, and it was desirable that this should be quite healed before we marched.

So it came about that I was really glad when Captain Robertson suggested that we should go down to a certain swamp formed, I gathered, by some small tributary of the Zambesi to take part in a kind of hippopotamus battue. It seemed that at this season of the year these great animals always frequented the place in numbers, also that by barring a neck of deep water through which they gained it, they, or a proportion of them, could be cut off and killed.

This had been done once or twice in the past, though not of late, perhaps because Captain Robertson had lacked the energy to organise such a hunt. Now he wished to do so again, taking advantage of my presence, both because of the value of the hides of the sea-cows which were cut up to be sent to the coast and sold as sjamboks or whips, and because of the sport of the thing. Also I think he desired to show me that he was not altogether sunk in sloth and drink.

I fell in with the idea readily enough, since in all my hunting life I had never seen anything of the sort, especially as I was told that the expedition would not take more than a week and I reckoned that the sick men and Hans would not be fit to travel sooner. So great preparations were made. The riverside natives, whose share of the spoil was to be the carcases of the slain sea-cows, were summoned by hundreds and sent off to their appointed stations to beat the swamps at a signal given by the firing of a great pile of reeds. Also many other things were done upon which I need not enter.

Then came the time for us to depart to the appointed spot over twenty miles away, most of which distance it seemed we could trek in the waggon. Captain Robertson, who for the time had cut off his gin, was as active about the affair as though he were once more in command of a mail-steamer. Nothing escaped his attention; indeed, in the care which he gave to details he reminded me of the captain of a great ship that is leaving port, and from it I learned how able a man he must once have been.

"Does your daughter accompany us?" I asked on the night before we started.

"Oh! no," he answered, "she would only be in the way. She will be quite safe here, especially as Thomaso, who is no hunter, remains in charge of the place with some of the older natives to look after the women and children."

Later I saw Inez herself, who said that she would have liked to come, although she hated to see great beasts killed, but that her father was against it because he thought she might catch fever. So she supposed that she had better remain where she was.

I agreed, though in my heart I was doubtful, and said that I would leave Hans, whose foot was not as yet quite well, and with whom she had made friends as she had done with Umslopogaas, to look after her. Also there would be with him the two great Zulus who were now recovering from their attack of stomach sickness, so that she would have nothing to fear. She answered with her slow smile that she feared nothing, still, she would have liked to come with us. Then we parted, as it proved for a long time.

It was quite a ceremony. Umslopogaas, "in the name of the Axe" solemnly gave over Inez to the charge of his two followers, bidding them guard her with so much earnestness that I began to suspect he feared something which he did not choose to mention. My mind went back indeed to the prophecy of the witch-doctor Goroko, of which it was possible that he might be thinking, but as while he spoke he kept his fierce eyes fixed upon the fat and pompous quarter-breed, Thomaso, I concluded that here was the object of his doubts.

It might have occurred to him that this Thomaso would take the opportunity of her father's absence to annoy Inez. If so I was sure that he was mistaken for various reasons, of which I need only quote one, namely, that even if such an idea had ever entered his head, Thomaso was far too great a coward to translate it into action. Still, suspecting something, I also gave Hans instructions to keep a sharp eye on Inez and generally to watch the place, and if he saw anything suspicious, to communicate with us at once.

"Yes, Baas," said Hans, "I will look after 'Sad-Eyes'"—for so with their usual quickness of observation our Zulus had named Inez—"as though she were my grandmother, though what there is to fear for her, I do not know. But, Baas, I would much rather come and look after you, as your reverend father, the Predikant, told me to do always, which is my duty, not girl-herding, Baas. Also my foot is now quite well and—I want to shoot sea-cows, and—" Here he paused.

"And what, Hans?"

"And Goroko said that there was going to be much fighting and if there should be fighting and you should come to harm because I was not there to protect you, what would your reverend father think of me then?"

All of which meant two things: that Hans never liked being separated from me if he could help it, and that he much preferred a shooting trip to stopping alone in this strange place with nothing to do except eat and sleep. So I concluded, though indeed I did not get quite to the bottom of the business. In reality Hans was putting up a most gallant struggle against temptation.

As I found out afterwards, Captain Robertson had been giving him strong drink on the sly, moved thereto by sympathy with a fellow toper. Also he had shown him where, if he wanted it, he could get more, and Hans always wanted gin very badly indeed. To leave it within his reach was like leaving a handful of diamonds lying about in the room of a thief. This he knew, but was ashamed to tell me the truth, and thence came much trouble.

"You will stop here, Hans, look after the young lady and nurse your foot," I said sternly, whereon he collapsed with a sigh and asked for some tobacco.

Meanwhile Captain Robertson, who I think had been taking a stirrup cup to cheer him on the road, was making his farewells down in what was known as "the village," for I saw him there kissing a collection of half-breed children, and giving Thomaso instructions to look after them and their mothers. Returning at length, he called to Inez, who remained upon the veranda, for she always seemed to shrink from her father after his visits to the village, to "keep a stiff upper lip" and not feel lonely, and commanded the cavalcade to start.

So off we went, about twenty of the village natives, a motley crew armed with every kind of gun, marching ahead and singing songs. Then came the waggon with Captain Robertson and myself seated on the driving-box, and lastly Umslopogaas and his Zulus, except the two who had been left behind.

We trekked along a kind of native road over fine veld of the same character as that on which Strathmuir stood, having the lower-lying bush-veld which ran down to the Zambesi on our right. Before nightfall we came to a ridge whereon this bush-veld turned south, fringing that tributary of the great river in the swamps of which we were to hunt for sea-cows. Here we camped and next morning, leaving the waggon in charge of my voorlooper and a couple of the Strathmuir natives, for the driver was to act as my gun-bearer—we marched down into the sea of bush-veld. It proved to be full of game, but at this we dared not fire for fearing of disturbing the hippopotami in the swamps beneath, whence in that event they might escape us back to the river.

About midday we passed out of the bush-veld and reached the place where the drive was to be. Here, bordered by steep banks covered with bush, was swampy ground not more than two hundred yards wide, down the centre of which ran a narrow channel of rather deep water, draining a vast expanse of morass above. It was up this channel that the sea-cows travelled to the feeding ground where they loved to collect at that season of the year.

There with the assistance of some of the riverside natives we made our preparations under the direction of Captain Robertson. The rest of these men, to the number of several hundreds, had made a wide détour to the head of the swamps, miles away, whence they were to advance at a certain signal. These preparations were simple. A quantity of thorn trees were cut down and by means of heavy stones fastened to their trunks, anchored in the narrow channel of deep water. To their tops, which floated on the placid surface, were tied a variety of rags which we had brought with us, such as old red flannel shirts, gay-coloured but worn-out blankets, and I know not what besides. Some of these fragments also were attached to the anchored ropes under water.

Also we selected places for the guns upon the steep banks that I have mentioned, between which this channel ran. Foreseeing what would happen, I chose one for myself behind a particularly stout rock and what is more, built a stone wall to the height of several feet on the landward side of it, as I guessed that the natives posted near to me would prove wild in their shooting.

These labours occupied the rest of that day, and at night we retired to higher ground to sleep. Before dawn on the following morning we returned and took up our stations, some on one side of the channel and some on the other which we had to reach in a canoe brought for the purpose by the river natives.

Then, before the sun rose, Captain Robertson fired a huge pile of dried reeds and bushes, which was to give the signal to the river natives far away to begin their beat. This done, we sat down and waited, after making sure that every gun had plenty of ammunition ready.

As the dawn broke, by climbing a tree near my schanze or shelter, I saw a good many miles away to the south a wide circle of little fires, and guessed that the natives were beginning to burn the dry reeds of the swamp. Presently these fires drew together into a thin wall of flame. Then I knew that it was time to return to the schanze and prepare. It was full daylight, however, before anything happened.

Watching the still channel of water, I saw ripples on it and bubbles of air rising. Suddenly there appeared the head of a great bull-hippopotamus which, having caught sight of our rag barricade, either above or below water, had risen to the surface to see what it might be. I put a bullet from an eight-bore rifle through its brain, whereon it sank, as I guessed, stone dead to the bottom of the channel, thus helping to increase the barricade by the bulk of its great body. Also it had another effect. I have observed that sea-cows cannot bear the smell and taint of blood, which frightens them horribly, so that they will expose themselves to almost any risk, rather than get it into their nostrils.

Now, in this still water where there was no perceptible current, the blood from the dead bull soon spread all about so that when the herd, following their leader, began to arrive they were much alarmed. Indeed, the first of them on winding or tasting it, turned and tried to get back up the channel where, however, they met others following, and there ensued a tremendous confusion. They rose to the surface, blowing, snorting, bellowing and scrambling over each other in the water, while continually more and more arrived behind them, till there was a perfect pandemonium in that narrow place.

All our guns opened fire wildly upon the mass; it was like a battle and through the smoke I caught sight of the riverside natives who were acting as beaters, advancing far away, fantastically dressed, screaming with excitement and waving spears, or sometimes torches of flaming reeds. Most of these were scrambling along the banks, but some of the bolder spirits advanced over the lagoon in canoes, driving the hippopotami towards the mouth of the channel by which alone they could escape into the great swamps below and so on to the river. In all my hunting experience I do not think I ever saw a more remarkable scene. Still, in a way, to me it was unpleasant, for I flatter myself that I am a sportsman and a battle of this sort is not sport as I understand the term.

At length it came to this; the channel for quite a long way was literally full of hippopotami—I should think there must have been a hundred of them or more of all sorts and sizes, from great bulls down to little calves. Some of these were killed, not many, for the shooting of our gallant company was execrable and almost at hazard. Also for every sea-cow that died, of which number I think that Captain Robertson and myself accounted for most—many were only wounded.

Still, the unhappy beasts, crazed with noise and fire and blood, did not seem to dare to face our frail barricade, probably for the reason that I have given. For a while they remained massed together in the water, or under it, making a most horrible noise. Then of a sudden they seemed to take a resolution. A few of them broke back towards the burning reeds, the screaming beaters and the advancing canoes. One of these, indeed, a wounded bull, charged a canoe, crushed it in its huge jaws and killed the rower, how exactly I do not know, for his body was never found. The majority of them, however, took another counsel, for emerging from the water on either side, they began to scramble towards us along the steep banks, or even to climb up them with surprising agility. It was at this point in the proceedings that I congratulated myself earnestly upon the solid character of the water-worn rock which I had selected as a shelter.

Behind this rock together with my gun-bearer and Umslopogaas, who, as he did not shoot, had elected to be my companion, I crouched and banged away at the unwieldy creatures as they advanced. But fire fast as I might with two rifles, I could not stop the half of them—they were drawing unpleasantly near. I glanced at Umslopogaas and even then was amused to see that probably for the first time in his life that redoubtable warrior was in a genuine fright.

"This is madness, Macumazahn," he shouted above the din. "Are we to stop here and be stamped flat by a horde of water-pigs?"

"It seems so," I answered, "unless you prefer to be stamped flat outside—or eaten," I added, pointing to a great crocodile that had also emerged from the channel and was coming along towards us with open jaws.

"By the Axe!" shouted Umslopogaas again, "I—a warrior—will not die thus, trodden on like a slug by an ox."

Now I have mentioned a tree which I climbed. In his extremity Umslopogaas rushed for that tree and went up it like a lamplighter, just as the crocodile wriggled past its trunk, snapping at his retreating legs.

After this I took no more note of him, partly because of the advancing sea-cows, and more for the reason that one of the village natives posted above me, firing wildly, put a large round bullet through the sleeve of my coat. Indeed, had it not been for the wall which I built that protected us, I am certain that both my bearer and I would have been killed, for afterwards I found it splashed over with lead from bullets which had struck the stones.

Well, thanks to the strength of my rock and to the wall, or as Hans said afterwards, to Zikali's Great Medicine, we escaped unhurt. The rush went by me; indeed, I killed one sea-cow so close that the powder from the rifle actually burned its hide. But it did go by, leaving us untouched. All, however, were not so fortunate, since of the village natives two were trampled to death, while a third had his leg broken.

Also, and this was really amusing—a bewildered bull charging at full speed, crashed into the trunk of Umslopogaas' tree, and as it was not very thick, snapped it in two. Down came the top in which the dignified chief was ensconced like a bird in a nest, though at that moment there was precious little dignity about him. However, except for scratches he was not hurt, as the hippopotamus had other business in urgent need of attention and did not stop to settle with him.

"Such are the things which happen to a man who mixes himself up with matters of which he knows nothing," said Umslopogaas sententiously to me afterwards. But all the same he could never bear any allusion to this tree-climbing episode in his martial career, which, as it happened, had taken place in full view of his retainers, among whom it remained the greatest of jokes. Indeed, he wanted to kill a man, the wag of the party, who gave him a slang name which, being translated, means "He-who-is-so-brave-that-he-dares-to-ride-a-water-horse-up-a-tree."

It was all over at last, for which I thanked Providence devoutly. A good many of the sea-cows were dead, I think twenty-one was out exact bag, but the majority of them had escaped in one way or another, many as I fear, wounded. I imagine that at the last the bulk of the herd overcame its fears and swimming through our screen, passed away down the channel. At any rate they were gone, and having ascertained that there was nothing to be done for the man who had been trampled on my side of the channel, I crossed it in the canoe with the object of returning quietly to our camp to rest.

But as yet there was to be no quiet for me, for there I found Captain Robertson, who I think had been refreshing himself out of a bottle and was in a great state of excitement about a native who had been killed near him who was a favourite of his, and another whose leg was broken. He declared vehemently that the hippopotamus which had done this had been wounded and rushed into some bushes a few hundred yards away, and that he meant to take vengeance upon it. Indeed, he was just setting off to do so.

Seeing his agitated state I thought it wisest to follow him. What happened need not be set out in detail. It is sufficient to say that he found that hippopotamus and blazed both barrels at it in the bushes, hitting it, but not seriously. Out lumbered the creature with its mouth open, wishing to escape. Robertson turned to fly as he was in its path, but from one cause or another, tripped and fell down. Certainly he would have been crushed beneath its huge feet had I not stepped in front of him and sent two solid eight-bore bullets down that yawning throat, killing it dead within three feet of where Robertson was trying to rise, and I may add, of myself.

This narrow escape sobered him, and I am bound to say that his gratitude was profuse.

"You are a brave man," he said, "and had it not been for you by now I should be wherever bad people go. I'll not forget it, Mr. Quatermain, and if ever you want anything that John Robertson can give, why, it's yours."

"Very well," I answered, being seized by an inspiration, "I do want something that you can give easily enough."

"Give it a name and it's yours, half my place, if you like."

"I want," I went on as I slipped new cartridges into the rifle, "I want you to promise to give up drink for your daughter's sake. That's what nearly did for you just now, you know."

"Man, you ask a hard thing," he said slowly. "But by God I'll try for her sake and for yours too."

Then I went to help to set the leg of the injured man, which was all the rest I got that morning.

CHAPTER VII

THE OATH

We spent three more days at that place. First it was necessary to allow time to elapse before the gases which generated in their great bodies caused those of the sea-cows which had been killed in the water, to float. Then they must be skinned and their thick hides cut into strips and pieces to be traded for sjamboks or to make small native shields for which some of the East Coast tribes will pay heavily.

All this took a long while, during which I amused, or disgusted myself in watching those river natives devouring the flesh of the beasts. The lean, what there was of it, they dried and smoked into a kind of "biltong," but a great deal of the fat they ate at once. I had the curiosity to weigh a lump which was given to one thin, hungry-looking fellow. It scaled quite twenty pounds. Within four hours he had eaten it to the last ounce and lay there, a distended and torpid log. What would not we white people give for such a digestion!

At last all was over and we started homewards, the man with a broken leg being carried in a kind of litter. On the edge of the bush-veld we found the waggon quite safe, also one of Captain Robertson's that had followed us from Strathmuir in order to carry the expected load of hippopotamus' hides and ivory. I asked my voorlooper if anything had happened during our absence. He answered nothing, but on the previous evening after dark, he had seen a glow in the direction of Strathmuir which lay on somewhat lower ground about twenty miles away, as though numerous fires had been lighted there. It struck him so much, he added, that he climbed a tree to observe it better. He did not think, however, that any building had been burned there, as the glow was not strong enough for that.

I suggested that it was caused by some grass fire or reed-burning, to which he replied indifferently that he did not think so as the line of the glow was not sufficiently continuous.

There the matter ended, though I confess that the story made me anxious, for what exact reason I could not say. Umslopogaas also, who had listened to it, for our talk was in Zulu, looked grave, but made no remark. But as since his tree-climbing experience he had been singularly silent, of this I thought little.

We had trekked at a time which we calculated would bring us to Strathmuir about an hour before sundown, allowing for a short halt half way. As my oxen were got in more quickly than those of the other waggon after this outspan, I was the first away, followed at a little distance by Umslopogaas, who preferred to walk with his Zulus. The truth was that I could not get that story about the glow of fires out of my mind and was anxious to push on, which had caused me to hurry up the inspanning.

Perhaps we had covered a couple of miles of the ten or twelve which still lay between us and Strathmuir, when far off on the crest of one of the waves of the veld which much resembled those of the swelling sea frozen while in motion, I saw a small figure approaching us at a rapid trot. Somehow that figure suggested Hans to my mind, so much so that I fetched my glasses to examine it more closely. A short scrutiny through them convinced me that Hans it was, Hans and no other, advancing at a great pace.

Filled with uneasiness, I ordered the driver to flog up the oxen, with the result that in a little over five minutes we met. Halting the waggon, I leapt from the waggon-box and calling to Umslopogaas who had kept up with us at a slow, swinging trot, went to Hans, who, when he saw me, stood still at a little distance, swinging his apology for a hat in his hand, as was his fashion when ashamed or perplexed.

"What is the matter, Hans?" I asked when we were within speaking distance.

"Oh! Baas, everything," he answered, and I noticed that he kept his eyes fixed upon the ground and that his lips twitched.

"Speak, you fool, and in Zulu," I said, for by now Umslopogaas had joined me.

"Baas," he answered in that tongue, "a terrible thing has come about at the farm of Red-Beard yonder. Yesterday afternoon at the time when people are in the habit of sleeping there till the sun grows less hot, a body of great men with fierce faces who carried big spears—perhaps there were fifty of them, Baas—crept up to the place through the long grass and growing crops, and attacked it."

"Did you see them come?" I asked.

"No, Baas. I was watching at a little distance as you bade me do and the sun being hot, I shut my eyes to keep out the glare of it, so that I did not see them until they had passed me and heard the noise."

"You mean that you were asleep or drunk, Hans, but go on."

"Baas, I do not know," he answered shamefacedly, "but after that I climbed a tall tree with a kind of bush at the top of it" (I ascertained afterwards that this was a sort of leafy-crowned palm), "and from it I saw everything without being seen."

"What did you see, Hans?" I asked him.

"I saw the big men run up and make a kind of circle round the village. Then they shouted, and the people in the village came out to see what was the matter. Thomaso and some of the men caught sight of them first and ran away fast into the hillside at the back where the trees grow, before the circle was complete. Then the women and the children came out and the big men killed them with their spears—all, all!"

"Good God!" I exclaimed. "And what happened at the house and to the lady?"

"Baas, some of the men had surrounded that also and when she heard the noise the lady Sad-Eyes came out on to the stoep and with her came the two Zulus of the Axe who had been left sick but were now quite recovered. A number of the big men ran as though to take her, but the two Zulus made a great fight in front of the little steps to the stoep, having their backs protected by the stoep, and killed six of them before they themselves were killed. Also Sad-Eyes shot one with a pistol she carried, and wounded another so that the spear fell out of his hand.

"Then the rest fell on her and tied her up, setting her in a chair on the stoep where two remained to watch her. They did her no hurt, Baas; indeed, they seemed to treat her as gently as they could. Also they went into the house and there they caught that tall fat yellow girl who always smiles and is called Janee, she who waits upon the Lady Sad-Eyes, and brought her out to her. I think they told her, Baas, that she must look after her mistress and that if she tried to run away she would be killed, for afterwards I saw Janee bring her food and other things."

"And then, Hans?"

"Then, Baas, most of the great men rested a while, though some of them went through the store gathering such things as they liked, blankets, knives and iron cooking-pots, but they set fire to nothing, nor did they try to catch the cattle. Also they took dry wood from the pile and lit big fires, eight or nine of them, and when the sun set they began to feast."

"What did they feast on, Hans, if they took no cattle?" I asked with a shiver, for I was afraid of I knew not what.

"Baas," answered Hans, turning his head away and looking at the ground, "they feasted on the children whom they had killed, also on some of the young women. These tall soldiers are men-eaters, Baas."

At this horrible intelligence I turned faint and felt as though I was going to fall, but recovering myself, signed to him to go on with his story.

"They feasted quite nicely, Baas," he continued, "making no noise. Then some of them slept while others watched, and that went on all night. As soon as it was dark, but before the moon rose, I slid down the tree and crept round to the back of the house without being seen or heard, as I can, Baas. I got into the house by the back door and crawled to the window of the sitting-room. It was open and peeping through I saw Sad-Eyes still tied to the seat on the stoep not more than a pace away, while the girl Janee crouched on the floor at her feet—I think she was asleep or fainting.

"I made a little noise, like a night-adder hissing, and kept on making it, till at last Sad-Eyes turned her head. Then I spoke in a very low whisper, for fear lest I should wake the two guards who were dozing on either side of her wrapped in their blankets, saying, 'It is I, Hans, come to help you.' 'You cannot,' she answered, also speaking very low. 'Get to your master and tell him and my father to follow. These men are called Amahagger and live far away across the river. They are going to take me to their home, as I understand, to rule them, because they want a white woman to be a queen over them who have always been ruled by a certain white queen, against whom they have rebelled. I do not think they mean to do me any harm, unless perhaps they want to marry me to their chief, but of this I am not sure from their talk which I understand badly. Now go, before they catch you.'

"'I think you might get away,' I whispered back. 'I will cut your bonds. When you are free, slip through the window and I will guide you.'

"'Very well, try it,' she said.

"So I drew my knife and stretched out my arm. But then, Baas, I showed myself a fool—if the Great Medicine had still been there I might have known better. I forgot the starlight which shone upon the blade of the knife. That girl Janee came out of her sleep or swoon, lifted her head and saw the knife. She screamed once, then at a word from her mistress was silent. But it was enough, for it woke up the guards who glared about them and threatened Janee with their great spears, also they went to sleep no more, but began to talk together, though what they said I could not hear, for I was hiding on the floor of the room. After this, knowing that I could do no good and might do harm and get myself killed, I crept out of the house as I had crept in, and crawled back to my tree."

"Why did you not come to me?" I asked.

"Because I still hoped I might be able to help Sad-Eyes, Baas. Also I wanted to see what happened, and I knew that I could not bring you here in time to be any good. Yet it is true I thought of coming though I did not know the road."

"Perhaps you were right."

"At the first dawn," continued Hans, "the great men who are called Amahagger rose and ate what was left over from the night before. Then they gathered themselves together and went to the house. Here they found a large chair, that seated with rimpis in which the Baas Red-Beard sits, and lashed two poles to the chair. Beneath the chair they tied the garments and other things of the Lady Sad-Eyes which they made Janee gather as Sad-Eyes directed her. This done, very gently they sat Sad-Eyes herself in the chair, bowing while they made her fast. After this eight of them set the poles upon their shoulders, and they all went away at a trot, heading for the bush-veld, driving with them a herd of goats which they had stolen from the farm, and making Janee run by the chair. I saw everything, Baas, for they passed just beneath my tree. Then I came to seek you, following the outward spoor of the waggons which I could not have done well at night. That is all, Baas."

"Hans," I said, "you have been drinking and because of it the lady Sad-Eyes is taken a prisoner by cannibals; for had you been awake and watching, you might have seen them coming and saved her and the rest. Still, afterwards you did well, and for the rest you must answer to Heaven."

"I must tell your reverend father, the Predikant, Baas, that the white master, Red-Beard, gave me the liquor and it is rude not to do as a great white master does, and drink it up. I am sure he will understand, Baas," said Hans abjectly.

I thought to myself that it was true and that the spear which Robertson cast had fallen upon his own head, as the Zulus say, but I made no answer, lacking time for argument.

"Did you say," asked Umslopogaas, speaking for the first time, "that my servants killed only six of these men-eaters?"

Hans nodded and answered, "Yes, six. I counted the bodies."

"It was ill done, they should have killed six each," said Umslopogaas moodily. "Well, they have left the more for us to finish," and he fingered the great axe.

Just then Captain Robertson arrived in his waggon, calling out anxiously to know what was the matter, for some premonition of evil seemed to have struck him. My heart sank at the sight of him, for how was I to tell such a story to the father of the murdered children and of the abducted girl?

In the end I felt that I could not. Yes, I turned coward and saying that I must fetch something out of the waggon, bolted into it, bidding Hans go forward and repeat his tale. He obeyed unwillingly enough and looking out between the curtains of the waggon tent I saw all that happened, though I could not hear the words that passed.

Robertson had halted the oxen and jumping from the waggon-box strode forward and met Hans, who began to speak with him, twitching his hat in his hands. Gradually as the tale progressed, I saw the Captain's face freeze into a mask of horror. Then he began to argue and deny, then to weep—oh! it was a terrible sight to see that great man weeping over those whom he had lost, and in such a fashion.

After this a kind of blind rage seized him and I thought he was going to kill Hans, who was of the same opinion, for he ran away. Next he staggered about, shaking his fists, cursing and shouting, till presently he fell of a heap and lay face downwards, beating his head against the ground and groaning.

Now I went to him and sat up.

"That's a pretty story, Quatermain, which this little yellow monkey has been gibbering at me. Man, do you understand what he says? He says that all those half-blood children of mine are dead, murdered by savages from over the Zambesi, yes, and eaten, too, with their mothers. Do you take the point? Eaten like lambs. Those fires your man saw last night were the fires on which they were cooked, my little so-and-so and so-and-so," and he mentioned half a dozen different names. "Yes, cooked, Quatermain. And that isn't all of it, they have taken Inez too. They didn't eat her, but they have dragged her off a captive for God knows what reason. I couldn't understand. The whole ship's crew is gone, except the captain absent on leave and the first officer, Thomaso, who deserted with some Lascar stokers, and left the women and children to their fate. My God, I'm going mad. I'm going mad! If you have any mercy in you, give me something to drink."

"All right," I said, "I will. Sit here and wait a minute."

Then I went to the waggon and poured out a stiff tot of spirits into which I put an amazing doze of bromide from a little medicine chest I always carry with me, and thirty drops of chlorodyne on the top of it. All this compound I mixed up with a little water and took it to him in a tin cup so that he could not see the colour.

He drank it at a gulp and throwing the pannikin aside, sat down on the veld, groaning while the company watched him at a respectful distance, for Hans had joined the others and his tale had spread like fire in drought-parched grass.

In a few minutes the drugs began to take effect upon Robertson's tortured nerves, for he rose and said quietly,

"What now?"

"Vengeance, or rather justice," I answered.

"Yes," he exclaimed, "vengeance. I swear that I will be avenged, or die—or both."

Again I saw my opportunity and said, "You must swear more than that, Robertson. Only sober men can accomplish great things, for drink destroys the judgment. If you wish to be avenged for the dead and to rescue the living, you must be sober, or I for one will not help you."

"Will you help me if I do, to the end, good or ill, Quatermain?" he added.

I nodded.

"That's as much as another's oath," he muttered. "Still, I will put my thought in words. I swear by God, by my mother—like these natives—and by my daughter born in honest marriage, that I will never touch another drop of strong drink, until I have avenged those poor women and their little children, and rescued Inez from their murderers. If I do you may put a bullet through me."

"That's all right," I said in an offhand fashion, though inwardly I glowed with pride at the success of my great idea, for at the time I thought it great, and went on,

"Now let us get to business. The first thing to do is to trek to Strathmuir and make preparations; the next to start upon the trail. Come to sit on the waggon with me and tell me what guns and ammunition you have got, for according to Hans those savages don't seem to have touched anything, except a few blankets and a herd of goats."

He did as I asked, telling me all he could remember. Then he said,

"It is a strange thing, but now I recall that about two years ago a great savage with a high nose, who talked a sort of Arabic which, like Inez, I understand, having lived on the coast, turned up one day and said he wanted to trade. I asked him what in, and he answered that he would like to buy some children. I told him that I was not a slave-dealer. Then he looked at Inez, who was moving about, and said that he would like to buy her to be a wife for his Chief, and offered some fabulous sum in ivory and in gold, which he said should be paid before she was taken away. I snatched his big spear from his hand, broke it over his head and gave him the best hiding with its shaft that he had ever heard of. Then I kicked him off the place. He limped away but when he was out of reach, turned and called out that one day he would come again with others and take her, meaning Inez, without leaving the price in ivory and gold. I ran for my gun, but when I got back he had gone and I never thought of the matter again from that day to this."

"Well, he kept his promise," I said, but Robertson made no answer, for by this time that thundering dose of bromide and laudanum had taken effect on him and he had fallen asleep, of which I was glad, for I thought that this sleep would save his sanity, as I believe it did for a while.

We reached Strathmuir towards sunset, too late to think of attempting the pursuit that day. Indeed, during our trek, I had thought the matter out carefully and come to the conclusion that to try to do so would be useless. We must rest and make preparations; also there was no hope of our overtaking these brutes who already had a clear twelve hours' start, by a sudden spurt. They must be run down patiently by following their spoor, if indeed they could be run down at all before they vanished into the vast recesses of unknown Africa. The most we could do this night was to get ready.

Captain Robertson was still sleeping when we passed the village and of this I was heartily glad, since the remains of a cannibal feast are not pleasant to behold, especially when they are—! Indeed, of these I determined to be rid at once, so slipping off the waggon with Hans and some of the farm boys, for none of the Zulus would defile themselves by touching such human remnants—I made up two of the smouldering fires, the light of which the voorlooper had seen upon the sky, and on to them cast, or caused to be cast, those poor fragments. Also I told the farm natives to dig a big grave and in it to place the other bodies and generally to remove the traces of murder.

Then I went on to the house, and not too soon. Seeing the waggons arrive and having made sure that the Amahagger were gone, Thomaso and the other cowards emerged from their hiding-places and returned. Unfortunately for the former the first person he met was Umslopogaas, who began to revile the fat half-breed in no measured terms, calling him dog, coward, and other opprobrious names, such as deserter of women and children, and so forth—all of which someone translated.

Thomaso, an insolent person, tried to swagger the matter out, saying that he had gone to get assistance. Infuriated at this lie, Umslopogaas leapt upon him with a roar and though he was a strong man, dealt with him as a lion does with a buck. Lifting him from his feet, he hurled him to the ground, then as he strove to rise and run, caught him again and as it seemed to me, was about to break his back across his knee. Just at this juncture I arrived.

"Let the man go," I shouted to him. "Is there not enough death here already?"

"Yes," answered Umslopogaas, "I think there is. Best that this jackal should live to eat his own shame," and he cast Thomaso to the ground, where he lay groaning.

Robertson, who was still asleep in the waggon, woke up at the noise, and descended from it, looking dazed. I got him to the house and in doing so made my way past, or rather between the bodies of the two Zulus and of the six men whom they had killed, also of him whom Inez had shot. Those Zulus had made a splendid fight for they were covered with wounds, all of them in front, as I found upon examination.

Having made Robertson lie down upon his bed, I took a good look at the slain Amahagger. They were magnificent men, all of them; tall, spare and shapely with very clear-cut features and rather frizzled hair. From these characteristics, as well as the lightness of their colour, I concluded that they were of a Semitic or Arab type, and that the admixture of their blood with that of the Bantus was but slight, if indeed there were any at all. Their spears, of which one had been cut through by a blow of a Zulu's axe, were long and broad, not unlike to those used by the Masai, but of finer workmanship.

By this time the sun was setting and thoroughly tired by all that I had gone through, I went into the house to get something to eat, having told Hans to find food and prepare a meal. As I sat down Robertson joined me and I made him also eat. His first impulse was to go to the cupboard and fetch the spirit bottle; indeed, he rose to do so.

"Hans is making coffee," I said warningly.

"Thank you," he answered, "I forgot. Force of habit, you know."

Here I may state that never from that moment did I see him touch another drop of liquor, not even when I drank my modest tot in front of him. His triumph over temptation was splendid and complete, especially as the absence of his accustomed potations made him ill for some time and of course depressed his spirits, with painful results that were apparent in due course.

In fact, the man became totally changed. He grew gloomy but resourceful, also full of patience. Only one idea obsessed him—to rescue his daughter and avenge the murder of his people; indeed, except his sins, he thought of and found interest in nothing else. Moreover, his iron constitution cast off all the effects of his past debauchery and he grew so strong that although I was pretty tough in those days, he could out-tire me.

To return; I engaged him in conversation and with his help made a list of what we should require on our vendetta journey, all of which served to occupy his mind. Then I sent him to bed, saying that I would call him before dawn, having first put a little more bromide into his third cup of coffee. After this I turned in and notwithstanding the sight of those remains of the cannibal feast and the knowledge of the dead men who lay outside my window, I slept like a top.

Indeed, it was the Captain who awakened me, not I the Captain, saying that daylight was on the break and we had better be stirring. So we went down to the Store, where I was thankful to find that everything had been tidied up in accordance with my directions.

On our way Robertson asked me what had become of the remains, whereon I pointed to the smouldering ashes of one of the great fires. He went to it and kneeling down, said a prayer in broad Scotch, doubtless one that he had learned at his mother's knee. Then he took some of the ashes from the edge of the pyre—for such it was—and threw them into the glowing embers where, as he knew, lay all that was left of those who had sprung from him. Also he tossed others of them into the air, though what he meant by this I did not understand and never asked. Probably it was some rite indicative of expiation or of revenge, or both, which he had learned from the savages among whom he had lived so long.

After this we went into the Store and with the help of some of the natives, or half-breeds, who had accompanied us on the sea-cow expedition, selected all the goods we wanted, which we sent to the house.

As we returned thither I saw Umslopogaas and his men engaged, with the usual Zulu ceremonies, in burying their two companions in a hole they had made in the hillside. I noted, however, that they did not inter their war-axes or their throwing-spears with them as usual, probably because they thought that these might be needed. In place of them they put with the dead little models roughly shaped of bits of wood, which models they "killed" by first breaking them across.

I lingered to watch the funeral and heard Goroko, the witch-doctor, make a little speech.

"O Father and Chief of the Axe," he said, addressing Umslopogaas, who stood silent leaning on his weapon and watching all, a portentous figure in the morning mist, "O Father, O Son of the Heavens" (this was an allusion to the royal blood of Umslopogaas of which the secret was well known, although it would never have been spoken aloud in Zululand), "O Slaughterer (Bulalio), O Woodpecker who picks at the hearts of men; O King-Slayer; O Conqueror of the Halakazi; O Victor in a hundred fights; O Gatherer of the Lily-bloom that faded in the hand; O Wolf-man, Captain of the Wolves that ravened; O Slayer of Faku; O Great One whom it pleases to seem small, because he must follow his blood to the end appointed—"

This was the opening of the speech, the "bonga-ing" or giving of Titles of Praise to the person addressed, of which I have quoted but a sample, for there were many more of them that I have forgotten. Then the speaker went on,

"It was told to me, though of it I remember nothing, that when my Spirit was in me a while ago I prophesied that this place would flow with blood, and lo! the blood has flowed, and with it that of these our brothers," and he gave the names of the two dead Zulus, also those of their forefathers for several generations.

"It seems, Father, that they died well, as you would have wished them to die, and as doubtless they desired to die themselves, leaving a tale behind them, though it is true that they might have died better, killing more of the men-eaters, as it is certain they would have done, had they not been sick inside. They are finished; they have gone beyond to await us in the Under-world among the ghosts. Their story is told and soon to their children they will be but names whispered in honour after the sun has set. Enough of them who have showed us how to die as our fathers did before them."

Goroko paused a while, then added with a waving of his hands,

"My Spirit comes to me again and I know that these our brothers shall not pass unavenged. Chief of the Axe, great glory awaits the Axe, for it shall feed full. I have spoken."

"Good words!" grunted Umslopogaas. Then he saluted the dead by raising Inkosikaas and came to me to consult about our journey.

CHAPTER VIII

PURSUIT

After all we did not get away much before noon, because first there was a great deal to be done. To begin with the loads had to be arranged. These consisted largely of ammunition, everything else being cut down to an irreducible minimum. To carry them we took two donkeys there were on the place, also half a dozen pack oxen, all of which animals were supposed to be "salted"—that is, to have suffered and recovered from every kind of sickness, including the bite of the deadly tsetse fly. I suspected, it is true, that they would not be proof against further attacks, still, I hoped that they would last for some time, as indeed proved to be the case.

In the event of the beasts failing us, we took also ten of the best of those Strathmuir men who had accompanied us on the sea-cow trip, to serve as bearers when it became necessary. It cannot be said that these snuff-and-butter fellows—for most, if not all of them had some dash of white blood in their veins—were exactly willing volunteers. Indeed, if a choice had been left to them, they would, I think, have declined this adventure.

But there was no choice. Their master, Robertson, ordered them to come and after a glance at the Zulus they concluded that the command was one which would be enforced and that if they stopped behind, it would not be as living men. Also some of them had lost wives or children in the slaughter, which, if they were not very brave, filled them with a desire for revenge. Lastly, they could all shoot after a fashion and had good rifles; moreover if I may say so, I think that they put confidence in my leadership. So they made the best of a bad business and got themselves ready.

Then arrangements must be made about the carrying on of the farm and store during our absence. These, together with my waggon and oxen, were put in the charge of Thomaso, since there was no one else who could be trusted at all—a very battered and crestfallen Thomaso, by the way. When he heard of it he was much relieved, since I think he feared lest he also should be expected to take part in the hunt of the Amahagger man-eaters. Also it may have occurred to him that in all probability none of us would ever come back at all, in which case by a process of natural devolution, he might find himself the owner of the business and much valuable property. However, he swore by sundry saints—for Thomaso was nominally a Catholic—that he would look after everything as though it were his own, as no doubt he hoped it might become.

"Hearken, fat pig," said Umslopogaas, Hans obligingly translating so that there might be no mistake, "if I come back, and come back I shall who travel with the Great Medicine—and find even one of the cattle of the white lord, Macumazahn, Watcher-by-Night, missing, or one article stolen from his waggon, or the fields of your master not cultivated or his goods wasted, I swear by the Axe that I will hew you into pieces with the axe; yes, if to do it I have to hunt you from where the sun rises to where it sets and down the length of the night between. Do you understand, fat pig, deserter of women and children, who to save yourself could run faster than a buck?"

Thomaso replied that he understood very clearly indeed, and that, Heaven helping him, all should be kept safe and sound. Still, I was sure that in his manly heart he was promising great gifts to the saints if they would so arrange matters that Umslopogaas and his axe were never seen at Strathmuir again, and reflecting that after all the Amahagger had their uses. However, as I did not trust him in the least, much against their will, I left my driver and voorlooper to guard my belongings.

At last we did get off, pursued by the fervent blessings of Thomaso and the prayers of the others that we would avenge their murdered relatives. We were a curious and motley procession. First went Hans, because at following a spoor he was, I believe, almost unequalled in Africa, and with him, Umslopogaas, and three of his Zulus to guard against surprise. These were followed by Captain Robertson, who seemed to prefer to walk alone and whom I thought it best to leave undisturbed. Then I came and after me straggled the Strathmuir boys with the pack animals, the cavalcade being closed by the remaining

Zulus under the command of Goroko. These walked last in case any of the mixed-bloods should attempt to desert, as we thought it quite probable that they would.

Less than an hour's tramp brought us to the bush-veld where I feared that our troubles might begin, since if the Amahagger were cunning, they would take advantage of it to confuse or hide their spoor. As it chanced, however, they had done nothing of the sort and a child could have followed their march. Just before nightfall we came to their first halting-place where they had made a fire and eaten one of the herd of farm goats which they had driven away with them, although they left the cattle, I suppose, because goats are docile and travel well.

Hans showed us everything that had happened; where the chair in which Inez was carried was set down, where she and Janee had been allowed to walk that she might stretch her stiff limbs, the dregs of some coffee that evidently Janee had made in a saucepan, and so forth.

He even told us the exact number of the Amahagger, which he said totalled forty-one, including the man whom Inez had wounded. His spoor he distinguished from that of the others both by an occasional drop of blood and because he walked lightly on his right foot, doubtless for the reason that he wished to avoid jarring his wound, which was on that side.

At this spot we were obliged to stay till daybreak, since it was impossible to follow the spoor by night, a circumstance that gave the cannibals a great advantage over us.

The next two days were repetitions of the first, but on the fourth we passed out of the bush-veld into the swamp country that bordered the great river. Here our task was still easy since the Amahagger had followed one of the paths made by the river-dwellers who had their habitations on mounds, though whether these were natural or artificial I am not sure, and sometimes on floating islands.

On our second day in the reeds we came upon a sad sight. To our left stood one of these mound villages, if a village it could be called, since it consisted only of four or five huts inhabited perhaps by twenty people. We went up to it to obtain information and stumbled across the body of an old man lying in the pathway. A few yards further on we found the ashes of a big fire and by it such remains as we had seen at Strathmuir. Here there had been another cannibal feast. The miserable huts were empty, but as at Strathmuir, had not been burnt.

We were going away when the acute ears of Hans caught the sound of groans. We searched about and in a clump of reeds near the foot of the mound, found an old woman with a great spear wound just above her skinny thigh piercing deep into the vitals, but of a nature which is not immediately mortal. One of Robertson's people who understood the language of these swamp-dwellers well, spoke to her. She told him that she wanted water. It was brought and she drank copiously. Then in answer to his questions she began to talk.

She said that the Amahagger had attacked the village and killed all who could not escape. They had eaten a young woman and three children. She had been wounded by a spear and fled away into the place where we found her, where none of them took the trouble to follow her as she "was not worth eating."

By my direction the man asked her whether she knew anything of these Amahagger. She replied that her grandfathers had, though she had heard nothing of them since she was a child, which must have been seventy years before. They were a fierce people who lived far up north across the Great River, the remnants of a race that had once "ruled the world."

Her grandfathers used to say that they were not always cannibals, but had become so long before because of a lack of food and now had acquired the taste. It was for this purpose that they still raided to get other people to eat, since their ruler would not allow them to eat one another. The flesh of cattle they did not care for, although they had plenty of them, but sometimes they ate goats and pigs because they said they tasted like man. According to her grandfathers they were a very evil people and full of magic.

All of this the old woman told us quite briskly after she had drunk the water, I think because her wound had mortified and she felt no pain. Her information, however, as is common with the aged, dealt entirely with the far past; of the history of the Amahagger since the days of her forebears she knew nothing, nor had she seen anything of Inez. All she could tell us was that some of them had attacked her village at dawn and that when she ran out of the hut she was speared.

While Robertson and I were wondering what we should do with the poor old creature whom it seemed cruel to leave here to perish, she cleared up the question by suddenly expiring before our eyes. Uttering the name of someone with whom, doubtless, she had been familiar in her youth, three or four times over, she just sank down and seemed to go to sleep and on examination we found that she was dead. So we left her and went on.

Next day we came to the edge of the Great River, here a sheet of placid running water about a mile across, for at this time of the year it was low. Perceiving quite a big village on our left, we went to it and made enquiries, to find that it had not been attacked by the cannibals, probably because it was too powerful, but that three nights before some of their canoes had been stolen, in which no doubt these had crossed the river.

As the people of this village had traded with Robertson at Strathmuir, we had no difficulty in obtaining other canoes from them in which to cross the Zambesi in return for one of our oxen that I could see was already sickening from tsetse bite. These canoes were large enough to take the donkeys that were patient creatures and stood still, but the cattle we could not get into them for fear of an upset. So we killed the two driven beasts that were left to us and took them with us as dead meat for food, while the three remaining pack oxen we tried to swim across, dragging them after the canoes with hide reims round their horns. As a result two were drowned, but one, a bold-hearted and enterprising animal, gained the other bank.

Here again we struck a sea of reeds in which, after casting about, Hans once more found the spoor of the Amahagger. That it was theirs beyond doubt was proved by the circumstance that on a thorny kind of weed we found a fragment of a cotton dress which, because of the pattern stamped on it, we all recognised as one that Inez had been wearing. At first I thought that this had been torn off by the thorns, but on examination we became certain that it had been placed there purposely, probably by Janee, to give us a clue. This conclusion was confirmed when at subsequent periods of the hunt we found other fragments of the same garment.

Now it would be useless for me to set out the details of this prolonged and arduous chase which in all endured for something over three weeks. Again and again we lost the trail and were only able to recover it by long and elaborate search, which occupied much time. Then, after we escaped from the reeds and swamps, we found ourselves upon stony uplands where the spoor was almost impossible to follow, indeed, we only rediscovered it by stumbling across the dead body of that cannibal whom Inez had wounded. Evidently he had perished from his hurt, which I could see had mortified. From the state of his remains we gathered that the raiders must be about two days' march ahead of us.

Striking their spoor again on softer ground where the impress of their feet remained—at any rate to the cunning sight of Hans—we followed them down across great valleys wherein trees grew sparsely, which valleys were separated from each other by ridges of high and barren land. On these belts of rocky soil our difficulties were great, but here twice we were put on the right track by more fragments torn from the dress of Inez.

At length we lost the spoor altogether; not a sign of it was to be found. We had no idea which way to go. All about us appeared these valleys covered with scattered bush running this way and that, so that we could not tell which of them to follow or to cross. The thing seemed hopeless, for how could we expect to find a little body of men in that immensity? Hans shook his head and even the fierce and steadfast Robertson was discouraged.

"I fear my poor lassie is gone," he said, and relapsed into brooding as had become his wont.

"Never say die! It's dogged as does it!" I replied cheerfully in the words of Nelson, who also had learned what it meant to hunt an enemy over trackless wastes, although his were of water.

I walked to the top of the rise where we were encamped, and sat down alone to think matters over. Our condition was somewhat parlous; all our beasts were now dead, even the second donkey, which was the last of them, having perished that morning, and been eaten, for food was scanty since of late we had met with little game. The Strathmuir men, who now must carry the loads, were almost worn out and doubtless would have deserted, except for the fact that there was no place to which they could go. Even the Zulus were discouraged, and said they had come away from home across the Great River to fight, not to run about in wildernesses and starve, though Umslopogaas made no complaint, being buoyed up by the promise of his soothsayer, Goroko, that battle was ahead of him in which he would win great glory.

Hans, however, remained cheerful, for the reason, as he remarked vacuously, that the Great Medicine was with us and that therefore, however bad things seemed to be, all in fact was well; an argument that carried no conviction to my soul.

It was on a certain evening towards sunset that I went away thus alone. I looked about me, east and west and north. Everywhere appeared the same bush-clad valleys and barren rises, miles upon miles of them. I bethought me of the map that old Zikali had drawn in the ashes, and remembered that it showed these valleys and rises and that beyond them there should be a great swamp, and beyond the swamp a mountain. So it seemed that we were on the right road to the home of his white Queen, if such a person existed, or at any rate we were passing over country similar to that which he had pictured or imagined.

But at this time I was not troubling my head about white queens. I was thinking of poor Inez. That she was alive a few days before we knew from the fragments of her dress. But where was she now? The spoor was utterly lost on that stony ground, or if any traces of it remained a heavy deluge of rain had washed them away. Even Hans had confessed himself beaten.

I stared about me helplessly, and as I did so a flying ray of light from the setting sun reflected downwards from a storm-cloud, fell upon a white patch on the crest of one of the distant land-waves. It struck me that probably limestone outcropped at this spot, as indeed proved to be the case; also that such a patch of white would be a convenient guide for any who were travelling across that sea of bush. Further, some instinct within seemed to impel me to steer for it, although I had all but made up my mind to go in a totally different direction many more points to the east. It was almost as though a voice were calling to me to take this path and no other. Doubtless this was an effect produced by weariness and mental overstrain. Still, there it was, very real and tangible, one that I did not attempt to combat.

So next morning at the dawn I headed north by west, laying my course for that white patch and for the first time breaking the straight line of our advance. Captain Robertson, whose temper had not been bettered by prolonged and frightful anxiety, or I may add, by his unaccustomed abstinence, asked me rather roughly why I was altering the course.

"Look here, Captain," I answered, "if we were at sea and you did something of the sort, I should not put such a question to you, and if by any chance I did, I should not expect you to answer. Well, by your own wish I am in command here and I think that the same argument holds."

"Yes," he replied. "I suppose you have studied your chart, if there is any of this God-forsaken country, and at any rate discipline is discipline. So steam ahead and don't mind me."

The others accepted my decision without comment; most of them were so miserable that they did not care which way we went, also they were good enough to repose confidence in my judgment.

"Doubtless the Baas has reasons," said Hans dubiously, "although the spoor, when last we saw it, headed towards the rising sun and as the country is all the same, I do not see why those man-eaters should have returned."

"Yes," I said, "I have reasons," although in fact I had none at all.

Hans surveyed me with a watery eye as though waiting for me to explain them, but I looked haughty and declined to oblige.

"The Baas has reasons," continued Hans, "for taking us on what I think to be the wrong side of that great ridge, there to hunt for the spoor of the men-eaters, and they are so deep down in his mind that he cannot dig them up for poor old Hans to look at. Well, the Baas wears the Great Medicine and perhaps it is there that the reasons sit. Those Strathmuir fellows say that they can go no further and wish to die. Umslopogaas has just gone to them with his axe to tell them that he is ready to help them to their wish. Look, he has got there, for they are coming quickly, who after all prefer to live."

Well, we started for my white patch of stones which no one else had noticed and of which I said nothing to anyone, and reached it by the following evening, to find, as I expected, that it was a lime outcrop.

By now we were in a poor way, for we had practically nothing left to eat, which did not tend to raise the spirits of the party. Also that lime outcrop proved to be an uninteresting spot overlooking a wide valley which seemed to suggest that there were other valleys of a similar sort beyond it, and nothing more.

Captain Robertson sat stern-faced and despondent at a distance muttering into his beard, as had become a habit with him. Umslopogaas leaned upon his axe and contemplated the heavens, also occasionally the Strathmuir men who cowered beneath his eye. The Zulus squatted about sharing such snuff as remained to them in economic pinches. Goroko, the witch-doctor, engaged himself in consulting his "Spirit," by means of bone-throwing, upon the humble subject of whether or no we should succeed in killing any game for food to-morrow, a point on which I gathered that his "Spirit" was quite uncertain. In short, the gloom was deep and universal and the sky looked as though it were going to rain.

Hans became sarcastic. Sneaking up to me in his most aggravating way, like a dog that means to steal something and cover up the theft with simulated affection, he pointed out one by one all the disadvantages of our present position. He indicated per contra, that if his advice had been followed, his conviction was that even if we had not found the man-eaters and rescued the lady called Sad-Eyes, our state would have been quite different. He was sure, he added, that the valley which he had suggested we should follow, was one full of game, inasmuch as he had seen their spoor at its entrance.

"Then why did you not say so?" I asked.

Hans sucked at his empty corn-cob pipe, which was his way of indicating that he would like me to give him some tobacco, much as a dog groans heavily under the table when he wants a bit to eat, and answered that it was not for him to point out things to one who knew everything, like the great Macumazahn, Watcher-by-Night, his honoured master. Still, the luck did seem to have gone a bit wrong. The privations could have been put up with (here he sucked very loudly at the empty pipe and looked at mine, which was alight), everything could have been put up with, if only there had been a chance of coming even with those men-eaters and rescuing the Lady Sad-Eyes, whose face haunted his sleep. As it was, however, he was convinced that by following the course I had mapped out we had lost their spoor finally and that probably they were now three days' march away in another direction. Still, the Baas had said that he had his reasons, and that of course was enough for him, Hans, only if the Baas would condescend to tell him, he would as a matter of curiosity like to know what the reasons were.

At that moment I confess that, much as I was attached to him, I should have liked to murder Hans, who, I felt, believing that he had me "on toast," to use a vulgar phrase, was taking advantage of my position to make a mock of me in his sly, Hottentot way.

I tried to continue to look grand, but felt that the attitude did not impress. Then I stared about me as though taking counsel with the Heavens, devoutly hoping that the Heavens would respond to my mute appeal. As a matter of fact they did.

"There is my reason, Hans," I said in my most icy voice, and I pointed to a faint line of smoke rising against the twilight sky on the further side of the intervening valley.

"You will perceive, Hans," I added, "that those Amahagger cannibals have forgotten their caution and lit a fire yonder, which they have not done for a long time. Perhaps you would like to know why this has happened. If so I will tell you. It is because for some days past I have purposely lost their spoor, which they knew we were following, and lit fires to puzzle them. Now, thinking that they have done with us, they have become incautious and shown us where they are. That is my reason, Hans."

He heard and, although of course he did not believe that I had lost the spoor on purpose, stared at me till I thought his little eyes were going to drop out of his head. But even in his admiration he contrived to convey an insult as only a native can.

"How wonderful is the Great Medicine of the Opener-of-Roads, that it should have been able thus to instruct the Baas," he said. "Without doubt the Great Medicine is right and yonder those men-eaters are encamped, who might just as well as have been anywhere else within a hundred miles."

"Drat the Great Medicine," I replied, but beneath my breath, then added aloud,

"Be so good, Hans, as to go to Umslopogaas and to tell him that Macumazahn, or the Great Medicine, proposes to march at once to attack the camp of the Amahagger, and—here is some tobacco."

"Yes, Baas," answered Hans humbly, as he snatched the tobacco and wriggled away like a worm.

Then I went to talk with Robertson.

The end of it was that within an hour we were creeping across that valley towards the spot where I had seen the line of smoke rising against the twilight sky.

Somewhere about midnight we reached the neighbourhood of this place. How near or how far we were from it, we could not tell since the moon was invisible, as of course the smoke was in the dark. Now the question was, what should we do?

Obviously there would be enormous advantages in a night attack, or at least in locating the enemy, so that it might be carried out at dawn before he marched. Especially was this so, since we were scarcely in a condition even if we could come face to face with them, to fight these savages when they were prepared and in the light of day. Only we two white men, with Hans, Umslopogaas and his Zulus, could be relied upon in such a case, since the Strathmuir mixed-bloods had become entirely demoralised and were not to be trusted at a pinch. Indeed, tired and half starving as we were, none of us was at his best. Therefore a surprise seemed our only chance. But first we must find those whom we wished to surprise.

Ultimately, after a hurried consultation, it was agreed that Hans and I should go forward and see if we could locate the Amahagger. Robertson wished to come too, but I pointed out that he must remain to look after his people, who, if he left them, might take the opportunity to melt away in the darkness, especially as they knew that heavy fighting was at hand. Also if anything happened to me it was desirable that one white man should remain to lead the party. Umslopogaas, too, volunteered, but knowing his character, I declined his help. To tell the truth, I was almost certain that if we came upon the men-eaters, he would charge the whole lot of them and accomplish a fine but futile end after hacking down a number of cannibal barbarians, whose extinction or escape remained absolutely immaterial to our purpose, namely, the rescue of Inez.

So it came about that Hans and I started alone, I not at all enjoying the job. I suppose that there lurks in my nature some of that primeval terror of the dark, which must continually have haunted our remote forefathers of a hundred or a thousand generations gone and still lingers in the blood of most of us. At any rate even if I am named the Watcher-by-Night, greatly do I prefer to fight or to face peril in the sunlight, though it is true that I would rather avoid both at any time.

In fact, I wished heartily that the Amahagger were at the other side of Africa, or in heaven, and that I, completely ignorant of the person called Inez Robertson, were seated smoking the pipe of peace on my own stoep in Durban. I think that Hans guessed my state of mind, since he suggested that he should go alone, adding with his usual unveiled rudeness, that he was quite certain that he would do much better without me, since white men always made a noise.

"Yes," I replied, determined to give him a Roland for his Oliver, "I have no doubt you would—under the first bush you came across, where you would sleep till dawn, and then return and say that you could not find the Amahagger."

Hans chuckled, quite appreciating the joke, and having thus mutually affronted each other, we started on our quest.

CHAPTER IX

THE SWAMP

Neither Hans nor I carried rifles that we knew would be in the way on our business, which was just to scout. Moreover, one is always tempted to shoot if a gun is at hand, and this I did not want to do at present. So, although I had my revolver in case of urgent necessity, my only other weapon was a Zulu axe, that formerly had belonged to one of those two men who died defending Inez on the veranda at Strathmuir, while Hans had nothing but his long knife. Thus armed, or unarmed, we crept forward towards that spot whence, as we conjectured, we had seen the line of smoke rising some hours before.

For about a quarter of a mile we went on thus without seeing or hearing anything, and a difficult job it was in that gloom among the scattered trees with no light save such as the stars gave us. Indeed, I was about to suggest that we had better abandon the enterprise until daybreak when Hans nudged me, whispering,

"Look to the right between those twin thorns."

I obeyed and following the line of sight which he had indicated, perceived, at a distance of about two hundred yards a faint glow, so faint indeed that I think only Hans would have noticed it. Really it might have been nothing more than the phosphorescence rising from a heap of fungus, or even from a decaying animal.

"The fire of which we saw the smoke that has burnt to ashes," whispered Hans again. "I think that they have gone, but let us look."

So we crawled forward very cautiously to avoid making the slightest noise; so cautiously, indeed, that it must have taken us nearly half an hour to cover those two hundred yards.

At length we were within about forty yards of that dying fire and, afraid to go further, came to a stand—or rather, a lie-still—behind some bushes until we knew more. Hans lifted his head and sniffed with his broad nostrils; then he whispered into my ear, but so low that I could scarcely hear him.

"Amahagger there all right, Baas, I smell them."

This of course was possible, since what wind there was blew from the direction of the fire, although I whose nose is fairly keen could smell nothing at all. So I determined to wait and watch a while, and indicated my decision to Hans, who, considering our purpose accomplished, showed signs of wishing to retreat.

Some minutes we lay thus, till of a sudden this happened. A branch of resinous wood of which the stem had been eaten through by the flames, fell upon the ashes of the fire and burnt up with a brilliant light. In it we saw that the Amahagger were sleeping in a circle round the fire wrapped in their blankets.

Also we saw another thing, namely that nearer to us, not more than a dozen yards away, indeed, was a kind of little tent, also made of fur rugs or blankets, which doubtless sheltered Inez. Indeed, this was evident from the fact that at the mouth of it, wrapped up in something, lay none other than her maid, Janee, for her face being towards us, was recognised by us both in the flare of the flaming branch. One more thing we noted, namely, that two of the cannibals, evidently a guard, were sleeping between us and the little tent. Of course they ought to have been awake, but fatigue had overcome them and there they slumbered, seated on the ground, their heads hanging forward almost upon their knees.

An idea came to me. If we could kill those men without waking the others in that gloom, it might be possible to rescue Inez at once. Rapidly I weighed the pros and cons of such an attempt. Its advantages, if successful, were that the object of our pursuit would be carried through without further trouble and that it was most doubtful whether we should ever get such a chance again. If we returned to fetch the others and attacked in force, the probability was that those Amahagger, or one of them, would hear some sound made by the advance of a number of men, and fly into the darkness; or, rather than lose Inez, they might kill her. Or if they stood and fought, she might be slain in the scrimmage. Or, as after all we had only about a dozen effectives, for the Strathmuir bearers could not be relied upon, they might defeat and kill us whom they outnumbered by two or three to one.

These were the arguments for the attempt. Those for not making it were equally obvious. To begin with it was one of extraordinary risk; the two guards or someone else behind them might wake up—for such people, like dogs, mostly sleep with one eye open, especially when they knew that they are being pursued. Or if they did not we might bungle the business so that they raised an outcry before they grew silent for ever, in which case both of us and perhaps Inez also would probably pay the penalty before we could get away.

Such was the horned dilemma upon one point or other of which we ran the risk of being impaled. For a full minute or more I considered the matter with an earnestness almost amounting to mental agony, and at last all but came to the conclusion that the danger was too enormous. It would be better, notwithstanding the many disadvantages of that plan, to go back and fetch the others.

But then it was that I made one of my many mistakes in life. Most of us do more foolish things than wise ones and sometimes I think that in spite of a certain reputation for caution and far-sightedness, I am exceptionally cursed in this respect. Indeed, when I look back upon my past, I can scarcely see the scanty flowers of wisdom that decorate its path because of the fat, ugly trees of error by which it is overshadowed.

On that occasion, forgetting past experiences where Hans was concerned, my natural tendency to blunder took the form of relying upon another's judgment instead of on my own. Although I had formed a certain view as to what should be done, the pros and cons seemed so evenly balanced that I determined to consult the little Hottentot and accept his verdict. This, after all, was but a form of gambling like pitch and toss, since, although it is true Hans was a clever, or at any rate a cunning man according to his lights, and experienced, it meant that I was placing my own judgment in abeyance, which no one considering a life-and-death enterprise should do, taking the chance of that of another, whatever it might be. However, not for the first time, I did so—to my grief.

In the tiniest of whispers with my lips right against his smelly head, I submitted the problem to Hans, asking him what we should do, go on or go back. He considered a while, then answered in a voice which he contrived to make like the drone of a night beetle.

"Those men are fast asleep, I know it by their breathing. Also the Baas has the Great Medicine. Therefore I say go on, kill them and rescue Sad-Eyes."

Now I saw that the Fates to which I had appealed had decided against me and that I must accept their decree. With a sick and sinking heart—for I did not at all like the business—I wondered for a moment what had led Hans to take this view, which was directly opposite to any I had expected from him. Of course his superstition about the Great Medicine had something to do with it, but I felt convinced that this was not all.

Even then I guessed that two arguments appealed to him, of which the first was that he desired, if possible, to put an end to this intolerable and unceasing hunt which had worn us all out, no matter what that end might be. The second and more powerful, however, was, I believed, and rightly, that the idea of this stealthy, midnight blow appealed irresistibly to the craft of his half-wild nature in which the strains of the leopard and the snake seemed to mingle with that of the human being. For be it remembered that notwithstanding his veneer of civilisation, Hans was a savage whose forefathers for countless ages had preserved themselves alive by means of such attacks and stratagems.

The die having been cast, in the same infinitesimal whispers we made our arrangements, which were few and simple. They amounted to this—that we were to creep on to the men and each of us to kill that one who was opposite to him, I with the axe and Hans with his knife, remembering that it must be done with a single stroke—that is, if they did not wake up and kill us—after which we were to get Inez out of her shelter, dressed or undressed, and make off with her into the darkness where we were pretty sure of being able to baffle pursuit until we reached our own camp.

Provided that we could kill the two guards in the proper fashion—rather a large proviso, I admit—the thing was simple as shelling peas which, notwithstanding the proverb, in my experience is not simple at all, since generally the shells crack the wrong way and at least one of the peas remained in the pod. So it happened in this case, for Janee, whom we had both forgotten, remained in the pod.

I am sure I don't know why we overlooked her; indeed, the error was inexcusable, especially as Hans had already experienced her foolishness and she was lying there before our eyes. I suppose that our minds were so concentrated upon the guard-killing and the tragic and impressive Inez that there was no room in them for the stolid and matter-of-fact Janee. At any rate she proved to be the pea that would not come out of the pod.

Often in my life I have felt terrified, not being by nature one of those who rejoices in dangers and wild adventures for their own sake, which only the stupid do, but who has, on the contrary, been forced to undertake them by the pressure of circumstances, a kind of hydraulic force that no one can resist, and who, having undertaken, has been carried through them, triumphing over the shrinkings of his flesh by some secret reserve of nerve power. Almost am I tempted to call it spirit-power, something that lives beyond and yet inspires our frail and fallible bodies.

Well, rarely have I been more frightened than I was at this moment. Actually I hung back until I saw that Hans slithering through the grass like a thick yellow snake with the great knife in his right hand, was quite a foot ahead of me. Then my pride came to the rescue and I spurted, if one can spurt upon one's stomach, and drew level with him. After this we went at a pace so slow that any able-bodied snail would have left us standing still. Inch by inch we crept forward, lying motionless a while after each convulsive movement, once for quite a long time, since the left-hand cannibal seemed about to wake up, for he opened his mouth and yawned. If so, he changed his mind and rolling from a sitting posture on to his side, went to sleep much more soundly than before.

A minute or so later the right-hand ruffian, my man, also stirred, so sharply that I thought he had heard something. Apparently, however, he was only haunted by dreams resulting from an evil life, or perhaps by the prescience of its end, for after waving his arm and muttering something in a frightened voice, he too, wearied out, poor devil, sank back into sleep.

At last we were on them, but paused because we could not see exactly where to strike and knew, each of us, that our first blow must be the last and fatal. A cloud had come up and dimmed what light there was, and we must wait for it to pass. It was a long wait, or so it seemed.

At length that cloud did pass and in faint outline I saw the classical head of my Amahagger bowed in deep sleep. With a heart beating as it does only in the fierce extremities of love or war, I hissed like a snake, which was our agreed signal. Then rising to my knees, I lifted the Zulu axe and struck with all my strength.

The blow was straight and true; Umslopogaas himself could not have dealt a better. The victim in front of me uttered no sound and made no movement; only sank gently on to his side, and there lay as dead as though he had never been born.

It appeared that Hans had done equally well, since the other man kicked out his long legs, which struck me on the knees. Then he also became strangely still. In short, both of them were stone dead and would tell no stories this side of Judgment Day.

Recovering my axe, which had been wrenched from my hand, I crept forward and opened the curtain-like rugs or blankets, I do not know which they were, that covered Inez. I heard her stir at once. The movement had wakened her, since captives sleep lightly.

"Make no noise, Inez," I whispered. "It is I, Allan Quatermain, come to rescue you. Slip out and follow me; do you understand?"

"Yes, quite," she whispered back and began to rise.

At this moment a blood-curdling yell seemed to fill earth and heaven, a yell at the memory of which even now I feel faint, although I am writing years after its echoes died away.

I may as well say at once that it came from Janee who, awaking suddenly, had perceived against the background of the sky, Hans standing over her, looking like a yellow devil with a long knife in his hand, which she thought was about to be used to murder her.

So, lacking self-restraint, she screamed in the most lusty fashion, for her lungs were excellent, and—the game was up.

Instantly every man sleeping round the fire leapt to his feet and rushed in the direction of the echoes of Janee's yell. It was impossible to get Inez free of her tent arrangement or to do anything, except whisper to her,

"Feign sleep and know nothing. We will follow you. Your father is with us."

Then I bolted back into the bushes, which Hans had reached already.

A minute or two later when we were clear of the hubbub and nearing our own camp, Hans remarked to me sententiously,

"The Great Medicine worked well, Baas, but not quite well enough, for what medicine can avail against a woman's folly?"

"It was our own folly we should blame," I answered. "We ought to have known that fool-girl would shriek, and taken precautions."

"Yes, Baas, we ought to have killed her too, for nothing else would have kept her quiet," replied Hans in cheerful assent. "Now we shall have to pay for our mistake, for the hunt must go on."

At this moment we stumbled across Robertson and Umslopogaas who, with the others, and every living thing within a mile or two had also heard Janee's yell, and briefly told our story. When he learned how near we had been to rescuing his daughter, Robertson groaned, but Umslopogaas only said,

"Well, there are two less of the men-eaters left to deal with. Still, for once your wisdom failed you, Macumazahn. When you had found the camp you should have returned, so that we might all attack it together. Had we done so, before the dawn there would not have been one of them left."

"Yes," I answered, "I think that my wisdom did fail me, if I have any to fail. But come; perhaps we may catch them yet."

So we advanced, Hans and I showing the road. But when we reached the place it was too late, for all that remained of the Amahagger, or of Inez and Janee, were the two dead men whom we had killed, and in that darkness pursuit was impossible. So we went back to our own camp to rest and await the dawn before taking up the trail, only to find ourselves confronted with a new trouble. All the Strathmuir half-breeds whom we had left behind as useless, had taken advantage of our absence and that of the Zulus, to desert. They had just bolted back upon our tracks and vanished into the sea of bush. What became of them I do not know, as we never saw them again, but my belief is that these cowardly fellows all perished, for certainly not one of them reached Strathmuir.

Fortunately for us, however, they departed in such a hurry that they left all their loads behind them, and even some of the guns they carried. Evidently Janee's yell was the last straw which broke the back of such nerve as remained to them. Doubtless they believed it to be the signal of attack by hordes of cannibals.

As there was nothing to said or done, since any pursuit of these curs was out of the question, we made the best of things as they were. It proved a simple business. From the loads we selected such articles as were essential, ammunition for the most part, to carry ourselves—and the rest we abandoned, hiding it under a pile of stones in case we should ever come that way again.

The guns they had thrown aside we distributed among the Zulus who had none, though the thought that they possessed them, so far as I was concerned, added another terror to life. The prospect of going into battle with those wild axemen letting off bullets in every direction was not pleasant, but fortunately when that crisis came, they cast them away and reverted to the weapons to which they were accustomed.

Now all this sounds much like a tale of disaster, or at any rate of failure. It is, however, wonderful by what strange ways good results are brought about, so much so that at times I think that these seeming accidents must be arranged by an Intelligence superior to our own, to fulfil through us purposes of which we know nothing, and frequently, be it admitted, of a nature sufficiently obscure. Of course this is a fatalistic doctrine, but then, as I have said before, within certain limits I am a fatalist.

To take the present case, for instance, the whole Inez episode at first sight might appear to be an excrescence on my narrative, of which the object is to describe how I met a certain very wonderful woman and what I heard and experienced in her company. Yet it is not really so, since had it not been for the Inez adventure, it is quite clear that I should never have reached the home of this woman, if woman she were, or have seen her at all. Before long this became very obvious to me, as shall be told.

From the night upon which Hans and I failed to rescue Inez we had no more difficulty in following the trail of the cannibals, who thenceforward were never more than a few hours ahead of us and had no time to be careful or to attempt to hide their spoor. Yet so fast did they travel that do what we would, burdened and wearied as we were, it proved impossible to overtake them.

For the first three days the track ran on through scattered, rolling bush-veld of the character that I have described, but tending continually down hill. When we broke camp on the morning of the fourth day, eating a hasty meal at dawn (for now game had become astonishingly plentiful, so that we did not lack food) the rising sun showed beneath us an endless sea of billowy mist stretching in every direction far as the sight could carry.

To the north, however, it did come to an end, for there, as I judged fifty or sixty miles away, rose the grim outline of what looked like a huge fortress, which I knew must be one of those extraordinary mountain formations, probably owing their origin to volcanic action, that are to be met with here and there in the vast expanses of Central and Eastern Africa. Being so distant it was impossible to estimate its size, which I guessed must be enormous, but in looking at it I bethought me of that great mountain in which Zikali said the marvellous white Queen lived, and wondered whether it could be the same, as from my memory of his map upon the ashes, it well might be, that is, if such a place existed at all. If so the map had shown it as surrounded by swamps and—well, surely that mist hid the face of a mighty swamp?

It did indeed, since before nightfall, following the spoor of those Amahagger, we had plunged into a morass so vast that in all my experience I have never seen or heard of its like. It was a veritable ocean of papyrus and other reeds, some of them a dozen or more feet high, so that it was impossible to see a yard in any direction.

Here it was that the Amahagger ahead of us proved our salvation, since without them to guide us we must soon have perished. For through that gigantic swamp there ran a road, as I think an ancient road, since in one or two places I saw stone work which must have been laid by man. Yet it was not a road which it would have been possible to follow without a guide, seeing that it also was overgrown with reeds. Indeed, the only difference between it and the surrounding swamp was that on the road the soil was comparatively firm, that is to say, one seldom sank into it above the knee, whereas on either side of it quagmires were often apparently bottomless, and what is more, partook of the nature of quicksand.

This we found out soon after we entered the swamp, since Robertson, pushing forward with the fierce eagerness which seemed to consume him, neglected to keep his eye upon the spoor and stepped off the edge on to land that appeared to be exactly similar to its surface. Instantly he began to sink in greasy and tenacious mud. Umslopogaas and I were only twenty yards behind, yet by the time we reached him in answer to his shouts, already he was engulfed up to his middle and going down so rapidly that in another minute he would have vanished altogether. Well, we got him out but not with ease, for that mud clung to him like the tentacles of an octopus. After this we were more careful.

Nor did this road run straight; on the contrary, it curved about and sometimes turned at right angles, doubtless to avoid a piece of swamp over which it had proved impossible for the ancients to construct a causeway, or to follow some out-crop of harder soil beneath.

The difficulties of that horrible place are beyond description, and indeed can scarcely be imagined. First there was that of a kind of grass which grew among the roots of the reeds and had edges like to those of knives. As Robertson and I wore gaiters we did not suffer so much from it, but the poor Zulus with their bare legs were terribly cut about and in some cases lame.

Then there were the mosquitoes which lived here by the million and all seemed anxious for a bite; also snakes of a peculiarly deadly kind were numerous. A Zulu was bitten by one of them of so poisonous a nature that he died within three minutes, for the venom seemed to go straight to his heart. We threw his body into the swamp, where it vanished at once.

Lastly there was the all-pervading stench and the intolerable heat of the place, since no breath of air could penetrate that forest of reeds, while a minor trouble was that of the multitude of leeches which fastened on to our bodies. By looking one could see the creatures sitting on the under side of leaves with their heads stretched out waiting to attack anything that went by. As wayfarers there could not have been numerous, I wondered what they had lived on for the last few thousand years. By the way, I found that paraffin, of which we had a small supply for our hand-lamps, rubbed over all exposed surfaces, was to some extent a protection against these blood-sucking worms and the gnats, although it did make one go about smelling like a dirty oil tin.

During the day, except for the occasional rush of some great iguana or other reptile, and the sound of the wings of the flocks of wildfowl passing over us from time to time, the march was deathly silent. But at night it was different, for then the bull-frogs boomed incessantly, as did the bitterns, while great swamp owls and other night-flying birds uttered their weird cries. Also there were mysterious sucking noises caused, no doubt, by the sinking of areas of swamp, with those of bursting bubbles of foul, up-rushing gas.

Strange lights, too, played about, will-o'-the-wisps or St. Elmo fires, as I believe they are called, that frightened the Zulus very much, since they believed them to be spirits of the dead. Perhaps this superstition had something to do with their native legend that mankind was "torn out of the reeds." If so, they may have imagined that the ghosts of men went back to the reeds, of which there were enough here to accommodate those of the entire Zulu nation. Any way they were much scared; even the bold witch-doctor, Goroko, was scared and went through incantations with the little bag of medicines he carried to secure protection for himself and his companions. Indeed, I think even the iron Umslopogaas himself was not as comfortable as he might have been, although he did inform me that he had come out to fight and did not care whether it were with man, or wizard, or spirit.

In short, of all the journeys that I have made, with the exception of the passage of the desert on our way to King Solomon's Mines, I think that through this enormous swamp was the most miserable. Heartily did I curse myself for ever having undertaken such a quest in a wild attempt to allay that sickness, or rather to quench that thirst of the soul which, I imagine, at times assails most of those who have hearts and think or dream.

For this was at the bottom of the business: this it was which had delivered me into the hands of Zikali, Opener-of-Roads, who, as now I am sure, was merely making use of me for his private occult purposes. He desired to consult the distant Oracle, if such a person existed, as to great schemes of his own, and therefore, to attain his end, made use of my secret longings which I had been so foolish as to reveal to him, quite careless of what happened to me in the process. [A bit narrow and uncharitable, this view. It seems to me that Zikali is taking a big risk in giving him the Great Medicine.—JB]

Well, I was in for the business and must follow it to the finish whatever that might be. After all it was very interesting and if there were anything in what Zikali said (if there were not I could not conceive what object he had in sending me on such a wild-goose chase through this home of geese and ducks), it might become more interesting still. For being pretty well fever-proof I did not think I should die in that morass, as of course nine white men out of ten would have done, and, beyond it lay the huge mountain which day by day grew larger and clearer.

Nor did Hans, who, with a childlike trust, pinned his faith to the Great Medicine. This, he remarked, was the worst veld through which he had ever travelled, but as the Great Medicine would never consent to be buried in that stinking mud, he had no doubt that we should come safely through it some time. I replied that this wonderful medicine of his had not saved one of our companions who had now made a grave in the same mud.

"No, Baas," he said, "but those Zulus have nothing to do with the Medicine which was given to you, and to me who accompanied you when we saw the Opener-of-Roads. Therefore perhaps they will all die, except Umslopogaas, whom you were told to take with you. If so, what does it matter, since there are plenty of Zulus, although there be but one Macumazahn or one Hans? Also the Baas may remember that he began by offending a snake and therefore it is quite natural that this snake's brother should have bitten the Zulu."

"If you are right, he should have bitten me, Hans."

"Yes, Baas, and so no doubt he would have done had you not been protected by the Great Medicine, and me too had not my grandfather been a snake-charmer, to say nothing of the smell of the Medicine being on me as well. The snakes know those that they should bite, Baas."

"So do the mosquitoes," I answered, grabbing a handful of them. "The Great Medicine has no effect upon them."

"Oh! yes, Baas, it has, since though it pleases them to bite, the bites do us no harm, or at least not much, and all are made happy. Still, I wish we could get out of these reeds of which I never want to see another, and Baas, please keep your rifle ready for I think I hear a crocodile stirring there."

"No need, Hans," I remarked sarcastically. "Go and tell him that I have the Great Medicine."

"Yes, Baas, I will; also that if he is very hungry, there are some Zulus camped a few yards further down the road," and he went solemnly to the reeds a little way off and began to talk to them.

"You infernal donkey!" I murmured, and drew my blanket over my head in a vain attempt to keep out the mosquitoes and smoking furiously with the same object, tried to get to sleep.

At last the swamp bottom began to slope upwards a little, with the result that as the land dried through natural drainage, the reeds grew thinner by degrees, until finally they ceased and we found ourselves on firmer ground; indeed, upon the lowest slopes of the great mountain that I have mentioned, that now towered above us, forbidden and majestic.

I had made a little map in my pocket-book of the various twists and turns of the road through that vast Slough of Despond, marking them from hour to hour as we followed its devious wanderings. On studying this at the end of that part of our journey I realised afresh how utterly impossible it would have been for us to thread that misty maze where a few false steps would always have meant death by suffocation, had it not been for the spoor of those Amahagger travelling immediately ahead of us who were acquainted with its secrets. Had they been friendly guides they could not have done us a better turn.

What I wondered was why they had not tried to ambush us in the reeds, since our fires must have shown them that we were close upon their heels. That they did try to burn us out was clear from certain evidences that I found, but fortunately at this season of the year in the absence of a strong wind the rank reeds were too green to catch fire. For the rest I was soon to learn the reason of their neglect to attack us in that dense cover.

They were waiting for a better opportunity!

CHAPTER X

THE ATTACK

We won out of the reeds at last, for which I fervently thanked God, since to have crossed that endless marsh unguided, with the loss of only one man, seemed little less than miraculous. We emerged from them late in the afternoon and being wearied out, stopped for a while to rest and eat of the flesh of a buck that I had been fortunate enough to shoot upon their fringe. Then we pushed forward up the slope, proposing to camp for the night on the crest of it a mile or so away where I thought we should escape from the deadly mist in which we had been enveloped for so long, and obtain a clear view of the country ahead.

Following the bank of a stream which here ran down into the marsh, we came at length to this crest just as the sun was sinking. Below us lay a deep valley, a fold, as it were, in the skin of the mountain, well but not densely bushed. The woods of this valley climbed up the mountain flank for some distance above it and then gave way to grassy slopes that ended in steep sides of rock, which were crowned by a black and frowning precipice of unknown height.

There was, I remember, something very impressive about this towering natural wall, which seemed to shut off whatever lay beyond the gaze of man, as though it veiled an ancient mystery. Indeed, the aspect of it thrilled me, I knew not why. I observed, however, that at one point in the mighty cliff there seemed to be a narrow cleft down which, no doubt, lava had flowed in a remote age, and it occurred to me that up this cleft ran a roadway, probably a continuation of that by which we had threaded the swamp. The fact that through my glasses I could see herds of cattle grazing on the slopes of the mountain went to confirm this view, since cattle imply owners and herdsmen, and search as I would, I could find no native villages on the slopes. The inference seemed to be that those owners dwelt beyond or within the mountain.

All of these things I saw and pointed out to Robertson in the light of the setting sun.

Meanwhile Umslopogaas had been engaged in selecting the spot where we were to camp for the night. Some soldierlike instinct, or perchance some prescience of danger, caused him to choose a place particularly suitable to defence. It was on a steep-sided mound that more or less resembled a gigantic ant-heap. Upon one side this mound was protected by the stream which because of a pool was here rather deep, while at the back of it stood a collection of those curious and piled-up water-worn rocks that are often to be found in Africa. These rocks, lying one upon another like the stones of a Cyclopean wall, curved round the western side of the mound, so that practically it was only open for a narrow space, say thirty or forty feet, upon that face of it which looked on to the mountain.

"Umslopogaas expects battle," remarked Hans to me with a grin, "otherwise with all this nice plain round us he would not have chosen to camp in a place which a few men could hold against many. Yes, Baas, he thinks that those cannibals are going to attack us."

"Stranger things have happened," I answered indifferently, and having seen to the rifles, went to lie down, observing as I did so that the tired Zulus seemed already to be asleep. Only Umslopogaas did not sleep. On the contrary, he stood leaning on his axe staring at the dim outlines of the opposing precipice.

"A strange mountain, Macumazahn," he said, "compared to it that of the Witch, beneath which my kraal lies, is but a little baby. I wonder what we shall find within it. I have always loved mountains, Macumazahn, ever since a dead brother of mine and I lived with the wolves in the Witch's lap, for on them I have had the best of my fighting."

"Perhaps it is not done with yet," I answered wearily.

"I hope not, Macumazahn, since some is due for us, after all these days of mud and stench. Sleep a while now, Macumazahn, for that head of yours which you use so much, must need rest. Fear not, I and the little yellow man who do not think as much as you do, will keep watch and wake you if there is need, as mayhap there will be before the dawn. Here none can come at us except in front, and the place is narrow."

So I lay down and slept as soundly as ever I had done in my life, for a space of four or five hours I suppose. Then, by some instinct perhaps, I awoke suddenly, feeling much refreshed in that sweet mountain air, a new man indeed, and in the moonlight saw Umslopogaas striding towards me.

"Arise, Macumazahn," he said, "I hear men stirring below us."

At this moment Hans slipped past him, whispering,

"The cannibals are coming, Baas, a good number of them. I think they mean to attack before dawn."

Then he passed behind me to warn the Zulus. As he went by, I said to him,

"If so, Hans, now is the time for your Great Medicine to show what it can do."

"The Great Medicine will look after you and me all right, Baas," he replied, pausing and speaking in Dutch, which Umslopogaas did not understand, "but I expect there will be fewer of those Zulus to cook for before the sun grows hot. Their spirits will be turned into snakes and go back into the reeds from which they say they were 'torn out,'" he added over his shoulder.

I should explain that Hans acted as cook to our party and it was a grievance with him that the Zulus ate so much of the meat which he was called upon to prepare. Indeed, there is never much sympathy between Hottentots and Zulus.

"What is the little yellow man saying about us?" asked Umslopogaas suspiciously.

"He is saying that if it comes to battle, you and your men will make a great fight," I replied diplomatically.

"Yes, we will do that, Macumazahn, but I thought he said that we should be killed and that this pleased him."

"Oh dear no!" I answered hastily. "How could he be pleased if that happened, since then he would be left defenceless, if he were not killed too. Now, Umslopogaas, let us make a plan for this fight."

So, together with Robertson, rapidly we discussed the thing. As a result, with the help of the Zulus, we dragged together some loose stones and the tops of three small thorn trees which we had cut down, and with them made a low breastwork, sufficient to give us some protection if we lay down to shoot. It was the work of a few minutes since we had prepared the material when we camped in case an emergency should arise.

Behind this breastwork we gathered and waited, Robertson and I being careful to get a little to the rear of the Zulus, who it will be remembered had the rifles which the Strathmuir bastards had left behind them when they bolted, in addition to their axes and throwing assegais. The question was how these cannibals would fight. I knew that they were armed with long spears and knives but I did not know if they used those spears for thrusting or for throwing. In the former case it would be difficult to get at them with the axes because they must have the longer reach. Fortunately as it turned out, they did both.

At length all was ready and there came that long and trying wait, the most disagreeable part of a fight in which one grows nervous and begins to reflect earnestly upon one's sins. Clearly the Amahagger, if they really intended business, did not mean to attack till just before dawn, after the common native fashion, thinking to rush us in the low and puzzling light. What perplexed me was that they should wish to attack us at all after having let so many opportunities of doing so go by. Apparently these men were now in sight of their own home, where no doubt they had many friends, and by pushing on could reach its shelter before us, especially as they knew the roads and we did not.

They had come out for a secret purpose that seemed to have to do with the abduction of a certain young white woman for reasons connected with their tribal statecraft or ritual, which is the kind of thing that happens not infrequently among obscure and ancient African tribes. Well, they had abducted their young woman and were in sight of safety and success in their objects, whatever these might be. For what possible reason, then, could they desire to risk a fight with the outraged friends and relatives of that young woman?

It was true that they outnumbered us and therefore had a good chance of victory, but on the other hand, they must know that it would be very dearly won, and if it were not won, that we should retake their captive, so that all their trouble would have been for nothing. Further they must be as exhausted and travel-worn as we were ourselves and in no condition to face a desperate battle.

The problem was beyond me and I gave it up with the reflection that either this threatened attack was a mere feint to delay us, or that behind it was something mysterious, such as a determination to prevent us at all hazards from discovering the secrets of that mountain stronghold.

When I put the riddle to Hans, who was lying next to me, he was ready with another solution.

"They are men-eaters, Baas," he said, "and being hungry, wish to eat us before they get to their own land where doubtless they are not allowed to eat each other."

"Do you think so," I answered, "when we are so thin?" and I surveyed Hans' scraggy form in the moonlight.

"Oh! yes, Baas, we should be quite good boiled—like old hens, Baas. Also it is the nature of cannibals to prefer thin man to fat beef. The devil that is in them gives them that taste, Baas, just as he makes me like gin, or you turn your head to look at pretty women, as those Zulus say you always did in their country, especially at a certain witch who was named Mameena and whom you kissed before everybody—"

Here I turned my head to look at Hans, proposing to smite him with words, or physically, since to have this Mameena myth, of which I have detailed the origin in the book called Child of Storm, re-arise out of his hideous little mouth was too much. But before I could get out a syllable he held up his finger and whispered,

"Hush! the dawn breaks and they come. I hear them."

I listened intently but could distinguish nothing. Only straining my eyes, presently I thought that about a hundred yards down the slope beneath us in the dim light I caught sight of ghostlike figures flitting from tree to tree; also that these figures were drawing nearer.

"Look out!" I said to Robertson on my right, "I believe they are coming."

"Man," he answered sternly, "I hope so, for whom else have I wanted to meet all these days?"

Now the figures vanished into a little fold of the ground. A minute or so later they re-appeared upon its hither side where such light as there was from the fading stars and the gathering dawn fell full upon them, for here were no trees. I looked and a thrill of horror went through me, for with one glance I recognised that these were not the men whom we had been following. To begin with, there were many more of them, quite a hundred, I should think, also they had painted shields, wore feathers in their hair, and generally so far as I could judge, seemed to be fat and fresh.

"We have been led into an ambush," I said first in Zulu to Umslopogaas immediately in front, and then in English to Robertson.

"If so, man, we must just do the best we can," answered the latter, "but God help my poor daughter, for those other devils will have taken her away, leaving their brethren to make an end of us."

"It is so, Macumazahn," broke in Umslopogaas. "Well, whatever the end of it, we shall have a better fight. Now do you give the word and we will obey."

The savages, for so I call them, although I admit that cannibals or not, they looked more like high-class Arabs than savages, came on in perfect silence, hoping, I suppose, to catch us asleep. When they were about fifty yards away, running in a treble line with spears advanced, I called out "Fire!" in Zulu, and set the example by loosing off both barrels of my express rifle at men whom I had picked out as leaders, with results that must have been more satisfactory to me than to the two Amahagger whose troubles in this world came to an end.

There followed a tremendous fusillade, the Zulus banging off their guns wildly, but even at that distance managing for the most part to shoot over the enemy's heads. Captain Robertson and Hans, however, did better and the general result was that the Amahagger, who appeared to be unaccustomed to firearms, retreated in a hurry to a fold of the ground whence they had emerged. Before the last of them got there I loaded again, so that two more stopped behind. Altogether we had put nine or ten of them out of action.

Now I hoped that they would give the business up. But this was not so, for being brave fellows, after a pause of perhaps five minutes, once more they charged in a body, hoping to overwhelm us. Again we greeted them with bullets and knocked out several, whereon the rest threw a volley of their long spears at us. I was glad to see them do this although one of the Zulus got his death from it, while two more were wounded. I myself had a very narrow escape, for a spear passed between my neck and shoulder. Each of them carried but one of these weapons and I knew that if they used them up in throwing, only their big knives would remain to them with which to attack us.

After this discharge of spears which was kept up for some time, they rushed at us and there followed a great fight. The Zulus, throwing down their guns, rose to their feet and holding their little fighting shields which had been carried in their mats, in the left hand, wielded their axes with the right. Umslopogaas, who stood in the centre of them, however, had no shield and swung his great axe with both arms. This was the first time that I had seen him fight and the spectacle was in a way magnificent. Again and again the axe crashed down and every time it fell it left one dead beneath the stroke, till at length those Amahagger shrank back out of his reach.

Meanwhile Robertson, Hans and I, standing on some stones at the back, kept up a continual fire upon them, shooting over the heads of the Zulus, who were playing their part like men. Yes, they shrank back, leaving many dead behind them. Then a captain tried to gather them for another rush, and once more they moved forward. I killed that captain with a revolver shot, for my rifle had become too hot to hold, and at the sight of his fall, they broke and ran back into the little hollow where our bullets could not reach them.

So far we had held our own, but at a price, for three of the Zulus were now dead and three more wounded, one of them severely, the other two but enough to cripple them. In fact, now there were left of them but three untouched men, and Umslopogaas, so that in all for fighting purposes we were but seven. What availed it that we had killed a great number of these Amahagger, when we were but seven? How could seven men withstand such another onslaught?

There in the pale light of the dawn we looked at each other dismayed.

"Now," said Umslopogaas, leaning on his red axe, "there remains but one thing to do, make a good end, though I would that it were in a greater cause. At least we must either fight or fly," and he looked down at the wounded.

"Think not of us, Father," murmured one of them, the man who had a mortal hurt. "If it is best, kill us and begone that you may live to bear the Axe in years to come."

"Well spoken!" said Umslopogaas, and again stood still a while, then added, "The word is with you, Macumazahn, who are our captain."

I set out the situation to Robertson and Hans as briefly as I could, showing that there was a chance of life if we ran, but so far as I could see, none if we stayed.

"Go if you like, Quatermain," answered the Captain, "but I shall stop and die here, for since my girl is gone I think I'm better dead."

I motioned to Hans to speak.

"Baas," he answered, "the Great Medicine is here with us upon the earth and your reverend father, the Predikant, is with us in the sky, so I think we had better stop here and do what we can, especially as I do not want to see those reeds any more at present."

"So do I," I said briefly, giving no reasons.

So we made ready for the next attack which we knew would be the last, strengthening our little wall and dragging the dead Amahagger up against it as an added protection. As we were thus engaged the sun rose and in its first beams, some miles away on the opposing slopes of the mountain looking tiny against the black background of the precipice, we saw a party of men creeping forward. Lifting my glasses I studied it and perceived that in its midst was a litter.

"There goes your daughter," I said, and handed the glasses to Robertson.

"Oh! my God," he answered, "those villains have outwitted us after all."

Another minute and the litter, or rather the chair with its escort, had vanished into the shadow of the great cliffs, probably up some pass which we could not see.

Next moment our thoughts were otherwise engaged, since from various symptoms we gathered that the attack was about to be renewed. Spears upon which shone the light of the rising sun, appeared above the edge of the ground-fold that I have mentioned, which to the east increased to a deep, bush-clad ravine. Also there were voices as of leaders encouraging their men to a desperate effort.

"They are coming," I said to Robertson.

"Yes," he answered, "they are coming and we are going. It's a queer end to the thing we call life, isn't it, Quatermain, and hang it all! I wonder what's beyond? Not much for me, I expect, but whatever it is could scarcely be worse than what I've gone through here below in one way and another."

"There's hope for all of us," I replied as cheerfully as I could, for the man's deep depression disturbed me.

"Mayhap, Quatermain, for who knows the infinite mercy of whatever made us as we are? My old mother used to preach of it and I remember her words now. But in my case I expect it will stop at hope, or sleep, and if it wasn't for Inez, I'd not mind so much, for I tell you I've had enough of the world and life. Look, there's one of them. Take that, you black devil!" and lifting his rifle he aimed and fired at an Amahagger who appeared upon the edge of the fold of ground. What is more he hit him, for I saw the man double up and fall backwards.

Then the game began afresh, for the cannibals (I suppose they were cannibals like their brethren) crept out of shelter, advancing on their stomachs or their hands and knees, so as to offer a smaller mark, and dragging between them a long and slender tree-trunk with which clearly they intended to batter down our wall.

Of course I blazed away at them, pretty carefully too, for I was determined that what I believed to be the last exercise of the gift of shooting that has been given to me, should prove a record. Therefore I selected my men and even where I would hit them, and as subsequent examination showed, I made no mistakes in the seven or eight shots that I fired. But all the while, like poor Captain Robertson, I was thinking of other things; namely, where I was bound for presently and if I should meet certain folk there and what was the meaning of this show called Life, which unless it leads somewhere, according to my judgment has none at all. Until these questions were solved, however, my duty was to kill as many of those ruffians as I could, and this I did with finish and despatch.

Robertson and Hans were firing also, with more or less success, but there were too many to be stopped by our three rifles. Still they came on till at length their fierce faces were within a few yards of our little parapet and Umslopogaas had lifted his great axe to give them greeting. They paused a moment before making their final rush, and so did we to slip in fresh cartridges.

"Die well, Hans," I said, "and if you get there first, wait for me on the other side."

"Yes, Baas, I always meant to do that, though not yet. We are not going to die this time, Baas. Those who have the Great Medicine don't die; it is the others who die, like that fellow," and he pointed to an Amahagger who went reeling round and round with a bullet from his Winchester through the middle, for he had fired in the midst of his remarks.

"Curse—I mean bless—the Great Medicine," I said as I lifted my rifle to my shoulder.

At that moment all those Amahagger—there were about sixty of them left—became seized with a certain perturbation. They stood still, they stared towards the fold of ground out of which they had emerged; they called to each other words which I did not catch, and then—they turned to run.

Umslopogaas saw, and with a leader's instinct, acted. Springing over the parapet, followed by his remaining Zulus of the Axe, he leapt upon them with a roar. Down they went before Inkosikaas, like corn before a sickle. The thing was marvellous to see, it was like the charge of a leopard, so swift was the rush and so lightning-like were the strokes or rather the pecks of that flashing axe, for now he was tapping at their heads or spines with the gouge-like point upon its back. Nor were these the only victims, for those brave followers of his also did their part. In a minute all who remained upon their feet of the Amahagger were in full flight, vanishing this way and that among the trees. Hans fired a parting shot after the last of them, then sat down upon a stone and finding his corn-cob pipe, proceeded to fill it.

"The Great Medicine, Baas," he began sententiously, "or perhaps your reverend father, the Predikant—" Here he paused and pointed doubtfully with the bowl of the pipe towards the fold in the ground, adding, "Here it is, but I think it must be your reverend father, not the Great Medicine, yes, the Predikant himself, returned from Heaven, the Place of Fires!"

Looking vaguely in the direction indicated, for I could not conceive what he meant and thought that the excitement must have made him mad, I perceived a venerable old man with a long white beard and clothed in a flowing garment, also white, who reminded me of Father Christmas at a child's party, walking towards us and radiating benignancy. Also behind him I perceived a whole forest of spear points emerging from the gully. He seemed to take it for granted that we should not shoot at him, for he came on quite unconcerned, carefully picking his way among the corpses. When he was near enough he stopped and said in a kind of Arabic which I could understand,

"I greet you, Strangers, in the name of her I serve. I see that I am just in time, but this does not surprise me, since she said that it would be so. You seem to have done very well with these dogs," and he prodded a dead Amahagger with his sandalled foot. "Yes, very well indeed. You must be great warriors."

Then he paused and we stared at each other.

CHAPTER XI

THROUGH THE MOUNTAIN WALL

"These do not seem to be friends of yours," I said, pointing to the fallen. "And yet," I added, nodding towards the spearmen who were now emerging from the gully, "they are very like your friends."

"Puppies from the same litter are often alike, yet when they grow up sometimes they fight each other," replied Father Christmas blandly. "At least these come to save and not to kill you. Look! they kill the others!" and he pointed to them making an end of some of the wounded men. "But who are these?" and he glanced with evident astonishment, first at the fearsome-looking Umslopogaas and then at the grotesque Hans. "Nay, answer not, you must be weary and need rest. Afterwards we can talk."

"Well, as a matter of fact we have not yet breakfasted," I replied. "Also I have business to attend to here," and I glanced at our wounded.

The old fellow nodded and went to speak to the captains of his force, doubtless as to the pursuit of the enemy, for presently I saw a company spring forward on their tracks. Then, assisted by Hans and the remaining Zulus, of whom one was Goroko, I turned to attend to our own people. The task proved lighter than I expected, since the badly injured man was dead or dying and the hurts of the two others were in their legs and comparatively slight, such as Goroko could doctor in his own native fashion.

After this, taking Hans to guard my back, I went down to the stream and washed myself. Then I returned and ate, wondering the while that I could do so with appetite after the terrible dangers which we had passed. Still, we had passed them, and Robertson, Umslopogaas with three of his men, I and Hans were quite unharmed, a fact for which I returned thanks in silence but sincerely enough to Providence.

Hans also returned thanks in his own fashion, after he had filled himself, not before, and lit his corn-cob pipe. But Robertson made no remark; indeed, when he had satisfied his natural cravings, he rose and walking a few paces forward, stood staring at the cleft in the mountain cliff into which he had seen the litter vanish that bore his daughter to some fate unknown.

Even the great fight that we had fought and the victory we had won against overpowering odds did not appear to impress him. He only glared at the mountain into the heart of which Inez had been raped away, and shook his fist. Since she was gone all else went for nothing, so much so that he did not offer to assist with the wounded Zulus or show curiosity about the strange old man by whom we had been rescued.

"The Great Medicine, Baas," said Hans in a bewildered way, "is even more powerful than I thought. Not only has it brought us safely through the fighting and without a scratch, for those Zulus there do not matter and there will be less cooking for me to do now that they are gone; it has also brought down your reverend father the Predikant from the Place of Fires in Heaven, somewhat changed from what I remember him, it is true, but still without doubt the same. When I make my report to him presently, if he can understand my talk, I shall—"

"Stop your infernal nonsense, you son of a donkey," I broke in, for at this moment old Father Christmas, smiling more benignly than before, re-appeared from the kloof into which he had vanished and advanced towards us bowing with much politeness.

Having seated himself upon the little wall that we had built up, he contemplated us, stroking his beautiful white beard, then said, addressing me,

"Of a certainty you should be proud who with a few have defeated so many. Still, had I not been ordered to come at speed, I think that by now you would have been as those are," and he looked towards the dead Zulus who were laid out at a distance like men asleep, while their companions sought for a place to bury them.

"Ordered by whom?" I asked.

"There is only one who can order," he answered with mild astonishment. "'She-who-commands, She-who-is-everlasting'!"

It occurred to me that this must be some Arabic idiom for the Eternal Feminine, but I only looked vague and said,

"It would appear that there are some whom this exalted everlasting She cannot command; those who attacked us; also those who have fled away yonder," and I waved my hand towards the mountain.

"No command is absolute; in every country there are rebels, even, as I have heard, in Heaven above us. But, Wanderer, what is your name?"

"Watcher-by-Night," I answered.

"Ah! a good name for one who must have watched well by night, and by day too, to reach this country living where She-who-commands says that no man of your colour has set foot for many generations. Indeed, I think she told me once that two thousand years had gone by since she spoke to a white man in the City of Kôr."

"Did she indeed?" I exclaimed, stifling a cough.

"You do not believe me," he went on, smiling. "Well, She-who-commands can explain matters for herself better than I who was not alive two thousand years ago, so far as I remember. But what must I call him with the Axe?"

"Warrior is his name."

"Again a good name, as to judge by the wounds on them, certain of those rebels I think are now telling each other in Hell. And this man, if indeed he be a man—" he added, looking doubtfully at Hans.

"Light-in-Darkness is his name."

"I see, doubtless because his colour is that of the winter sun in thick fog, or a bad egg broken into milk. And the other white man who mutters and whose brow is like a storm?"

"He is called Avenger; you will learn why later on," I answered impatiently, for I grew tired of this catechism, adding, "And what are you called and, if you are pleased to tell it to us, upon what errand do you visit us in so fortunate an hour?"

"I am named Billali," he answered, "the servant and messenger of She-who-commands, and I was sent to save you and to bring you safely to her."

"How can this be, Billali, seeing that none knew of our coming?"

"Yet She-who-commands knew," he said with his benignant smile. "Indeed, I think that she learned of it some moons ago through a message that was sent to her and so arranged all things that you should be guided safely to her secret home; since otherwise how would you have passed a great pathless swamp with the loss, I think she said, of but one man whom a snake bit?"

Now I stared at the old fellow, for how could he know of the death of this man, but thought it useless to pursue the conversation further.

"When you are rested and ready," he went on, "we will start. Meanwhile I leave you that I may prepare litters to carry those wounded men, and you also, Watcher-by-Night, if you wish." Then with a dignified bow, for everything about this old fellow was stately, he turned and vanished into the kloof.

The next hour or so was occupied in the burial of the dead Zulus, a ceremony in which I took no part beyond standing up and raising my hat as they were borne away, for as I have said somewhere, it is best to leave natives alone on these occasions. Indeed, I lay down, reflecting that strangely enough there seemed to be something in old Zikali's tale of a wonderful white Queen who lived in a mountain fastness, since there was the mountain as he had drawn it on the ashes, and the servants of that Queen who, apparently, had knowledge of our coming, appeared in the nick of time to rescue us from one of the tightest fixes in which ever I found myself.

Moreover, the antique and courteous individual called Billali, spoke of her as "She-who-is-everlasting." What the deuce could he mean by that, I wondered? Probably that she was very old and therefore disagreeable to look on, which I confessed to myself would be a disappointment.

And how did she know that we were coming? I could not guess and when I asked Robertson, he merely shrugged his shoulders and intimated that he took no interest in the matter. The truth is that nothing moved the man, whose whole soul was wrapped in one desire, namely to rescue, or avenge, the daughter against whom he knew he had so sorely sinned.

In fact, this loose-living but reformed seaman was becoming a monomaniac, and what is more, one of the religious type. He had a Bible with him that had been given to him by his mother when he was a boy, and in this he read constantly; also he was always on his knees and at night I could hear him groaning and praying aloud. Doubtless now that the chains of drink had fallen off him, the instincts and the blood of the dour old Covenanters from whom he was descended, were asserting themselves. In a way this was a good thing though for some time past I had feared lest it should end in his going mad, and certainly as a companion he was more cheerful in his unregenerate days.

Abandoning speculation as useless and taking my chance of being murdered where I lay, for after all Billali's followers were singularly like the men with whom we had been fighting and for aught I knew might be animated by identical objects—I just went to sleep, as I can do at any time, to wake up an hour or so later feeling wonderfully refreshed. Hans, who when I closed my eyes was already asleep slumbering at my feet curled up like a dog on a spot where the sun struck hotly, roused me by saying:

"Awake, Baas, they are here!"

I sprang up, snatching at my rifle, for I thought that he meant that we were being attacked again, to see Billali advancing at the head of a train of four litters made of bamboo with grass mats for curtains and coverings, each of which was carried by stalwart Amahagger, as I supposed that they must be. Two of these, the finest, Billali indicated were for Robertson and myself, and the two others for the wounded. Umslopogaas and the remaining Zulus evidently were expected to walk, as was Hans.

"How did you make these so quickly," I asked, surveying their elegant and indeed artistic workmanship.

"We did not make them, Watcher-by-Night, we brought them with us folded up. She-who-commands looked in her glass and said that four would be needed, besides my own which is yonder, two for white lords and two for wounded black men, which you see is the number required."

"Yes," I answered vaguely, marvelling what kind of a glass it was that gave the lady this information.

Before I could inquire upon the point Billali added,

"You will be glad to learn that my men caught some of those rebels who dared to attack you, eight or ten of them who had been hurt by your missiles or axe-cuts, and put them to death in the proper fashion—yes, quite the proper fashion," and he smiled a little. "The rest had gone too far where it would have been dangerous to follow them among the rocks. Enter now, my lord Watcher-by-Night, for the road is steep and we must travel fast if we would reach the place where She-who-commands is camped in the ancient holy city, before the moon sinks behind the cliffs to-night."

So having explained matters to Robertson and Umslopogaas, who announced that nothing would induce him to be carried like an old woman, or a corpse upon a shield, and seen that the hurt Zulus were comfortably accommodated, Robertson and I got into our litters, which proved to be delightfully easy and restful.

Then when our gear was collected by the hook-nosed bearers to whom we were obliged to trust, though we kept with us our rifles and a certain amount of ammunition, we started. First went a number of Billali's spearmen, then came the litters with the wounded alongside of which Umslopogaas and his three uninjured Zulus talked or trotted, then another litter containing Billali, then my own by which ran Hans, and Robertson's, and lastly the rest of the Amahagger and the relief bearers.

"I see now, Baas," said Hans, thrusting his head between my curtains, "that yonder Whitebeard cannot be your reverend father, the Predikant, after all."

"Why not?" I asked, though the fact was fairly obvious.

"Because, Baas, if he were, he would not have left Hans, of whom he always thought so well, to run in the sun like a dog, while he and others travel in carriages like great white ladies."

"You had better save your breath instead of talking nonsense, Hans," I said, "since I believe that you have a long way to go."

In fact, it proved to be a very long way indeed, especially as after we began to breast the mountain, we must travel slowly. We started about ten o'clock in the morning, for the fight which after all did not take long—had, it will be remembered, begun shortly after dawn, and it was three in the afternoon before we reached the base of the towering cliff which I have mentioned.

Here, at the foot of a remarkable, isolated column of rock, on which I was destined to see a strange sight in the after days, we halted and ate of the remaining food which we had brought with us, while the Amahagger consumed their own, that seemed to consist largely of curdled milk, such as the Zulus call maas, and lumps of a kind of bread.

I noted that they were a very curious people who fed in silence and on whose handsome, solemn faces one never saw a smile. Somehow it gave me the creeps to look at them. Robertson was affected in the same way, for in one of the rare intervals of his abstraction he remarked that they were "no canny." Then he added,

"Ask yon old wizard who might be one of the Bible prophets come to life—what those man-eating devils have done with my daughter."

I did so, and Billali answered,

"Say that they have taken her away to make a queen of her, since having rebelled against their own queen, they must have another who is white. Say too that She-who-commands will wage war on them and perhaps win her back, unless they kill her first."

"Ah!" Robertson repeated when I had translated, "unless they kill her first—or worse." Then he relapsed into his usual silence.

Presently we started on again, heading straight for what looked like a sheer wall of black rock a thousand feet or more in height, up a path so steep that Robertson and I got out and walked, or rather scrambled, in order to ease the bearers. Billali, I noticed, remained in his litter. The convenience of the bearers did not trouble him; he only ordered an extra gang to the poles. I could not imagine how we were to negotiate this precipice. Nor could Umslopogaas, who looked at it and said,

"If we are to climb that, Macumazahn, I think that the only one who will live to get to the top will be that little yellow monkey of yours," and he pointed with his axe at Hans.

"If I do," replied that worthy, much nettled, for he hated to be called a "yellow monkey" by the Zulus, "be sure that I will roll down stones upon any black butcher whom I see sprawling upon the cliff below."

Umslopogaas smiled grimly, for he had a sense of humour and could appreciate a repartee even when it hit him hard. Then we stopped talking for the climb took all our breath.

At length we came to the cliff face where, to all appearance, our journey must end. Suddenly, however, out of the blind black wall in front of us started the apparition of a tall man armed with a great spear and wearing a white robe, who challenged us hoarsely.

Suddenly he stood before us, as a ghost might do, though whence he came we could not see. Presently the mystery was explained. Here in the cliff face there was a cleft, though one invisible even from a few paces away, since its outer edge projected over the inner wall of rock. Moreover, this opening was not above four feet in width, a mere split in the huge mountain mass caused by some titanic convulsion in past ages. For it was a definite split since, once entered, far, far above could be traced a faint line of light coming from the sky, although the gloom of the passage was such that torches, which were stored at hand, must be used by those who threaded it. One man could have held the place against a hundred— until he was killed. Still, it was guarded, not only at the mouth where the warrior had appeared, but further along at every turn in the jagged chasm, and these were many.

Into this grim place we went. The Zulus did not like it at all, for they are a light-loving people and I noted that even Umslopogaas seemed scared and hung back a little. Nor did Hans, who with his usual suspicion, feared some trap; nor, for the matter of that, did I, though I thought it well to appear much interested. Only Robertson seemed quite indifferent and trudged along stolidly after a man carrying a torch.

Old Billali put his head out of the litter and shouted back to me to fear nothing, since there were no pitfalls in the path, his voice echoing strangely between those narrow walls of measureless height.

For half an hour or more we pursued this dreary, winding path round the corners of which the draught tore in gusts so fierce that more than once the litters with the wounded men and those who bore them were nearly blown over. It was safe enough, however, since on either side of us, smooth and without break, rose the sheer walls of rock over which lay the tiny ribbon of blue sky. At length the cleft widened somewhat and the light grew stronger, making the torches unnecessary.

Then of a sudden we came to its end and found ourselves upon a little plateau in the mountainside. Behind us for a thousand feet or so rose the sheer rock wall as it did upon the outer face, while in front and beneath, far beneath, was a beautiful plain circular in shape and of great extent, which plain was everywhere surrounded, so far as I could see, by the same wall of rock. In short, notwithstanding its enormous size, without doubt it was neither more nor less than the crater of a vast extinct volcano. Lastly, not far from the centre of this plain was what appeared to be a city, since through my glasses I could see great walls built of stone, and what I thought were houses, all of them of a character more substantial than any that I had discovered in the wilds of Africa.

I went to Billali's litter and asked him who lived in the city.

"No one," he answered, "it has been dead for thousands of years, but She-who-commands is camped there at present with an army, and thither we go at once. Forward, bearers."

So, Robertson and I having re-entered our litters, we started on down hill at a rapid pace, for the road, though steep, was safe and kept in good order. All the rest of that afternoon we travelled and by sunset reached the edge of the plain, where we halted a while to rest and eat, till the light of the growing moon grew strong enough to enable us to proceed. Umslopogaas came up and spoke to me.

"Here is a fortress indeed, Macumazahn," he said, "since none can climb that fence of rock in which the holes seem to be few and small."

"Yes," I answered, "but it is one out of which those who are in, would find it difficult to get out. We are buffaloes in a pit, Umslopogaas."

"That is so," he answered, "I have thought it already. But if any would meddle with us we still have our horns and can toss for a while."

Then he went back to his men.

The sunset in that great solemn place was a wonderful thing to see. First of all the measureless crater was filled with light like a bowl with fire. Then as the great orb sank behind the western cliff, half of the plain became quite dark while shadows seemed to rush forward over the eastern part of its surface, till that too was swallowed up in gloom and for a little while there remained only a glow reflected from the cliff face and from the sky above, while on the crest of the parapet of rock played strange and glorious fires. Presently these too vanished and the world was dark.

Then the half moon broke from behind a bank of clouds and by its silver, uncertain light we struggled forward across the flat plain, rather slowly now, for even the iron muscles of those bearers grew tired. I could not see much of it, but I gathered that we were passing through crops, very fine crops to judge by their height, as doubtless they would be upon this lava soil; also once or twice we splashed through streams.

At length, being tired and lulled by the swaying of the litter and by the sound of a weird, low chant that the bearers had set up now that they neared home and were afraid of no attack, I sank into a doze. When I awoke again it was to find that the litter had halted and to hear the voice of Billali say,

"Descend, White Lords, and come with your companions, the black Warrior and the yellow man who is named Light-in-Darkness. She-who-commands desires to see you at once before you eat and sleep, and must not be kept waiting. Fear not for the others, they will be cared for till you return."

CHAPTER XII

THE WHITE WITCH

I descended from the litter and told the others what the old fellow had said. Robertson did not want to come, and indeed refused to do so until I suggested to him that such conduct might prejudice a powerful person against us. Umslopogaas was indifferent, putting, as he remarked, no faith in a ruler who was a woman.

Only Hans, although he was so tired, acquiesced with some eagerness, the fact being that his brain was more alert and that he had all the curiosity of the monkey tribe which he so much resembled in appearance, and wanted to see this queen whom Zikali revered.

In the end we started, conducted by Billali and by men who carried torches whereof the light showed me that we were passing between houses, or at any rate walls that had been those of houses, and along what seemed to be a paved street.

Walking under what I took to be a great arch or portico, we came into a court that was full of towering pillars but unroofed, for I could see the stars above. At its end we entered a building of which the doorway was hung with mats, to find that it was lighted with lamps and that all down its length on either side guards with long spears stood at intervals.

"Oh, Baas," said Hans hesitatingly, "this is the mouth of a trap," while Umslopogaas glared about him suspiciously, fingering the handle of his great axe.

"Be silent," I answered. "All this mountain is a trap, therefore another does not matter, and we have our pistols."

Walking forward between the double line of guards who stood immovable as statues, we came to some curtains hung at the end of a long, narrow hall which, although I know little of such things, were, I noted, made of rich stuff embroidered in colours and with golden threads. Before these curtains Billali motioned us to halt.

After a whispered colloquy with someone beyond carried on through the join of the curtains, he vanished between them, leaving us alone for five minutes or more. At length they opened and a tall and elegant woman with an Arab cast of countenance and clad in white robes, appeared and beckoned to us to enter. She did not speak or answer when I spoke to her, which was not wonderful as afterwards I discovered that she was a mute. We went in, I wondering very much what we were going to see.

On the further side of the curtains was a room of no great size illumined with lamps of which the light fell upon sculptured walls. It looked to me as though it might once have been the inmost court or a sanctuary of some temple, for at its head was a dais upon which once perhaps had stood the shrine or statue of a god. On this dais there was now a couch and on the couch—a goddess!

There she sat, straight and still, clothed in shining white and veiled, but with her draperies so arranged that they emphasised rather than concealed the wonderful elegance of her tall form. From beneath the veil, which was such as a bride wears, appeared two plaits of glossy, raven hair of great length, to the end of each of which was suspended a single large pearl. On either side of her stood a tall woman like to her who had led us through the curtains, and on his knees in front, but to the right, knelt Billali.

About this seated personage there was an air of singular majesty, such as might pervade a queen as fancy paints her, though she had a nobler figure than any queen I ever saw depicted. Mystery seemed to flow from her; it clothed her like the veil she wore, which of course heightened the effect. Beauty flowed from her also; although it was shrouded I knew that it was there, no veil or coverings could obscure it—at least, to my imagination. Moreover she breathed out power also; one felt it in the air as one feels a thunderstorm before it breaks, and it seemed to me that this power was not quite human, that it drew its strength from afar and dwelt a stranger to the earth.

To tell the truth, although my curiosity, always strong, was enormously excited and though now I felt glad that I had attempted this journey with all its perils, I was horribly afraid, so much afraid that I should have liked to turn and run away. From the beginning I knew myself to be in the presence of an unearthly being clothed in soft and perfect woman's flesh, something alien, too, and different from our human race.

What a picture it all made! There she sat, quiet and stately as a perfect marble statue; only her breast, rising and falling beneath the white robe, showed that she was alive and breathed as others do. Another thing showed it also—her eyes. At first I could not see them through the veil, but presently either because I grew accustomed to the light, or because they brightened as those of certain animals have power to do when they watch intently, it ceased to be a covering to them. Distinctly I saw them now, large and dark and splendid with a tinge of deep blue in the iris; alluring and yet awful in their majestic aloofness which seemed to look through and beyond, to embrace all without seeking and without effort. Those eyes were like windows through which light flows from within, a light of the spirit.

I glanced round to see the effect of this vision upon my companions. It was most peculiar. Hans had sunk to his knees; his hands were joined in the attitude of prayer and his ugly little face reminded me of that of a big fish out of water and dying from excess of air. Robertson, startled out of his abstraction, stared at the royal-looking woman on the couch with his mouth open.

"Man," he whispered, "I've got them back although I have touched nothing for weeks, only this time they are lovely. For yon's no human lady, I feel it in my bones."

Umslopogaas stood great and grim, his hands resting on the handle of his tall axe; and he stared also, the blood pulsing against the skin that covered the hole in his head.

"Watcher-by-Night," he said to me in his deep voice, but also speaking in a whisper, "this chieftainess is not one woman, but all women. Beneath those robes of hers I seem to see the beauty of one who has 'gone Beyond,' of the Lily who is lost to me. Do you not feel it thus, Macumazahn?"

Now that he mentioned it, certainly I did; indeed, I had felt it all along although amid the rush of sensations this one had scarcely disentangled itself in my mind. I looked at the draped shape and saw—well, never mind whom I saw; it was not one only but several in sequence; also a woman who at that time I did not know although I came to know her afterwards, too well, perhaps, or at any rate quite enough to puzzle me. The odd thing was that in this hallucination the personalities of these individuals seemed to overlap and merge, till at last I began to wonder whether they were not parts of the same entity or being, manifesting itself in sundry shapes, yet springing from one centre, as different coloured rays flow from the same crystal, while the beams from their source of light shift and change. But the fancy is too metaphysical for my poor powers to express as clearly as I would. Also no doubt it was but a hallucination that had its origin, perhaps, in the mischievous brain of her who sat before us.

At length she spoke and her voice sounded like silver bells heard over water in a great calm. It was low and sweet, oh! so sweet that at its first notes for a moment my senses seemed to swoon and my pulse to stop. It was to me that she addressed herself.

"My servant here," and ever so slightly she turned her head towards the kneeling Billali, "tells me that you who are named Watcher-in-the-Night, understand the tongue in which I speak to you. Is it so?"

"I understand Arabic of a kind well enough, having learned it on the East Coast and from Arabs in past years, but not such Arabic as you use, O—" and I paused.

"Call me Hiya," she broke in, "which is my title here, meaning, as you know, She, or Woman. Or if that does not please you, call me Ayesha. It would rejoice me after so long to hear the name I bore spoken by the lips of one of my colour and of gentle blood."

I blushed at the compliment so artfully conveyed, and repeated stupidly enough,

"—Not such Arabic as you use, O—Ayesha."

"I thought that you would like the sound of the word better than that of Hiya, though afterwards I will teach you to pronounce it as you should, O—have you any other name save Watcher-by-Night, which seems also to be a title?"

"Yes," I answered. "Allan."

"—O—Allan. Tell me of these," she went on quickly, indicating my companions with a sweep of her slender hand, "for they do not speak Arabic, I think. Or stay, I will tell you of them and you shall say if I do so rightly. This one," and she nodded towards Robertson, "is a man bemused. There comes from him a colour which I see if you cannot, and that colour betokens a desire for revenge, though I think that in his time he has desired other things also, as I remember men always did from the beginning, to their ruin. Human nature does not change, Allan, and wine and women are ancient snares. Enough of him for this time. The little yellow one there is afraid of me, as are all of you. That is woman's greatest power, although she is so weak and gentle, men are still afraid of her just because they are so foolish that they cannot understand her. To them after a million years she still remains the Unknown and to us all the Unknown is also the awful. Do you remember the proverb of the Romans that says it well and briefly?"

I nodded, for it was one of the Latin tags that my father had taught me.

"Good. Well, he is a little wild man, is he not, nearer to the apes from whose race our bodies come? But do you know that, Allan?"

I nodded again, and said,

"There are disputes upon the point, Ayesha."

"Yes, they had begun in my day and we will discuss them later. Still, I say—nearer to the ape than you or I, and therefore of interest, as the germ of things is always. Yet he has qualities, I think; cunning, and fidelity and love which in its round is all in all. Do you understand, Allan, that love is all in all?"

I answered warily that it depended upon what she meant by love, to which she replied that she would explain afterwards when we had leisure to talk, adding,

"What this little yellow monkey understands by it at least has served you well, or so I believe. You shall tell me the tale of it some day. Now of the last, this Black One. Here I think is a man indeed, a warrior of warriors such as there used to be in the early world, if a savage. Well, believe me, Allan, savages are often the best. Moreover, all are still savage at heart, even you and I. For what is termed culture is but coat upon coat of paint laid on to hide our native colour, and often there is poison in the paint. That axe of his has drunk deep, I think, though always in fair fight, and I say that it shall drink deeper yet. Have I read these men aright, Allan?"

"Not so ill," I answered.

"I thought it," she said with a musical laugh, "although at this place I rust and grow dull like an unused sword. Now you would rest. Go—all of you. To-morrow you and I will talk alone. Fear nothing for your safety; you are watched by my slaves and I watch my slaves. Until to-morrow, then, farewell. Go now, eat and sleep, as alas we all must do who linger on this ball of earth and cling to a life we should do well to lose. Billali, lead them hence," and she waved her hand to signify that the audience was ended.

At this sign Hans, who apparently was still much afraid, rose from his knees and literally bolted through the curtains. Robertson followed him. Umslopogaas stood a moment, drew himself up and lifting the great axe, cried Bayéte, after which he too turned and went.

"What does that word mean, Allan?" she asked.

I explained that it was the salutation which the Zulu people only give to kings.

"Did I not say that savages are often the best?" she exclaimed in a gratified voice. "The white man, your companion, gave me no salute, but the Black One knows when he stands before a woman who is royal."

"He too is of royal blood in his own land," I said.

"If so, we are akin, Allan."

Then I bowed deeply to her in my best manner and rising from her couch for the first time she stood up, looking very tall and commanding, and bowed back.

After this I went to find the others on the further side of the curtains, except Hans, who had run down the long narrow hall and through the mats at its end. We followed, marching with dignity behind Billali and between the double line of guards, who raised their spears as we passed them, and on the further side of the mats discovered Hans, still looking terrified.

"Baas," he said to me as we threaded our way through the court of columns, "in my life I have seen all kinds of dreadful things and faced them, but never have I been so much afraid as I am of that white witch. Baas, I think that she is the devil of whom your reverend father, the Predikant, used to talk so much, or perhaps his wife."

"If so, Hans," I answered, "the devil is not so black as he is painted. But I advise you to be careful of what you say as she may have long ears."

"It doesn't matter at all what one says, Baas, because she reads thoughts before they pass the lips. I felt her doing it there in that room. And do you be careful, Baas, or she will eat up your spirit and make you fall in love with her, who, I expect, is very ugly indeed, since otherwise she would not wear a veil. Whoever saw a pretty woman tie up her head in a sack, Baas?"

"Perhaps she does this because she is so beautiful, Hans, that she fears the hearts of men who look upon her would melt."

"Oh, no, Baas, all women want to melt men's hearts; the more the better. They seem to have other things in their minds, but really they think of nothing else until they are too old and ugly, and it takes them a long while to be sure of that."

So Hans went on talking his shrewd nonsense till, following so far as I could see, the same road as that by which we had come, we reached our quarters, where we found food prepared for us, broiled goat's flesh with corncakes and milk, I think it was; also beds for us two white men covered with skin rugs and blankets woven of wool.

These quarters, I should explain, consisted of rooms in a house built of stone of which the walls had once been painted. The roof of the house was gone now, for we could see the stars shining above us, but as the air was very soft in this sheltered plain, this was an advantage rather than otherwise. The largest room was reserved for Robertson and myself, while another at the back was given to Umslopogaas and his Zulus, and a third to the two wounded men.

Billali showed us these arrangements by the light of lamps and apologised that they were not better because, as he explained, the place was a ruin and there had been no time to build us a house. He added that we might sleep without fear as we were guarded and none would dare to harm the guests of She-who-commands, on whom he was sure we, or at any rate I and the black Warrior, had produced an excellent impression. Then he bowed himself out, saying that he would return in the morning, and left us to our own devices.

Robertson and I sat down on stools that had been set for us, and ate, but he seemed so overcome by his experiences, or by his sombre thoughts, that I could not draw him into conversation. All he remarked was that we had fallen into queer company and that those who supped with Satan needed a long spoon. Having delivered himself of this sentiment he threw himself upon the bed, prayed aloud for a while as had become his fashion, to be "protected from warlocks and witches," amongst other things, and went to sleep.

Before I turned in I visited Umslopogaas's room to see that all was well with him and his people, and found him standing in the doorway staring at the star-spangled sky.

"Greeting, Macumazahn," he said, "you who are white and wise and I am black and a fighter have seen many strange things beneath the sun, but never such a one as we have looked upon to-night. Who and what is that chieftainess, Macumazahn?"

"I do not know," I said, "but it is worth while to have lived to see her, even though she be veiled."

"Nor do I, Macumazahn. Nay, I do know, for my heart tells me that she is the greatest of all witches and that you will do well to guard your spirit lest she should steal it away. If she were not a witch, should I have seemed to behold the shape of Nada the Lily who was the wife of my youth, beneath those white robes of hers, and though the tongue in which she spoke was strange to me, to hear the murmur of Nada's voice between her lips, of Nada who has gone further from me than those stars. It is good that you wear the Great Medicine of Zikali upon your breast, Macumazahn, for perhaps it will shield you from harm at those hands that are shaped of ivory."

"Zikali is another of the tribe," I answered, laughing, "although less beautiful to see. Also I am not afraid of any of them, and from this one, if she be more than some white woman whom it pleases to veil herself, I shall hope to gather wisdom."

"Yes, Macumazahn, such wisdom as Spirits and the dead have to give."

"Mayhap, Umslopogaas, but we came here to seek Spirits and the dead, did we not?"

"Aye," answered Umslopogaas, "these and war, and I think that we shall find enough of all three. Only I hope that war will come the first, lest the Spirits and the dead should bewitch me and take away my skill and courage."

Then we parted, and too tired even to wonder any more, I threw myself down on my bed and slept.

I was awakened when the sun was already high, by the sound of Robertson, who was on his knees, praying aloud as usual, a habit of his which I confess got on my nerves. Prayer, in my opinion, is a private matter between man and his Creator, that is, except in church; further, I did not in the least wish to hear all about Robertson's sins, which seemed to have been many and peculiar. It is bad enough to have to bear the burden of one's own transgressions without learning of those of other people, that is, unless one is a priest and must do so professionally. So I jumped up to escape and make arrangements for a wash, only to butt into old Billali, who was standing in the doorway contemplating Robertson with much interest and stroking his white beard.

He greeted me with his courteous bow and said,

"Tell your companion, O Watcher, that it is not necessary for him to go upon his knees to She-who-commands—and must be obeyed," he added with emphasis, "when he is not in her presence, and that even then he would do well to keep silent, since so much talking in a strange tongue might trouble her."

I burst out laughing and answered,

"He does not go upon his knees and pray to She-who-commands, but to the Great One who is in the sky."

"Indeed, Watcher. Well, here we only know a Great One who is upon the earth, though it is true that perhaps she visits the skies sometimes."

"Is it so, Billali?" I answered incredulously. "And now, I would ask you to take me to some place where I can bathe."

"It is ready," he replied. "Come."

So I called to Hans, who was hanging about with a rifle on his arm, to follow with a cloth and soap, of which fortunately we had a couple of pieces left, and we started along what had once been a paved roadway running between stone houses, whereof the time-eaten ruins still remained on either side.

"Who and what is this Queen of yours, Billali?" I asked as we went. "Surely she is not of the Amahagger blood."

"Ask it of herself, O Watcher, for I cannot tell you. All I know is that I can trace my own family for ten generations and that my tenth forefather told his son on his deathbed, for the saying has come down through his descendants—that when he was young She-who-commands had ruled the land for more scores of years than he could count months of life."

I stopped and stared at him, since the lie was so amazing that it seemed to deprive me of the power of motion. Noting my very obvious disbelief he continued blandly,

"If you doubt, ask. And now here is where you may bathe."

Then he led me through an arched doorway and down a wrecked passage to what very obviously once had been a splendid bath-house such as some I have seen pictures of that were built by the Romans. Its size was that of a large room; it was constructed of a kind of marble with a sloping bottom that varied from three to seven feet in depth, and water still ran in and out of it through large glazed pipes. Moreover round it was a footway about five feet across, from which opened chambers, unroofed now, that the bathers used as dressing-rooms, while between these chambers stood the remains of statues. One at the end indeed, where an alcove had protected it from sun and weather, was still quite perfect, except for the outstretched arms which were gone (the right hand I noticed lying at the bottom of the bath). It was that of a nude young woman in the attitude of diving, a very beautiful bit of work, I thought, though of course I am no judge of sculpture. Even the smile mingled with trepidation upon the girl's face was most naturally portrayed.

This statue showed two things, that the bath was used by females and that the people who built it were highly civilised, also that they belonged to an advanced if somewhat Eastern race, since the girl's nose was, if anything, Semitic in character, and her lips, though prettily shaped, were full. For the rest, the basin was so clean that I presume it must have been made ready for me or other recent bathers, and at its bottom I discovered gratings and broken pipes of earthenware which suggested that in the old days the water could be warmed by means of a furnace.

This relic of a long-past civilisation excited Hans even more than it did myself, since having never seen anything of the sort, he thought it so strange that, as he informed me, he imagined that it must have been built by witchcraft. In it I had a most delightful and much-needed bath. Even Hans was persuaded to follow my example—a thing I had rarely known him to do before—and seated in its shallowest part, splashed some water over his yellow, wrinkled anatomy. Then we returned to our house, where I found an excellent breakfast had been provided which was brought to us by tall, silent, handsome women who surveyed us out of the corners of their eyes, but said nothing.

Shortly after I had finished my meal, Billali, who had disappeared, came back again and said that She-who-commands desired my presence as she would speak with me; also that I must come alone. So, after attending to the wounded, who both seemed to be getting on well, I went, followed by Hans armed with his rifle, though I only carried my revolver. Robertson wished to accompany me, as he did not seem to care about being left alone with the Zulus in that strange place, but this Billali would not allow. Indeed, when he persisted, two great men stepped forward and crossed their spears before him in a somewhat threatening fashion. Then at my entreaty, for I feared lest trouble should arise, he gave in and returned to the house.

Following our path of the night before, we walked up a ruined street which I could see was only one of scores in what had once been a very great city, until we came to the archway that I have mentioned, a large one now overgrown with plants that from their yellow, sweet-scented bloom I judged to be a species of wallflower, also with a kind of houseleek or saxifrage.

Here Hans was stopped by guards, Billali explaining to me that he must await my return, an order which he obeyed unwillingly enough. Then I went on down the narrow passage, lined as before by guards who stood silent as statues, and came to the curtains at the end. Before these at a motion from Billali, who did not seem to dare to speak in this place, I stood still and waited.

CHAPTER XIII

ALLAN HEARS A STRANGE TALE

For some minutes I remained before those curtains until, had it not been for something electric in the air which got into my bones, a kind of force that, perhaps in my fancy only, seemed to pervade the place, I should certainly have grown bored. Indeed I was about to ask my companion why he did not announce our arrival instead of standing there like a stuck pig with his eyes shut as though in prayer or meditation, when the curtains parted and from between them appeared one of those tall waiting women whom we had seen on the previous night. She contemplated us gravely for a few moments, then moved her hand twice, once forward, towards Billali as a signal to him to retire, which he did with great rapidity, and next in a beckoning fashion towards myself to invite me to follow her.

I obeyed, passing between the thick curtains which she fastened in some way behind me, and found myself in the same roofed and sculptured room that I have already described. Only now there were no lamps, such light as penetrated it coming from an opening above that I could not see, and falling upon the dais at its head, also on her who sat upon the dais.

Yes, there she was in her white robes and veil, the point and centre of a little lake of light, a wondrous and in a sense a spiritual vision, for in truth there was something about her which was not of the world, something that drew and yet frightened me. Still as a statue she sat, like one to whom time is of no account and who has grown weary of motion, and on either side of her yet more still, like caryatides supporting a shrine, stood two of the stately women who were her attendants.

For the rest a sweet and subtle odour pervaded the chamber which took hold of my senses as hasheesh might do, which I was sure proceeded from her, or from her garments, for I could see no perfumes burning. She spoke no word, yet I knew she was inviting me to come nearer and moved forward till I reached a curious carved chair that was placed just beneath the dais, and there halted, not liking to sit down without permission.

For a long while she contemplated me, for as before I could feel her eyes searching me from head to foot and as it were looking through me as though she would discover my very soul. Then at length she moved, waving those two ivory arms of hers outwards with a kind of swimming stroke, whereon the women to right and left of her turned and glided away, I know not whither.

"Sit, Allan," she said, "and let us talk, for I think we have much to say to each other. Have you slept well? And eaten?—though I fear that the food is but rough. Also was the bath made ready for you?"

"Yes, Ayesha," I answered to all three questions, adding, for I knew not what to say, "It seems to be a very ancient bath."

"When I last saw it," she replied, "it was well enough with statues standing round it worked by a sculptor who had seen beauty in his dreams. But in two thousand years—or is it more?—the tooth of Time bites deep, and doubtless like all else in this dead place it is now a ruin."

I coughed to cover up the exclamation of disbelief that rose to my lips and remarked blandly that two thousand years was certainly a long time.

"When you say one thing, Allan, and mean another, your Arabic is even more vile than usual and does not serve to cloak your thought."

"It may be so, Ayesha, for I only know that tongue as I do many other of the dialects of Africa by learning it from common men. My own speech is English, in which, if you are acquainted with it, I should prefer to talk."

"I know not English, which doubtless is some language that has arisen since I left the world. Perhaps later you shall teach it to me. I tell you, you anger me whom it is not well to anger, because you believe nothing that passes my lips and yet do not dare to say so."

"How can I believe one, Ayesha, who if I understand aright, speaks of having seen a certain bath two thousand years ago, whereas one hundred years are the full days of man? Forgive me therefore if I cannot believe what I know to be untrue."

Now I thought that she would be very angry and was sorry that I had spoken. But as it happened she was not.

"You must have courage to give me the lie so boldly—and I like courage," she said, "who have been cringed to for so long. Indeed, I know that you are brave, who have heard how you bore yourself in the fight yesterday, and much else about you. I think that we shall be friends, but—seek no more."

"What else should I seek, Ayesha?" I asked innocently.

"Now you are lying again," she said, "who know well that no man who is a man sees a woman who is beautiful and pleases him, without wondering whether, should he desire it, she could come to love him, that is, if she be young."

"Which at least is not possible if she has lived two thousand years. Then naturally she would prefer to wear a veil," I said boldly, seeking to avoid the argument into which I saw she wished to drag me.

"Ah!" she answered, "the little yellow man who is named Light-in-Darkness put that thought into your heart, I think. Oh, do not trouble as to how I know it, who have many spies here, as he guessed well enough. So a woman who has lived two thousand years must be hideous and wrinkled, must she? The stamp of youth and loveliness must long have fled from her; of that you, the wise man, are sure. Very well. Now you tempt me to do what I had determined I would not do and you shall pluck the fruit of that tree of curiosity which grows so fast within you. Look, Allan, and say whether I am old and hideous, even though I have lived two thousand years upon the earth and mayhap many more."

Then she lifted her hands and did something to her veil, so that for a moment—only one moment—her face was revealed, after which the veil fell into its place.

I looked, I saw, and if that chair had lacked a back I believe that I should have fallen out of it to the ground. As for what I saw—well, it cannot be described, at any rate by me, except perhaps as a flash of glory.

Every man has dreamed of perfect beauty, basing his ideas of it perhaps on that of some woman he has met who chanced to take his fancy, with a few accessories from splendid pictures or Greek statues thrown in, plus a garnishment of the imagination. At any rate I have, and here was that perfect beauty multiplied by ten, such beauty, that at the sight of it the senses reeled. And yet I repeat that it is not to be described.

I do not know what the nose or the lips were like; in fact, all that I can remember with distinctness is the splendour of the eyes, of which I had caught some hint through her veil on the previous night. Oh, they were wondrous, those eyes, but I cannot tell their colour save that the groundwork of them was black. Moreover they seemed to be more than eyes as we understand them. They were indeed windows of the soul, out of which looked thought and majesty and infinite wisdom, mixed with all the allurements and the mystery that we are accustomed to see or to imagine in woman.

Here let me say something at once. If this marvellous creature expected that the revelation of her splendour was going to make me her slave; to cause me to fall in love with her, as it is called, well, she must have been disappointed, for it had no such effect. It frightened and in a sense humbled me, that is all, for I felt myself to be in the presence of something that was not human, something alien to me as a man, which I could fear and even adore as humanity would adore that which is Divine, but with which I had no desire to mix. Moreover, was it divine, or was it something very different? I did not know, I only knew that it was not for me; as soon should I have thought of asking for a star to set within my lantern.

I think that she felt this, felt that her stroke had missed, as the French say, that is if she meant to strike at all at this moment. Of this I am not certain, for it was in a changed voice, one with a suspicion of chill in it that she said with a little laugh,

"Do you admit now, Allan, that a woman may be old and still remain fair and unwrinkled?"

"I admit," I answered, although I was trembling so much that I could hardly speak with steadiness, "that a woman may be splendid and lovely beyond anything that the mind of man can conceive, whatever her age, of which I know nothing. I would add this, Ayesha, that I thank you very much for having revealed to me the glory that is hid beneath your veil."

"Why?" she asked, and I thought that I detected curiosity in her question.

"For this reason, Ayesha. Now there is no fear of my troubling you in such a fashion as you seemed to dread a little while ago. As soon would a man desire to court the moon sailing in her silver loveliness through heaven."

"The moon! It is strange that you should compare me to the moon," she said musingly. "Do you know that the moon was a great goddess in Old Egypt and that her name was Isis and—well, once I had to do with Isis? Perhaps you were there and knew it, since more lives than one are given to most of us. I must search and learn. For the rest, all have not thought as you do, Allan. Many, on the contrary, love and seek to win the Divine."

"So do I at a distance, Ayesha, but to come too near to it I do not aspire. If I did perhaps I might be consumed."

"You have wisdom," she replied, not without a note of admiration in her voice. "The moths are few that fear the flame, but those are the moths which live. Also I think that you have scorched your wings before and learned that fire hurts. Indeed, now I remember that I have heard of three such fires of love through which you have flown, Allan, though all of them are dead ashes now, or shine elsewhere. Two burned in your youth when a certain lady died to save you, a great woman that, is it not so? And the third, ah! she was fire indeed, though of a copper hue. What was her name? I cannot remember, but I think it had something to do with the wind, yes, with the wind when it wails."

I stared at her. Was this Mameena myth to be dug up again in a secret place in the heart of Africa? And how the deuce did she know anything about Mameena? Could she have been questioning Hans or Umslopogaas? No, it was not possible, for she had never seen them out of my presence.

"Perhaps," she went on in a mocking voice, "perhaps once again you disbelieve, Allan, whose cynic mind is so hard to open to new truths. Well, shall I show you the faces of these three? I can," and she waved her hand towards some object that stood on a tripod to the right of her in the shadow—it looked like a crystal basin. "But what would it serve when you who know them so well, believed that I drew their pictures out of your own soul? Also perchance but one face would appear and that one strange to you. [Lady Ragnall perhaps?—JB]

"Have you heard, Allan, that among the wise some hold that not all of us is visible at once here on earth within the same house of flesh; that the whole self in its home above, separates itself into sundry parts, each of which walks the earth in different form, a segment of life's circle that can never be dissolved and must unite again at last?"

I shook my head blankly, for I had never heard anything of the sort.

"You have still much to learn, Allan, although doubtless there are some who think you wise," she went on in the same mocking voice. "Well, I hold that this doctrine is built upon a rock of truth; also," she added after studying me for a minute, "that in your case these three women do not complete that circle. I think there is a fourth who as yet is strange to you in this life, though you have known her well enough in others."

I groaned, imagining that she alluded to herself, which was foolish of me, for at once she read my mind and went on with a rather acid little laugh,

"No, no, not the humble slave who sits before you, whom, as you have told me, it would please you to reject as unworthy were she brought to you in offering, as in the old days was done at the courts of the great kings of the East. O fool, fool! who hold yourself so strong and do not know that if I chose, before yon shadow had moved a finger's breadth, I could bring you to my feet, praying that you might be suffered to kiss my robe, yes, just the border of my robe."

"Then I beg of you not to choose, Ayesha, since I think that when there is work to be done by both of us, we shall find more comfort side by side than if I were on the ground seeking to kiss a garment that doubtless then it would delight you to snatch away."

At these words her whole attitude seemed to change. I could see her lovely shape brace itself up, as it were, beneath her robes and felt in some way that her mind had also changed; that it had rid itself of mockery and woman's pique and like a shifting searchlight, was directed upon some new objective.

"Work to be done," she repeated after me in a new voice. "Yes, I thank you who bring it to my mind, since the hours pass and that work presses. Also I think there is a bargain to be made between us who are both of the blood that keeps bargains, even if they be not written on a roll and signed and sealed. Why do you come to me and what do you seek of me, Allan, Watcher-in-the-Night? Say it and truthfully, for though I may laugh at lies and pass them by when they have to do with the eternal sword-play which Nature decrees between man and woman, until these break apart or, casting down the swords, seek arms in which they agree too well, when they have to do with policy and high purpose and ambition's ends, why then I avenge them upon the liar."

Now I hesitated, as what I had to tell her seemed so foolish, indeed so insane, while she waited patiently as though to give me time to shape my thoughts. Speaking at last because I must, I said,

"I come to ask you, Ayesha, to show me the dead, if the dead still live elsewhere."

"And who told you, Allan, that I could show you the dead, if they are not truly dead? There is but one, I think, and if you are his messenger, show me his token. Without it we do not speak together of this business."

"What token?" I asked innocently, though I guessed her meaning well enough.

She searched me with her great eyes, for I felt, and indeed saw them on me through the veil, then answered,

"I think—nay, let me be sure," and half rising from the couch, she bent her heard over the tripod that I have described, and stared into what seemed to be a crystal bowl. "If I read aright," she said, straightening herself presently, "it is a hideous thing enough, the carving of an abortion of a man such as no woman would care to look on lest her babe should bear its stamp. It is a charmed thing also that has virtues for him who wears it, especially for you, Allan, since something tells me that it is dyed with the blood of one who loved you. If you have it, let it be revealed, since without it I do not talk with you of these dead you seek."

Now I drew Zikali's talisman from its hiding-place and held it towards her.

"Give it to me," she said.

I was about to obey when something seemed to warn me not to do so.

"Nay," I answered, "he who lent me this carving for a while, charged me that except in emergency and to save others, I must wear it night and day till I returned it to his hand, saying that if I parted from it fortune would desert me. I believe none of this talk and tried to be rid of it, whereon death drew near to me from a snake, such a snake as I see you wear about you, which doubtless also has poison in its fangs, if of another sort, Ayesha."

"Draw near," she said, "and let me look. Man, be not afraid."

So I rose from my chair and knelt before her, hoping secretly that no one would see me in that ridiculous position, which the most unsuspicious might misinterpret. I admit, however, that it proved to have compensations, since even through the veil I saw her marvellous eyes better than I had done before, and something of the pure outline of her classic face; also the fragrance of her hair was wonderful.

She took the talisman in her hand and examined it closely.

"I have heard of this charm and it is true that the thing has power," she said, "for I can feel it running through my veins, also that it is a shield of defence to him who wears it. Yes, and now I understand what perplexed me somewhat, namely, how it came about that when you vexed me into unveiling—but let that matter be. The wisdom was not your own, but another's, that is all. Yes, the wisdom of one whose years have borne him beyond the shafts that fly from woman's eyes, the ruinous shafts which bring men down to doom and nothingness. Tell me, Allan, is this the likeness of him who gave it to you?"

"Yes, Ayesha, the very picture, as I think, carved by himself, though he said that it is ancient, and others tell that it has been known in the land for centuries."

"So perchance has he," she answered drily, "since some of our company live long. Now tell me this wizard's names. Nay, wait awhile for I would prove that indeed you are his messenger with whom I may talk about the dead, and other things, Allan. You can read Arabic, can you not?"

"A little," I answered.

Then from a stool at her side she took paper, or rather papyrus and a reed pen, and on her knee wrote something on the sheet which she gave to me folded up.

"Now tell me the names," she said, "and then let us see if they tally with what I have written, for if so you are a true man, not a mere wanderer or a spy."

"The principal names of this doctor are Zikali, the Opener-of-Roads, the 'Thing-that-should-never-have-been-born,'" I answered.

"Read the writing, Allan," she said.

I unfolded the sheet and read Arabic words which meant, "Weapons, Cleaver-of-Rocks, One-at-whom-dogs-bark-and-children-wail."

"The last two are near enough," she said, "but the first is wrong."

"Nay, Ayesha, since in this man's tongue the word 'Zikali' means 'Weapons'"; intelligence at which she clapped her hands as a merry girl might do. "The man," I went on, "is without doubt a great doctor, one who sees and knows things that others do not, but I do not understand why this token carved in his likeness should have power, as you say it has."

"Because with it goes his spirit, Allan. Have you never heard of the Egyptians, a very wise people who, as I remember, declared that man has a Ka or Double, a second self, that can either dwell in his statue or be sent afar?"

I answered that I had heard this.

"Well the Ka of this Zikali goes with that hideous image of him, which is perhaps why you have come safe through many dangers and why also I seemed to dream so much of him last night. Tell me now, what does Zikali want of me whose power he knows very well?"

"An oracle, the answer to a riddle, Ayesha."

"Then set it out another time. So you decide to see the dead, and this old dwarf, who is a home of wisdom, desires an oracle from one who is greater than he. Good. And what are you, or both of you, prepared to pay for these boons? Know, Allan, that I am a merchant who sells my favours dear. Tell me then, will you pay?"

"I think that it depends upon the price," I answered cautiously. "Set out the price, Ayesha."

"Be not afraid, O cunning dealer," she mocked. "I do not ask your soul or even that love of yours which you guard so jealously, since these things I could take without the asking. Nay, I ask only what a brave and honest man may give without shame: your help in war, and perhaps," she added with a softer tone, "your friendship. I think, Allan, that I like you well, perhaps because you remind me of another whom I knew long ago."

I bowed at the compliment, feeling proud and pleased at the prospect of a friendship with this wonderful and splendid creature, although I was aware that it had many dangers. Then I sat still and waited. She also waited, brooding.

"Listen," she said after a while, "I will tell you a story and when you have heard it you shall answer, even if you do not believe it, but not before. Does it please you to listen to something of the tale of my life which I am moved to tell you, that you may know with whom you have to deal?"

Again I bowed, thinking to myself that I knew nothing that would please me more, who was eaten up with a devouring curiosity about this woman.

Now she rose from her couch and descending off the dais, began to walk up and down the chamber. I say, to walk, but her movements were more like the gliding of an eagle through the air or the motion of a swan upon still water, so smooth were they and gracious. As she walked she spoke in a low and thrilling voice.

"Listen," she said again, "and even if my story seems marvellous to you, interrupt, and above all, mock me not, lest I should grow angry, which might be ill for you. I am not as other women are, O Allan, who having conquered the secrets of Nature," here I felt an intense desire to ask what secrets, but remembered and held my tongue, "to my sorrow have preserved my youth and beauty through many ages. Moreover in the past, perhaps in payment for my sins, I have lived other lives of which some memory remains with me.

"By my last birth I am an Arab lady of royal blood, a descendant of the Kings of the East. There I dwelt in the wilderness and ruled a people, and at night I gathered wisdom from the stars and the spirits of the earth and air. At length I wearied of it all and my people too wearied of me and besought me to depart, for, Allan, I would have naught to do with men, yet men went mad because of my beauty and slew each other out of jealousy. Moreover other peoples made war upon my people, hoping to take me captive that I might be a wife to their kings. So I left them, and being furnished with great wealth in hoarded gold and jewels, together with a certain holy man, my master, I wandered through the world, studying the nations and their worships. At Jerusalem I tarried and learned of Jehovah who is, or was, its God.

"At Paphos in the Isle of Chitim I dwelt a while till the folk of that city thought that I was Aphrodite returned to earth and sought to worship me. For this reason and because I made a mock of Aphrodite, I, who, as I have said, would have naught to do with men, she through her priests cursed me, saying that her yoke should lie more heavily upon my neck from age to age than on that of any woman who had breathed beneath the sun.

"It was a wondrous scene," she added reflectively, "that of the cursing, since for every word I gave back two. Moreover I told the hoary villain of a high-priest to make report to his goddess that long after she was dead in the world, I would live on, for the spirit of prophecy was on me in that hour. Yet the curse fell in its season, since in her day, doubt it or not, Aphrodite had strength, as indeed under other names she has and will have while the world endures, and for aught I know, beyond it. Do they worship her now in any land, Allan?"

"No, only her statues because of their beauty, though Love is always worshipped."

"Yes, who can testify to that better than you yourself, Allan, if he who is called Zikali tells me the truth concerning you in the dreams he sends? As for the statues, I saw some of them as they left the master's hand in Greece, and when I told him that he might have found a better model, once I was that model. If this marble still endures, it must be the most famous of them all, though perchance Aphrodite has shattered it in her jealous rage. You shall tell me of these statues afterwards; mine had a mark on the left shoulder like to a mole, but the stone was imperfect, not my flesh, as I can prove if you should wish."

Thinking it better not to enter on a discussion as to Ayesha's shoulder, I remained silent and she went on.

"I dwelt in Egypt also, and there, to be rid of men who wearied me with their sighs and importunities, also to acquire more wisdom of which she was the mistress, I entered the service of the goddess Isis, Queen of Heaven, vowing to remain virgin for ever. Soon I became her high-priestess and in her most sacred shrines upon the Nile, I communed with the goddess and shared her power, since from me her daughter, she withheld none of her secrets. So it came about that though Pharaohs held the sceptre, it was I who ruled Egypt and brought it and Sidon to their fall, it matters not how or why, as it was fated that I must do. Yes, kings would come to seek counsel from me where I sat throned, dressed in the garb of Isis and breathing out her power. Yet, my task accomplished, of it all I grew weary, as men will surely do of the heavens that they preach, should they chance to find them."

I wondered what this "task" might be, but only asked, "Why?"

"Because in their pictured heaven all things lie to their hands and man, being man, cannot be happy without struggle, and woman, being woman, without victory over others. What is cheaply bought, or given, has no value, Allan; to be enjoyed, it must first be won. But I bade you not to break my thought."

I asked pardon and she went on,

"Then it was that the shadow of the curse of Aphrodite fell upon me, yes, and of the curse of Isis also, so that these twin maledictions have made me what I am, a lost soul dwelling in the wilderness waiting the fulfilment of a fate whereof I know not the end. For though I have all wisdom, all knowledge of the Past and much power together with the gift of life and beauty, the future is as dark to me as night without its moon and stars.

"Hearken, this chanced to me. Though it be to my shame I tell it you that all may be clear. At a temple of Isis on the Nile where I ruled, there was a certain priest, a Greek by birth, vowed like myself to the service of the goddess and therefore to wed none but her, the goddess herself—that is, in the spirit. He was named Kallikrates, a man of courage and of beauty, such an one as those Greeks carved in the statues of their god Apollo. Never, I think, was a man more beautiful in face and form, though in soul he was not great, as often happens to men who have all else, and well-nigh always happens to women, save myself and perhaps one or two others that history tells of, doubtless magnifying their fabled charms.

"The Pharaoh of that day, the last of the native blood, him whom the Persians drove to doom, had a daughter, the Princess of Egypt, Amenartas by name, a fair woman in her fashion, though somewhat swarthy. In her youth this Amenartas became enamoured of Kallikrates and he of her, when he was a captain of the Grecian Mercenaries at Pharaoh's Court. Indeed, she brought blood upon his hands because of her, wherefore he fled to Isis for forgiveness and for peace. Thither in after time she followed him and again urged her love.

"Learning of the thing and knowing it for sacrilege, I summoned this priest and warned him of his danger and of the doom which awaited him should he continue in that path. He grew affrighted. He flung himself upon the ground before me with groans and supplications, and kissing my feet, vowed most falsely to me that his dealings with the royal Amenartas were but a veil and that it was I whom he worshipped. His unhallowed words filled me with horror and sternly I bade him begone and do penance for his crime, saying that I would pray the goddess on behalf of him.

"He went, leaving me alone lost in thought in the darkening shrine. Then sleep fell on me and in my sleep I dreamed a dream, or saw a vision. For suddenly there stood before me a woman beauteous as myself clad in nothing save a golden girdle and a veil of gossamer.

"'O Ayesha,' she said in a honeyed voice, 'priestess of Isis of the Egyptians, sworn to the barren worship of Isis and fed on the ashes of her unprofitable wisdom, know that I am Aphrodite of the Greeks whom many times thou hast mocked and defied, and Queen of the breathing world, as Isis is Queen of the world that is dead. Now because thou didst despise me and pour contempt upon my name, I smite thee with my strength and lay a curse upon thee. It is that thou shalt love and desire this man who but now hath kissed thy feet, ever longing till the world's end to kiss his lips in payment, although thou art as far above him as the moon thou servest is above the Nile. Think not that thou shalt escape my doom, for know that however strong the spirit, here upon the earth the flesh is stronger still and of all flesh I am the queen.'

"Then she laughed softly and smiting me across the eyes with a lock of her scented hair, was gone.

"Allan, I awoke from my sleep and a great trouble fell upon me, for I who had never loved before now was rent with a rage of love and for this man who till that moment had been naught to me but as some beauteous image of gold and ivory. I longed for him, my heart was racked with jealousy because of the Egyptian who favoured him, an eating flame possessed my breast. I grew mad. There in the shrine of Isis the divine I cast myself upon my knees and cried to Aphrodite to return and give me him I sought, for whose sake I would renounce all else, even if I must pour my wisdom into a beauteous, empty cup. Yes, thus I prayed and lay upon the ground and wept until, outworn, once more sleep fell upon me.

"Now in the darkness of the holy place once more there came a dream or vision, since before me in her glory stood the goddess Isis crowned with the crescent of the young moon and holding in her hand the jewelled sistrum that is her symbol, from which came music like to the melody of distant bells. She gazed at me and in her great eyes were scorn and anger.

"'O Ayesha, Daughter of Wisdom,' she said in a solemn voice, 'whom I, Isis, had come to look upon rather as a child than a servant, since in none other of my priestesses was such greatness to be found, and whom in a day to be I had purposed to raise to the very steps of my heavenly throne, thou hast broken thine oath and, forsaking me, hast worshipped false Aphrodite of the Greeks who is mine enemy. Yea, in the eternal war between the spirit and the flesh, thou hast chosen the part of flesh. Therefore I hate thee and add my doom to that which Aphrodite laid upon thee, which, hadst thou prayed to me and not to her, I would have lifted from thy heart.

"'Hearken! The Grecian whom thou hast chosen, by Aphrodite's will, thou shalt love as the Pathian said. More, thy love shall bring his blood upon thy hands, nor mayest thou follow him to the grave. For I will show thee the Source of Life and thou shalt drink of it to make thyself more fair even than thou art and thus outpace thy rival, and when thy lover is dead, in a desolate place thou shalt wait in grief and solitude till he is born again and find thee there.

"'Yet shall this be but the beginning of thy sorrows, since through all time thou shalt pursue thy fate till at length thou canst draw up this man to the height on which thine own soul stands by the ropes of love and loss and suffering. Moreover through it all thou shalt despise thyself, which is man's and woman's hardest lot, thou who having the rare feast of spirit spread out before thee, hast chosen to fill thyself from the troughs of flesh.'

"Then, Allan, in my dream I made a proud answer to the goddess, saying, 'Hear me, mighty mistress of many Forms who dost appear in all that lives! An evil fate has fallen upon me, but was it I who chose that fate? Can the leaf contend against the driving gale? Can the falling stone turn upwards to the sky, or when Nature draws it, can the tide cease to flow? A goddess whom I have offended, that goddess whose strength causes the whole world to be, has laid her curse upon me and because I have bent before the storm, as bend I must, or break, another goddess whom I serve, thou thyself, Mother Isis, hast added to the curse. Where then is Justice, O Lady of the Moon?'

"'Not here, Woman,' she answered. 'Yet far away Justice lives and shall be won at last and mayhap because thou art so proud and high-stomached, it is laid upon thee to seek her blinded eyes through many an age. Yet at last I think thou shalt set thy sins against her weights and find the balance even. Therefore cease from questioning the high decrees of destiny which thou canst not understand and be content to suffer, remembering that all joy grows from the root of pain. Moreover, know this for thy comfort, that the wisdom which thou hast shall grow and gather on thee and with it thy beauty and thy power; also that at the last thou shalt look upon my face again, in token whereof I leave to thee my symbol, the sistrum that I bear, and with it this command. Follow that false priest of mine wherever he may go and avenge me upon him, and if thou lose him there, wait while the generations pass till he return again. Such and no other is thy destiny.'

"Allan, the vision faded and when I awoke the lights of dawn played upon the image of the goddess in the sanctuary. They played, moreover, upon the holy jewelled thing that in my dream her hand had held, the sistrum of her worship, shaped like the loop of life, the magic symbol that she had vowed to me, wherewith goes her power, which henceforth was mine.

"I took it and followed after the priest Kallikrates, to whom thenceforward I was bound by passion's ties that are stronger than all the goddesses in this wide universe."

Here I, Allan, could contain myself no longer and asked, "What for?" then, fearing her wrath, wished that I had been silent.

But she was not angry, perhaps because this tale of her interviews with goddesses, doubtless fabled, had made her humble, for she answered quietly,

"By Aphrodite, or by Isis, or both of them I did not know. All I knew was that I must seek him, then and evermore, as seek I do to-day and shall perchance through æons yet unborn. So I followed, as I was taught and commanded, the sistrum being my guide, how it matters not, and giving me the means, and so at last I came to this ancient land whereof the ruin in which you sit was once known as Kôr."

CHAPTER XIV

ALLAN MISSES OPPORTUNITY

All the while that she was talking thus the Lady or the Queen or the Witch-woman, Ayesha, had been walking up and down the place from the curtains to the foot of the dais, sweeping me with her scented robes as she passed to and fro, and as she walked she waved her arms as an orator might do to emphasise the more moving passages of her tale. Now at the end of it, or what I took to be the end, she stepped on to the dais and sank upon the couch as if exhausted, though I think her spirit was weary rather than her body.

Here she sat awhile, brooding, her chin resting on her hand, then suddenly looked up and fixing her glance upon me—for I could see the flash of it through her thin veil—said,

"What think you of this story, Allan? Do you believe it and have you ever heard its like?"

"Never," I answered with emphasis, "and of course I believe every word. Only there are one or two questions that with your leave I would wish to ask, Ayesha."

"By which you mean, Allan, that you believe nothing, being by nature without faith and doubtful of all that you cannot see and touch and handle. Well, perhaps you are wise, since what I have told you is not all the truth. For example, it comes back to me now that it was not in the temple on the Nile, or indeed upon the Earth, that I saw the vision of Aphrodite and of Isis, but elsewhere; also that it was here in Kôr that I was first consumed by passion for Kallikrates whom hitherto I had scorned. In two thousand years one forgets much, Allan. Out with your questions and I will answer them, unless they be too long."

"Ayesha," I said humbly, reflecting to myself that my questions would, at any rate, be shorter than her varying tale, "even I who am not learned have heard of these goddesses of whom you speak, of the Grecian Aphrodite who rose from the sea upon the shores of Cyprus and dwelt at Paphos and elsewhere—"

"Yes, doubtless like most men you have heard of her and perchance also have been struck across the eyes with her hair, like your betters before you," she interrupted with sarcasm.

"—Also," I went on, avoiding argument, "I have heard of Isis of the Egyptians, Lady of the Moon, Mother of Mysteries, Spouse of Osiris whose child was Horus the Avenger."

"Aye, and I think will hear more of her before you have done, Allan, for now something comes back to me concerning you and her and another. I am not the only one who has broken the oaths of Isis and received her curse, Allan, as you may find out in the days to come. But what of these heavenly queens?"

"Only this, Ayesha; I have been taught that they were but phantasms fabled by men with many another false divinity, and could have sworn that this was true. And yet you talk of them as real and living, which perplexes me."

"Being dull of understanding doubtless it perplexes you, Allan. Yet if you had imagination you might understand that these goddesses are great Principles of Nature; Isis, of throned Wisdom and strait virtue, and Aphrodite, of Love, as it is known to men and women who, being human, have it laid upon them that they must hand on the torch of Life in their little hour. Also you would know that such Principles can seem to take shape and form and at certain ages of the world appear to their servants visible in majesty, though perchance to-day others with changed names wield their sceptres and work their will. Now you are answered on this matter. So to the next."

Privately I did not feel as though I were answered at all and I was sure that I know nothing of the kind she indicated, but thinking it best to leave the subject, I went on,

"If I understood rightly, Ayesha, the events which you have been pleased first to describe to me, and then to qualify or contradict, took place when the Pharaohs reigned. Now no Pharaoh has sat upon the throne of Egypt for near two thousand years, for the last was a Grecian woman whom the Romans conquered and drove to death. And yet, Ayesha, you speak as though you have lived all through that gulf of time, and in this there must be error, because it is impossible. Therefore I suppose you to mean that this history has come down to you in writing, or perhaps in dreams. I believe that even in such far-off times there were writers of romance, and we all know of what stuff dreams are made. At least this thought comes to me," I added hurriedly, fearing lest I had said too much, "and one so wise as you are, I repeat, knows well that a woman who says she has lived two thousand years must be mad or—suffer from delusions, because I repeat, it is impossible."

At these quite innocent remarks she sprang to her feet in a rage that might truly be called royal in every sense.

"Impossible! Romance! Dreams! Delusions! Mad!" she cried in a ringing voice. "Oh! of a truth you weary me, and I have a mind to send you whither you will learn what is impossible and what is not. Indeed, I would do it, and now, only I need your services, and if I did there would be none left for me to talk with, since your companion is moonstruck and the others are but savages of whom I have seen enough.

"Hearken, fool! Nothing is impossible. Why do you seek, you who talk of the impossible, to girdle the great world in the span of your two hands and to weigh the secrets of the Universe in the balance of your petty mind and, of that which you cannot understand, to say that it is not? Life you admit because you see it all about you. But that it should endure for two thousand years, which after all is but a second's beat in the story of the earth, that to you is 'impossible,' although in truth the buried seed or the sealed-up toad can live as long. Doubtless, also, you have some faith which promises you this same boon to all eternity, after the little change called Death.

"Nay, Allan, it is possible enough, like to many other things of which you do not dream to-day that will be common to the eyes of those who follow after you. Mayhap you think it impossible that I should speak with and learn of you from yonder old black wizard who dwells in the country whence you came. And yet whenever I will I do so in the night because he is in tune with me, and what I do shall be done by all men in the years unborn. Yes, they shall talk together across the wide spaces of the earth, and the lover shall hear her lover's voice although great seas roll between them. Nor perchance will it stop at this; perchance in future time men shall hold converse with the denizens of the stars, and even with the dead who have passed into silence and the darkness. Do you hear and understand me?"

"Yes, yes," I answered feebly.

"You lie, as you are too prone to do. You hear but you do not understand nor believe, and oh! you vex me sorely. Now I had it in my mind to tell you the secret of this long life of mine; long, mark you, but not endless, for doubtless I must die and change and return again, like others, and even to show you how it may be won. But you are not worthy in your faithlessness."

"No, no, I am not worthy," I answered, who at that moment did not feel the least desire to live two thousand years, perhaps with this woman as a neighbour, rating me from generation to generation. Yet it is true, that now when I am older and a certain event cannot be postponed much longer, I do often regret that I neglected to take this unique chance, if in truth there was one, of prolonging an existence which after all has its consolations—especially when one has made one's pile. Certainly it is a case, a flagrant case, of neglected opportunities, and my only consolation for having lost them is that this was due to the uprightness of my nature which made it so hard for me to acquiesce in alternative statements that I had every cause to disbelieve and thus to give offence to a very powerful and petulant if attractive lady.

"So that is done with," she went on with a little stamp of indignation, "as soon you will be also, who, had you not crossed and doubted me, might have lived on for untold time and become one of the masters of the world, as I am."

Here she paused, choked, I think, with her almost childish anger, and because I could not help it, I said,

"Such place and power, if they be yours, Ayesha, do not seem to bring you much reward. If I were a master of the world I do not think that I should choose to dwell unchangingly among savages who eat men and in a pile of ruins. But perhaps the curses of Aphrodite and of Isis are stronger masters still?" and I paused inquiringly.

This bold argument—for now I see that it was bold—seemed to astonish and even bewilder my wonderful companion.

"You have more wisdom than I thought," she said reflectively, "who have come to understand that no one is really lord of anything, since above there is always a more powerful lord who withers all his pomp and pride to nothingness, even as the great kings learned in olden days, and I, who am higher than they are, am learning now. Hearken. Troubles beset me wherein I would have your help and that of your companions, for which I will pay each of you the fee that he desires. The brooding white man who is with you shall free his daughter and unharmed; though that he will be unharmed I do not promise. The black savage captain shall fight his fill and gain the glory that he seeks, also something that he seeks still more. The little yellow man asks nothing save to be with his master like a dog and to satisfy at once his stomach and his apish curiosity. You, Allan, shall see those dead over whom you brood at night, though the other guerdon that you might have won is now passed from your reach because you mock me in your heart."

"What must we do to gain these things?" I asked. "How can we humble creatures help one who is all powerful and who has gathered in her breast the infinite knowledge of two thousand years?"

"You must make war under my banner and rid me of my foes. As for the reason, listen to the end of my tale and you shall learn."

I reflected that it was a marvellous thing that this queen who claimed supernatural powers should need our help in a war, but thinking it wiser to keep my meditations to myself, said nothing. As a matter of fact I might just as well have spoken, since as usual she read my thoughts.

"You are thinking that it is strange, Allan, that I, the Mighty and Undying, should seek your aid in some petty tribal battle, and so it would be were my foes but common savages. But they are more; they are men protected by the ancient god of this immemorial city of Kôr, a great god in his day whose spirit still haunts these ruins and whose strength still protects the worshippers who cling to him and practise his unholy rites of human sacrifice."

"How was this god named?" I asked.

"Rezu was his name, and from him came the Egyptian Re or Ra, since in the beginning Kôr was the mother of Egypt and the conquering people of Kôr took their god with them when they burst into the valley of the Nile and subdued its peoples long before the first Pharaoh, Menes, wore Egypt's crown."

"Ra was the sun, was he not?" I asked.

"Aye, and Rezu also was a sun-god whom from his throne in the fires of the Lord of Day, gave life to men, or slew them if he willed with his thunderbolts of drought and pestilence and storm. He was no gentle king of heaven, but one who demanded blood-sacrifice from his worshippers, yes, even that of maids and children. So it came about that the people of Kôr, who saw their virgins slain and eaten by the priests of Rezu, and their infants burned to ashes in the fires that his rays lit, turned themselves to the worship of the gentle moon, the goddess whom they named Lulala, while some of them chose Truth for their queen, since Truth, they said, was greater and more to be desired than the fierce Sun-King or even the sweet Moon-Lady, Truth, who sat above them both throned in the furthest stars of Heaven. Then the demon, Rezu, grew wroth and sent a pestilence upon Kôr and its subject lands and slew their people, save those who clung to him in the great apostasy, and with them some others who served Lulala and Truth the Divine, that escaped I know not how."

"Did you see this great pestilence?" I asked, much interested.

"Nay, it befell generations before I came to Kôr. One Junis, a priest, wrote a record of it in the caves yonder where I have my home and where is the burying-place of the countless thousands that it slew. In my day Kôr, of which, should you desire to hear it, I will tell you the history, was a ruin as it is now, though scattered in the lands amidst the tumbled stones which once built up her subject cities, a people named the Amahagger dwelt in Households, or Tribes and there sacrificed men by fire and devoured them, following the rites of the demon Rezu. For these were the descendants of those who escaped the pestilence. Also there were certain others, children of the worshippers of Lulala whose kingdom is the moon, and of Truth the Queen, who clung to the gentle worship of their forefathers and were ever at war with the followers of Rezu."

"What brought you to Kôr, Ayesha?" I asked irrelevantly.

"Have I not said that I was led hither by the command and the symbol of great Isis whom I serve? Also," she added after a pause, "that I might find a certain pair, one of whom had broken his oaths to her, tempted thereto by the other."

"And did you find them, Ayesha?" I asked.

"Aye, I found them, or rather they found me, and in my presence the goddess executed her decree upon her false priest and drove his temptress back to the world."

"That must have been dreadful for you, Ayesha, since I understood that you also—liked this priest."

She sprang from her couch and in a low, hissing voice which resembled the sound made by an angry snake and turned my blood cold to hear, exclaimed,

"Man, do you dare to mock me? Nay, you are but a blundering, curious fool, and it is well for you that this is so, since otherwise like Kallikrates, never should you leave Kôr living. Cease from seeking that which you may not learn. Suffice it for you to know that the doom of Isis fell upon the lost Kallikrates, her priest forsworn, and that on me also fell her doom, who must dwell here, dead yet living, till he return again and the play begins afresh.

"Stranger," she went on in a softer voice, "perchance your faith, whate'er it be, parades a hell to terrify its worshippers and give strength to the arms of its prophesying priests, who swear they hold the keys of doom or of the eternal joys. I see you sign assent" (I had nodded at her extremely accurate guess) "and therefore can understand that in such a hell as this, here upon the earth I have dwelt for some two thousand years, expiating the crime of Powers above me whereof I am but the hand and instrument, since those Powers which decreed that I should love, decree also that I must avenge that love."

She sank down upon the couch as though exhausted by emotion, of which I could only guess the reasons, hiding her face in her hands. Presently she let them fall again and continued,

"Of these woes ask me no more. They sleep till the hour of their resurrection, which I think draws nigh; indeed, I thought that you perchance—But let that be. 'Twas near the mark; nearer, Allan, than you know, not in it! Therefore leave them to their sleep as I would if I might—ah! if I might, whose companions they are throughout the weary ages. Alas! that through the secret which was revealed to me I remain undying on the earth who in death might perhaps have found a rest, and being human although half divine, must still busy myself with the affairs of earth.

"Look you, Wanderer, after that which was fated had happened and I remained in my agony of solitude and sorrow, after, too, I had drunk of the cup of enduring life and like the Prometheus of old fable, found myself bound to this changeless rock, whereon day by day the vultures of remorse tear out my living heart which in the watches of the night is ever doomed to grow again within my woman's breast, I was plunged into petty troubles of the flesh, aye and welcomed them because their irk at times gave me forgetfulness. When the savage dwellers in this land came to know that a mighty one had arisen among them who was the servant of the Lady of the Moon, those of them who still worshipped their goddess Lulala, gathered themselves about me, while those of them who worshipped Rezu sought to overthrow me.

"'Here,' they said, 'is the goddess Lulala come to earth. In the name of Rezu let us slay her and make an end,' for these fools thought that I could be killed. Allan, I conquered them, but their captain, who also is named Rezu and whom they held and hold to be an emanation of the god himself walking the earth, I could not conquer."

"Why not?" I asked.

"For this reason, Allan. In some past age his god showed him the same secret that was shown to me. He too had drunk of the Cup of Life and lives on unharmed by Time, so that being in strength my equal, no spear of mine can reach his heart clad in the armour of his evil god."

"Then what spear can?" I inquired helplessly, who was bewildered.

"None at all, Allan, yet an axe may, as you shall hear, or so I think. For many generations there has been peace of a sort between the worshippers of Lulala who dwell with me in the Plain of Kôr, or rather of myself, since to these people I am Lulala, and the worshippers of Rezu, who dwell in the strongholds beyond the mountain crest. But of late years their chief Rezu, having devastated the lands about, has grown restless and threatened to attack on Kôr, which is not strong enough to stand against him. Moreover he has sought for a white queen to rule under him, purposing to set her up to mock my majesty."

"Is that why those cannibals carried away the daughter of my companion, the Sea-Captain who is named Avenger?" I asked.

"It is, Allan, since presently he will give it out that I am dead or fled, if he has not done so already, and that this new queen has arisen in my place. Thereby he hopes to draw away many who cling to me ere he advances upon Kôr, carrying with him this girl veiled as I am, so that none may know the difference between us, since not a man of them has ever looked upon my face, Allan. Therefore this Rezu must die, if die he can; otherwise, although it is impossible that he should harm me, he may slay or draw away my people and leave me with none to rule in this place where by the decree of Fate I must dwell on until he whom I seek returns. You are thinking in your heart that such savages would be little loss and this is so, but still they serve as slaves to me in my loneliness. Moreover I have sworn to protect them from the demon Rezu and they have trusted in me and therefore my honour is at stake, for never shall it be said that those who trusted in She-who-commands, were overthrown because they put faith in one who was powerless."

"What do you mean about an axe, Ayesha?" I asked. "Why can an axe alone kill Rezu?"

"The thing is a mystery, O Allan, of which I may not tell you all, since to do so I must reveal secrets which I have determined you shall not learn. Suffice it to you to know that when this Rezu drank of the Cup of Life he took with him his axe. Now this axe was an ancient weapon rumoured to have been fashioned by the gods and, as it chanced, that axe drew to itself more and stronger life than did Rezu, how, it does not matter, if indeed the tale be more than a fable. At least this I know is true, for he who guarded the Gate of Life, a certain Noot, a master of mysteries, and mine also in my day of youth, who being a philosopher and very wise, chose never to pass that portal which was open to him, said it to me himself ere he went the way of flesh. He told this Rezu also that now he had naught to fear save his own axe and therefore he counselled him to guard it well, since if it was lifted against him in another's hands it would bring him down to death, which nothing else could do. Like to the heel of Achilles whereof the great Homer sings—have you read Homer, Allan?"

"In a translation," I answered.

"Good, then you will remember the story. Like to the heel of Achilles, I say, that axe would be the only gate by which death could enter his invulnerable flesh, or rather it alone could make the gate."

"How did Noot know that?" I asked.

"I cannot say," she answered with irritation. "Perchance he did not know it. Perchance it is all an idle tale, but at least it is true that Rezu believed and believes it, and what a man believes is true for him and will certainly befall. If it were otherwise, what is the use of faith which in a thousand forms supports our race and holds it from the horrors of the Pit? Only those who believe nothing inherit what they believe—nothing, Allan."

"It may be so," I replied prosaically, "but what happened about the axe?"

"In the end it was lost, or as some say stolen by a woman whom Rezu had deserted, and therefore he walks the world in fear from day to day. Nay, ask no more empty questions" (I had opened my mouth to speak) "but hear the end of the tale. In my trouble concerning Rezu I remembered this wild legend of the axe and since, when lost in a forest every path that may lead to safety should be explored, I sent my wisdom forth to make inquiry concerning it, as I who am great, have the power to do, of certain who are in tune with me throughout this wide land of Africa. Amongst others, I inquired of that old wizard whom you named Zikali, Opener of Roads, and he gave me an answer that there lived in his land a certain warrior who ruled a tribe called the People of the Axe by right of the Axe, of which axe none, not even he, knew the beginning or the legend. On the chance, though it was a small one, I bade the wizard send that warrior here with his axe. Last night he stood before me and I looked upon him and the axe, which at least is ancient and has a story. Whether it be the same that Rezu bore I do not know who never saw it, yet perchance he who bears it now is prepared to hold it aloft in battle even against Rezu, though he be terrible to see, and then we shall learn."

"Oh! yes," I answered, "he is quite prepared, for that is his nature. Also among this man's people, the holder of the Axe is thought to be unconquerable."

"Yet some must have been conquered who held it," she replied musingly. "Well, you shall tell me that tale later. Now we have talked long and you are weary and astonished. Go, eat and rest yourself. To-night when the moon rises I will come to where you are, not before, for I have much that must be done, and show you those with whom you must fight against Rezu, and make a plan of battle."

"But I do not want to fight," I answered, "who have fought enough and came here to seek wisdom, not bloodshed."

"First the sacrifice, then the reward," she answered, "that is if any are left to be rewarded. Farewell."

CHAPTER XV

ROBERTSON IS LOST

So I went and was conducted by Billali, the old chamberlain, for such seemed to be his office, who had been waiting patiently without all this while, back to our rest-house. On my way I picked up Hans, whom I found sitting outside the arch, and found that as usual that worthy had been keeping his eyes and ears open.

"Baas," he said, "did the White Witch tell you that there is a big impi encamped over yonder outside the houses, in what looks like a great dry ditch, and on the edge of the plain beyond?"

"No, Hans, but she said that this evening she would show us those in whose company we must fight."

"Well, Baas, they are there, some thousands of them, for I crept through the broken walls like a snake and saw them. And, Baas, I do not think they are men, I think that they are evil spirits who walk at night only."

"Why, Hans?"

"Because when the sun is high, Baas, as it is now, they are all sleeping. Yes, there they lie abed, fast asleep, as other people do at night, with only a few sentries out on guard, and these are yawning and rubbing their eyes."

"I have heard that there are folk like that in the middle of Africa where the sun is very hot, Hans," I answered, "which perhaps is why She-who-commands is going to take us to see them at night. Also these people, it seems, are worshippers of the moon."

"No, Baas, they are worshippers of the devil and that White Witch is his wife."

"You had better keep your thoughts to yourself, Hans, for whatever she is I think that she can read thoughts from far away, as you guessed last night. Therefore I would not have any if I were you."

"No, Baas, or if I must think, henceforth, it shall be only of gin which in this place is also far away," he replied, grinning.

Then we came to the rest-house where I found that Robertson had already eaten his midday meal and like the Amahagger gone to sleep, while apparently Umslopogaas had done the same; at least I saw nothing of him. Of this I was glad, since that wondrous Ayesha seemed to draw vitality out of me and after my long talk with her I felt very tired. So I too ate and then went to lie down under an old wall in the shade at a little distance, and to reflect upon the marvellous things that I had heard.

Here be it said at once that I believed nothing of them, or at least very little indeed. All the involved tale of Ayesha's long life I dismissed at once as incredible. Clearly she was some beautiful woman who was more or less mad and suffered from megalomania; probably an Arab, who had wandered to this place for reasons of her own, and become the chieftainess of a savage tribe whose traditions she had absorbed and reproduced as personal experiences, again for reasons of her own.

For the rest, she was now threatened by another tribe and knowing that we had guns and could fight from what happened on the yesterday, wished naturally enough for our assistance in the coming battle. As for the marvellous chief Rezu, or rather for his supernatural attributes and all the cock-and-bull story about an axe—well, it was humbug like the rest, and if she believed in it she must be more foolish than I took her to be—even if she were unhinged on certain points. For the rest, her information about myself and Umslopogaas doubtless had reached her from Zikali in some obscure fashion, as she herself acknowledged.

But heavens! how beautiful she was! That flash of loveliness when out of pique or coquetry she lifted her veil, blinded like the lightning. But thank goodness, also like the lightning it frightened; instinctively one felt that it was very dangerous, even to death, and with it I for one wished no closer acquaintance. Fire may be lovely and attractive, also comforting at a proper distance, but he who sits on the top of it is cremated, as many a moth has found.

So I argued, knowing well enough all the while that if this particular human—or inhuman—fire desired to make an holocaust of me, it could do so easily enough, and that in reality I owed my safety so far to a lack of that desire on its part. The glorious Ayesha saw nothing to attract her in an insignificant and withered hunter, or at any rate in his exterior, though with his mind she might find some small affinity.

Moreover to make a fool of him just for the fun of it would not serve her purpose, since she needed his assistance in a business that necessitated clear wits and unprejudiced judgment.

Lastly she had declared herself to be absorbed in some tiresome complication with another man, of which it was rather difficult to follow the details. It is true that she described him as a handsome but somewhat empty-headed person whom she had last seen two thousand years ago, but probably this only meant that she thought poorly of him because he had preferred some other woman to herself, while the two thousand years were added to the tale to give it atmosphere.

The worst of scandals becomes romantic and even respectable in two thousand years; witness that of Cleopatra with Cæsar, Mark Antony and other gentlemen. The most virtuous read of Cleopatra with sympathy, even in boarding-schools, and it is felt that were she by some miracle to be blotted out of the book of history, the loss would be enormous. The same applied to Helen, Phryne, and other bad lots. In fact now that one comes to think of it, most of the attractive personages in history, male or female, especially the latter, were bad lots. When we find someone to whose name is added "the good" we skip. No doubt Ayesha, being very clever, appreciated this regrettable truth, and therefore moved her murky entanglements of the past decade or so back for a couple of thousand years, as many of us would like to do.

There remained the very curious circumstance of her apparent correspondence with old Zikali who lived far away. This, however, after all was not inexplicable. In the course of a great deal of experience I have observed that all the witch-doctor family, to which doubtless she belonged, have strange means of communication.

In most instances these are no doubt physical, carried on by help of messengers, or messages passed from one to the other. But sometimes it is reasonable to assume what is known as telepathy, as their link of intercourse. Between two such highly developed experts as Ayesha and Zikali, it might for the sake of argument safely be supposed that it was thus they learned each other's mind and co-operated in each other's projects, though perhaps this end was effected by commoner methods.

Whatever its interpretations, the issue of the business seemed to be that I was to be let in for more fighting. Well, in any case this could not be avoided, since Robertson's daughter, Inez, had to be saved at all costs, if it could possibly be done, even if we lost our lives in the attempt. Therefore fight we must, so there was nothing more to be said. Also without doubt this adventure was particularly interesting and I could only hope that good luck, or Zikali's Great Medicine, or rather Providence, would see me through it safely.

For the rest the fact that our help was necessary to her in this war-like venture showed me clearly enough that all this wonderful woman's pretensions to supernatural powers were the sheerest nonsense. Had they been otherwise she would not have needed our help in her tribal fights, notwithstanding the rubbish she talked about the chief, Rezu, who according to her account of him, must resemble one of the fabulous "trolls," half-human and half-ghostly evil creatures, of whom I have read in the Norse Sagas, who could only be slain by some particular hero armed with a particular weapon.

Reflecting thus I went to sleep and did not wake until the sun was setting. Finding that Hans was also sleeping at my feet just like a faithful dog, I woke him up and we went back together to the rest-house, which we reached as the darkness fell with extraordinary swiftness, as it does in those latitudes, especially in a place surrounded by cliffs.

Not finding Robertson in the house, I concluded that he was somewhere outside, possibly making a reconnaissance on his own account, and told Hans to get supper ready for both of us. While he was doing so, by aid of the Amahagger lamps, Umslopogaas suddenly appeared in the circle of light, and looking about him, said,

"Where is Red-Beard, Macumazahn?"

I answered that I did not know and waited, for I felt sure that he had something to say.

"I think that you had better keep Red-Beard close to you, Macumazahn," he went on. "This afternoon, when you had returned from visiting the white doctoress and having eaten, had gone to sleep under the wall yonder, I saw Red-Beard come out of the house carrying a gun and a bag of cartridges. His eyes rolled wildly and he turned first this way and then that, sniffing at the air, like a buck that scents danger. Then he began to talk aloud in his own tongue and as I saw that he was speaking with his Spirit, as those do who are mad, I went away and left him."

"Why?" I asked.

"Because, as you know, Macumazahn, it is a law among us Zulus never to disturb one who is mad and engaged in talking with his Spirit. Moreover, had I done so, probably he would have shot me, nor should I have complained who would have thrust myself in where I had no right to be."

"Then why did you not come to call me, Umslopogaas?"

"Because then he might have shot you, for, as I have seen for some time he is inspired of heaven and knows not what he does upon the earth, thinking only of the Lady Sad-Eyes who has been stolen away from him, as is but natural. So I left him walking up and down, and when I returned later to look, saw that he was gone, as I thought into this walled hut. Now when Hansi tells me that he is not here, I have come to speak to you about him."

"No, certainly he is not here," I said, and I went to look at the bed where Robertson slept to see if it had been used that evening.

Then for the first time I saw lying on it a piece of paper torn from a pocketbook and addressed to myself. I seized and read it. It ran thus:

"The merciful Lord has sent me a vision of Inez and shown me where she is over the cliff-edge away to the west, also the road to her. In my sleep I heard her talking to me. She told me that she is in great danger—that they are going to marry her to some brute—and called to me to come at once and save her; yes, and to come alone without saying anything to anyone. So I am going at once. Don't be frightened or trouble about me. All will be well, all will be quite well. I will tell you the rest when we meet."

Horrorstruck I translated this insane screed to Umslopogaas and Hans. The former nodded gravely.

"Did I not tell you that he was talking with his Spirit, Macumazahn?" (I had rendered "the merciful Lord" as the Good Spirit.) "Well, he has gone and doubtless his Spirit will take care of him. It is finished."

"At any rate we cannot, Baas," broke in Hans, who I think feared that I might send him out to look for Robertson. "I can follow most spoors, but not on such a night as this when one could cut the blackness into lumps and build a wall of it."

"Yes," I answered, "he has gone and nothing can be done at present," though to myself I reflected that probably he had not gone far and would be found when the moon rose, or at any rate on the following morning.

Still I was most uneasy about the man who, as I had noted for a long while, was losing his balance more and more. The shock of the barbarous and dreadful slaughter of his half-breed children and of the abduction of Inez by these grim, man-eating savages began the business, and I think that it was increased and accentuated by his sudden conversion to complete temperance after years of heavy drinking.

When I persuaded him to this course I was very proud of myself, thinking that I had done a clever thing, but now I was not so sure. Perhaps it would have been better if he had continued to drink something, at any rate for a while, but the trouble is that in such cases there is generally no half-way house. A man, or still more a woman, given to this frailty either turns aggressively sober or remains very drunken. At any rate, even if I had made a mess of it, I had acted for the best and could not blame myself.

For the rest it was clear that in his new phase the religious associations of his youth had re-asserted themselves with remarkable vigour, for I gathered that he had been brought up almost as a Calvinist, and in the rush of their return, had overset his equilibrium. As I have said, he prayed night and day without any of those reserves which most people prefer in their religious exercises, and when he talked of matters outside our quest, his conversation generally revolved round the devil, or hell and its torments, which, to say the truth, did not make him a cheerful companion. Indeed in this respect I liked him much better in his old, unregenerate days, being, I fear, myself a somewhat worldly soul.

Well, the sum of it was that the poor fellow had gone mad and given us the slip, and as Hans said, to search for him at once in that darkness was impossible. Indeed, even if it had been lighter, I do not think that it would have been safe among these Amahagger nightbirds whom I did not trust. Certainly I could not have asked Hans to undertake the task, and if I had, I do not think he would have gone since he was afraid of the Amahagger. Therefore there was nothing to be done except wait and hope for the best.

So I waited till at last the moon came and with it Ayesha, as she had promised. Clad in a rich, dark cloak she arrived in some pomp, heralded by Billali, followed by women, also cloaked, and surrounded by a guard of tall spearmen. I was seated outside the house, smoking, when suddenly she arrived from the shadows and stood before me.

I rose respectfully and bowed, while Umslopogaas, Goroko and the other Zulus who were with me, gave her the royal salute, and Hans cringed like a dog that is afraid of being kicked.

After a swift glance at them, as I guessed by the motion of her veiled head, she seemed to fix her gaze upon my pipe that evidently excited her curiosity, and asked me what it was. I explained as well as I could, expatiating on the charms of smoking.

"So men have learned another useless vice since I left the world, and one that is filthy also," she said, sniffing at the smoke and waving her hand before her face, whereon I dropped the pipe into my pocket, where, being alight, it burnt a hole in my best remaining coat.

I remember the remark because it showed me what a clever actress she was who, to keep up her character of antiquity, pretended to be astonished at a habit with which she must have been well acquainted, although I believe that it was unknown in the ancient world.

"You are troubled," she went on, swiftly changing the subject, "I read it in your face. One of your company is missing. Who is it? Ah! I see, the white man you name Avenger. Where is he gone?"

"That is what I wish to ask you, Ayesha," I said.

"How can I tell you, Allan, who in this place lack any glass into which to look for things that pass afar. Still, let me try," and pressing her hands to her forehead, she remained silent for perhaps a minute, then spoke slowly.

"I think that he has gone over the mountain lip towards the worshippers of Rezu. I think that he is mad; sorrow and something else which I do not understand have turned his brain; something that has to do with the Heavens. I think also that we shall recover him living, if only for a little while, though of this I cannot be sure since it is not given to me to read the future, but only the past, and sometimes the things that happen in the present though they be far away."

"Will you send to search for him, O Ayesha?" I asked anxiously.

"Nay, it is useless, for he is already distant. Moreover those who went might be taken by the outposts of Rezu, as perchance has happened to your companion wandering in his madness. Do you know what he went to seek?"

"More or less," I answered and translated to her the letter that Robertson had left for me.

"It may be as the man writes," she commented, "since the mad often see well in their dreams, though these are not sent by a god as he imagines. The mind in its secret places knows all things, O Allan, although it seems to know little or nothing, and when the breath of vision or the fury of a soul distraught blows away the veils or burns through the gates of distance, then for a while it sees and learns, since, whatever fools may think, often madness is true wisdom. Now follow me with the little yellow man and the Warrior of the Axe. Stay, let me look upon that axe."

I interpreted her wish to Umslopogaas who held it out to her but refused to loose it from his wrist to which it was attached by the leathern thong.

"Does the Black One think that I shall cut him down with his own weapon, I who am so weak and gentle?" she asked, laughing.

"Nay, Ayesha, but it is his law not to part with this Drinker of Lives, which he names 'Chieftainess and Groan-maker,' and clings to closer by day and night than a man does to his wife."

"There he is wise, Allan, since a savage captain may get more wives but never such another axe. The thing is ancient," she added musingly after examining its every detail, "and who knows? It may be that whereof the legend tells which is fated to bring Rezu to the dust. Now ask this fierce-eyed Slayer whether, armed with his axe he can find courage to face the most terrible of all men and the strongest, one who is a wizard also, of whom it is prophesied that only by such an axe as this can he be made to bite the dust."

I obeyed. Umslopogaas laughed grimly and answered,

"Say to the White Witch that there is no man living upon the earth whom I would not face in war, I who have never been conquered in fair fight, though once a chance blow brought me to the doors of death," and he touched the great hole in his forehead. "Say to her also that I have no fear of defeat, I from whom doom is, as I think, still far away, though the Opener-of-Roads has told me that among a strange people I shall die in war at last, as I desire to do, who from my boyhood have lived in war."

"He speaks well," she answered with a note of admiration in her voice. "By Isis, were he but white I would set him to rule these Amahagger under me. Tell him, Allan, that if he lays Rezu low he shall have a great reward."

"And tell the White Witch, Macumazahn," Umslopogaas replied when I had translated, "that I seek no reward, save glory only, and with it the sight of one who is lost to me but with whom my heart still dwells, if indeed this Witch has strength to break the wall of blackness that is built between me and her who is 'gone down.'"

"Strange," reflected Ayesha when she understood, "that this grim Destroyer should yet be bound by the silken bonds of love and yearn for one whom the grave has taken. Learn from it, Allan, that all humanity is cast in the same mould, since my longings and your longings are his also, though the three of us be far apart as are the sun and the moon and the earth, and as different in every other quality. Yet it is true that sun and moon and earth are born of the same black womb of chaos. Therefore in the beginning they were identical, as doubtless they will be in the end when, their journeyings done, they rush together to light space with a flame at which the mocking gods that made them may warm their hands. Well, so it is with men, Allan, whose soul-stuff is drawn from the gulf of Spirit by Nature's hand, and, cast upon the cold air of this death-driven world, freezes into a million shapes each different to the other and yet, be sure, the same. Now talk no more, but follow me. Slave" (this was addressed to Billali), "bid the guards lead on to the camp of the servants of Lulala."

So we went through the silent ruins. Ayesha walked, or rather glided a pace or two ahead, then came Umslopogaas and I side by side, while at our heels followed Hans, very close at our heels since he did not wish to be out of reach of the virtue of the Great Medicine and incidentally of the protection of axe and rifle.

Thus we marched surrounded by the solemn guard for something between a quarter and half a mile, till at length we climbed the debris of a mighty wall that once had encompassed the city, and by the moonlight saw beneath us a vast hollow which clearly at some unknown time had been the bed of an enormous moat and filled with water.

Now, however, it was dry and all about its surface were dotted numerous camp-fires round which men were moving, also some women who appeared to be engaged in cooking food. At a little distance too, upon the further edge of the moat-like depression were a number of white-robed individuals gathered in a circle about a large stone upon which something was stretched that resembled the carcase of a sheep or goat, and round these a great number of spectators.

"The priests of Lulala who make sacrifice to the moon, as they do night by night, save when she is dead," said Ayesha, turning back towards me as though in answer to the query which I had conceived but left unuttered.

What struck me about the whole scene was its extraordinary animation and briskness. All the folk round the fires and outside of them moved about quickly and with the same kind of liveliness which might animate a camp of more natural people at the rising of the sun. It was as though they had just got up full of vigour to commence their daily, or rather their nightly round, which in truth was the case, since as Hans discovered, by habitude these Amahagger preferred to sleep during the day unless something prevented them, and to carry on the activities of life at night. It only remains to add that there seemed to be a great number of them, for their fires following the round of the dry moat, stretched further than I could see.

Scrambling down the crumpled wall by a zig-zag pathway, we came upon the outposts of the army beneath us who challenged, then seeing with whom they had to do, fell flat upon their faces, leaving their great spears, which had iron spikes on their shafts like to those of the Masai, sticking in the ground beside them.

We passed on between some of the fires and I noted how solemn and gloomy, although handsome, were the countenances of the folk by whom these were surrounded. Indeed, they looked like denizens of a different world to ours, one alien to the kindly race of men. There was nothing social about these Amahagger, who seemed to be a people labouring under some ancient ancestral curse of which they could never shake off the memory. Even the women rarely smiled; their clear-cut, stately countenances remained stern and set, except when they glowered at us incuriously. Only when Ayesha passed they prostrated themselves like the rest.

We went on through them and across the moat, climbing its further slope and here suddenly came upon a host of men gathered in a hollow square, apparently in order to receive us. They stood in ranks of five or six deep and their spear-points glimmering in the moonlight looked like long bands of level steel. As we entered the open side of the square all these spears were lifted. Thrice they were lifted and at each uplifting there rose a deep-throated cry of Hiya, which is the Arabic for She, and I suppose was a salutation to Ayesha.

She swept on taking no heed, till we came to the centre of the square where a number of men were gathered who prostrated themselves in the usual fashion. Motioning to them to rise she said,

"Captains, this very night within two hours we march against Rezu and the sun-worshippers, since otherwise as my arts tell me, they march against us. She-who-commands is immortal, as your fathers have known from generation to generation, and cannot be destroyed; but you, her servants, can be destroyed, and Rezu, who also has drunk of the Cup of Life, out-numbers you by three to one and prepares a queen to set up in my place over his own people and such of you as remain. As though," she added with a contemptuous laugh, "any woman of a day could take my place."

She paused and the spokesman of the captains said,

"We hear, O Hiya, and we understand. What wouldst thou have us do, O Lulala-come-to-earth? The armies of Rezu are great and from the beginning he has hated thee and us, also his magic is as thy magic and his length of days as thy length of days. How then can we who are few, three thousand men at the most, match ourselves against Rezu, Son of the Sun? Would it not be better that we should accept the terms of Rezu, which are light, and acknowledge him as our king?"

As she heard these words I saw the tall shape of Ayesha quiver beneath her robes, as I think, not with fear but with rage, because the meaning of them was clear enough, namely that rather than risk a battle with Rezu, these people were contemplating surrender and her own deposition, if indeed she could be deposed. Still she answered in a quiet voice,

"It seems that I have dealt too gently with you and with your fathers, Children of Lulala, whose shadow I am here upon the earth, so that because you only see the scabbard, you have forgotten the sword within and that it can shine forth and smite. Well, why should I be wrath because the brutish will follow the law of brutes, though it be true that I am minded to slay you where you stand? Hearken! Were I less merciful I would leave you to the clutching hands of Rezu, who would drag you one by one to the stone of sacrifice and there offer up your hearts to his god of fire and devour your bodies with his heat. But I bethink me of your wives and children and of your forefathers whom I knew in the dead days, and therefore, if I may, I still would save you from yourselves and your heads from the glowing pot.

"Take counsel together now and say—Will you fight against Rezu, or will you yield? If that is your desire, speak it, and by to-morrow's sun I will begone, taking these with me," and she pointed to us, "whom I have summoned to help us in the war. Aye, I will begone, and when you are stretched upon the stone of sacrifice, and your women and children are the slaves of the men of Rezu, then shall you cry,

"'Oh, where is Hiya whom our fathers knew? Oh, will she not return and save us from this hell?'

"Yes, so shall you cry but there shall come no answer, since then she will have departed to her own habitations in the moon and thence appear no more. Now consult together and answer swiftly, since I weary of you and your ways."

The captains drew apart and began to talk in low voices, while Ayesha stood still, apparently quite unconcerned, and I considered the situation.

It was obvious to me that these people were almost in rebellion against their strange ruler, whose power over them was of a purely moral nature, one that emanated from her personality alone. What I wondered was, being what she seemed to be, why she thought it worth while to exercise it at all. Then I remembered her statement that here and nowhere else she must abide for some secret reason, until a certain mystical gentleman with a Greek name came to fetch her away from this appointed rendezvous. Therefore I supposed she had no choice, or rather, suffering as she did from hallucinations, believed herself to have no choice and was obliged to put up with a crowd of disagreeable savages in quarters which were sadly out of repair.

Presently the spokesman returned, saluted with his spear, and asked,

"If we go up to fight against Rezu, who will lead us in the battle, O Hiya?"

"My wisdom shall be your guide," she answered, "this white man shall be your General and there stands the warrior who shall meet Rezu face to face and bring him to the dust," and she pointed to Umslopogaas leaning upon his axe and watching them with a contemptuous smile.

This reply did not seem to please the man for he withdrew to consult again with his companions. After a debate which I suppose was animated for the Amahagger, men of few words who did not indulge in oratory, all of them advanced on us and the spokesman said,

"The choice of a General does not please us, Hiya. We know that the white man is brave because of the fight he made against the men of Rezu over the mountain yonder; also that he and his followers have weapons that deal death from afar. But there is a prophecy among us of which none know the beginning, that he who commands in the last great battle between Lulala and Rezu must produce before the eyes of the People of Lulala a certain holy thing, a charm of power, without which defeat will be the portion of Lulala. Of this holy thing, this spirit-haunted shape of power, we know the likeness and the fashion, for these have come down among our priests, though who told it to them we cannot tell, but of it I will say this only, that it speaks both of the spirit and the body, of man and yet of more than man."

"And if this wondrous charm, this talisman of might, cannot be shown by the white lord here, what then?" asked Ayesha coldly.

"Then, Hiya, this is the word of the People of Lulala, that we will not serve under him in the battle, and this also is their word that we will not go up against Rezu. That thou art mighty we know well, Hiya, also that thou canst slay if thou wilt, but we know also that Rezu is mightier and that against him thou hast no power. Therefore kill us if thou dost so desire, until thy heart is satisfied with death. For it is better that we should perish thus than upon the altar of sacrifice wearing the red-hot crowns of Rezu."

"So say we all," exclaimed the rest of the company when he had finished.

"The thought comes to me to begin to satisfy my heart with thy coward blood and that of thy companions," said Ayesha contemptuously. Then she paused and turning to me, added, "O Watcher-by-Night, what counsel? Is there aught that will convince these chicken-hearted ones over whom I have spread my feathers for so long?"

I shook my head blankly, whereat they murmured together and made as though they would go.

Then it was that Hans, who understood something of Arabic as he did of most African tongues, pulled my sleeve and whispered in my ear.

"The Great Medicine, Baas! Show them Zikali's Great Medicine."

Here was an idea. The description of the article required, a "spirit-haunted shape of power" that spoke "both of the spirit and the body of man and yet of more than man," was so vague that it might mean anything or nothing. And yet—

I turned to Ayesha and prayed her to ask them if what they wanted should be produced, whether they would follow me bravely and fight Rezu to the death. She did so and with one voice they replied,

"Aye, bravely and to the death, him and the Bearer of the Axe of whom also our legend tells."

Then with deliberation I opened my shirt and holding out the image of Zikali as far as the chain of elephant hair would allow, I asked,

"Is this the holy thing, the charm of power, of which your legend tells, O People of the Amahagger and worshippers of Lulala?"

The spokesman glanced at it, then snatching a brand from a watch-fire that burnt near by held it over the carving and stared, and stared again; and as he did, so did the others bending over him.

"Dog! would you singe my beard?" I cried in affected rage, and seizing the brand from his hand I smote him with it over the head.

But he took no heed of the affront which I had offered to him merely to assert my authority. Still for a few moments he stared although the sparks from the wood were frizzling in his greasy hair, then of a sudden went down on his face before me, as did all the others and cried out,

"It is the Holy Thing! It is the spirit-haunted Shape of Power itself, and we the Worshippers of Lulala will follow thee to the death, O white lord, Watcher-by-Night. Yes, where thou goest and he goes who bears the Axe, thither will we follow till not one of us is left upon his feet."

"Then that's settled," I said, yawning, since it is never wise to show concern about anything before savages. Indeed personally I had no wish to be the leader of this very peculiar tribe in an adventure of which I knew nothing, and therefore had hoped that they would leave that honour to someone else. Then I turned and told Umslopogaas what had passed, a tale at which he only shrugged his great shoulders, handling his axe as though he were minded to try its edge upon some of these "Dark-lovers," as he named the Amahagger people because of their nocturnal habits.

Meanwhile Ayesha gave certain orders. Then she came to me and said,

"These men march at once, three thousand strong, and by dawn will camp on the northern mountain crest. At sunrise litters will come to bear you and those with you if they will, to join them, which you should do by midday. In the afternoon marshall them as you think wise, for the battle will take place in the small hours of the following morning, since the People of Lulala only fight at night. I have said."

"Do you not come with us?" I asked, dismayed.

"Nay, not in a war against Rezu, why it matters not. Yet my Spirit will go with you, for I shall watch all that passes, how it matters not and perchance you may see it there—I know not. On the third day from to-morrow we shall meet again in the flesh or beyond it, but as I think in the flesh, and you can claim the reward which you journeyed here to seek. A place shall be prepared for the white lady whom Rezu would have set up as a rival queen to me. Farewell, and farewell also to yonder Bearer of the Axe that shall drink the blood of Rezu, also to the little yellow man who is rightly named Light-in-Darkness, as you shall learn ere all is done."

Then before I could speak she turned and glided away, swiftly surrounded by her guards, leaving me astonished and very uncomfortable.

CHAPTER XVI

ALLAN'S VISION

The old chamberlain, Billali, conducted us back to our camp. As we went he discoursed to me of these Amahagger, of whom it seemed he was himself a developed specimen, one who threw back, perhaps tens of generations, to some superior ancestor who lived before they became debased. In substance he told me that they were a wild and lawless lot who lived amongst ruins or in caves, or some of them in swamp dwellings, in small separate communities, each governed by its petty headman who was generally a priest of their goddess Lulala.

Originally they and the people of Rezu were the same, in times when they worshipped the sun and the moon jointly, but "thousands of years" ago, as he expressed it, they had separated, the Rezuites having gone to dwell to the north of the Great Mountain, whence they continually threatened the Lulalaites whom, had it not been for She-who-commands, they would have destroyed long before. The Rezuites, it seemed, were habitual cannibals, whereas the Lulalaite branch of the Amahagger only practised cannibalism occasionally when by a lucky chance they got hold of strangers. "Such as yourself, Watcher-by-Night, and your companions," he added with meaning. If their crime were discovered, however, Hiya, She-who-commands, punished it by death.

I asked if she exercised an active rule over these people. He answered that she did not, as she lacked sufficient interest in them; only when she was angry with individuals she would destroy some of them by "her arts," as she had power to do if she chose. Most of them indeed had never seen her and only knew of her existence by rumour. To them she was a spirit or a goddess who inhabited the ancient tombs that lay to the south of the old city whither she had come because of the threatened war with Rezu, whom alone she feared, he did not know why. He told me again, moreover, that she was the greatest magician who had ever been, and that it was certain she did not die, since their forefathers knew her generations ago. Still she seemed to be under some curse, like the Amahagger themselves, who were the descendants of those who had once inhabited Kôr and the country round it, as far as the sea-coast and for hundreds of miles inland, having been a mighty people in their day before a great plague destroyed them.

For the rest he thought that she was a very unhappy woman who "lived with her own soul mourning the dead" and consorting with none upon the earth.

I asked him why she stayed here, whereat he shook his head and replied, he supposed because of the "curse," since he could conceive of no other reason. He informed me also that her moods varied very much. Sometimes she was fierce and active and at others by comparison mild and low-spirited. Just now she was passing through one of the latter stages, perhaps because of the Rezu trouble, for she did not wish her people to be destroyed by this terrible person; or perhaps for some other reason with which he was not acquainted.

When she chose, she knew all things, except the distant future. Thus she knew that we were coming, also the details of our march and that we should be attacked by the Rezuites who were going out to meet their returning company that had been sent afar to find a white queen. Therefore she had ordered him to go with soldiers to our assistance. I asked why she went veiled, and he replied, because of her beauty which drove even savage men mad, so that in old days she had been obliged to kill a number of them.

That was all he seemed to know about her, except that she was kind to those who served her well, like himself, and protected them from evil of every sort.

Then I asked him about Rezu. He answered that he was a dreadful person, undying, it was said, like She-who-commands, though he had never seen the man himself and never wanted to do so. His followers being cannibals and having literally eaten up all those that they could reach, were now desirous of conquering the people of Lulala that they might eat them also at their leisure. Each other they did not eat, because dog does not eat dog, and therefore they were beginning to grow hungry, although they had plenty of grain and cattle of which they used the milk and hides.

As for the coming battle, he knew nothing about it or what would happen, save that She-who-commands said that it would go well for the Lulalaites under my direction. She was so sure that it would go well, that she did not think it worth while to accompany the army, for she hated noise and bloodshed.

It occurred to me that perhaps she was afraid that she too would be taken captive and eaten, but I kept my reflection to myself.

Just then we arrived at our camp-house, where Billali bade me farewell, saying that he wished to rest as he must be back at dawn with litters, when he hoped to find us ready to start. Then he departed. Umslopogaas and Hans also went away to sleep, leaving me alone who, having taken my repose in the afternoon, did not feel drowsy at the moment. So lovely was the night indeed that I made up my mind to take a little walk during the midnight hours, after the manner of the Amahagger themselves, for having now been recognised as Generalissimo of their forces, I had little fear of being attacked, especially as I carried a pistol in my pocket. So off I set strolling slowly down what seemed to have been a main street of the ancient city, which in its general appearance resembled excavated Pompeii, only on an infinitely larger scale.

As I went I meditated on the strange circumstances in which I found myself. Really they tempted me to believe that I was suffering from delusions and perhaps all the while in fact lay stretched upon a bed in the delirium of fever. That marvellous woman, for instance—even rejecting her tale of miraculously extended life, which I did—what was I to make of her? I did not know, except that wondrous as she was, it remained clear that she claimed a great deal more power than she possessed. This was evident from her tone in the interview with the captains, and from the fact that she had shuffled off the command of her tribe on to my shoulders. If she were so mighty, why did she not command it herself and bring her celestial, or infernal, powers to bear upon the enemy? Again, I could not say, but one fact emerged, namely that she was as interesting as she was beautiful, and uncommonly clever into the bargain.

But what a task was this that she had laid upon me, to lead into battle, with a foe of unascertained strength, a mob of savages probably quite undisciplined, of whose fighting qualities I knew nothing and whom I had no opportunity of organising. The affair seemed madness and I could only hope that luck or destiny would take me through somehow.

To tell the truth, I believed it would, for I had grown almost as superstitious about Zikali and his Great Medicine as was Hans himself. Certainly the effect of it upon those captains was very odd, or would have been had not the explanation come to me in a flash. On the first night of our meeting, as I have described, I showed this talisman to Ayesha, as a kind of letter of credentials, and now I could see that it was she who had arranged all the scene with the captains, or their tribal magician, in order to get her way about my appointment to the command.

Everything about her conduct bore this out, even her feigning ignorance of the existence of the charm and the leaving of it to Hans to suggest its production, which perhaps she did by influencing his mind subconsciously. No doubt more or less it fitted in with one of those nebulous traditions which are so common amongst ancient savage races, and therefore once shown to her confederate, or confederates, would be accepted by the common people as a holy sign, after which the rest was easy.

Such an obvious explanation involved the death of any illusions I might still cherish about this Arab lady, Ayesha, and it is true that I parted with them with regret, as we all do when we think we have discovered something wonderful in the female line. But there it was, and to bother any more about her, her history and aims, seemed useless.

So dismissing her and all present anxieties from my mind, I began to look about me and to wonder at the marvellous scene which unfolded itself before me in the moonlight. That I might see it better, although I was rather afraid of snakes which might hide among the stones, by an easy ascent I climbed a mount of ruins and up the broad slope of a tumbled massive wall, which from its thickness I judged must have been that of some fort or temple. On the crest of this wall, some seventy or eighty feet above the level of the streets, I sat down and looked about me.

Everywhere around me stretched the ruins of the great city, now as fallen and as deserted as Babylon herself. The majestic loneliness of the place was something awful. Even the vision of companies and battalions of men crossing the plain towards the north with the moonlight glistening on their spear-points, did little to lessen this sense of loneliness. I knew that these were the regiments which I was destined to command, travelling to the camp where I must meet them. But in such silence did they move that no sound came from them even in the deathly stillness of the perfect night, so that almost I was tempted to believe them to be the shadow-ghosts of some army of old Kôr.

They vanished, and musing thus I think I must have dozed. At any rate it seemed to me that of a sudden the city was as it had been in the days of its glory. I saw it brilliant with a hundred colours; everywhere was colour, on the painted walls and roofs, the flowering trees that lined the streets and the bright dresses of the men and women who by thousands crowded them and the marts and squares. Even the chariots that moved to and fro were coloured as were the countless banners which floated from palace walls and temple tops.

The enormous place teemed with every activity of life; brides being borne to marriage and dead men to burial; squadrons marching, clad in glittering armour; merchants chaffering; white-robed priests and priestesses passing in procession (who or what did they worship? I wondered); children breaking out of school; grave philosophers debating in the shadow of a cool arcade; a royal person making a progress preceded by runners and surrounded by slaves, and lastly the multitudes of citizens going about the daily business of life.

Even details were visible, such as those of officers of the law chasing an escaped prisoner who had a broken rope tied to his arm, and a collision between two chariots in a narrow street, about the wrecks of which an idle mob gathered as it does to-day if two vehicles collide, while the owners argued, gesticulating angrily, and the police and grooms tried to lift a fallen horse on to its feet. Only no sound of the argument or of anything else reached me. I saw, and that was all. The silence remained intense, as well it might do, since those chariots must have come to grief thousands upon thousands of years ago.

A cloud seemed to pass before my eyes, a thin, gauzy cloud which somehow reminded me of the veil that Ayesha wore. Indeed at the moment, although I could not see her, I would have sworn that she was present at my side, and what is more, that she was mocking me who had set her down as so impotent a trickstress, which doubtless was part of the dream.

At any rate I returned to my normal state, and there about me were the miles of desolate streets and the thousands of broken walls, and the black blots of roofless houses and the wide, untenanted plain bounded by the battlemented line of encircling mountain crests, and above all, the great moon shining softly in a tender sky.

I looked and thrilled, though oppressed by the drear and desolate beauty of the scene around me, descended the wall and the ruined slope and made my way homewards, afraid even of my own shadow. For I seemed to be the only living thing among the dead habitations of immemorial Kôr.

Reaching our camp I found Hans awake and watching for me.

"I was just coming to look for you, Baas," he said. "Indeed I should have done so before, only I knew that you had gone to pay a visit to that tall white 'Missis' who ties up her head in a blanket, and thought that neither of you would like to be disturbed."

"Then you thought wrong," I answered, "and what is more, if you had made that visit I think it might have been one from which you would never have come back."

"Oh yes, Baas," sniggered Hans. "The tall white lady would not have minded. It is you who are so particular, after the fashion of men whom Heaven made very shy."

Without deigning to reply to the gibes of Hans I went to lie down, wondering what kind of a bed poor Robertson occupied that night, and soon fell asleep, as fortunately for myself I have the power to do, whatever my circumstances at the moment. Men who can sleep are those who do the work of the world and succeed, though personally I have had more of the work than of the success.

I was awakened at the first grey dawn by Hans, who informed me that Billali was waiting outside with litters, also that Goroko had already made his incantations and doctored Umslopogaas and his two men for war after the Zulu fashion when battle was expected. He added that these Zulus had refused to be left behind to guard and nurse their wounded companions, and said that rather than do so, they would kill them.

Somehow, he informed me, in what way he could not guess, this had come to the ears of the White Lady who "hid her face from men because it was so ugly," and she had sent women to attend to the sick ones, with word that they should be well cared for. All of this proved to be true enough, but I need not enter into the details.

In the end off we went, I in my litter following Billali's, with an express and a repeating rifle and plenty of ammunition for both, and Hans, also well armed, in that which had been sent for Umslopogaas, who preferred to walk with Goroko and the two other Zulus.

For a little while Hans enjoyed the sensation of being carried by somebody else, and lay upon the cushions smoking with a seraphic smile and addressing sarcastic remarks to the bearers, who fortunately did not understand them. Soon, however, he wearied of these novel delights and as he was still determined not to walk until he was obliged, climbed on to the roof of the litter, astride of which he sat as though it were a horse, looking for all the world like a toy monkey on a horizontal stick.

Our road ran across the level, fertile plain but a small portion of which was cultivated, though I could see that at some time or other, when its population was greater, every inch of it had been under crop. Now it was largely covered by trees, many of them fruit-bearing, between which meandered streams of water which once, I think, had been irrigation channels.

About ten o'clock we reached the foot of the encircling cliffs and began the climb of the escarpment, which was steep, tortuous and difficult. By noon we reached its crest and here found all our little army encamped and, except for the sentries, sleeping, as seemed to be the invariable custom of these people in the daytime.

I caused the chief captains to be awakened and with them made a circuit of the camp, reckoning the numbers of the men which came to about 3,250 and learning what I could concerning them and their way of fighting. Then, accompanied by Umslopogaas and Hans with the Zulus as a guard, also by three of the head-captains of the Amahagger, I walked forward to study the lie of the land.

Coming to the further edge of the escarpment, I found that at this place two broad-based ridges, shaped like those that spring from the boles of certain tropical forest trees, ran from its crest to the plain beneath at a gentle slope. Moreover I saw that on this plain between the ends of the ridges an army was encamped which, by the aid of my glasses, I examined and estimated to number at least ten thousand men.

This army, the Amahagger captains informed me, was that of Rezu, who, they said, intended to commence his attack at dawn on the following morning, since the People of Rezu, being sun-worshippers, would never fight until their god appeared above the horizon. Having studied all there was to see I asked the captains to set out their plan of battle, if they had a plan.

The chief of them answered that it was to advance halfway down the right-hand ridge to a spot where there was a narrow flat piece of ground, and there await attack, since at this place their smaller numbers would not so much matter, whereas these made it impossible for them to assail the enemy.

"But suppose that Rezu should choose to come up to the other ridge and get behind you. What would happen then?" I inquired.

He replied that he did not know, his ideas of strategy being, it was clear, of a primitive order.

"Do your people fight best at night or in the day?" I went on.

He said undoubtedly at night, indeed in all their history there was no record of their having done so in the daytime.

"And yet you propose to let Rezu join battle with you when the sun is high, or in other words to court defeat," I remarked.

Then I went aside and discussed things for a while with Umslopogaas and Hans, after which I returned and gave my orders, declining all argument. Briefly these were that in the dusk before the rising of the moon, our Amahagger must advance down the right-hand ridge in complete silence, and hide themselves among the scrub which I saw grew thickly near its root. A small party, however, under the leadership of Goroko, whom I knew to be a brave and clever captain, was to pass halfway down the left-hand ridge and there light fires over a wide area, so as to make the enemy think that our whole force had encamped there. Then at the proper moment which I had not yet decided upon, we would attack the army of Rezu.

The Amahagger captains did not seem pleased with this plan which I think was too bold for their fancy, and began to murmur together. Seeing that I must assert my authority at once, I walked up to them and said to their chief man,

"Hearken, my friend. By your own wish, not mine, I have been appointed your general and I expect to be obeyed without question. From the moment that the advance begins you will keep close to me and to the Black One, and if so much as one of your men hesitates or turns back, you will die," and I nodded towards the axe of Umslopogaas. "Moreover, afterwards She-who-commands will see that others of you die, should you escape in the fight."

Still they hesitated. Thereon without another word, I produced Zikali's Great Medicine and held it before their eyes, with the result that the sight of this ugly thing did what even the threat of death could not do. They went flat on the ground, every one of them, and swore by Lulala and by She-who-commands, her priestess, that they would do all I said, however mad it seemed to them.

"Good," I answered. "Now go back and make ready, and for the rest, by this time to-morrow we shall know who is or is not mad."

From that moment till the end I had no more trouble with these Amahagger.

I will get on quickly with the story of this fight whereof the preliminary details do not matter. At the proper time Goroko went off with two hundred and fifty men and one of the two Zulus to light the fires and, at an agreed signal, namely the firing of two shots in rapid succession by myself, to begin shouting and generally make as much noise as they could.

We also went off with the remaining three thousand, and before the moon rose, crept as quietly as ghosts down the right-hand ridge. Being such a silent folk who were accustomed to move at night and could see in the dark almost as well as cats, the Amahagger executed this manoeuvre splendidly, wrapping their spear-blades in bands of dry grass lest light should glint on them and betray our movements. So in due course we came to the patch of bush where the ridge widened out about five hundred yards from the plain beneath, and there lay down in four companies or regiments, each of them about seven hundred and fifty strong.

Now the moon had risen, but because of the mist which covered the surface of the plain, we could see nothing of the camp of Rezu which we knew must be within a thousand yards of us, unless indeed it had been moved, as the silence seemed to suggest.

This circumstance gave me much anxiety, since I feared lest abandoning their reputed habits, these Rezuites were also contemplating a night attack. Umslopogaas, too, was disturbed on the subject, though because of Goroko and his men whose fires began to twinkle on the opposing ridge something over a mile away, they could not pass up there without our knowledge.

Still, for aught I knew there might be other ways of scaling this mountain. I did not trust the Amahagger, who declared that none existed, since their local knowledge was slight as they never visited these northern slopes because of their fear of Rezu. Supposing that the enemy gained the crest and suddenly assaulted us in the rear! The thought of it made me feel cold down the back.

While I was wondering how I could find out the truth, Hans, who was squatted behind a bush, suddenly rose and gave the rifle he was carrying to the remaining Zulu.

"Baas," he said, "I am going to look and find out what those people are doing, if they are still there, and then you will know how and when to attack them. Don't be afraid for me, Baas, it will be easy in that mist and you know I can move like a snake. Also if I should not come back, it does not matter and it will tell you that they are there."

I hesitated who did not wish to expose the brave little Hottentot to such risks. But when he understood, Umslopogaas said,

"Let the man go. It is his gift and duty to spy, as it is mine to smite with the axe, and yours to lead, Macumazahn. Let him go, I say."

I nodded my head, and having kissed my hand in his silly fashion in token of much that he did not wish to say, Hans slipped out of sight, saying that he hoped to be back within an hour. Except for his great knife, he went unarmed, who feared that if he took a pistol he might be tempted to fire it and make a noise.

CHAPTER XVII

THE MIDNIGHT BATTLE

That hour went by very slowly. Again and again I consulted my watch by the light of the moon, which was now rising high in the heavens, and thought that it would never come to an end. Listen as I would, there was nothing to be heard, and as the mist still prevailed the only thing I could see except the heavens, was the twinkling of the fires lit by Goroko and his party.

At length it was done and there was no sign of Hans. Another half hour passed and still no sign of Hans.

"I think that Light-in-Darkness is dead or taken prisoner," said Umslopogaas.

I answered that I feared so, but that I would give him another fifteen minutes and then, if he did not appear, I proposed to order an advance, hoping to find the enemy where we had last seen them from the top of the mountain.

The fifteen minutes went by also, and as I could see that the Amahagger captains who sat at a little distance were getting very nervous, I picked up my double-barrelled rifle and turned round so that I faced up hill with a view of firing it as had been agreed with Goroko, but in such a fashion that the flashes perhaps would not be seen from the plain below. For this purpose I moved a few yards to the left to get behind the trunk of a tree that grew there, and was already lifting the rifle to my shoulder, when a yellow hand clasped the barrel and a husky voice said,

"Don't fire yet, Baas, as I want to tell you my story first."

I looked down and there was the ugly face of Hans wearing a grin that might have frightened the man in the moon.

"Well," I said with cold indifference, assumed I admit to hide my excessive joy at his safe return, "tell on, and be quick about it. I suppose you lost your way and never found them."

"Yes, Baas, I lost my way for the fog was very thick down there. But in the end I found them all right, by my nose, Baas, for those man-eating people smell strong and I got the wind of one of their sentries. It was easy to pass him in the mist, Baas, so easy that I was tempted to cut his throat as I went, but I didn't for fear lest he should make a noise. No, I walked on right into the middle of them, which was easy too, for they were all asleep, wrapped up in blankets. They hadn't any fires perhaps because they didn't want them to be seen, or perhaps because it is so hot down in that low land, I don't know which.

"So I crept on taking note of all I saw, till at last I came to a little hill of which the top rose above the level of the mist, so that I could see on it a long hut built of green boughs with the leaves still fresh upon them. Now I thought that I would crawl up to the hut since it came into my mind that Rezu himself must be sleeping there and that I might kill him. But while I stood hesitating I heard a noise like to that made by an old woman whose husband had thrown a blanket over her head to keep her quiet, or to that of a bee in a bottle, a sort of droning noise that reminded me of something.

"I thought a while and remembered that when Red Beard was on his knees praying to Heaven, as is his habit when he has nothing else to do, Baas, he makes a noise just like that. I crept towards the sound and presently there I found Red Beard himself tied upon a stone and looking as mad as a buffalo bull stuck in a swamp, for he shook his head and rolled his eyes about, just as though he had had two bottles of bad gin, Baas, and all the while he kept saying prayers. Now I thought that I would cut him loose, and bent over him to do so, when by ill-luck he saw my face and began to shout, saying,

"'Go away, you yellow devil. I know you have come to take me to hell, but you are too soon, and if my hands were loose I would twist your head off your shoulders.'

"He said this in English, Baas, which as you know I can understand quite well, after which I was sure that I had better leave him alone. Whilst I was thinking, there came out of the hut above two old men dressed in night-shirts, such as you white people wear, with yellow things upon their heads that had a metal picture of the sun in front of them."

"Medicine-men," I suggested.

"Yes, Baas, or Predikants of some sort, for they were rather like your reverend father when he dressed himself up and went into a box to preach. Seeing them I slipped back a little way to where the mist began, lay down and listened. They looked at Red Beard, for his shouts at me had brought them out, but he took no notice of them, only went on making a noise like a beetle in a tin can.

"'It is nothing,' said one of the Predikants to the other in the same tongue that these Amahagger use. 'But when is he to be sacrificed? Soon, I hope, for I cannot sleep because of the noise he makes.'

"'When the edge of the sun appears, not before,' answered the other Predikant. 'Then the new queen will be brought out of the hut and this white man will be sacrificed to her.'

"'I think it is a pity to wait so long,' said the first Predikant, 'for never shall we sleep in peace until the red-hot pot is on his head.'

"'First the victory, then the feast,' answered the second Predikant, 'though he will not be so good to eat as that fat young woman who was with the new queen.'

"Then, Baas, they both smacked their lips and one of them went back towards the hut. But the other did not go back. No, he sat down on the ground and glowered at Baas Red-Beard upon the stone. More, he struck him on the face to make him quiet.

"Now, Baas, when I saw this and remembered that they had said that they had eaten Janee whom I liked although she was such a fool, the spirit in me grew so very angry and I thought that I would give this old skellum (i.e. rascal) of a Predikant a taste of sacrifice himself, after which I purposed to creep to the hut and see if I could get speech with the Lady Sad-Eyes, if she was there.

"So I wriggled up behind the Predikant as he sat glowering over Red-Beard, and stuck my knife into his back where I thought it would kill him at once. But it didn't, Baas, for he fell on to his face and began to make a noise like a wounded hyena before I could finish him. Then I heard a sound of shouts, and to save my life was obliged to run away into the mist, without loosing Red-Beard or seeing Lady Sad-Eyes. I ran very hard, Baas, making a wide circle to the left, and so at last got back here. That's all, Baas."

"And quite enough, too," I answered, "though if they did not see you, the death of the Medicine-man may frighten them. Poor Janee! Well, I hope to come even with those devils before they are three hours older."

Then I called up Umslopogaas and the Amahagger captains and told them the substance of the story, also that Hans had located the army, or part of it.

The end of it was that we made up our minds to attack at once; indeed I insisted on this, as I was determined if I could to save that unfortunate man, Robertson, who, from Hans' account, evidently was now quite mad and raving. So I fired the two shots as had been arranged and presently heard the sound of distant shoutings on the slope of the opposing ridge. A few minutes later we started, Umslopogaas and I leading the vanguard and the Amahagger captains following with the three remaining companies.

Now the reader, presuming the existence of such a person, will think that everything is sure to go right; that this cunning old fellow, Allan Quatermain, is going to surprise and wipe the floor with those Rezuites, who were already beguiled by the trick he had instructed Goroko to play. That after this he will rescue Robertson who doubtless shortly recovers his mind, also Inez with the greatest ease, in fact that everything will happen as it ought to do if this were a romance instead of a mere record of remarkable facts. But being the latter, as it happened, matters did not work out quite in this convenient way.

To begin with, when those Amahagger told me that the Rezuites never fought in the dark or before the sun was well up, either they lied or they were much mistaken, for at any rate on this occasion they did the exact contrary. All the while that we thought we were stalking them, they were stalking us. The Goroko manoeuvre had not deceived them in the least, since from their spies they knew its exact significance.

Here, I may add that those spies were in our own ranks, traitors, in short, who were really in the pay of Rezu and possibly belonged to his abominable faith, some of whom slipped away from time to time to the enemy to report our progress and plans, so far as they knew them.

Further, what Hans had stumbled on was a mere rear guard left around the place of sacrifice and the hut where Inez was confined. The real army he never found at all. That was divided into two bodies and hidden in bush to the right and left of the ridge which we were descending just at the spot where it joined the plain beneath, and into the jaws of these two armies we marched gaily.

Now that hypothetical reader will say, "Why didn't that silly old fool, Allan, think of all these things? Why didn't he remember that he was commanding a pack of savages with whom he had no real acquaintance, among whom there were sure to be traitors, especially as they were of the same blood as the Rezuites, and take precautions?"

Ah! my dear reader, I will only answer that I wish you had handled the job yourself, and enjoyed the opportunity of seeing what you could do in the circumstances. Do you suppose I didn't think of all these points? Of course I did. But have you ever heard of the difficulty of making silk purses out of sows' ears, or of turning a lot of gloomy and disagreeable barbarians whom you had never even drilled, into trustworthy and efficient soldiers ready to fight three times their own number and beat them?

Also I beg to observe that I did get through somehow, as you shall learn, which is more than you might have done, Mr. Wisdom, though I admit, not without help from another quarter. It is all very well for you to sit in your armchair and be sapient and turn up your learned nose, like the gentlemen who criticise plays and poems, an easy job compared to the writing of them. From all of which, however, you will understand that I am, to tell the truth, rather ashamed of what followed, since qui s'excuse, s'accuse.

As we slunk down that hill in the moonlight, a queer-looking crowd, I admit also that I felt very uncomfortable. To begin with I did not like that remark of the Medicine-man which Hans reported, to the effect that the feast must come after the victory, especially as he had said just before that

Robertson was to be sacrificed as the sun rose, which would seem to suggest that the "victory" was planned to take place before that event.

While I was ruminating upon this subject, I looked round for Hans to cross-examine him as to the priest's exact words, only to find that he had slunk off somewhere. A few minutes later he reappeared running back towards us swiftly and, I noticed, taking shelter behind tree trunks and rocks as he came.

"Baas," he gasped, for he was out of breath, "be careful, those Rezu men are on either side ahead. I went forward and ran into them. They threw many spears at me. Look!" and he showed a slight cut on his arm from which blood was flowing.

Instantly I understood that we were ambushed and began to think very hard indeed. As it chanced we were passing across a large flat space upon the ridge, say seven or eight acres in extent, where the bush grew lightly, though owing to the soil being better, the trees were tall.

On the steep slope below this little plain it seemed to be denser and there it was, according to Hans, that the ambush was set. I halted my regiment and sent back messengers to the others that they were to halt also as they came up, on the pretext of giving them a rest before they were marshalled and we advanced to the battle.

Then I told Umslopogaas what Hans said and asked him to send out his Zulu soldier whom he could trust, to see if he could obtain confirmation of the report. This he did at once. Also I asked him what he thought should be done, supposing that it was true.

"Form the Amahagger into a ring or a square and await attack," he answered.

I nodded, for that was my own opinion, but replied,

"If they were Zulus, the plan would be good. But how do we know that these men will stand?"

"We know nothing, Macumazahn, and therefore can only try. If they run it must be up-hill."

Then I called the captains and told them what was toward, which seemed to alarm them very much. Indeed one or two of them wanted to retreat at once, but I said I would shoot the first man who tried to do so. In the end they agreed to my plan and said that they would post their best soldiers above, at the top of the square, with the orders to stop any attempt at a flight up the mountain.

After this we formed up the square as best we could, arranging it in a rather rough, four-fold line. While we were doing this we heard some shouts below and presently the Zulu returned, who reported that all was as Hans had said and that Rezu's men were moving round us, having discovered, as he thought, that we had halted and escaped their ambush.

Still the attack did not develop at once, for the reason that the Rezu army was crawling up the steep flanks of the spur on either side of the level piece of ground, with a view of encircling us altogether, so as to make a clean sweep of our force. As a matter of fact, considered from our point of view, this was a most fortunate move, since thereby they stopped any attempt at a retreat on the part of our Amahagger, whose bolt-hole was now blocked.

When we had done all we could, we sat down, or at least I did, and waited. The night, I remember, was strangely still, only from the slopes on either side of our plateau came a kind of rustling sound which in fact was caused by the feet of Rezu's people, as they marched to surround us.

It ceased at last and the silence grew complete, so much so that I could hear the teeth of some of our tall Amahagger chattering with fear, a sound that gave me little confidence and caused Umslopogaas to remark that the hearts of these big men had never grown; they remained "as those of babies." I told the captains to pass the word down the ranks that those who stood might live, but those who fled would certainly die. Therefore if they wished to see their homes again they had better stand and fight like men. Otherwise most of them would be killed and the rest eaten by Rezu. This was done, and I observed that the message seemed to produce a steadying effect upon our ranks.

Suddenly all around us, from below, from above and on either side there broke a most awful roar which seemed to shape itself into the word, Rezu, and next minute also from above, below and either side, some ten thousand men poured forth upon our square.

In the moonlight they looked very terrible with their flowing white robes and great gleaming spears. Hans and I fired some shots, though for all the effect they produced, we might as well have pelted a breaker with pebbles. Then, as I thought that I should be more useful alive than dead, I retreated within the square, Umslopogaas, his Zulu, and Hans coming with me.

On the whole our Amahagger stood the attack better than I expected. They beat back the first rush with considerable loss to the enemy, also the second after a longer struggle. Then there was a pause during which we re-formed our ranks, dragging the wounded men into the square.

Scarcely had we done this when with another mighty shout of "Rezu!" the enemy attacked again—that was about an hour after the battle had begun. But now they had changed their tactics, for instead of trying to rush all sides of the square at once, they concentrated their efforts on the western front, that which faced towards the plain below.

On they came, and among them in the forefront of the battle, now and again I caught sight of a gigantic man, a huge creature who seemed to me to be seven feet high and big in proportion. I could not see him clearly because of the uncertain moonlight, but I noted his fierce aspect, also that he had an enormous beard, black streaked with grey, that flowed down to his middle, and that his hair hung in masses upon his shoulders.

"Rezu himself!" I shouted to Umslopogaas.

"Aye, Macumazahn, Rezu himself without doubt, and I rejoice to see him for he will be a worthy foe to fight. Look! he carries an axe as I do. Now I must save my strength for when we come face to face I shall need it all."

I thought that I would spare Umslopogaas this exertion and watched my opportunity to put a bullet through this giant. But I could never get one. Once when I had covered him an Amahagger rushed in front of my gun so that I could not shoot, and when a second chance came a little cloud floated over the face of the moon and made him invisible. After that I had other things to which to attend, since, as I expected would happen, the western face of our square gave, and yelling like devils, the enemy began to pour in through the gap.

A cold thrill went through me for I saw that the game was up. To re-form these undisciplined Amahagger was impossible; nothing was to be expected except panic, rout and slaughter. I cursed my folly for ever having had anything to do with the business, while Hans screamed to me in a thin voice that the only chance was for us three and the Zulu to bolt and hide in the bush.

I did not answer him because, apart from any nasty pride, the thing was impossible, for how could we get through those struggling masses of men which surrounded us on every side? No, my clock had struck, so I went on making a kind of mental sandwich of prayers and curses; prayers for my soul and forgiveness for my sins, and curses on the Amahagger and everything to do with them, especially Zikali and the woman called Ayesha, who, between them, had led me into this affair.

"Perhaps the Great Medicine of Zikali," piped Hans again as he fired a rifle at the advancing foe.

"Hang the Great Medicine," I shouted back, "and Ayesha with it. No wonder she declined to take a hand in this business."

As I spoke the words I saw old Billali, who not being a man of war was keeping as close to us as he could, go flat onto his venerable face, and reflected that he must have got a thrown spear through him. Casting a hurried glance at him to see if he were done for or only wounded, out of the corner of my eye I caught sight of something diaphanous which gleamed in the moonlight and reminded me of I knew not what at the moment.

I looked round quickly to see what it might be and lo! there, almost at my side was the veiled Ayesha herself, holding in her hand a little rod made of black wood inlaid with ivory not unlike a field marshal's baton, or a sceptre.

I never saw her come and to this day I do not know how she did so; she was just there and what is more she must have put luminous paint or something else on her robes, for they gleamed with a sort of faint, phosphorescent fire, which in the moonlight made her conspicuous all over the field of battle. Nor did she speak a single word, she only waved the rod, pointed with it towards the fierce hordes who were drawing near to us, killing as they came, and began to move forward with a gliding motion.

Now from every side there went up a roar of "She-who-commands! She-who-commands!" while the people of Rezu in front shouted "Lulala! Lulala! Fly, Lulala is upon us with the witchcrafts of the moon!"

She moved forward and by some strange impulse, for no order was given, we all began to move after her. Yes, the ranks that a minute before were beginning to give way to wild panic, became filled with a marvellous courage and moved after her.

The men of Rezu also, and I suppose with them Rezu himself, for I saw no more of him at that time, began to move uncommonly fast over the edge of the plateau towards the plain beneath. In fact they broke into flight and leaping over dead and dying, we rushed after them, always following the gleaming robe of Ayesha, who must have been an extremely agile person, since without any apparent exertion she held her place a few steps ahead of us.

There was another curious circumstance about this affair, namely, that terrified though they were, those Rezuites, after the first break, soon seemed to find it impossible to depart with speed. They kept turning round to look behind them at that following vision, as though they were so many of Lot's wives. Moreover, the same fate overtook many of them which fell upon that scriptural lady, since they appeared to become petrified and stood there quite still, like rabbits fascinated by a snake, until our people came up and killed them.

This slaying went on all down the last steep slope of the ridge, on which I suppose at least two-thirds of the army of Rezu must have perished, since our Amahagger showed themselves very handy men when it came to exterminating foes who were too terror-struck to fight, and, exhilarated by the occupation, gained courage every moment.

CHAPTER XVIII

THE SLAYING OF REZU

At last we were on the plain, the bemused remnant of Rezu's army still doubling before us like a mob of game pursued by wild dogs. Here we halted to re-form our ranks; it seemed to me, although still she spoke no word, that some order reached me from the gleaming Ayesha that I should do this. The business took twenty minutes or so, and then, numbering about two thousand five hundred strong, for the rest had fallen in the fight of the square, we advanced again.

Now there came that dusk which often precedes the rising of the sun, and through it I could see that the battle was not yet over, since gathered in front of us was still a force about equal to our own. Ayesha pointed towards it with her wand and we leapt forward to the attack. Here the men of Rezu stood awaiting us, for they seemed to overcome their terror with the approach of day.

The battle was fierce, a very strange battle in that dim, uncertain light, which scarcely showed us friend from foe. Indeed I am not sure that we should have won it, since Ayesha was no longer visible to give our Amahagger confidence, and as the courage of the Rezuites increased, so theirs seemed to lessen with the passing of the night.

Fortunately, however, just as the issue hung doubtful, there was a shout to our left and looking, I made out the tall shape of Goroko, the witch-doctor, with the other Zulu, followed by his two hundred and fifty men, and leaping on to the flank of the line of Rezu.

That settled the business. The enemy crumpled up and melted, and just then the first lights of dawn appeared in the sky. I looked about me for Ayesha, but she had gone, where to I knew not, though at the moment I feared that she must have been killed in the mêlée.

Then I gave up looking and thinking, since now or never was the time for action. Signalling and shouting to those hatchet-faced Amahagger to advance, accompanied by Umslopogaas with Goroko who had joined us, and Hans, I sprang forward to give them an example, which, to be just to them, they took.

"This is the mound on which Red-Beard should be," cried Hans as we faced a little slope.

I ran up it and through the gloom which precedes the actual dawn, saw a group of men gathered round something, as people collect about a street accident.

"Red-Beard on the stone. They are killing him," screeched Hans again.

It was so; at least several white-robed priests were bending over a prostrate figure with knives in their hands, while behind stood the huge fellow whom I took to be Rezu, staring towards the east as though he were waiting for the rim of the sun to appear before he gave some order. At that very moment it did appear, just a thin edge of bright light on the horizon, and he turned, shouting the order.

Too late! For we were on them. Umslopogaas cut down one of the priests with his axe, and the men about me dealt with the others, while Hans with a couple of sweeps of his long knife, severed the cords with which Robertson was tied.

The poor man who in the growing light I could see was raving mad, sprang up, calling out something in Scotch about "the deil." Seizing a great spear which had fallen from the hand of one of the priests, he rushed furiously at the giant who had given the order, and with a yell drove it at his heart. I saw the spear snap, from which I concluded that this man, whom rightly I took to be Rezu, wore some kind of armour.

Next instant the axe he held, a great weapon, flashed aloft and down went Robertson before its awful stroke, stone dead, for as we found out afterwards, he was cloven almost in two. At the sight of the death of my poor friend rage took hold of me. In my hand was a double-barrelled rifle, an Express loaded with hollow-pointed bullets. I covered the giant and let drive, first with one barrel and then with the other, and what is more, distinctly I heard both bullets strike upon him.

Yet he did not fall. He rocked a little, that is all, then turned and marched off towards a hut, that whereof Hans had told me, which stood about fifty yards away.

"Leave him to me," shouted Umslopogaas. "Steel cuts where bullets cannot pierce," and with a bound like to that of a buck, the great Zulu leapt away after him.

I think that Rezu meant to enter the hut for some purpose of his own, but Umslopogaas was too hard upon his tracks. At any rate he ran past it and down the other slope of the little hill on to the plain behind where the remnants of his army were trying to re-form. There in front of them the giant turned and stood at bay.

Umslopogaas halted also, waiting for us to come up, since, cunning old warrior as he was, he feared lest should he begin the fight before that happened, the horde of them would fall on him. Thirty seconds later we arrived and found him standing still with bent body, small shield advanced and the great axe raised as though in the act of striking, a wondrous picture outlined as it was against the swiftly rising-sun.

Some ten paces away stood the giant leaning on the axe he bore, which was not unlike to that with which woodmen fell big trees. He was an evil man to see and at this, my first full sight of him, I likened him in my mind to Goliath whom David overthrew. Huge he was and hairy, with deep-set, piercing eyes and a great hooked nose. His face seemed thin and ancient also, when with a motion of the great head, he tossed his long locks back from about it, but his limbs were those of a Hercules and his movements full of a youthful vigour. Moreover his aspect as a whole was that of a devil rather than of a man; indeed the sight of it sickened me.

"Let me shoot him," I cried to Umslopogaas, for I had reloaded the rifle as I ran.

"Nay, Watcher-by-Night," answered the Zulu without moving his head, "rifle has had its chance and failed. Now let us see what axe can do. If I cannot kill this man, I will be borne hence feet first who shall have made a long journey for nothing."

Then the giant began to talk in a low, rumbling voice that reverberated from the slope of the little hill behind us.

"Who are you?" he asked, speaking in the same tongue that the Amahagger use, "who dare to come face to face with Rezu? Black hound, do you not know that I cannot be slain who have lived a year for every week of your life's days, and set my foot upon the necks of men by thousands. Have you not seen the spear shatter and the iron balls melt upon my breast like rain-drops, and would you try to bring me down with that toy you carry? My army is defeated—I know it. But what matters that when I can get me more? Because the sacrifice was not completed and the white queen was not wed, therefore my army was defeated by the magic of Lulala, the White Witch who dwells in the tombs. But I am not defeated who cannot be slain until I show my back, and then only by a certain axe which long ago has rusted into dust."

Now of this long speech Umslopogaas understood nothing, so I answered for him, briefly enough, but to the point, for there flashed into my mind all Ayesha's tale about an axe.

"A certain axe!" I cried. "Aye, a certain axe! Well, look at that which is held by the Black One, the captain who is named Slaughterer, the ancient axe whose title is Chieftainess, because if so she wills, she takes the lives of all. Look at it well, Rezu, Giant and Wizard, and say whether it is not that which your forefather lost, that which is destined to bring you to your doom?"

Thus I spoke, very loudly that all might hear, slowly also, pausing between each word because I wished to give time for the light to strengthen, seeing as I did that the rays of the rising sun struck upon the face of the giant, whereas the eyes of Umslopogaas were less dazzled by it.

Rezu heard, and stared at the axe which Umslopogaas held aloft, causing it to quiver slightly by an imperceptible motion of his arm. As he stared I saw his hideous face change, and that on it for the first time gathered a look of something resembling fear. Also his followers behind him who were also studying the axe, began to murmur together.

For here I should say that as though by common consent the battle had been stayed; we no longer attacked and the enemy no longer ran. They, or whose who were left of them, stood still as though they felt that the real and ultimate issue of the fight depended upon the forthcoming duel between these two champions, though of that issue they had little doubt since, as I learned afterwards, they believed their king to be invulnerable.

For quite a while Rezu went on staring. Then he said aloud as if he were thinking to himself.

"It is like, very like. The horn haft is the same; the pointed gouge is the same; the blade shaped like the young moon is the same. Almost could I think that before me shook the ancient holy axe. Nay, the gods have taken that back long ago and this is but a trick of the witch, Lulala of the Caves."

Thus he spoke, but still for a moment hesitated.

"Umslopogaas," I said in the deep silence that followed, "hear me."

"I hear you," he answered without turning his head or moving his arms. "What counsel, Watcher-by-Night?"

"This, Slaughterer. Strike not at that man's face and breast, for there I think he is protected by witchcraft or by armour. Get behind him and strike at his back. Do you understand?"

"Nay, Macumazahn, I understand not. Yet I will do your bidding because you are wiser than I and utter no empty words. Now be still."

Then Umslopogaas threw the axe into the air and caught it as it fell, and as he did so began to chant his own praises Zulu fashion.

"Oho!" he said, "I am the child of the Lion, the Black-maned Lion, whose claws never loosened of their prey. I am the Wolf-king, he who hunted with the wolves upon the Witch-mountain with my brother, Bearer of the Club named Watcher-of-the-Fords, I am he who slew him called the Unconquered, Chief of the People of the Axe, he who bore the ancient Axe before me; I am he who smote the Halakazi tribe in their caves and won me Nada the Lily to wife. I am he who took to the King Dingaan a gift that he loved little, and afterward with Mopo, my foster-sire, hurled this Dingaan down to death. I am the Royal One, named Bulalio the Slaughterer, named Woodpecker, named Umhlopekazi the Captain, before whom never yet man has stood in fair and open fight. Now, thou Wizard Rezu, now thou Giant, now thou Ghost-man, come on against me and before the sun has risen by a hand's breadth, all those who watch shall see which of us is better at the game of war. Come on, then! Come on, for I say that my blood boils over and my feet grow cold. Come on, thou grinning dog, thou monster grown fat with eating the flesh of men, thou hook-beaked vulture, thou old, grey-whiskered wolf!"

Thus he changed in his fierce, boastful way, while his two remaining Zulus clapped their hands and sentence by sentence echoed his words, and Goroko, the witch-doctor, muttered incantations behind him.

While he sang thus Umslopogaas began to stir. First only his head and shoulders moved gently, swaying from side to side like a reed shaken in the wind or a snake about to strike. Then slowly he put out first one foot and next the other and drew them back again, as a dancer might do, tempting Rezu to attack.

But the giant would not, his shield held before him, he stood still and waited to see what this black warrior would do.

The snake struck. Umslopogaas darted in and let drive with the long axe. Rezu raised his shield above his head and caught the blow. From the clank it made I knew that this shield which seemed to be of hide, was lined with iron. Rezu smote back, but before the blow could fall the Zulu was out of his reach. This taught me how great was the giant's strength, for though the stroke was heavy, like the steel-hatted axe he bore, still when he saw that it had missed he checked the weapon in mid air, which only a mighty man could have done.

Umslopogaas saw these things also and changed his tactics. His axe was six or eight inches longer in the haft than that of Rezu, and therefore he could reach where Rezu could not, for the giant was short-armed. He twisted it round in his hand so that the moon-shaped blade was uppermost, and keeping it almost at full length, began to peck with the gouge-shaped point on the back at the head and arms of Rezu, that as I knew was a favourite trick of his in fight from which he won his name of "Woodpecker." Rezu defended his head with his shield as best he could against the sharp points of steel which flashed all about him.

Twice it seemed to me that the Zulu's pecks went home upon the giant's breast, but if so they did no harm. Either Rezu's thick beard, or armour beneath it stopped them from penetrating his body. Still he roared out as though with pain, or fury, or both, and growing mad, charged at Umslopogaas and smote with all his strength.

The Zulu caught the blow upon his shield, through which it shore as though the tough hide were paper. Stay the stroke it could not, yet it turned its direction, so that the falling axe slid past Umslopogaas's shoulder, doing him no hurt. Next instant, before Rezu could strike again, the Zulu threw the severed shield into his face and seizing the axe with both hands, leapt in and struck. It was a mighty blow, for I saw the rhinoceros-horn handle of the famous axe bend like a drawn bow, and it went home with a dull thud full upon Rezu's breast. He shook, but no more. Evidently the razor edge of Inkosikaas had failed to pierce. There was a sound as though a hollow tree had been smitten and some strands of the long beard, shorn off, fell to the ground, but that was all.

"Tagati! (bewitched)," cried the watching Zulus. "That stroke should have cut him in two!" while I thought to myself that this man knew how to make good armour.

Rezu laughed aloud, a bellowing kind of laugh, while Umslopogaas sprang back astonished.

"Is it thus!" he cried in Zulu. "Well, all wizards have some door by which their Spirit enters and departs. I must find the door, I must find the door!"

So he spoke and with springing movements tried to get past Rezu, first to the right and then to the left, all the while keeping out of reach. But Rezu ever turned and faced him, as he did so retreating step by step down the slope of the little hill and striking whenever he found a chance, but without avail, for always Umslopogaas was beyond his reach. Also the sunlight which now grew strong, dazzled him, or so I thought. Moreover he seemed to tire somewhat—or so I thought also.

At any rate he determined to make an end of the play, for with a swift motion, as Umslopogaas had done, he threw away his shield and grasping the iron handle of his axe with both hands, charged the Zulu like a bull. Umslopogaas leapt back out of reach. Then suddenly he turned and ran up the rise. Yes, Bulalio the Slaughterer ran!

A roar of mockery went up from the sun-worshippers behind, while our Amahagger laughed and Goroko and the two Zulus stared astonished and ashamed. Only I read his mind aright and wondered what guile he had conceived.

He ran, and Rezu ran after him, but never could he catch the swiftest-footed man in Zululand. To and fro he followed him, for Umslopogaas was taking a zig-zag path towards the crest of the slope, till at length

Rezu stopped breathless. But Umslopogaas still ran another twenty yards or so until he reached the top of the slope and there halted and wheeled round.

For ten seconds or more he stood drawing his breath in great gasps, and, looking at his face, I saw that it had become as the face of a wolf. His lips were drawn up into a terrible grin, showing the white teeth between; his cheeks seemed to have fallen in and his eyes glared, while the skin over the hole in his forehead beat up and down.

There he stood, gathering himself together for some mighty effort.

"Run on!" shouted the spectators. "Run back to Kôr, black dog!"

Umslopogaas knew that they were mocking him, but he took no heed, only bent down and rubbed his sweating hand in the grit of the dry earth. Then he straightened himself and charged down on Rezu.

I, Allan Quatermain, have seen many things in battle, but never before or since did I see aught like to this charge. It was swift as that of a lioness, so swift that the Zulu's feet scarcely seemed to touch the ground. On he sped like a thrown spear, till, when within about a dozen feet of Rezu who stood staring at him, he bent his frame almost double and leapt into the air.

Oh! what a leap was that. Surely he must have learnt it from the lion, or the spring-buck. High he rose and now I saw his purpose; it was to clear the tall shape of Rezu. Aye, and he cleared him with half a foot to spare, and as he passed above, smote downwards with the axe so that the blow fell upon the back of Rezu's head. Moreover it went home this time, for I saw the red blood stream and Rezu fell forward on his face. Umslopogaas landed far beyond him, ran a little way because he must, then wheeled round and charged again.

Rezu was rising, but before he gained his feet, the axe Inkosikaas thundered down where the neck joins the shoulder and sank in. Still, so great was his strength that Rezu found his feet and smote out wildly. But now his movements were slow and again Umslopogaas got behind him, smiting at his back. Once, twice, thrice, he smote, and at the third blow it seemed as though the massive spine were severed, for his weapon fell from Rezu's hand and slowly he sank down to the ground, and lay there, a huddled heap.

Believing that all was over I ran to where he lay with Umslopogaas standing over him, as it seemed to me, utterly exhausted, for he supported himself by the axe and tottered upon his feet. But Rezu was not yet dead. He opened his cavernous eyes and glared at the Zulu with a look of hellish hate.

"Thou hast not conquered me, Black One," he gasped. "It is thine axe which gave thee victory; the ancient, holy axe that once was mine until the woman stole it, yes, that and the craft of the Witch of the Caves who told thee to smite where the Spirit of Life which I feared to enter wholly, had not kissed my flesh, and there only left me mortal. Wolf of a black man, may we meet elsewhere and fight this fray again. Ah! would that I could get these hands about thy throat and take thee with me down into the Darkness. But Lulala wins if only for a while, since her fate, I think, shall be worse than mine. Ah! I see the magic beauty that she boasts turn to shameful—"

Here of a sudden life left him and throwing his great arms wide, a last breath passed bubbling from his lips.

As I stooped to examine the man's huge and hairy carcase that to me looked only half human, with a thunder of feet our Amahagger rushed down upon us and thrusting me aside, fell upon the body of their ancient foe like hounds upon a helpless fox, and with hands and spears and knives literally tore and hacked it limb from limb, till no semblance of humanity remained.

It was impossible to stop them; indeed I was too outworn with labours and emotions to make any such attempt. This I regret the more since I lost the opportunity of making an examination of the body of this troll-like man, and of ascertaining what kind of armour it was he wore beneath that great beard of his, which was strong enough to stop my bullets, and even the razor edge of the axe Inkosikaas driven with all the might of the arms of the Zulu, Bulalio. For when I looked again at the sickening sight the giant was but scattered fragments and the armour, whatever it might have been, was gone, rent to little pieces and carried off, doubtless, by the Amahagger, perhaps to be divided between them to serve as charms.

So of Rezu I know only that he was the hugest, most terrible-looking man I have ever seen, one too who carried his vast strength very late in life, since from the aspect of his countenance I imagine that he must have been nigh upon seventy years of age, though his supposed unnatural antiquity of course was nothing but a fable put about by the natives for their own purposes.

Presently Umslopogaas seemed to recover from the kind of faint into which he had fallen and opening his eyes, looked about him. The first person they fell on was old Billali who stood stroking his white beard and contemplating the scene with an air which was at once philosophic and satisfied. This seemed to anger Umslopogaas, for he cried,

"I think it was you, ancient bag of words and sweeper of paths for the feet of the great, who made a mock of me but now, when you thought that I fled before the horns of yonder man-eating bull—" and he nodded towards the fragments of what once had been Rezu. "Find now his axe and though I am weak and weary, I will wash away the insult with your blood."

"What does this glorious black hero say, Watcher-by-Night?" asked Billali in his most courteous tones.

I told him word by word, whereon Billali lifted his hands in horror, turned and fled. Nor did I see him again until we arrived at Kôr.

At the sight of the fall of their giant chief Rezu whom they believed to be invulnerable, his followers, who were watching the fray, set up a great wailing, a most mournful and uncanny noise to hear. Then, as I think did the hosts of the Philistines when David brought down Goliath by his admirable shot with a stone, they set out for their homes wherever these may have been, at an absolutely record pace and in the completest disarray.

Our Amahagger followed them for a while, but soon were left standing still. So they contented themselves with killing any wounded they could find and returned. I did not accompany them; indeed the battle being won, metaphorically I washed my hands of them, and in my thoughts consigned them to a certain locality as a people of whom it might well be said that manners they had none and their customs were simply beastly. Also, although fierce and cruel, these night-bats were not good fighting men and in short never did I wish to have to do with such another company.

Moreover, a very different matter pressed. The object of this business so far as I was concerned, had been to rescue poor Inez, since had it not been for her sake, never would I have consented to lead those Amahagger against their fellow blackguards, the Rezuites.

But where was Inez? If Hans had understood the medicine-man aright, she was, or had been, in the hut, where it was my earnest hope that she still remained, since otherwise the hunt must be continued. This at any rate was easy to discover. Calling Hans, who was amusing himself by taking long shots at the flying enemy, so that they might not forget him, as he said, and the Zulus, I walked up the slope to the hut, or rather booth of boughs, for it was quite twenty feet long by twelve or fifteen broad.

At its eastern end was a doorway or opening closed with a heavy curtain. Here I paused full of tremors, and listened, for to tell the truth I dreaded to draw that curtain, fearing what I might see within. Gathering up my courage at length I tore it aside and, a revolver in my hand, looked in. At first after the strong light without, for the sun was now well up, I could see nothing, since those green boughs and palm leaves were very closely woven. As my eyes grew accustomed to the gloom, however, I perceived a glittering object seated on a kind of throne at the end of the booth, while in a double row in front knelt six white-robed women who seemed to wear chains about their necks and carried large knives slung round their middles. On the floor between these women and the throne lay a dead man, a priest of some sort as I gathered from his garb, who still held a huge spear in his hand. So silent were the figure on the throne and those that knelt before it, that at first I thought that all of them must be dead.

"Lady Sad-Eyes," whispered Hans, "and her bride-women. Doubtless that old Predikant came to kill her when he saw that the battle was lost, but the bride-women killed him with their knives."

Here I may state that Hans' suppositions proved to be quite correct, which shows how quick and deductive was his mind. The figure on the throne was Inez; the priest in his disappointed rage had come to kill her, and the bride-women had killed him with their knives before he could do so.

I bade the Zulus tear down the curtain and pull away some of the end boughs, so as to let in more light. Then we advanced up the place, holding our pistols and spears in readiness. The kneeling women turned their heads to look at us and I saw that they were all young and handsome in their fashion, although fierce-faced. Also I saw their hands go to the knives they wore. I called to them to let these be and come out, and that if they did so they had nothing to fear. But if they understood, they did not heed my words.

On the contrary while Hans and I covered them with our pistols, fearing lest they should stab the person on the throne whom we took to be Inez, at some word from one of them, they bowed simultaneously towards her, then at another word, suddenly they drew the knives and plunged them to their own hearts!

It was a dreadful sight and one of which I never saw the like. Nor to this day do I know why the deed was done, unless perhaps the women were sworn to the service of the new queen and feared that if they failed to protect her, they would be doomed to some awful end. At any rate we got them out dead or dying, for their blows had been strong and true, and not one of them lived for more than a few minutes.

Then I advanced to the figure on the throne, or rather foot-stooled chair of black wood inlaid with ivory, which sat so silent and motionless that I was certain it was that of a dead woman, especially when I perceived that she was fastened to the chair with leather straps, which were sewn over with gold wire.

Also she was veiled and, with one exception, made up, if I may use the term, exactly to resemble the lady Ayesha, even down to the two long plaits of black hair, each finished with some kind of pearl and to the sandalled feet.

The exception was that about her hung a great necklace of gold ornaments from which were suspended pendants also of gold representing the rayed disc of the sun in rude but bold and striking workmanship.

I went to her and having cut the straps, since I could not stop to untie their knots, lifted the veil.

Beneath it was Inez sure enough, and Inez living, for her breast rose and fell as she breathed, but Inez senseless. Her eyes were wide open, yet she was quite senseless. Probably she had been drugged, or perhaps some of the sights of horror which she saw, had taken away her mind. I confess that I was glad that this was so, who otherwise must have told her the dreadful story of her father's end.

We bore her out and away from that horrible place, apparently quite unhurt, and laid her under the shadow of a tree till a litter could be procured. I could do no more who knew not how to treat her state, and had no spirits with me to pour down her throat.

This was the end of our long pursuit, and thus we rescued Inez, whom the Zulus called the Lady Sad-Eyes.

CHAPTER XIX

THE SPELL

Of our return to Kôr I need say nothing, except that in due course we reached that interesting ruin. The journey was chiefly remarkable for one thing, that on this occasion, I imagine for the first and last time in his life, Umslopogaas consented to be carried in a litter, at least for part of the way. He was, as I have said, unwounded, for the axe of his mighty foe had never once so much as touched his skin. What he suffered from was shock, a kind of collapse, since, although few would have thought it, this great and utterly fearless warrior was at bottom a nervous, highly-strung man.

It is only the nervous that climb the highest points of anything, and this is true of fights as of all others. That fearful fray with Rezu had been a great strain on the Zulu. As he put it himself, "the wizard had sucked the strength" out of him, especially when he found that owing to his armour he could not harm him in front, and owing to his cunning could not get at him behind. Then it was that he conceived the desperate expedient of leaping over his head and smiting backwards as he leapt, a trick, he told me, that he had once played years before when he was young, in order to break a shield ring and reach one who stood in its centre.

In this great leap over Rezu's head Umslopogaas knew that he must succeed, or be slain, which in turn would mean my death and that of the others. For this reason he faced the shame of seeming to fly in order to gain the higher ground, whence alone he could gather the speed necessary to such a terrific spring.

Well, he made it and thereby conquered, and this was the end, but as he said, it had left him, "weak as a snake when it crawls out of its hole into the sun after the long winter sleep."

Of one thing, Umslopogaas added, he was thankful, namely that Rezu had never succeeded in getting his arms round him, since he was quite certain that if he had he would have broken him "as a baboon breaks a mealie-stalk." No strength, not even his, could have resisted the iron might of that huge, gorilla-like man.

I agreed with him who had noted Rezu's vast chest and swelling muscles, also the weight of the blows that he struck with the steel-hafted axe (which, by the way, when I sought for it, was missing, stolen, I suppose, by one of the Amahagger).

Whence did that strength come, I wondered, in one who from his face appeared to be old? Was there perchance, after all, some truth in the legend of Samson and did it dwell in that gigantic beard and those long locks of his? It was impossible to say and probably the man was but a Herculean freak, for that he was as strong as Hercules all the stories that I heard afterwards of his feats, left little room for doubt.

About one thing only was I certain in connection with him, namely, that the tales of his supernatural abilities were the merest humbug. He was simply one of the representatives of the family of "strong men," of whom examples are still to be seen doing marvellous feats all over the earth.

For the rest, he was dead and broken up by those Amahagger blood-hounds before I could examine him, or his body-armour either, and there was an end of him and his story. But when I looked at the corpse of poor Robertson, which I did as we buried it where he fell, and saw that though so large and thick-set, it was cleft almost in two by a single blow of Rezu's axe, I came to understand what the might of this savage must have been.

I say savage, but I am not sure that this is a right description of Rezu. Evidently he had a religion of a sort, also imagination, as was shown by the theft of the white woman to be his queen; by his veiling of her to resemble Ayesha whom he dreaded; by the intended propitiatory sacrifice; by the guard of women sworn to her service who slew the priest that tried to kill her, and afterwards committed suicide when they had failed in their office, and by other things. All this indicated something more than savagery, perhaps survivals from a forgotten civilisation, or perhaps native ability on the part of an individual ruler. I do not know and it matters nothing.

Rezu is dead and the world is well rid of him, and those who want to learn more of his people can go to study such as remain of them in their own habitat, which for my part I never wish to visit any more.

During our journey to Kôr poor Inez never stirred. Whenever I went to look at her in the litter, I found her lying there with her eyes open and a fixed stare upon her face which frightened me very much, since I began to fear lest she should die. However I could do nothing to help her, except urge the bearers to top speed. So swiftly did we travel down the hill and across the plain that we reached Kôr just as the sun was setting. As we crossed the moat I perceived old Billali coming to meet us. This he did with many bows, keeping an anxious eye upon the litter which he had learned contained Umslopogaas. Indeed his attitude and that of the Amahagger towards the two of us, and even Hans, thenceforward became almost abject, since after our victory over Rezu and his death beneath the axe, they looked upon us as half divine and treated us accordingly.

"O mighty General," he said, "She-who-commands bids me conduct the lady who is sick to the place that has been made ready for her, which is near your own so that you may watch over her if you will."

I wondered how Ayesha knew that Inez was sick, but being too tired to ask questions, merely bade him lead on. This he did, taking us to another ruined house next to our own quarters which had been swept, cleaned and furnished after a fashion, and moreover cleverly roofed in with mats, so that it was really quite comfortable. Here we found two middle-aged women of a very superior type, who, Billali informed me, were by trade nurses of the sick. Having seen her laid upon her bed, I committed Inez to their charge, since the case was not one that I dared to try to doctor myself, not knowing what drug of the few I possessed should be administered to her. Moreover Billali comforted me with the information that soon She-who-commands would visit her and "make her well again," as she could do.

I answered that I hoped so and went to our quarters where I found an excellent meal ready cooked and with it a stone flagon, of the contents of which Billali said we were all three to drink by the command of Ayesha, who declared that it would take away our weariness.

I tried the stuff, which was pale yellow in colour like sherry and, for aught I knew, might be poison, to find it most comforting, though it did not seem to be very strong to the taste. Certainly, too, its effects were wonderful, since presently all my great weariness fell from me like a discarded cloak, and I found myself with a splendid appetite and feeling better and stronger than I had done for years. In short that drink was a "cocktail" of the best, one of which I only wish I possessed the recipe, though Ayesha told me afterwards that it was distilled from quite harmless herbs and not in any sense a spirit.

Having discovered this, I gave some of it to Hans, also to Umslopogaas, who was with the wounded Zulus, who, we found, were progressing well towards complete recovery, and lastly to Goroko who also was worn out. On all of these the effect of that magical brew proved most satisfactory.

Then, having washed, I ate a splendid dinner, though in this respect Hans, who was seated on the ground nearby, far outpassed my finest efforts.

"Baas," he said, "things have gone very well with us when they might have gone very ill. The Baas Red-Beard is dead, which is a good thing, since a madman would have been difficult to look after, and a brain full of moonshine is a bad companion for any one. Oh! without doubt he is better dead, though your reverend father the Predikant will have a hard job looking after him there in the Place of Fires."

"Perhaps," I said with a sigh, "since it is better to be dead than to live a lunatic. But what I fear is that the lady his daughter will follow him."

"Oh, no! Baas," replied Hans cheerfully, "though I daresay that she will always be a little mad also, because you see it is in her blood and doubtless she has looked on dreadful things. But the Great Medicine will see to it that she does not die after we have taken so much trouble and gone into such big dangers to save her. That Great Medicine is very wonderful, Baas. First of all it makes you General over those Amahagger who without you would never have fought, as the Witch who ties up her head in a cloth knew well enough. Then it brings us safe through the battle and gives strength to Umslopogaas to kill the old man-eating giant."

"Why did it not give me strength to kill him, Hans? I let him have two Express bullets on his chest, which hurt him no more than a tap upon the horns with a dancing stick would hurt a bull-buffalo."

"Oh! Baas, perhaps you missed him, who because you hit things sometimes, think that you do so always."

Having waited to see if I would rise to this piece of insolence, which of course I did not, he went on by way of letting me down easily, "Or perhaps he wore very good armour under his beard, for I saw some of those Amahagger who pulled his hair off and cut him to pieces, go away with what looked like little bits of brass. Also the Great Medicine meant that he should be killed by Umslopogaas and not by you, since otherwise Umslopogaas would have been sad for the rest of his life, whereas now he will walk about the world as proud as a cock with two tails and crow all night as well as all day. Then, Baas, when Rezu broke the square and the Amahagger began to run, without doubt it was the Great Medicine which changed their hearts and made them brave again, so that they charged at the right moment when they saw it going forward on your breast, and instead of being eaten up, ate up the cannibals."

"Indeed! I thought that the Lady who dwells yonder had something to do with that business. Did you see her, Hans?"

"Oh, yes! I saw her, Baas, and I think that without doubt she lifted the cloth from over her head and when the people of Rezu saw how ugly was the face beneath, it did frighten them a little. But doubtless the Great Medicine put that thought into her also, for, Baas, what could a silly woman do in such a case? Did you ever know of a woman who was of any use in a battle, or for anything else except to nurse babies, and this one does not even do that, no doubt because being so hideous under that sheet, no man can be found to marry her."

Now I looked up by chance and in the light of the lamps saw Ayesha standing in the room, which she had entered through the open doorway, within six feet of Hans' back indeed.

"Be sure Baas," he went on, "that this bundle of rags is nothing but a common old cheat who frightens people by pretending to be a spook, as, if she dared to say that it was she who made those stinking Amahagger charge, and not the Great Medicine of the Opener-of-Roads, I would tell her to her face."

Now I was too paralysed to speak, and while I was reflecting that it was fortunate Ayesha did not understand Dutch, she moved a little so that one of the lamps behind her caused her shadow to fall on to the back of the squatting Hans and over it on to the floor beyond. He saw it and stared at the distorted shape of the hooded head, then slowly screwed his neck round and looked upwards behind him.

For a moment he went on staring as though he were frozen, then uttering a wild yell, he scrambled to his feet, bolted out of the house and vanished into the night.

"It seems, Allan," said Ayesha slowly, "that yonder yellow ape of yours is very bold at throwing sticks when the leopardess is not beneath the tree. But when she comes it is otherwise with him. Oh! make no excuse, for I know well that he was speaking ill things of me, because being curious, as apes are, he burns to learn what is behind my veil, and being simple, believes that no woman would hide her face unless its fashion were not pleasing to the nice taste of men."

Then, to my relief, she laughed a little, softly, which showed me that she had a sense of humour, and went on, "Well, let him be, for he is a good ape and courageous in his fashion, as he showed when he went out to spy upon the host of Rezu, and stabbed the murderer-priest by the stone of sacrifice."

"How can you know the words of Hans, Ayesha," I asked, "seeing that he spoke in a tongue which you have never learned?"

"Perchance I read faces, Allan."

"Or backs," I suggested, remembering that his was turned to her.

"Or backs, or voices, or hearts. It matters little which, since read I do. But have done with such childish talk and lead me to this maiden who has been snatched from the claws of Rezu and a fate that is worse than death. Do you understand, Allan, that ere the demon Rezu took her to wife, the plan was to sacrifice her own father to her and then eat him as the woman with her was eaten, and before her eyes? Now the father is dead, which is well, as I think the little yellow man said to you—nay, start not, I read it from his back [Ha!—JB]—since had he lived whose brain was rotted, he would have raved till his death's day. Better, therefore, that he should die like a man fighting against a foe unconquerable by all save one. But she still lives."

"Aye, but mindless, Ayesha."

"Which, in great trouble such as she has passed, is a blessed state, O Allan. Bethink you, have there not been days, aye and months, in your own life when you would have rejoiced to sleep in mindlessness? And should we not, perchance, be happier, all of us, if like the beasts we could not remember, foreknow and understand? Oh! men talk of Heaven, but believe me, the real Heaven is one of dreamless sleep, since life and wakefulness, however high their scale and on whatever star, mean struggle, which being so oft mistaken, must breed sorrow—or remorse that spoils all. Come now."

So I preceded her to the next ruined house where we found Inez lying on the bed still clothed in her barbaric trappings, although the veil had been drawn off her face. There she lay, wide-eyed and still, while the women watched her. Ayesha looked at her a while, then said to me,

"So they tricked her out to be Ayesha's mock and image, and in time accepted by those barbarians as my very self, and even set the seals of royalty on her," and she pointed to the gold discs stamped with the likeness of the sun. "Well, she is a fair maiden, white and gently bred, the first such that I have seen for many an age. Nor did she wish this trickery. Moreover she has taken no hurt; her soul has sunk deep into a sea of horror and that is all, whence doubtless it can be drawn again. Yet I think it best that for a while she should remember naught, lest her brain break, as did her father's, and therefore no net of mine shall drag her back to memory. Let that return gently in future days, and then of it not too much, for so shall all this terror become to her a void in which sad shapes move like shadows, and as shadows are soon forgot and gone, no more to be held than dreams by the awakening sense. Stand aside, Allan, and you women, leave us for a while."

I obeyed, and the women bowed and went. Then Ayesha drew up her veil, and knelt down by the bed of Inez, but in such a fashion that I could not see her face although I admit that I tried to do so. I could see, however, that she set her lips against those of Inez and as I gathered by her motions, seemed to breathe into her lips. Also she lifted her hands and placing one of them upon the heart of Inez, for a minute or more swayed the other from side to side above her eyes, pausing at times to touch her upon the forehead with her finger-tips.

Presently Inez stirred and sat up, whereon Ayesha took a vessel of milk which stood upon the floor and held it to her lips. Inez drank to the last drop, then sank on to the bed again. For a while longer Ayesha continued the motions of her hands, then let fall her veil and rose.

"Look, I have laid a spell upon her," she said, beckoning to me to draw near.

I did so and perceived that now the eyes of Inez were shut and that she seemed to be plunged in a deep and natural sleep.

"So she will remain for this night and that day which follows," said Ayesha, "and when she wakes it will be, I think, to believe herself once more a happy child. Not until she sees her home again will she find her womanhood, and then all this story will be forgotten by her. Of her father you must tell her that he died when you went out to hunt the river-beasts together, and if she seeks for certain others, that they have gone away. But I think that she will ask little more when she learns that he is dead, since I have laid that command upon her soul."

"Hypnotic suggestion," thought I to myself, "and I only hope to heaven that it will work."

Ayesha seemed to guess what was passing through my mind, for she nodded and said,

"Have no fear, Allan, for I am what the black axe-bearer and the little yellow man called a 'witch' which means, as you who are instructed know, one who has knowledge of medicine and other things and who holds a key to some of the mysteries that lie hid in Nature."

"For instance," I suggested, "of how to transport yourself into a battle at the right moment, and out of it again—also at the right moment."

"Yes, Allan, since watching from afar, I saw that those Amahagger curs were about to flee and that I was needed there to hearten them and to put fear into the army of Rezu. So I came."

"But how did you come, Ayesha?"

She laughed as she answered,

"Perhaps I did not come at all. Perhaps you only thought I came; since I seemed to be there the rest matters nothing."

As I still looked unconvinced she went on,

"Oh! foolish man, seek not to learn of that which is too high for you. Yet listen. You in your ignorance suppose that the soul dwells within the body, do you not?"

I answered that I had always been under this impression.

"Yet, Allan, it is otherwise, for the body dwells within the soul."

"Like the pearl in an oyster," I suggested.

"Aye, in a sense, since the pearl which to you is beautiful, is to the oyster a sickness and a poison, and so is the body to the soul whose temple it troubles and defiles. Yet round it is the white and holy soul that ever seeks to bring the vile body to its own purity and colour, yet oft-times fails. Learn, Allan, that flesh and spirit are the deadliest foes joined together by a high decree that they may forget their hate and perfect each other, or failing, be separate to all eternity, the spirit going to its own place and the flesh to its corruption."

"A strange theory," I said.

"Aye, Allan, and one which is so new to you that never will you understand it. Yet it is true and I set it out for this reason. The soul of man, being at liberty and not cooped within his narrow breast, is in touch with that soul of the Universe, which men know as God Whom they call by many names. Therefore it has all knowledge and perhaps all power, and at times the body within it, if it be a wise body, can draw from this well of knowledge and abounding power. So at least can I. And now you will understand why I am so good a doctoress and how I came to appear in the battle, as you said, at the right time, and to leave it when my work was done."

"Oh! yes," I answered, "I quite understand. I thank you much for putting it so plainly."

She laughed a little, appreciating my jest, looked at the sleeping Inez, and said,

"The fair body of this lady dwells in a large soul, I think, though one of a somewhat sombre hue, for souls have their colours, Allan, and stain that which is within them. She will never be a happy woman."

"The black people named her Sad-Eyes," I said.

"Is it so? Well, I name her Sad-Heart, though for such often there is joy at last. Meanwhile she will forget; yes, she will forget the worst and how narrow was the edge between her and the arms of Rezu."

"Just the width of the blade of the axe, Inkosikaas," I answered. "But tell me, Ayesha, why could not that axe cut and why did my bullets flatten or turn aside when these smote the breast of Rezu?"

"Because his front-armour was good, Allan, I suppose," she replied indifferently, "and on his back he wore none."

"Then why did you fill my ears with such a different tale about that horrible giant having drunk of a Cup of Life, and all the rest?" I asked with irritation.

"I have forgotten, Allan. Perhaps because the curious, such as you are, like to hear tales even stranger than their own, which in the days to be may become their own. Therefore you will be wise to believe only what I do, and of what I tell you, nothing."

"I don't," I exclaimed exasperated.

She laughed again and replied,

"What need to say to me that which I know already? Yet perhaps in the future it may be different, since often by the alchemy of the mind the fables of our youth are changed into the facts of our age, and we come to believe in anything, as your little yellow man believes in some savage named Zikali, and those Amahagger believe in the talisman round your neck, and I who am the maddest of you all, believe in Love and Wisdom, and the black warrior, Umslopogaas, believes in the virtue of that great axe of his, rather than in those of his own courage and of the strength that wields it. Fools, every one of us, though perchance I am the greatest fool among them. Now take me to the warrior, Umslopogaas, whom I would thank, as I thank you, Allan, and the little yellow man, although he jeers at me with his sharp tongue, not knowing that if I were angered, with a breath I could cause him to cease to be."

"Then why did you not choose Rezu to cease to be, and his army also, Ayesha?"

"It seems that I have done these things through the axe of Umslopogaas and by the help of your generalship, Allan. Why then, waste my own strength when yours lay to my hand?"

"Because you had no power over Rezu, Ayesha, or so you told me."

"Have I not said that my words are snowflakes, meant to melt and leave no trace, hiding my thoughts as this veil hides my beauty? Yet as the beauty is beneath the veil, perchance there is truth beneath the words, though not that truth you think. So you are well answered, and for the rest, I wonder whether Rezu thought I had no power over him when yonder on the mountain spur he saw me float down upon his companies like a spirit of the night. Well, perchance some day I shall learn this and many other things."

I made no answer, since what was the use of arguing with a woman who told me frankly that all she said was false. So, although I longed to ask her why these Amahagger had such reverence for the talisman that Hans called the Great Medicine, since now I guessed that her first explanations concerning it were quite untrue, I held my tongue.

Yet as we went out of the house, by some coincidence she alluded to this very matter.

"I wish to tell you, Allan," she said, "why it was those Amahagger would not accept you as a General till their eyes had seen that which you wear upon your breast. Their tale of a legend of this very thing seemed that of savages or of their cunning priests, not to be believed by a wise man such as you are, like some others that you have heard in Kôr. Yet it has in it a grain of truth, for as it chanced a little while ago, about a hundred years ago, I think, the old wizard whose picture is cut upon the wood, came to visit her who held my place before me as ruler of this tribe—she was very like me and as I believe, my mother, Allan—because of her repute for wisdom.

"At that time I have heard there was a question of war between the worshippers of Lulala and the grandfather of Rezu. But this Zikali told the People of Lulala that they must not fight the People of Rezu until in a day to come a white man should visit Kôr and bring with him a piece of wood on which was cut the image of a dwarf like to that of Zikali himself. Then and not before they must fight and conquer the People of Rezu. Now this story came down among them and you who may have thought the first tale magical, will understand it in its simplicity: is it not so, you wise Allan?"

"Oh! yes," I answered, "except that I do not see how Zikali can have come here a hundred years ago, since men do not live as long, although he pretends to have done so."

"No, Allan, nor do I, but perhaps it was his father, or his grandfather who came, since being observant, you will have noted that if the parent is mis-formed, so often are the descendants; also that the pretence of wizardry at times comes down with the blood."

Again I made no answer for I saw that Ayesha was fooling me, and before she could exhaust that amusement we reached the place where Umslopogaas and his men were gathered round a camp fire. He sat silent, but Goroko with much animation was telling the story of the fight in picturesque and colourful language, or that part of it which he had seen, for the benefit of the two wounded men who took no share in it and who, lying on their blankets with heads thrust forward, were listening with eagerness to the entrancing tale. Suddenly they caught sight of Ayesha, and those of the party who could stand sprang to their feet, while one and all they gave her the royal salute of Bayéte.

She waited till the sound had died away. Then she said,

"I come to thank you and your men, O Wielder of the Axe, who have shown yourself very great in battle, and to say to you that my Spirit tells me that every one of you, yes, even those who are still sick, will come safe to your own land again and live out your years with honour."

Again they saluted at this pleasing intelligence, when I had translated it to them, for of course they knew no Arabic. Then she went on,

"I am told, Umslopogaas, Son of the Lion, as a certain king was named in your land, that the fight you made against Rezu was a very great fight, and that such a leap as yours above his head when you smote him with the axe on the hinder parts where he wore no armour, and brought him to his death, has not been seen before, nor will be again."

I rendered the words, and Umslopogaas, preferring truth to modesty, replied emphatically that this was the case.

"Because of that fight and that leap," Ayesha went on, "as for other deeds that you have done and will do, my Spirit tells me that your name will live in story for many generations. Yet of what use is fame to the dead? Therefore I make you an offer. Bide here with me and you shall rule these Amahagger, and with them the remnant of the People of Rezu. Your cattle shall be countless and your wives the fairest in the land, and your children many, for I will lift a certain curse from off you so that no more shall you be childless. Do you accept, O Holder of the Axe?"

When he understood, Umslopogaas, after pondering a moment, asked if I meant to stay in this land and marry the white chieftainess who spoke such wise words and could appear and disappear in the battle at her will, and like a mountain-top hid her head in a cloud, which was his way of alluding to her veil.

I answered at once and with decision that I intended to do nothing of the sort and immediately regretted my words, since, although I spoke in Zulu, I suppose she read their meaning from my face. At any rate she understood the drift of them.

"Tell him, Allan," she said with a kind of icy politeness, "that you will not stop here and marry me, because if ever I chose a husband he would not be a little man at the doors of whose heart so many women's hands have knocked—yes, even those that are black—and not, I think, in vain. One, moreover, who holds himself so clever that he believes he has nothing left to learn, and in every flower of truth that is shown to him, however fair, smells only poison, and beneath, nurturing it, sees only the gross root of falsehood planted in corruption. Tell him these things, Allan, if it pleases you."

"It does not please me," I answered in a rage at her insults.

"Nor is it needful, Allan, since if I caught the meaning of that barbarous tongue you use aright, you have told him already. Well, let the jest pass, O man who least of all things desires to be Ayesha's husband, and whom Ayesha least of all things desires as her spouse, and ask the Axe-bearer nothing since I perceive that without you he will not stay at Kôr. Nor indeed is it fated that he should do so, for now my Spirit tells me what it hid from me when I spoke a moment gone, that this warrior shall die in a great fight far away and that between then and now much sorrow waits him who save that of one, knows not how to win the love of women. Let him say moreover what reward he desires since if I can give it to him, it shall be his."

Again I translated. Umslopogaas received her prophecies in stoical silence, and as I thought with indifference, and only said in reply,

"The glory that I have won is my reward and the only boon I seek at this queen's hands is that if she can she should give me sight of a woman for whom my heart is hungry, and with it knowledge that this woman lives in that land whither I travel like all men."

When she heard these words Ayesha said,

"True, I had forgotten. Your heart also is hungry, I think, Allan, for the vision of sundry faces that you see no more. Well, I will do my best, but since only faith fulfils itself, how can I who must strive to pierce the gates of darkness for one so unbelieving, know that they will open at my word? Come to me, both of you, at the sunset to-morrow."

Then as though to change the subject, she talked to me for a long while about Kôr, of which she told me a most interesting history, true or false, that I omit here.

At length, as though suddenly she had grown tired, waving her hand to show that the conversation was ended, Ayesha went to the wounded men and touched them each in turn.

"Now they will recover swiftly," she said, and leaving the place was gone into the darkness.

CHAPTER XX

THE GATE OF DEATH

Before turning in I examined these wounded men for myself. The truth is that I was anxious to learn their exact condition in order that I might make an estimate as to when it would be possible for us to leave this valley or crater bottom of Kôr, of which I was heartily tired. Who could desire to stay in a place where he had not only been involved in a deal of hard, doubtful, and very dangerous fighting from which all personal interest was absent, but where also he was meshed in a perfect spider's web of bewilderment, and exposed to continual insult into the bargain?

For that is what it came to; this Ayesha took every opportunity to jeer at and affront me. And why? Just because I had conceived doubts, which somehow she discovered, of the amazing tales with which it had amused her to stuff me, as a farmer's wife does a turkey poult with meal pellets. How could she expect me, a man, after all, of some experience, to believe such lies, which, not half an hour before, in the coolest possible fashion she had herself admitted to be lies and nothing else, told for the mere pleasure of romancing?

The immortal Rezu, for instance, who had drunk of the Cup of Life or some such rubbish, now turned out to be nothing but a brawny savage descended from generations of chiefs also called Rezu. Moreover the immemorial Ayesha, who also had drunk of Cups of Life, and according to her first story, had lived in this place for thousands of years, had come here with a mother, who filled the same mystic rôle before her for the benefit of an extremely gloomy and disagreeable tribe of Semitic savages. Yet she was cross with me because I had not swallowed her crude and indigestible mixture of fable and philosophy without a moment's question.

At least I supposed that this was the reason, though another possible explanation did come into my mind. I had refused to be duly overcome by her charms, not because I was unimpressed, for who could be, having looked upon that blinding beauty even for a moment? but rather because, after sundry experiences, I had at last attained to some power of judgment and learned what it is best to leave alone. Perhaps this had annoyed her, especially as no white man seemed to have come her way for a long while and the fabulous Kallikrates had not put in his promised appearance.

Also it was unfortunate that in one way or another—how did she do it, I wondered—she had interpreted Umslopogaas' question to me about marrying her, and my compromising reply. Not that for one moment, as I saw very clearly, did she wish to marry me. But that fact, intuition suggested to my mind, did not the least prevent her from being angry because I shared her views upon this important subject.

Oh! the whole thing was a bore and the sooner I saw the last of that veiled lady and the interesting but wearisome ruins in which she dwelt, the better I should be pleased, although apparently I must trek homewards with a poor young woman who was out of her mind, leaving the bones of her unfortunate father behind me. I admitted to myself, however, that there were consolations in the fact that Providence had thus decreed, for Robertson since he gave up drink had not been a cheerful companion, and two mad people would really have been more than I could manage.

To return, for these reasons I examined the two wounded Zulus with considerable anxiety, only to discover another instance of the chicanery which it amused this Ayesha to play off upon me. For what did I find? That they were practically well. Their hurts, which had never been serious, had healed wonderfully in that pure air, as those of savages have a way of doing, and they told me themselves that they felt quite strong again. Yet with colossal impudence Ayesha had managed to suggest to my mind that she was going to work some remarkable cure upon them, who were already cured.

Well, it was of a piece with the rest of her conduct and there was nothing to do except go to bed, which I did with much gratitude that my resting place that night was not of another sort. The last thing I remember was wondering how on earth Ayesha appeared and disappeared in the course of that battle, a problem as to which I could find no solution, though, as in the case of the others, I was sure that one would occur to me in course of time.

I slept like a top, so soundly indeed that I think there was some kind of soporific in the pick-me-up which looked like sherry, especially as the others who had drunk of it also passed an excellent night.

About ten o'clock on the following morning I awoke feeling particularly well and quite as though I had been enjoying a week at the seaside instead of my recent adventures, which included an abominable battle and some agonising moments during which I thought that my number was up upon the board of Destiny.

I spent the most of that day lounging about, eating, talking over the details of the battle with Umslopogaas and the Zulus and smoking more than usual. (I forgot to say that these Amahagger grew some capital tobacco of which I had obtained a supply, although like most Africans, they only used it in the shape of snuff.) The truth was that after all my marvellings and acute anxieties, also mental and physical exertions, I felt like the housemaid who caused to be cut upon her tombstone that she had gone to a better land where her ambition was to do nothing "for ever and ever." I just wanted to be completely idle and vacuous-minded for at least a month, but as I knew that all I could expect in that line was a single bank holiday, like a City clerk on the spree, of it I determined to make the most.

The result was that before the evening I felt very bored indeed. I had gone to look at Inez, who was still fast asleep, as Ayesha said would be the case, but whose features seemed to have plumped up considerably. The reason of this I gathered from her Amahagger nurses, was that at certain intervals she had awakened sufficiently to swallow considerable quantities of milk, or rather cream, which I hoped would not make her ill. I had chatted with the wounded Zulus, who were now walking about, more bored even than I was myself, and heaping maledictions on their ancestral spirits because they had not been well enough to take part in the battle against Rezu.

I even took a little stroll to look for Hans, who had vanished in his mysterious fashion, but the afternoon was so hot and oppressive with coming thunder, that soon I came back again and fell into a variety of reflections that I need not detail.

While I was thus engaged and meditating, not without uneasiness, upon the ordeal that lay before me after sunset, for I felt sure that it would be an ordeal, Hans appeared and said that the Amahagger impi or army was gathered on that spot where I had been elected to the proud position of their General. He added that he believed—how he got this information I do not know—that the White Lady was going to hold a review of them and give them the rewards that they had earned in the battle.

Hearing this, Umslopogaas and the other Zulus said that they would like to see this review if I would accompany them. Although I did not want to go nor indeed desired ever to look at another Amahagger, I consented to save the trouble of argument, on condition that we should do so from a distance.

So, including the wounded men, we strolled off and presently came to the crumbled wall of the old city, beyond which lay the great moat now dry, that once had encircled it with water.

Here on the top of this wall we sat down where we could see without being seen, and observed the Amahagger companies, considerably reduced during the battle, being marshalled by their captains beneath us and about a couple of hundred yards away. Also we observed several groups of men under guard. These we took to be prisoners captured in the fight with Rezu, who, as Hans remarked with a smack of his lips, were probably awaiting sacrifice.

I said I hoped not and yawned, for really the afternoon was intensely hot and the weather most peculiar. The sun had vanished behind clouds, and vapours filled the still air, so dense that at times it grew almost dark; also when these cleared for brief intervals, the landscape in the grey, unholy light looked distorted and unnatural, as it does during an eclipse of the sun.

Goroko, the witch-doctor, stared round him, sniffed the air and then remarked ocularly that it was "wizard's weather" and that there were many spirits about. Upon my word I felt inclined to agree with him, for my feelings were very uncomfortable, but I only replied that if so, I should be obliged if he, as a professional, would be good enough to keep them off me. Of course I knew that electrical charges were about, which accounted for my sensations, and wished that I had never left the camp.

It was during one of these periods of dense gloom that Ayesha must have arrived upon the review ground. At least, when it lifted, there she was in her white garments, surrounded by women and guards, engaged apparently in making an oration, for although I could not hear a word, I could see by the motions of her arms that she was speaking.

Had she been the central figure in some stage scene, no limelights could have set her off to better advantage, than did those of the heavens above her. Suddenly, through the blanket of cloud, flowing from a hole in it that looked like an eye, came a blood-red ray which fell full upon her, so that she alone was fiercely visible whilst all around was gloom in which shapes moved dimly. Certainly she looked strange and even terrifying in that red ray which stained her robe till I who had but just come out of battle with its "confused noise," began to think of "the garments rolled in blood" of which I often read in my favourite Old Testament. For crimson was she from head to foot; a tall shape of terror and of wrath.

The eye in heaven shut and the ray went out. Then came one of the spaces of grey light and in it I saw men being brought up, apparently from the groups of prisoners, under guard, and, to the number of a dozen or more, stood in a line before Ayesha.

Then I saw nothing more for a long while, because blackness seemed to flow in from every quarter of the heavens and to block out the scene beneath. At least after a pause of perhaps five minutes, during which the stillness was intense, the storm broke.

It was a very curious storm; in all my experience of African tempests I cannot recall one which it resembled. It began with the usual cold and wailing wind. This died away, and suddenly the whole arch of heaven was alive with little lightnings that seemed to strike horizontally, not downwards to the earth, weaving a web of fire upon the surface of the sky.

By the illumination of these lightnings which, but for the swiftness of their flashing and greater intensity, somewhat resembled a dense shower of shooting stars, I perceived that Ayesha was addressing the men that had been brought before her, who stood dejectedly in a long line with their heads bent, quite unattended, since their guards had fallen back.

"If I were going to receive a reward of cattle or wives, I should look happier than those moon-worshippers, Baas," remarked Hans reflectively.

"Perhaps it would depend," I answered, "upon what the cattle and wives were like. If the cattle had red-water and would bring disease into your herd, or wild bulls that would gore you, and the wives were skinny old widows with evil tongues, then I think you would look as do those men, Hans."

I don't quite know what made me speak thus, but I believe it was some sense of pending death or disaster, suggested, probably, by the ominous character of the setting provided by Nature to the curious drama of which we were witnesses.

"I never thought of that, Baas," commented Hans, "but it is true that all gifts are not good, especially witches' gifts."

As he spoke the little net-like lightnings died away, leaving behind them a gross darkness through which, far above us, the wind wailed again.

Then suddenly all the heaven was turned into one blaze of light, and by it I saw Ayesha standing tall and rigid with her hand pointed towards the line of men in front of her. The blaze went out, to be followed by blackness, and to return almost instantly in a yet fiercer blaze which seemed to fall earthwards in a torrent of fire that concentrated itself in a kind of flame-spout upon the spot where Ayesha stood.

Through that flame or rather in the heart of it, I saw Ayesha and the file of men in front of her, as the great King saw the prophets in the midst of the furnace that had been heated sevenfold. Only these men did not walk about in the fire; no, they fell backwards, while Ayesha alone remained upon her feet with outstretched hand.

Next came more blackness and crash upon crash of such thunder that the earth shook as it reverberated from the mountain cliffs. Never in my life did I hear such fearful thunder. It frightened the Zulus so much, that they fell upon their faces, except Goroko and Umslopogaas, whose pride kept them upon their feet, the former because he had a reputation to preserve as a "Heaven-herd," or Master of tempests.

I confess that I should have liked to follow their example, and lie down, being dreadfully afraid lest the lightning should strike me. But there—I did not.

At last the thunder died away and in the most mysterious fashion that violent tempest came to a sudden end, as does a storm upon the stage. No rain fell, which in itself was surprising enough and most unusual, but in place of it a garment of the completest calm descended upon the earth. By degrees, too, the darkness passed and the westering sun reappeared. Its rays fell upon the place where the Amahagger companies had stood, but now not one of them was to be seen.

They were all gone and Ayesha with them. So completely had they vanished away that I should have thought that we suffered from illusions, were it not for the line of dead men which lay there looking very small and lonesome on the veld; mere dots indeed at that distance.

We stared at each other and at them, and then Goroko said that he would like to inspect the bodies to learn whether lightning killed at Kôr as it did elsewhere, also whether it had smitten them altogether or leapt from man to man. This, as a professional "Heaven-herd," he declared he could tell from the marks upon these unfortunates.

As I was curious also and wanted to make a few observations, I consented. So with the exception of the wounded men, who I thought should avoid the exertion, we scrambled down the débris of the tumbled wall and across the open space beyond, reaching the scene of the tragedy without meeting or seeing anyone.

There lay the dead, eleven of them, in an exact line as they had stood. They were all upon their backs with widely-opened eyes and an expression of great fear frozen upon their faces. Some of these I recognised, as did Umslopogaas and Hans. They were soldiers or captains who had marched under me to attack Rezu, although until this moment I had not seen any of them after we began to descend the ridge where the battle took place.

"Baas," said Hans, "I believe that these were the traitors who slipped away and told Rezu of our plans so that he attacked us on the ridge, instead of our attacking him on the plain as we had arranged so nicely. At least they were none of them in the battle and afterwards I heard the Amahagger talking of some of them."

I remarked that if so the lightning had discriminated very well in this instance.

Meanwhile Goroko was examining the bodies one by one, and presently called out,

"These doomed ones died not by lightning but by witchcraft. There is not a burn upon one of them, nor are their garments scorched."

I went to look and found that it was perfectly true; to all outward appearance the eleven were quite unmarked and unharmed. Except for their frightened air, they might have died a natural death in their sleep.

"Does lightning always scorch?" I asked Goroko.

"Always, Macumazahn," he answered, "that is, if he who has been struck is killed, as these are, and not only stunned. Moreover, most of yonder dead wear knives which should have melted or shattered with the sheaths burnt off them. Yet those knives are as though they had just left the smith's hammer and the whet-stone," and he drew some of them to show me.

Again it was quite true and here I may remark that my experience tallied with that of Goroko, since I have never seen anyone killed by lightning on whom or on whose clothing there was not some trace of its passage.

"Ow!" said Umslopogaas, "this is witchcraft, not Heaven-wrath. The place is enchanted. Let us get away lest we be smitten also who have not earned doom like those traitors."

"No need to fear," said Hans, "since with us is the Great Medicine of Zikali which can tie up the lightning as an old woman does a bundle of sticks."

Still I observed that for all his confidence, Hans himself was the first to depart and with considerable speed. So we went back to our camp without more conversation, since the Zulus were scared and I confess that myself I could not understand the matter, though no doubt it admitted of some quite simple explanation.

However that might be, this Kôr was a queer place with its legends, its sullen Amahagger and its mysterious queen, to whom at times, in spite of my inner conviction to the contrary, I was still inclined to attribute powers beyond those that are common even among very beautiful and able women.

This reflection reminded me that she had promised us a further exhibition of those powers and within an hour or two. Remembering this I began to regret that I had ever asked for any such manifestations, for who knew what these might or might not involve?

So much did I regret it that I determined, unless Ayesha sent for us, as she had said she would do, I would conveniently forget the appointment. Luckily Umslopogaas seemed to be of the same way of thinking; at any rate he went off to eat his evening meal without alluding to it at all. So I made up my mind that I would not bring the matter to his notice and having ascertained that Inez was still asleep, I followed his example and dined myself, though without any particular appetite.

As I finished the sun was setting in a perfectly clear sky, so as there was no sign of any messenger, I thought that I would go to bed early, leaving orders that I was not to be disturbed. But on this point my luck was lacking, for just as I had taken off my coat, Hans arrived and said that old Billali was without and had come to take me somewhere.

Well, there was nothing to do but to put it on again. Before I had finished this operation Billali himself arrived with undignified and unusual haste. I asked him what was the matter, and he answered inconsequently that the Black One, the slayer of Rezu, was at the door "with his axe."

"That generally accompanies him," I replied. Then, remembering the cause of Billali's alarm, I explained to him that he must not take too much notice of a few hasty words spoken by an essentially gentle-natured person whose nerve had given way beneath provocation and bodily effort. The old fellow bowed in assent and stroked his beard, but I noticed that while Umslopogaas was near, he clung to me like a shadow. Perhaps he thought that nervous attacks might be recurrent, like those of fever.

Outside the house I found Umslopogaas leaning on his axe and looking at the sky in which the last red rays of evening lingered.

"The sun has set, Macumazahn," he said, "and it is time to visit this white queen as she bade us, and to learn whether she can indeed lead us 'down below' where the dead are said to dwell."

So he had not forgotten, which was disconcerting. To cover up my own doubts I asked him with affected confidence and cheerfulness whether he was not afraid to risk this journey "down below," that is, to the Realm of Death.

"Why should I fear to tread a road that awaits the feet of all of us and at the gate of which we knock day by day, especially if we chance to live by war, as do you and I, Macumazahn?" he inquired with a quiet dignity, which made me feel ashamed.

"Why indeed?" I answered, adding to myself, "though I should much prefer any other highway."

After this we started without more words, I keeping up my spirits by reflecting that the whole business was nonsense and that there could be nothing to dread.

All too soon we passed the ruined archway and were admitted into Ayesha's presence in the usual fashion. As Billali, who remained outside of them, drew the curtains behind us, I observed, to my astonishment, that Hans had sneaked in after me, and squatted down quite close to them, apparently in the hope of being overlooked.

It seemed, as I gathered later, that somehow or other he had guessed, or become aware of the object of our visit, and that his burning curiosity had overcome his terror of the "White Witch." Or possibly he hoped to discover whether or not she were so ugly as he supposed her veil-hidden face to be. At any rate there he was, and if Ayesha noticed him, as I think she did, for I saw by the motion of her head, that she was looking in his direction, she made no remark.

For a while she sat still in her chair contemplating us both. Then she said,

"How comes it that you are late? Those that seek their lost loves should run with eager feet, but yours have tarried."

I muttered some excuse to which she did not trouble to listen, for she went on,

"I think, Allan, that your sandals, which should be winged like to those of the Roman Mercury, are weighted with the grey lead of fear. Well, it is not strange, since you have come to travel through the Gates of Death that are feared by all, even by Ayesha's self, for who knows what he may find beyond them? Ask the Axe-Bearer if he also is afraid."

I obeyed, rendering all that she had said into the Zulu idiom as best I could.

"Say to the Queen," answered Umslopogaas, when he understood, "that I fear nothing, except women's tongues. I am ready to pass the Gates of Death and, if need be, to come back no more. With the white people I know it is otherwise because of some dark teachings to which they listen, that tell of terrors to be, such as we who are black do not dread. Still, we believe that there are ghosts and that the spirits of our fathers live on and as it chances I would learn whether this is so, who above all things desire to met a certain ghost, for which reason I journeyed to this far land.

"Say these things to the white Queen, Macumazahn, and tell her that if she should send me to a place whence there is no return, I who do not love the world, shall not blame her overmuch, though it is true that I should have chosen to die in war. Now I have spoken."

When I had passed on all this speech to Ayesha, her comment on it was,

"This black Captain has a spirit as brave as his body, but how is it with your spirit, Allan? Are you also prepared to risk so much? Learn that I can promise you nothing, save that when I loose the bonds of your mortality and send out your soul to wander in the depths of Death, as I believe that I can do, though even of this I am not certain—you must pass through a gate of terrors that may be closed behind you by a stronger arm than mine. Moreover, what you will find beyond it I do not know, since be sure of this, each of us has his own heaven or his own hell, or both, that soon or late he is doomed to travel. Now will you go forward, or go back? Make choice while there is still time."

At all this ominous talk I felt my heart shrivel like a fire-withered leaf, if I may use that figure, and my blood assume the temperature and consistency of ice-cream. Earnestly did I curse myself for having allowed my curiosity about matters which we are not meant to understand to bring me to the edge of such a choice. Swiftly I determined to temporise, which I did by asking Ayesha whether she would accompany me upon this eerie expedition.

She laughed a little as she answered,

"Bethink you, Allan. Am I, whose face you have seen, a meet companion for a man who desires to visit the loves that once were his? What would they say or think, if they should see you hand in hand with such a one?"

"I don't know and don't care," I replied desperately, "but this is the kind of journey on which one requires a guide who knows the road. Cannot Umslopogaas go first and come back to tell me how it has fared with him?"

"If the brave and instructed white lord, panoplied in the world's last Faith, is not ashamed to throw the savage in his ignorance out like a feather to test the winds of hell and watch the while to learn whether these blow him back unscorched, or waft him into fires whence there is no return, perchance it might so be ordered, Allan. Ask him yourself, Allan, if he is willing to run this errand for your sake. Or perhaps the little yellow man—" and she paused.

At this point Hans, who having a smattering of Arabic understood something of our talk, could contain himself no longer.

"No, Baas," he broke in from his corner by the curtain, "not me. I don't care for hunting spooks, Baas, which leave no spoor that you can follow and are always behind when you think they are in front. Also there are too many of them waiting for me down there and how can I stand up to them until I am a spook myself and know their ways of fighting? Also if you should die when your spirit is away, I want to be left that I may bury you nicely."

"Be silent," I said in my sternest manner. Then, unable to bear more of Ayesha's mockery, for I felt that as usual she was mocking me, I added with all the dignity that I could command,

"I am ready to make this journey through the gate of Death, Ayesha, if indeed you can show me the road. For one purpose and no other I came to Kôr, namely to learn, if so I might, whether those who have died upon the world, live on elsewhere. Now, what must I do?"

CHAPTER XXI

THE LESSON

"Yes," answered Ayesha, laughing very softly, "for that purpose alone, O truth-seeking Allan, whose curiosity is so fierce that the wide world cannot hold it, did you come to Kôr and not to seek wealth or new lands, or to fight more savages. No, not even to look upon a certain Ayesha, of whom the old wizard told you, though I think you have always loved to try to lift the veil that hides women's hearts, if not their faces. Yet it was I who brought you to Kôr for my own purposes, not your desire, nor Zikali's map and talisman, since had not the white lady who lies sick been stolen by Rezu, never would you have pursued the journey nor found the way hither."

"How could you have had anything to do with that business?" I asked testily, for my nerves were on edge and I said the first thing that came into my mind.

"That, Allan, is a question over which you will wonder for a long while either beneath or beyond the sun, as you will wonder concerning much that has to do with me, which your little mind, shut in its iron box of ignorance and pride, cannot understand to-day.

"For example, you have been wondering, I am sure, how the lightning killed those eleven men whose bodies you went to look on an hour or two ago, and left the rest untouched. Well, I will tell you at once that it was not lightning that killed them, although the strength within me was manifest to you in storm, but rather what that witch-doctor of your following called wizardry. Because they were traitors who betrayed your army to Rezu, I killed them with my wrath and by the wand of my power. Oh! you do not believe, yet perhaps ere long you will, since thus to fulfil your prayer I must also kill you—almost. That is the trouble, Allan. To kill you outright would be easy, but to kill you just enough to set your spirit free and yet leave one crevice of mortal life through which it can creep back again, that is most difficult; a thing that only I can do and even of myself I am not sure."

"Pray do not try the experiment—" I began thoroughly alarmed, but she cut me short.

"Disturb me no more, Allan, with the tremors and changes of your uncertain mind, lest you should work more evil than you think, and making mine uncertain also, spoil my skill. Nay, do not try to fly, for already the net has thrown itself about you and you cannot stir, who are bound like a little gilded wasp in the spider's web, or like birds beneath the eyes of basilisks."

This was true, for I found that, strive as I would, I could not move a limb or even an eyelid. I was frozen to that spot and there was nothing for it except to curse my folly and say my prayers.

All this while she went on talking, but of what she said I have not the faintest idea, because my remaining wits were absorbed in these much-needed implorations.

Presently, of a sudden, I appeared to see Ayesha seated in a temple, for there were columns about her, and behind her was an altar on which a fire burned. All round her, too, were hooded snakes like to that which she wore about her middle, fashioned in gold. To these snakes she sang and they danced to her singing; yes, with flickering tongues they danced upon their tails! What the scene signified I cannot conceive, unless it meant that this mistress of magic was consulting her familiars.

Then that vision vanished and Ayesha's voice began to seem very far away and dreamy, also her wondrous beauty became visible to me through her veil, as though I had acquired a new sense that overcame the limitations of mortal sight. Even in this extremity I reflected it was well that the last thing I looked on should be something so glorious. No, not quite the last thing, for out of the corners of my eyes I saw that Umslopogaas from a sitting position had sunk on to his back and lay, apparently dead, with his axe still gripped tightly and held above his head, as though his arm had been turned to ice.

After this terrible things began to happen to me and I became aware that I was dying. A great wind seemed to catch me up and blow me to and fro, as a leaf is blown in the eddies of a winter gale. Enormous rushes of darkness flowed over me, to be succeeded by vivid bursts of brightness that dazzled like lightning. I fell off precipices and at the foot of them was caught by some fearful strength and tossed to the very skies.

From those skies I was hurled down again into a kind of whirlpool of inky night, round which I spun perpetually, as it seemed for hours and hours. But worst of all was the awful loneliness from which I suffered. It seemed to me as though there were no other living thing in all the Universe and never had been and never would be any other living thing. I felt as though I were the Universe rushing solitary through space for ages upon ages in a frantic search for fellowship, and finding none.

Then something seemed to grip my throat and I knew that I had died—for the world floated away from beneath me.

Now fear and every mortal sensation left me, to be replaced by a new and spiritual terror. I, or rather my disembodied consciousness, seemed to come up for judgment, and the horror of it was that I appeared to be my own judge. There, a very embodiment of cold justice, my Spirit, grown luminous, sat upon a throne and to it, with dread and merciless particularity I set out all my misdeeds. It was as if some part of me remained mortal, for I could see my two eyes, my mouth and my hands, but nothing else—and strange enough they looked. From the eyes came tears, from the mouth flowed words and the hands were joined, as though in prayer to that throned and adamantine Spirit which was ME.

It was as though this Spirit were asking how my body had served its purposes and advanced its mighty ends, and in reply—oh! what a miserable tale I had to tell. Fault upon fault, weakness upon weakness, sin upon sin; never before did I understand how black was my record. I tried to relieve the picture with some incidents of attempted good, but that Spirit would not hearken. It seemed to say that it had gathered up the good and knew it all. It was of the evil that it would learn, not of the good that had bettered it, but of the evil by which it had been harmed.

Hearing this there rose up in my consciousness some memory of what Ayesha had said; namely, that the body lived within the temple of the spirit which is oft defied, and not the spirit in the body.

The story was told and I hearkened for the judgment, my own judgment on myself, which I knew would be accepted without question and registered for good or ill. But none came, since ere the balance sank this way or that, ere it could be uttered, I was swept afar.

Through Infinity I was swept, and as I fled faster than the light, the meaning of what I had seen came home to me. I knew, or seemed to know for the first time, that at the last man must answer to himself, or perhaps to a divine principle within himself, that out of his own free-will, through long æons and by a million steps, he climbs or sinks to the heights or depths dormant in his nature; that from what he was, springs what he is, and what he is, engenders what he shall be for ever and aye.

Now I envisaged Immortality and splendid and awful was its face. It clasped me to its breast and in the vast circle of its arms I was up-borne, I who knew myself to be without beginning and without end, and yet of the past and of the future knew nothing, save that these were full of mysteries.

As I went I encountered others, or overtook them, making the same journey. Robertson swept past me, and spoke, but in a tongue I could not understand. I noted that the madness had left his eyes and that his fine-cut features were calm and spiritual. The other wanderers I did not know.

I came to a region of blinding light; the thought rose in me that I must have reached the sun, or a sun, though I felt no heat. I stood in a lovely, shining valley about which burned mountains of fire. There were huge trees in that valley, but they glowed like gold and their flowers and fruit were as though they had been fashioned of many-coloured flames.

The place was glorious beyond compare, but very strange to me and not to be described. I sat me down upon a boulder which burned like a ruby, whether with heat or colour I do not know, by the edge of a stream that flowed with what looked like fire and made a lovely music. I stooped down and drank of this water of flames and the scent and the taste of it were as those of the costliest wine.

There, beneath the spreading limbs of a fire-tree I sat, and examined the strange flowers that grew around, coloured like rich jewels and perfumed above imagining. There were birds also which might have been feathered with sapphires, rubies and amethysts, and their song was so sweet that I could have wept to hear it. The scene was wonderful and filled me with exaltation, for I thought of the land where it is promised that there shall be no more night.

People began to appear; men, women, and even children, though whence they came I could not see. They did not fly and they did not walk; they seemed to drift towards me, as unguided boats drift upon the tide. One and all they were very beautiful, but their beauty was not human although their shapes and faces resembled those of men and women made glorious. None were old, and except the children, none seemed very young; it was as though they had grown backwards or forwards to middle life and rested there at their very best.

Now came the marvel; all these uncounted people were known to me, though so far as my knowledge went I had never set eyes on most of them before. Yet I was aware that in some forgotten life or epoch I had been intimate with every one of them; also that it was the fact of my presence and the call of my sub-conscious mind which drew them to this spot. Yet that presence and that call were not visible or audible to them, who, I suppose, flowed down some stream of sympathy, why or whither they did not know. Had I been as they were perchance they would have seen me, as it was they saw nothing and I could not speak and tell them of my presence.

Some of this multitude, however, I knew well enough even when they had departed years and years ago. But about these I noted this, that every one of them was a man or a woman or a child for whom I had felt love or sympathy or friendship. Not one was a person whom I had disliked or whom I had no wish to see again. If they spoke at all I could not hear—or read—their speech, yet to a certain extent I could hear their thoughts.

Many of these were beyond the power of my appreciation on subjects which I had no knowledge, or that were too high for me, but some were of quite simple things such as concern us upon the earth, such as of friendship, or learning, or journeys made or to be made, or art, or literature, or the wonders of Nature, or of the fruits of the earth, as they knew them in this region.

This I noted too, that each separate thought seemed to be hallowed and enclosed in an atmosphere of prayer or heavenly aspiration, as a seed is enclosed in the heart of a flower, or a fruit in its odorous rind, and that this prayer or aspiration presently appeared to bear the thought away, whither I knew not. Moreover, all these thoughts, even of the humblest things, were beauteous and spiritual, nothing cruel or impure or even coarse was to be found among them: they radiated charity, purity and goodness.

Among them I perceived were none that had to do with our earth; this and its affairs seemed to be left far behind these thinkers, a truth that chilled my soul was alien to their company. Worse still, so far as I could discover, although I knew that all these bright ones had been near to me at some hour in the measurements of time and space, not one of their musings dwelt upon me or on aught with which I had to do.

Between me and them there was a great gulf fixed and a high wall built.

Oh, look! One came shining like a star, and from far away came another with dove-like eyes and beautiful exceedingly, and with this last a maiden, whose eyes were as hers who my own heart told me was her mother.

Well, I knew them both; they were those whom I had come to seek, the women who had been mind upon the earth, and at the sight of them my spirit thrilled. Surely they would discover me. Surely at least they would speak of me and feel my presence.

But, although they stayed within a pace or two of where I rested, alas! it was not so. They seemed to kiss and to exchange swift thoughts about many things, high things of which I will not write, and common things; yes, even of the shining robes they wore, but never a one of me! I strove to rise and go to them, but could not; I strove to speak and could not; I strove to throw out my thought to them and could not; it fell back upon my head like a stone hurled heavenward.

They were remote from me, utterly apart. I wept tears of bitterness that I should be so near and yet so far; a dull and jealous rage burned in my heart, and this they did seem to feel, or so I fancied; at any rate, apparently by mutual consent, they moved further from me as though something pained them. Yes, my love could not reach their perfected natures, but my anger hurt them.

As I sat chewing this root of bitterness, a man appeared, a very noble man, in whom I recognised my father grown younger and happier-looking, but still my father, with whom came others, men and women whom I knew to be my brothers and sisters who had died in youth far away in Oxfordshire. Joy leapt up in me, for I thought—these will surely know me and give me welcome, since, though here sex has lost its power, blood must still call to blood.

But it was not so. They spoke, or interchanged their thoughts, but not one of me. I read something that passed from my father to them. It was a speculation as to what had brought them all together there, and read also the answer hazarded, that perhaps it might be to give welcome to some unknown who was drawing near from below and would feel lonely and unfriended. Thereon my father replied that he did not see or feel this wanderer, and thought that it could not be so, since it was his mission to greet such on their coming.

Then in an instant all were gone and that lovely, glowing plain was empty, save for myself seated on the ruby-like stone, weeping tears of blood and shame and loss within my soul.

So I sat a long while, till presently I was aware of a new presence, a presence dusky and splendid and arrayed in rich barbaric robes. Straight she came towards me, like a thrown spear, and I knew her for a certain royal and savage woman who on earth was named Mameena, or "Wind-that-wailed." Moreover she divined me, though see me she could not.

"Art there, Watcher-in-the-Night, watching in the light?" she said or thought, I know not which, but the words came to me in the Zulu tongue.

"Aye," she went on, "I know that thou art there; from ten thousand leagues away I felt thy presence and broke from my own place to welcome thee, though I must pay for it with burning chains and bondage. How did those welcome thee whom thou camest out to seek? Did they clasp thee in their arms and press their kisses on thy brow? Or did they shrink away from thee because the smell of earth was on thy hands and lips?"

I seemed to answer that they did not appear to know that I was there.

"Aye, they did not know because their love is not enough, because they have grown too fine for love. But I, the sinner, I knew well, and here am I ready to suffer all for thee and to give thee place within this stormy heart of mine. Forget them, then, and come to rule with me who still am queen in my own house that thou shalt share. There we will live royally and when our hour comes, at least we shall have had our day."

Now before I could reply, some power seemed to seize this splendid creature and whirl her thence so that she departed, flashing these words from her mind to mine,

"For a little while farewell, but remember always that Mameena, the Wailing Wind, being still as a sinful woman in a woman's love and of the earth, earthy, found thee, whom all the rest forgot. O Watcher-in-the-Night, watch in the night for me, for there thou shalt find me, the Child of Storm, again, and yet again."

She was gone and once more I sat in utter solitude upon that ruby stone, staring at the jewelled flowers and the glorious flaming trees and the lambent waters of the brook. What was the meaning of it all, I wondered, and why was I deserted by everyone save a single savage woman, and why had she a power to find me which was denied to all the rest? Well, she had given me an answer, because she was "as a sinful woman with a woman's love and of the earth, earthy," while with the rest it was otherwise. Oh! this was clear, that in the heavens man has no friend among the heavenly, save perhaps the greatest Friend of all Who understands both flesh and spirit.

Thus I mused in this burning world which was still so beautiful, this alien world into which I had thrust myself unwanted and unsought. And while I mused this happened. The fiery waters of the stream were disturbed by something and looking up I saw the cause.

A dog had plunged into them and was swimming towards me. At a glance I knew that dog on which my eyes had not fallen for decades. It was a mongrel, half spaniel and half bull-terrier, which for years had been the dear friend of my youth and died at last on the horns of a wounded wildebeeste that attacked me when I had fallen from my horse upon the veld. Boldly it tackled the maddened buck, thus giving me time to scramble to my rifle and shoot it, but not before the poor hound had yielded its life for mine, since presently it died disembowelled, but licking my hand and forgetful of its agonies. This dog, Smut by name, it was that swam or seemed to swim the brook of fire. It scrambled to the hither shore, it nosed the earth and ran to the ruby stone and stared about it whining and sniffing.

At last it seemed to see or feel me, for it stood upon its hind legs and licked my face, yelping with mad joy, as I could see though I heard nothing. Now I wept in earnest and bent down to hug and kiss the faithful beast, but this I could not do, since like myself it was only shadow.

Then suddenly all dissolved in a cataract of many-coloured flames and I fell down into an infinite gulf of blackness.

Surely Ayesha was talking to me! What did she say? What did she say? I could not catch her words, but I caught her laughter and knew that after her fashion she was making a mock of me. My eyelids were dragged down as though with heavy sleep; it was difficult to lift them. At last they were open and I saw Ayesha seated on her couch before me and—this I noted at once—with her lovely face unveiled. I looked about me, seeking Umslopogaas and Hans. But they were gone as I guessed they must be, since otherwise Ayesha would not have been unveiled. We were quite alone. She was addressing me and in a new fashion, since now she had abandoned the formal "you" and was using the more impressive and intimate "thou," much as is the manner of the French.

"Thou hast made thy journey, Allan," she said, "and what thou hast seen there thou shalt tell me presently. Yet from thy mien I gather this—that thou art glad to look upon flesh and blood again and, after the company of spirits, to find that of mortal woman. Come then and sit beside me and tell thy tale."

"Where are the others?" I asked as I rose slowly to obey, for my head swam and my feet seemed feeble.

"Gone, Allan, who as I think have had enough of ghosts, which is perhaps thy case also. Come, drink this and be a man once more. Drink it to me whose skill and power have brought thee safe from lands that human feet were never meant to tread," and taking a strange-shaped cup from a stool that stood beside her, she offered it to me.

I drank to the last drop, neither knowing nor caring whether it were wine or poison, since my heart seemed desperate at its failure and my spirit crushed beneath the weight of its great betrayal. I suppose it was the former, for the contents of that cup ran through my veins like fire and gave me back my courage and the joy of life.

I stepped to the dais and sat me down upon the couch, leaning against its rounded end so that I was almost face to face with Ayesha who had turned towards me, and thence could study her unveiled loveliness. For a while she said nothing, only eyed me up and down and smiled and smiled, as though she were waiting for that wine to do its work with me.

"Now that thou art a man again, Allan, tell me what thou didst see when thou wast more—or less—than man."

So I told her all, for some power within her seemed to draw the truth out of me. Nor did the tale appear to cause her much surprise.

"There is truth in thy dream," she said when I had finished; "a lesson also."

"Then it was all a dream?" I interrupted.

"Is not everything a dream, even life itself, Allan? If so, what can this be that thou hast seen, but a dream within a dream, and itself containing other dreams, as in the old days the ball fashioned by the eastern workers of ivory would oft be found to contain another ball, and this yet another and another and another, till at the inmost might be found a bead of gold, or perchance a jewel, which was the prize of him who could draw out ball from ball and leave them all unbroken. That search was difficult and rarely was the jewel come by, if at all, so that some said there was none, save in the maker's mind. Yes, I have seen a man go crazed with seeking and die with the mystery unsolved. How much harder, then, is it to come at the diamond of Truth which lies at the core of all our nest of dreams and without which to rest upon they could not be fashioned to seem realities?"

"But was it really a dream, and if so, what were the truth and the lesson?" I asked, determined not to allow her to bemuse or escape me with her metaphysical talk and illustrations.

"The first question has been answered, Allan, as well as I can answer, who am not the architect of this great globe of dreams, and as yet cannot clearly see the ineffable gem within, whose prisoned rays illuminate their substance, though so dimly that only those with the insight of a god can catch their glamour in the night of thought, since to most they are dark as glow-flies in the glare of noon."

"Then what are the truth and the lesson?" I persisted, perceiving that it was hopeless to extract from her an opinion as to the real nature of my experiences and that I must content myself with her deductions from them.

"Thou tellest me, Allan, that in thy dream or vision thou didst seem to appear before thyself seated on a throne and in that self to find thy judge. That is the Truth whereof I spoke, though how it found its way through the black and ignorant shell of one whose wit is so small, is more than I can guess, since I believed that it was revealed to me alone."

(Now I, Allan, thought to myself that I began to see the origin of all these fantasies and that for once Ayesha had made a slip. If she had a theory and I developed that same theory in a hypnotic condition, it was not difficult to guess its fount. However, I kept my mouth shut, and luckily for once she did not seem to read my mind, perhaps because she was too much occupied in spinning her smooth web of entangling words.)

"All men worship their own god," she went on, "and yet seem not to know that this god dwells within them and that of him they are a part. There he dwells and there they mould him to their own fashion, as the potter moulds his clay, though whatever the shape he seems to take beneath their fingers, still he remains the god infinite and unalterable. Still he is the Seeker and the Sought, the Prayer and its Fulfilment, the Love and the Hate, the Virtue and the Vice, since all these qualities the alchemy of his spirit turns into an ultimate and eternal Good. For the god is in all things and all things are in the god, whom men clothe with such diverse garments and whose countenance they hide beneath so many masks.

"In the tree flows the sap, yet what knows the great tree it nurtures of the sap? In the world's womb burns the fire that gives life, yet what of the fire knows the glorious earth it conceived and will destroy; in the heavens the great globes swing through space and rest not, yet what know they of the Strength that sent them spinning and in a time to come will stay their mighty motions, or turn them to another course? Therefore of everything this all-present god is judge, or rather, not one but many judges, since of each living creature he makes its own magistrate to deal out justice according to that creature's law which in the beginning the god established for it and decreed. Thus in the breast of everyone there is a rule and by that rule, at work through a countless chain of lives, in the end he shall be lifted up to Heaven, or bound about and cast down to Hell and death."

"You mean a conscience," I suggested rather feebly, for her thoughts and images overpowered me.

"Aye, a conscience, if thou wilt, and canst only understand that term, though it fits my theme but ill. This is my meaning, that consciences, as thou namest them, are many. I have one; thou, Allan, hast another; that black Axe-bearer has a third; the little yellow man a fourth, and so on through the tale of living things. For even a dog such as thou sawest has a conscience and—like thyself or I—must in the end be its own judge, because of the spark that comes to it from above, the same spark which in me burns as a great fire, and in thee as a smouldering ember of green wood."

"When you sit in judgment on yourself in a day to come, Ayesha," I could not help interpolating, "I trust that you will remember that humility did not shine among your virtues."

She smiled in her vivid way—only twice or thrice did I see her smile thus and then it was like a flash of summer lightning illumining a clouded sky, since for the most part her face was grave and even sombre.

"Well answered," she said. "Goad the patient ox enough and even it will grow fierce and paw the ground.

"Humility! What have I to do with it, O Allan? Let humility be the part of the humble-souled and lowly, but for those who reign as I do, and they are few indeed, let there be pride and the glory they have earned. Now I have told thee of the Truth thou sawest in thy vision and wouldst thou hear the Lesson?"

"Yes," I answered, "since I may as well be done with it at once, and doubtless it will be good for me."

"The Lesson, Allan, is one which thou preachest—humility. Vain man and foolish as thou art, thou didst desire to travel the Underworld in search of certain ones who once were all in all to thee—nay, not all in all since of them there were two or more—but at least much. Thus thou wouldst do because, as thou saidest, thou didst seek to know whether they still lived on beyond the gates of Blackness. Yes, thou saidest this, but what thou didst hope to learn in truth was whether they lived on in thee and for thee only. For thou, thou in thy vanity, didst picture these departed souls as doing naught in that Heaven they had won, save think of thee still burrowing on the earth, and, at times lightening thy labours with kisses from other lips than theirs."

"Never!" I exclaimed indignantly. "Never! it is not true."

"Then I pray pardon, Allan, who only judged of thee by others that were as men are made, and being such, not to be blamed if perchance from time to time, they turned to look on women, who alas! were as they are made. So at least it was when I knew the world, but mayhap since then its richest wine has turned to water, whereby I hope it has been bettered. At the least this was thy thought, that those women who had been thine for an hour, through all eternity could dream of naught else save thy perfections, and hope for naught else than to see thee at their sides through that eternity, or such part of thee as thou couldst spare to each of them. For thou didst forget that where they have gone there may be others even more peerless than thou art and more fit to hold a woman's love, which as we know on earth was ever changeful, and perhaps may so remain where it is certain that new lights must shine and new desires beckon. Dost understand me, Allan?"

"I think so," I answered with a groan. "I understand you to mean that worldly impressions soon wear out and that people who have departed to other spheres may there form new ties and forget the old."

"Yes, Allan, as do those who remain upon this earth, whence these others have departed. Do men and women still re-marry in the world, Allan, as in my day they were wont to do?"

"Of course—it is allowed."

"As many other things, or perchance this same thing, may be allowed elsewhere, for when there are so many habitations from which to choose, why should we always dwell in one of them, however strait the house or poor the prospect?"

Now understanding that I was symbolised by the "strait house" and the "poor prospect" I should have grown angry, had not a certain sense of humour come to my rescue, who remembered that after all Ayesha's satire was profoundly true. Why, beyond the earth, should anyone desire to remain unalterably tied to and inextricably wrapped up in such a personality as my own, especially if others of superior texture abounded about them? Now that I came to think of it, the thing was absurd and not to be the least expected in the midst of a thousand new and vivid interests. I had met with one more disillusionment, that was all.

"Dost understand, Allan," went on Ayesha, who evidently was determined that I should drink this cup to the last drop, "that these dwellers in the sun, or the far planet where thou hast been according to thy tale, saw thee not and knew naught of thee? It may chance therefore that at this time thou wast not in their minds which at others dream of thee continually. Or it may chance that they never dream of thee at all, having quite forgotten thee, as the weaned cub forgets its mother."

"At least there was one who seemed to remember," I exclaimed, for her poisoned mocking stung the words out of me, "one woman and—a dog."

"Aye, the savage, who being Nature's child, a sinner that departed hence by her own act" (how Ayesha knew this I cannot say, I never told her), "has not yet put on perfection and therefore still remembers him whose kiss was last upon her lips. But surely, Allan, it is not thy desire to pass from the gentle, ordered claspings of those white souls for the tumultuous arms of such a one as this. Still, let that be, for who knows what men will or will not do in jealousy and disappointed love? And the dog, it remembered also and even sought thee out, since dogs are more faithful and single-hearted than is mankind. There at least thou hast thy lesson, namely to grow more humble and never to think again that thou holdest all a woman's soul for aye, because once she was kind to thee for a little while on earth."

"Yes," I answered, jumping up in a rage, "as you say, I have my lesson, and more of it than I want. So by your leave, I will now bid you farewell, hoping that when it comes to be your turn to learn this lesson, or a worse, Ayesha, as I am sure it will one day, for something tells me so, you may enjoy it more than I have done."

CHAPTER XXII

AYESHA'S FAREWELL

Thus I spoke whose nerves were on edge after all that I had seen or, as even then I suspected, seemed to see. For how could I believe that these visions of mine had any higher origin than Ayesha's rather malicious imagination? Already I had formed my theory.

It was that she must be a hypnotist of power, who, after she had put a spell upon her subject, could project into his mind such fancies as she chose together with a selection of her own theories. Only two points remained obscure. The first was—how did she get the necessary information about the private affairs of a humble individual like myself, for these were not known even to Zikali with whom she seemed to be in some kind of correspondence, or to Hans, at any rate in such completeness?

I could but presume that in some mysterious way she drew them from, or rather excited them in my own mind and memory, so that I seemed to see those with whom once I had been intimate, with modifications and in surroundings that her intelligence had carefully prepared. It would not be difficult for a mind like hers familiar, as I gathered it was, with the ancient lore of the Greeks and the Egyptians, to create a kind of Hades and, by way of difference, to change it from one of shadow to one of intense illumination, and into it to plunge the consciousness of him upon whom she had laid her charm of sleep. I had seen nothing and heard nothing that she might not thus have moulded, always given that she had access to the needful clay of facts which I alone could furnish.

Granting this hypothesis, the second point was—what might be the object of her elaborate and most bitter jest? Well, I thought that I could guess. First, she wished to show her power, or rather to make me believe that she had power of a very unusual sort. Secondly, she owed Umslopogaas and myself a debt for our services in the war with Rezu which we had been told would be repaid in this way. Thirdly, I had offended her in some fashion and she took her opportunity of settling the score. Also there was a fourth possibility—that really she considered herself a moral instructress and desired, as she said, to teach me a lesson by showing how futile were human hopes and vanities in respect to the departed and their affections.

Now I do not pretend that all this analysis of Ayesha's motives occurred to me at the moment of my interview with her; indeed, I only completed it later after much careful thought, when I found it sound and good. At that time, although I had inklings, I was too bewildered to form a just judgment.

Further, I was too angry and it was from this bow of my anger that I loosed a shaft at a venture as to some lesson which awaited her. Perhaps certain words spoken by the dying Rezu had shaped that shaft. Or perhaps some shadow of her advancing fate fell upon me.

The success of the shot, however, was remarkable. Evidently it pierced the joints of her harness, and indeed went home to Ayesha's heart. She turned pale; all the peach-bloom hues faded from her lovely face, her great eyes seemed to lessen and grow dull and her cheeks to fall in. Indeed, for a moment she looked old, very old, quite an aged woman. Moreover she wept, for I saw two big tears drop upon her white raiment and I was horrified.

"What has happened to you?" I said, or rather gasped.

"Naught," she answered, "save that thou hast hurt me sore. Dost thou not know, Allan, that it is cruel to prophesy ill to any, since such words feathered from Fate's own wing and barbed with venom, fester in the breast and mayhap bring about their own accomplishment. Most cruel of all is it when with them are repaid friendship and gentleness."

I reflected to myself—yes, friendship of the order that is called candid, and gentleness such as is hid in a cat's velvet paw, but contented myself with asking how it was that she who said she was so powerful, came to fear anything at all.

"Because as I have told thee, Allan, there is no armour that can turn the spear of Destiny which, when I heard those words of thine, it seemed to me, I know not why, was directed by thy hand. Look now on Rezu who thought himself unconquerable and yet was slain by the black Axe-bearer and whose bones to-night stay the famine of the jackals. Moreover I am accursed who sought to steal its servant from Heaven to be my love, and how know I when and where vengeance will fall at last? Indeed, it has fallen already on me, who through the long ages amid savages must mourn widowed and alone, but not all of it—oh! I think, not all."

Then she began to weep in good earnest, and watching her, for the first time I understood that this glorious creature who seemed to be so powerful, was after all one of the most miserable of women and as much a prey to loneliness, every sort of passion and apprehensive fear, as can be any common mortal. If, as she said, she had found the secret of life, which of course I did not believe, at least it was obvious that she had lost that of happiness.

She sobbed softly and wept and while she did so the loveliness, which had left her for a little while, returned to her like light to a grey and darkened sky. Oh, how beautiful she seemed with the abundant locks in disorder over her tear-stained face, how beautiful beyond imagining! My heart melted as I studied her; I could think of nothing else except her surpassing charm and glory.

"I pray you, do not weep," I said; "it hurts me and indeed I am sorry if I said anything to give you pain."

But she only shook that glorious hair further about her face and behind its veil wept on.

"You know, Ayesha," I continued, "you have said many hard things to me, making me the target of your bitter wit, therefore it is not strange that at last I answered you."

"And hast thou not deserved them, Allan?" she murmured in soft and broken tones from behind that veil of scented locks.

"Why?" I asked.

"Because from the beginning thou didst defy me, showing in thine every accent that thou heldest me a liar and one of no account in body or in spirit, one not worthy of thy kind look, or of those gentle words which once were my portion among men. Oh! thou hast dealt hardly with me and therefore perchance—I know not—I paid thee back with such poor weapons as a woman holds, though all the while I liked thee well."

Then again she fell to sobbing, swaying herself gently to and fro in her sweet sorrow.

It was too much. Not knowing what else to do to comfort her, I patted her ivory hand which lay upon the couch beside me, and as this appeared to have no effect, I kissed it, which she did not seem to resent. Then suddenly I remembered and let it fall.

She tossed back her hair from her face and fixing her big eyes on me, said gently enough, looking down at her hand,

"What ails thee, Allan?"

"Oh, nothing," I answered; "only I remembered the story you told me about some man called Kallikrates."

She frowned.

"And what of Kallikrates, Allan? Is it not enough that for my sins, with tears, empty longings and repentance, I must wait for him through all the weary centuries? Must I also wear the chains of this Kallikrates, to whom I owe many a debt, when he is far away? Say, didst thou see him in that Heaven of thine, Allan, for there perchance he dwells?"

I shook my head and tried to think the thing out while all the time those wonderful eyes of hers seemed to draw the soul from me. It seemed to me that she bent forward and held up her face to me. Then I lost my reason and also bent forward. Yes, she made me mad, and, save her, I forgot all.

Swiftly she placed her hand upon my heart, saying,

"Stay! What meanest thou? Dost love me, Allan?"

"I think so—that is—yes," I answered.

She sank back upon the couch away from me and began to laugh very softly.

"What words are these," she said, "that they pass thy lips so easily and so unmeant, perchance from long practice? Oh! Allan, I am astonished. Art thou the same man who some few days ago told me, and this unasked, that as soon wouldst thou think of courting the moon as of courting me? Art thou he who not a minute gone swore proudly that never had his heart and his lips wandered from certain angels whither they should not? And now, and now—?"

I coloured to my eyes and rose, muttering,

"Let me be gone!"

"Nay, Allan, why? I see no mark here," and she held up her hand, scanning it carefully. "Thou art too much what thou wert before, except perhaps in thy soul, which is invisible," she added with a touch of malice. "Nor am I angry with thee; indeed, hadst thou not tried to charm away my woe, I should have thought but poorly of thee as a man. There let it rest and be forgotten—or remembered as thou wilt. Still, in answer to thy words concerning my Kallikrates, what of those adored ones that, according to thy tale, but now thou didst find again in a place of light? Because they seemed faithless, shouldst thou be faithless also? Shame on thee, thou fickle Allan!"

She paused, waiting for me to speak.

Well, I could not. I had nothing to say who was utterly disgraced and overwhelmed.

"Thou thinkest, Allan," she went on, "that I have cast my net about thee, and this is true. Learn wisdom from it, Allan, and never again defy a woman—that is, if she be fair, for then she is stronger than thou art, since Nature for its own purpose made her so. Whatever I have done by tears, that ancient artifice of my sex, as in other ways, is for thy instruction, Allan, that thou mayest benefit thereby."

Again I sprang up, uttering an English exclamation which I trust Ayesha did not understand, and again she motioned to me to be seated, saying,

"Nay, leave me not yet since, even if the light fancy of a man that comes and goes like the evening wind and for a breath made me dear to thee, has passed away, there remains certain work which we must do together. Although, thinking of thyself alone, thou hast forgotten it, having been paid thine own fee, one is yet due to that old wizard in a far land who sent thee to visit Kôr and me, as indeed he has reminded me and within an hour."

This amazing statement aroused me from my personal and painful pre-occupation and caused me to stare at her blankly.

"Again thou disbelievest me," she said, with a little stamp. "Do so once more, Allan, and I swear I'll bring thee to grovel on the ground and kiss my foot and babble nonsense to a woman sworn to another man, such as never for all thy days thou shalt think of without a blush of shame."

"Oh! no," I broke in hurriedly, "I assure you that you are mistaken. I believe every word you have said, or say or will say; I do in truth."

"Now thou liest. Well, what is one more falsehood among so many? Let it pass."

"What, indeed?" I echoed in eager affirmation, "and as for Zikali's message—" and I paused.

"It was to recall to my mind that he desired to learn whether a certain great enterprise of his will succeed, the details of which he says thou canst tell me. Repeat them to me."

So, glad enough to get away from more dangerous topics, I narrated to her as briefly and clearly as I could, the history of the old witch-doctor's feud with the Royal House of Zululand. She listened, taking in every word, and said,

"So now he yearns to know whether he will conquer or be conquered; and that is why he sent, or thinks that he sent thee on this journey, not for thy sake, Allan, but for his own. I cannot tell thee, for what have I do to with the finish of this petty business, which to him seems so large? Still, as I owe him a debt for luring the Axe-Bearer here to rid me of mine enemy, and thee to lighten my solitude for an hour by the burnishing of thy mind, I will try. Set that bowl before me, Allan," and she pointed to a marble tripod on which stood a basin half full of water, "and come, sit close by me and look into it, telling me what thou seest."

I obeyed her instructions and presently found myself with my head over the basin, staring into the water in the exact attitude of a person who is about to be shampooed.

"This seems rather foolish," I said abjectly, for at that moment I resembled the Queen of Sheba in one particular, if in no other, namely, that there was no more spirit in me. "What am I supposed to do? I see nothing at all."

"Look again," she said, and as she spoke the water grew clouded. Then on it appeared a picture. I saw the interior of a Kaffir hut dimly lighted by a single candle set in the neck of a bottle. To the left of the door of the hut was a bedstead and on it lay stretched a wasted and dying man, in whom, to my astonishment, I recognised Cetywayo, King of the Zulus. At the foot of the bed stood another man—myself grown older by many years, and leaning over the bed, apparently whispering into the dying man's ear, was a grotesque and malevolent figure which I knew to be that of Zikali, Opener-of-Roads, whose glowing eyes were fixed upon the terrified and tortured face of Cetywayo. All was as it happened afterwards, as I have written down in the book called "Finished."

I described what I saw to Ayesha, and while I was doing so the picture vanished away, so that nothing remained save the clear water in the marble bowl. The story did not seem to interest her; indeed, she leaned back and yawned a little.

"Thy vision is good, Allan," she said indifferently, "and wide also, since thou canst see what passes in the sun or distant stars, and pictures of things to be in the water, to say nothing of other pictures in a woman's eyes, all within an hour. Well, this savage business concerns me not and of it I want to know no more. Yet it would appear that here the old wizard who is thy friend, has the answer that he desires. For there in the picture the king he hates lies dying while he hisses in his ear and thou dost watch the end. What more can he seek? Tell him it when ye meet, and tell him also it is my will that in future he should trouble me less, since I love not to be wakened from my sleep to listen to his half-instructed talk and savage vapourings. Indeed, he presumes too much. And now enough of him and his dark plots. Ye have your desires, all of you, and are paid in full."

"Over-paid, perhaps," I said with a sigh.

"Ah, Allan, I think that Lesson thou hast learned pleases thee but little. Well, be comforted for the thing is common. Hast never heard that there is but one morsel more bitter to the taste than desire denied, namely, desire fulfilled? Believe me that there can be no happiness for man until he attains a land where all desire is dead."

"That is what the Buddha preaches, Ayesha."

"Aye, I remember the doctrines of that wise man well, who without doubt had found a key to the gate of Truth, one key only, for, mark thou, Allan, there are many. Yet, man being man must know desires, since without them, robbed of ambitions, strivings, hopes, fears, aye and of life itself, the race must die, which is not the will of the Lord of Life who needs a nursery for his servant's souls, wherein his swords of Good and Ill shall shape them to his pattern. So it comes about, Allan, that what we think the worst is oft the best for us, and with that knowledge, if we are wise, let us assuage our bitterness and wipe away our tears."

"I have often thought that," I said.

"I doubt it not, Allan, since though it has pleased me to make a jest of thee, I know that thou hast thy share of wisdom, such little share as thou canst gather in thy few short years. I know, too, that thy heart is good and aspires high, and Friend—well, I find in thee a friend indeed, as I think not for the first time, nor certainly for the last. Mark, Allan, what I say, not a lover, but a friend, which is higher far. For when passion dies with the passing of the flesh, if there be no friendship what will remain save certain memories that, mayhap, are well forgot? Aye, how would those lovers meet elsewhere who were never more than lovers? With weariness, I hold, as they stared into each other's empty soul, or even with disgust.

"Therefore the wise will seek to turn those with whom Fate mates them into friends, since otherwise soon they will be lost for aye. More, if they are wiser still, having made them friends, they will suffer them to find lovers where they will. Good maxims, are they not? Yet hard to follow, or so, perchance, thou thinkest them—as I do."

She grew silent and brooded a while, resting her chin upon her hand and staring down the hall. Thus the aspect of her face was different from any that I had seen it wear. No longer had it the allure of Aphrodite or the majesty of Hera; rather might it have been that of Athene herself. So wise it seemed, so calm, so full of experience and of foresight, that almost it frightened me.

What was this woman's true story, I wondered, what her real self, and what the sum of her gathered knowledge? Perhaps it was accident, or perhaps, again, she guessed my mind. At any rate her next words seemed in some sense an answer to these speculations. Lifting her eyes she contemplated me a while, then said,

"My friend, we part to meet no more in thy life's day. Often thou wilt wonder concerning me, as to what in truth I am, and mayhap in the end thy judgment will be to write me down some false and beauteous wanderer who, rejected of the world or driven from it by her crimes, made choice to rule among savages, playing the part of Oracle to that little audience and telling strange tales to such few travellers as come her way. Perhaps, indeed, I do play this part among many others, and if so, thou wilt not judge me wrongly.

"Allan, in the old days, mariners who had sailed the northern seas, told me that therein amidst mist and storm float mountains of ice, shed from dizzy cliffs which are hid in darkness where no sun shines. They told me also that whereas above the ocean's breast appears but a blue and dazzling point, sunk beneath it is oft a whole frozen isle, invisible to man.

"Such am I, Allan. Of my being thou seest but one little peak glittering in light or crowned with storm, as heaven's moods sweep over it. But in the depths beneath are hid its white and broad foundations, hollowed by the seas of time to caverns and to palaces which my spirit doth inhabit. So picture me, therefore, as wise and fair, but with a soul unknown, and pray that in time to come thou mayest see it in its splendour.

"Hadst thou been other than thou art, I might have shown thee secrets, making clear to thee the parable of much that I have told thee in metaphor and varying fable, aye, and given thee great gifts of power and enduring days of which thou knowest nothing. But of those who visit shrines, O Allan, two things are required, worship and faith, since without these the oracles are dumb and the healing waters will not flow.

"Now I, Ayesha, am a shrine; yet to me thou broughtest no worship until I won it by a woman's trick, and in me thou hast no faith. Therefore for thee the oracle will not speak and the waters of deliverance will not flow. Yet I blame thee not, who art as thou wast made and the hard world has shaped thee.

"And so we part: Think not I am far from thee because thou seest me not in the days to come, since like that Isis whose majesty alone I still exercise on earth, I, whom men name Ayesha, am in all things. I tell thee that I am not One but Many and, being many, am both Here and Everywhere. When thou standest beneath the sky at night and lookest on the stars, remember that in them mine eyes behold thee; when the soft winds of evening blow, that my breath is on thy brow and when the thunder rolls, that there am I riding on the lightnings and rushing with the gale."

"Do you mean that you are the goddess Isis?" I asked, bewildered. "Because if so why did you tell me that you were but her priestess?"

"Have it as thou wilt, Allan. All sounds do not reach thine ears; all sights are not open to thy eyes and therefore thou art both half deaf and blind. Perchance now that her shrines are dust and her worship is forgot, some spark of the spirit of that immortal Lady whose chariot was the moon, lingers on the earth in this woman's shape of mine, though her essence dwells afar, and perchance her other name is Nature, my mother and thine, O Allan. At the least hath not the World a soul—and of that soul am I not mayhap a part, aye, and thou also? For the rest are not the priest and the Divine he bows to, oft the same?"

It was on my lips to answer, Yes, if the priest is a knave or a self-deceiver, but I did not.

"Farewell, Allan, and let Ayesha's benison go with thee. Safe shalt thou reach thy home, for all is prepared to take thee hence, and thy companions with thee. Safe shalt thou live for many a year, till thy time comes, and then, perchance, thou wilt find those whom thou hast lost more kind than they seemed to be to-night."

She paused awhile, then added,

"Hearken unto my last word! As I have said, much that I have told thee may bear a double meaning, as is the way of parables, to be interpreted as thou wilt. Yet one thing is true. I love a certain man, in the old days named Kallikrates, to whom alone I am appointed by a divine decree, and I await him here. Oh, shouldest thou find him in the world without, tell him that Ayesha awaits him and grows weary in the waiting. Nay, thou wilt never find him, since even if he be born again, by what token would he be known to thee? Therefore I charge thee, keep my secrets well, lest Ayesha's curse should fall on thee. While thou livest tell naught of me to the world thou knowest. Dost thou swear to keep my secrets, Allan?"

"I swear, Ayesha."

"I thank thee, Allan," she answered, and grew silent for a while.

At length Ayesha rose and drawing herself up to the full of her height, stood there majestic. Next she beckoned to me to come near, for I too had risen and left the dais.

I obeyed, and bending down she held her hands over me as though in blessing, then pointed towards the curtains which at this moment were drawn asunder, by whom I do not know.

I went and when I reached them, turned to look my last on her.

There she stood as I had left her, but now her eyes were fixed upon the ground and her face once more was brooding absently as though no such a man as I had ever been. It came into my mind that already she had forgotten me, the plaything of an hour, who had served her turn and been cast aside.

CHAPTER XXIII

WHAT UMSLOPOGAAS SAW

Like one who drams I passed down the outer hall where stood the silent guards as statues might, and out through the archway. Here I paused for a moment, partly to calm my mind in the familiar surroundings of the night, and partly because I thought that I heard someone approaching me through the gloom, and in such a place where I might have many enemies, it was well to be prepared.

As it chanced, however, my imaginary assailant was only Hans, who emerged from some place where he had been hiding; a very disturbed and frightened Hans.

"Oh, Baas," he said in a low and shaky whisper, "I am glad to see you again, and standing on your feet, not being carried with them sticking straight in front of you as I expected."

"Why?" I asked.

"Oh, Baas, because of the things that happened in that place where the tall vrouw with her head tied up as though she had tooth-ache, sits like a spider in a web."

"Well, what happened, Hans?" I asked as we walked forward.

"This, Baas. The Doctoress talked and talked at you and Umslopogaas, and as she talked, your faces began to look as though you had drunk half a flask too much of the best gin, such as I wish I had some of here to-night, at once wise and foolish, and full and empty, Baas. Then you both rolled over and lay there quite dead, and whilst I was wondering what I should do and how I should get out your bodies to bury them, the Doctoress came down off her platform and bent, first over you and next over Umslopogaas, whispering into the ears of both of you. Then she took off a snake that looked as though it were made of gold with green eyes, which she wears about her middle beneath the long dish-cloth, Baas, and held it to your lips and next to those of Umslopogaas."

"Well, and what then, Hans?"

"After that all sorts of things came about, Baas, and I felt as though the whole house were travelling through the air, Baas, twice as fast as a bullet does from a rifle. Suddenly, too, the room became filled with fire so hot that it scorched me, and so bright that it made my eyes water, although they can look at the sun without winking. And, Baas, the fire was full of spooks which walked around; yes, I saw some of them standing on your head and stomach, Baas, also on that of Umslopogaas, whilst others went and talked to the white Doctoress as quietly as though they had met her in the market-place and wanted to sell her eggs or butter. Then, Baas, suddenly I saw your reverend father, the Predikant, who looked as though he were red-hot, as doubtless he is in the Place of Fires. I thought he came up to me, Baas, and said, 'Get out of this, Hans. This is no place for a good Hottentot like you, Hans, for here only the very best Christians can bear the heat for long.'

"That finished me, Baas. I just answered that I handed you, the Baas Allan his son, over to his care, hoping that he would see that you did not burn in that oven, whatever happened to Umslopogaas. Then I shut my eyes and mouth and held my nose, and wriggled beneath those curtains as a snake does, Baas, and ran down the hall and across the kraal-yard and through the archway out into the night, where I have been sitting cooling myself ever since, waiting for you to be carried away, Baas. And now you have come alive and with not even your hair burnt off, which shows how wonderful must be the Great Medicine of Zikali, Baas, since nothing else could have saved you in that fire, no, not even your reverend father, the Predikant."

"Hans," I said when he had finished, "you are a very wonderful fellow, for you can get drunk on nothing at all. Please remember, Hans, that you have been drunk to-night, yes, very drunk indeed, and never dare to repeat anything that you thought you saw while you were drunk."

"Yes, Baas, I understand that I was drunk and already have forgotten everything. But, Baas, there is still a bottle full of brandy and if I could have just one more tot I should forget so much better!"

By now we had reached our camp and here I found Umslopogaas sitting in the doorway and staring at the sky.

"Good-evening to you, Umslopogaas," I said in my most unconcerned manner, and waited.

"Good-evening, Watcher-by-Night, who I thought was lost in the night, since in the end the night is stronger than any of its watchers."

At this cryptic remark I looked bewildered but said nothing. At length Umslopogaas, whose nature, for a Zulu, was impulsive and lacking in the ordinary native patience, asked,

"Did you make a journey this evening, Macumazahn, and if so, what did you see?"

"Did you have a dream this evening, Umslopogaas?" I inquired by way of answer, "and if so, what was it about? I thought that I saw you shut your eyes in the House of the White One yonder, doubtless because you were weary of talk which you did not understand."

"Aye, Macumazahn, as you suppose I grew weary of that talk which flowed from the lips of the White Witch like the music that comes from a little stream babbling over stones when the sun is hot, and being weary, I fell asleep and dreamed. What I dreamed does not much matter. It is enough to say that I felt as though I were thrown through the air like a stone cast from his sling by a boy who is set upon a stage to scare the birds out of a mealie garden. Further than any stone I went, aye, further than a shooting star, till I reached a wonderful place. It does not much matter what it was like either, and indeed I am already beginning to forget, but there I met everyone I have ever known. I met the Lion of the Zulus, the Black One, the Earth-Shaker, he who had a 'sister' named Baleka, which sister," here he dropped his voice and looked about him suspiciously, "bore a child, which child was fostered by one Mopo, that Mopo who afterwards slew the Black one with the Princes. Now, Macumazahn, I had a score to settle with this Black One, aye, even though our blood be much of the same colour, I had a score to settle with him, because of the slaying of this sister of his, Baleka, together with the Langeni tribe.[*] So I walked up to him and took him by the head-ring and spat in his face and bade him find a spear and shield, and meet me as man to man. Yes, I did this."

[*] For the history of Baleka, the mother of Umslopogaas, and Mopo, see the book called "Nada the Lily."—Editor.

"And what happened then, Umslopogaas?" I said, when he paused in his narrative.

"Macumazahn, nothing happened at all. My hand seemed to go through his head-ring and the skull beneath, and to shut upon itself while he went on talking to someone else, a captain whom I recognised, yes, one Faku, whom in the days of Dingaan, the Black One's brother, I myself slew upon the Ghost-Mountain.

"Yes, Macumazahn, and Faku was telling him the tale of how I killed him and of the fight that I and my blood-brother and the wolves made, there on the knees of the old witch who sits aloft on the Ghost Mountain waiting for the world to die, for I could understand their talk, though mine went by them like the wind.

"Macumazahn, they passed away and there came others, Dingaan among them, aye, Dingaan who also knows something of the Witch-Mountain, seeing that there Mopo and I hurled him to his death. With him also I would have had words, but it was the same story, only presently he caught sight of the Black One, yes, of Chaka whom he slew, stabbing him with the little red assegai, and turned and fled, because in that land I think he still fears Chaka, Macumazahn, or so the dream told.

"I went on and met others, men I had fought in my day, most of them, among them was Jikiza, he who ruled the People of the Axe before me whom I slew with his own axe. I lifted the axe and made me ready to fight again, but not one of them took any note of me. There they walked about, or sat drinking beer or taking snuff, but never a sup of the beer or a pinch of the snuff did they offer me, no, not even those among them whom I chanced not to have killed. So I left them and walked on, seeking for Mopo, my foster-father, and a certain man, my blood-brother, by whose side I hunted with the wolves, yes, for them, and for another."

"Well, and did you find them?" I asked.

"Mopo I found not, which makes me think, Macumazahn, that, as once you hinted to me, he whom I thought long dead, perchance still lingers on the earth. But the others I did find . . ." and he ceased, brooding.

Now I knew enough of Umslopogaas's history to be aware that he had loved this man and woman of whom he spoke more than any others on the earth. The "blood-brother," whose name he would not utter, by which he did not mean that he was his brother in blood but one with whom he had made a pact of eternal friendship by the interchange of blood or some such ceremony, according to report, had dwelt with him on the Witch-Mountain where legend told, though this I could scarcely believe, that they had hunted with a pack of hyenas. There, it said also, they fought a great fight with a band send out by Dingaan the king under the command of that Faku whom Umslopogaas had mentioned, in which fight the "Blood-Brother," wielder of a famous club known as Watcher-of-the-Fords, got his death after doing mighty deeds. There also, as I had heard, Nada the Lily, whose beauty was still famous in the land, died under circumstances strange as they were sad.

Naturally, remembering my own experiences, or rather what seemed to be my experiences, for already I had made up my mind that they were but a dream, I was most anxious to learn whether these two who had been so dear to this fierce Zulu, had recognised him.

"Well, and what did they say to you, Umslopogaas?" I asked.

"Macumazahn, they said nothing at all. Hearken! There stood this pair, or sometimes they moved to and fro; my brother, an even greater man than he used to be, with the wolfskin girt about him and the club, Watcher-of-the-Fords, which he alone could wield, upon his shoulder, and Nada, grown lovelier even than she was of old, so lovely, Macumazahn, that my heart rose into my throat when I saw her and stopped my breath. Yes, Macumazahn, there they stood, or walked about arm in arm as lovers might, and looked into each other's eyes and talked of how they had known each other on the earth, for I could understand their words or thoughts, and how it was good to be at rest together where they were."

"You see, they were old friends, Umslopogaas," I said.

"Yes, Macumazahn, very old friends as I thought. So much so that they had never had a word to say of me who also was the old friend of both of them. Aye, my brother, whose name I am sworn not to speak, the woman-hater who vowed he loved nothing save me and the wolves, could smile into the face of Nada the Lily, Nada the bride of my youth, yet never a word of me, while she could smile back and tell him how great a warrior he had been and never a word of me whose deeds she was wont to praise, who saved her in the Halakazi caves and from Dingaan; no, never a word of me although I stood there staring at them."

"I suppose that they did not see you, Umslopogaas."

"That is so, Macumazahn; I am sure that they did not see me, for if they had they would not have been so much at ease. But I saw them and as they would not take heed when I shouted, I ran up calling to my brother to defend himself with his club. Then, as he still took no note, I lifted the axe Inkosikaas, making it circle in the light, and smote with all my strength."

"And what happened, Umslopogaas?"

"Only this, Macumazahn, that the axe went straight through my brother from the crown of his head to the groin, cutting him in two, and he just went on talking! Indeed, he did more, for stooping down he gathered a white lily-bloom which grew there and gave it to Nada, who smelt at it, smiled and thanked him, and then thrust it into her girdle, still thanking him all the while. Yes, she did this for I saw it with my eyes, Macumazahn."

Here the Zulu's voice broke and I think that he wept, for in the faint light I saw him draw his long hand across his eyes, whereon I took the opportunity to turn my back and light a pipe.

"Macumazahn," he went on presently, "it seems that madness took hold of me for a long while, for I shouted and raved at them, thinking that words and rage might hurt where good steel could not, and as I did so they faded away and disappeared, still smiling and talking, Nada smelling at the lily which, having a long stalk, rose up above her breast. After this I rushed away and suddenly met that savage king, Rezu, whom I slew a few days gone. At him I went with the axe, wondering whether he would put up a better fight this second time."

"And did he, Umslopogaas?"

"Nay, but I think he felt me for he turned and fled and when I tried to follow I could not see him. So I ran on and presently who should I find but Baleka, Baleka, Chaka's 'sister' who—repeat it not, Macumazahn—was my mother; and, Macumazahn, she saw me. Yes, though I was but little when last she looked on me who now am great and grim, she saw and knew me, for she floated up to me and smiled at me and seemed to press her lips upon my forehead, though I could feel no kiss, and to draw the soreness out of my heart. Then she, too, was gone and of a sudden I fell down through space, having, I suppose, stepped into some deep hole, or perchance a well.

"The next thing I knew was that I awoke in the house of the White Witch and saw you sleeping at my side and the Witch leaning back upon her bed and smiling at me through the thin blanket with which she covers herself up, for I could see the laughter in her eyes.

"Now I grew mad with her because of the things that I had seen in the Place of Dreams, and it came into my heart that it would be well to kill her that the world might be rid of her and her evil magic which can show lies to men. So, being distraught, I sprang up and lifted the axe and stepped towards her, whereon she rose and stood before me, laughing out loud. Then she said something in the tongue I cannot understand, and pointed with her finger, and lo! next moment it was as if giants had seized me and were whirling me away, till presently I found myself breathless but unharmed beyond the arch and—what does it all mean, Macumazahn?"

"Very little, as I think, Umslopogaas, except that this queen has powers to which those of Zikali are as nothing, and can cause visions to float before the eyes of men. For know that such things as you saw, I saw, and in them those whom I have loved also seemed to take no thought of me but only to be concerned with each other. Moreover when I awoke and told this to the queen who is called She-who-commands, she laughed at me as she did at you, and said that it was a good lesson for my pride who in that pride had believed that the dead only thought of the living. But I think that the lesson came from her who wished to humble us, Umslopogaas, and that it was her mind that shaped these visions which we saw."

"I think so too, Macumazahn, but how she knew of all the matters of your life and mine, I do not know, unless perchance Zikali told them to her, speaking in the night-watches as wizards can."

"Nay, Umslopogaas, I believe that by her magic she drew our stories out of our own hearts and then set them forth to us afresh, putting her own colour on them. Also it may be that she drew something from Hans, and from Goroko and the other Zulus with you, and thus paid us the fee that she had promised for our service, but in lung-sick oxen and barren cows, not in good cattle, Umslopogaas."

He nodded and said,

"Though at the time I seemed to go mad and though I know that women are false and men must follow where they lead them, never will I believe that my brother, the woman-hater, and Nada are lovers in the land below and have there forgotten me, the comrade of one of them and the husband of the other. Moreover I hold, Macumazahn, that you and I have met with a just reward for our folly.

"We have sought to look through the bottom of the grave at things which the Great-Great in Heaven above did not mean that men should see, and now that we have seen we are unhappier than we were, since such dreams burn themselves upon the heart as a red-hot iron burns the hide of an ox, so that the hair will never grow again where it has been and the hide is marred.

"To you, Watcher-by-Night, I say, 'Content yourself with your watching and whatever it may bring to you in fame and wealth.' And to myself I say, 'Holder of the Axe, content yourself with the axe and what it may bring to you in fair fight and glory'; and to both of us I say, 'Let the Dead sleep unawakened until we go to join them, which surely will be soon enough.'"

"Good words, Umslopogaas, but they should have been spoken ere ever we set out on this journey."

"Not so, Macumazahn, since that journey we were fated to make to save one who lies yonder, the Lady Sad-Eyes, and, as they tell me, is well again. Also Zikali willed it, and who can resist the will of the Opener-of-Roads? So it is made and we have seen many strange things and won some glory and come to know how deep is the pool of our own foolishness, who thought that we could search out the secrets of Death, and there have only found those of a witch's mind and venom, reflected as in water. And now having discovered all these things I wish to be gone from this haunted land. When do we march, Macumazahn?"

"To-morrow morning, I believe, if the Lady Sad-Eyes and the others are well enough, as She-who-commands says they will be."

"Good. Then I would sleep who am more weary than I was after I had killed Rezu in the battle on the mountain."

"Yes," I answered, "since it is harder to fight ghosts than men, and dreams, if they be bad, are more dreadful than deeds. Good-night, Umslopogaas."

He went, and I too went to see how it fared with Inez. I found that she was fast asleep but in a quite different sleep to that into which Ayesha seemed to have plunged her. Now it was absolutely natural and looking at her lying there upon the bed, I thought how young and healthy was her appearance. The women in charge of her also told me that she had awakened at the hour appointed by She-who-commands, as it seemed, quite well and very hungry, although she appeared to be puzzled by her surroundings. After she had eaten, they added that she had "sung a song," which was probably a hymn, and prayed upon her knees, "making signs upon her breast" and then gone quietly to bed.

My anxiety relieved as regards Inez, I returned to my own quarters. Not feeling inclined for slumber, however, instead of turning in I sat at the doorway contemplating the beauty of the night while I watched the countless fireflies that seemed to dust the air with sparks of burning gold; also the great owls and other fowl that haunt the dark. These had come out in numbers from their hiding-places among the ruins and sailed to and fro like white-winged spirits, now seen and now lost in the gloom.

While I sat thus many reflections came to me as to the extraordinary nature of my experiences during the past few days. Had any man ever known the like, I wondered? What could they mean and what could this marvellous woman Ayesha be? Was she perhaps a personification of Nature itself, as indeed to some extent all women are? Was she human at all, or was she some spirit symbolising a departed people, faith and civilisation, and haunting the ruins where once she reigned as queen? No, the idea was ridiculous, since such beings do not exist, though it was impossible to doubt that she possessed powers beyond those of common humanity, as she possessed beauty and fascination greater than are given to any other woman.

Of one thing I was certain, however, that the Shades I had seemed to visit had their being in the circle of her own imagination and intelligence. There Umslopogaas was right; we had seen no dead, we had only seen pictures and images that she drew and fashioned.

Why did she do this, I wondered. Perhaps to pretend to powers which she did not possess, perhaps out of sheer elfish mischief, or perhaps, as she asserted, just to teach us a lesson and to humble us in our own sight. Well, if so she had succeeded, for never did I feel so crushed and humiliated as at that moment.

I had seemed to descend, or ascend, into Hades, and there had only seen things that gave me little joy and did but serve to reopen old wounds. Then, on awaking, I had been bewitched; yes, fresh from those visions of the most dear dead, I had been bewitched by the overpowering magic of this woman's loveliness and charm, and made a fool of myself, only to be brought back to my senses by her triumphant mockery. Oh, I was humbled indeed, and yet the odd thing is that I could not feel angry with her, and what is more that, perhaps from vanity, I believed in her profession of friendship towards myself.

Well, the upshot of it was that, like Umslopogaas, more than anything else in the world did I desire to depart from this haunted Kôr and to bury all its recollections in such activities as fortune might bring to me. And yet, and yet it was well to have seen it and to have plucked the flower of such marvellous experience, nor, as I knew even then, could I ever inter the memory of Ayesha the wise, the perfect in all loveliness, and the half-divine in power.

When I awoke the next morning the sun was well up and after I had taken a swim in the old bath and dressed myself, I went to see how it fared with Inez. I found her sitting at the door of her house looking extremely well and with a radiant face. She was engaged in making a chain of some small and beautiful blue flowers of the iris tribe, of which quantities grew about, that she threaded together upon stalks of dry grass.

This chain, which was just finished, she threw over her head so that it hung down upon her white robe, for now she was dressed like an Arab woman though without the veil. I watched her unseen for a little while then came forward and spoke to her. She started at the sight of me and rose as though to run away; then, apparently reassured by my appearance, selected a particularly fine flower and offered it to me.

I saw at once that she did not know me in the least and thought that she had never seen me before, in short, that her mind had gone, exactly as Ayesha had said that it would do. By way of making conversation I asked her if she felt well. She replied, Oh, yes, she had never felt better, then added,

"Daddy has gone on a long journey and will not be back for weeks and weeks."

An idea came to me and I answered,

"Yes, Inez, but I am a friend of his and he has sent me to take you to a place where I hope that we shall find him. Only it is far away, so you also must make a long journey."

She clapped her hands and answered,

"Oh, that will be nice, I do so love travelling, especially to find Daddy, who I expect will have my proper clothes with him, not these which, although they are very comfortable and pretty, seem different to what I used to wear. You look very nice too and I am sure that we shall be great friends, which I am glad of, for I have been rather lonely since my mother went to live with the saints in Heaven, because, you see, Daddy is so busy and so often away, that I do not see much of him."

Upon my word I could have wept when I heard her prattle on thus. It is so terribly unnatural, almost dreadful indeed, to listen to a full grown woman who talks in the accents and expresses the thoughts of a child. However, under all the circumstances I recognised that her calamity was merciful, and remembering that Ayesha had prophesied the recovery of her mind as well as its loss and how great seemed to be her powers in these directions, I took such comfort as I could.

Leaving her I went to see the two Zulus who had been wounded and found to my joy that they were now quite well and fit to travel, for here, too, Ayesha's prophecy had proved good. The other men also were completely rested and anxious to be gone like Umslopogaas and myself.

While I was eating my breakfast Hans announced the venerable Billali, who with a sweeping bow informed me that he had come to inquire when we should be ready to start, as he had received orders to see to all the necessary arrangements. I replied—within an hour, and he departed in a hurry.

But little after the appointed time he reappeared with a number of litters and their bearers, also with a bodyguard of twenty-five picked men, all of whom we recognised as brave fellows who had fought well in the battle. These men and the bearers old Billali harangued, telling them that they were to guide, carry and escort us to the other side of the great swamp, or further if we needed it, and that it was the word of She-who-commands that if so much as the smallest harm came to any one of us, even by accident, they should die every man of them "by the hot-pot," whatever that might be, for I was not sure of the significance of this horror.[*] Then he asked them if they understood. They replied with fervour that they understood perfectly and would lead and guard us as though we were their own mothers.

[*] For this see the book called "She."—Editor.

As a matter of fact they did, and I think would have done so independently of Ayesha's command, since they looked upon Umslopogaas and myself almost as gods and thought that we could destroy them all if we wished, as we had destroyed Rezu and his host.

I asked Billali if he were not coming with us, to which he replied, No, as She-who-commands had returned to her own place and he must follow her at once. I asked him again where her own place might be, to which he answered vaguely that it was everywhere and he stared first at the heavens and then at the earth as though she inhabited most of them, adding that generally it was "in the Caves," though what he meant by that I did not know. Then he said that he was very glad to have met us and that the sight of Umslopogaas killing Rezu was a spectacle that he would remember with pleasure all his life. Also he asked me for a present. I gave him a spare pencil that I possessed in a little German silver case, with which he was delighted. Thus I parted with old Billali, of whom I shall always think with a certain affection.

I noticed even then that he kept very clear indeed of Umslopogaas, thinking, I suppose, that he might take a last opportunity to fulfil his threats and introduce him to his terrible Axe.

CHAPTER XXIV

UMSLOPOGAAS WEARS THE GREAT MEDICINE

A little while later we started, some of us in litters, including the wounded Zulus, who I insisted should be carried for a day or two, and some on foot. Inez I caused to be borne immediately in front of myself so that I could keep an eye upon her. Moreover I put her in the especial charge of Hans, to whom fortunately she took a great fancy at once, perhaps because she remembered subconsciously that she knew him and that he had been kind to her, although when they met after her long sleep, as in my own case, she did not recognise him in the least.

Soon, however, they were again the fastest of friends, so much so that within a day or two the little Hottentot practically filled the place of a maid to her, attending to her every want and looking after her exactly as a nurse does after a child, with the result that it was quite touching to see how she came to depend upon him, "her monkey," as she called him, and how fond he grew of her.

Once, indeed, there was trouble, since hearing a noise, I came up to find Hans bristling with fury and threatening to shoot one of the Zulus, who stupidly, or perhaps rudely, had knocked against the litter of Inez and nearly turned it over. For the rest, the Lady Sad-Eyes, as they called her, had for the time became the Lady Glad-Eyes, since she was merry as the day was long, laughing and singing and playing just as a healthy happy child should do.

Only once did I see her wretched and weep. It was when a kitten which she had insisted on bringing with her, sprang out of the litter and vanished into some bush where it could not be found. Even when she was soon consoled and dried her tears, when Hans explained to her in a mixture of bad English and worse Portuguese, that it had only run away because it wished to get back to its mother which it loved, and that it was cruel to separate it from its mother.

We made good progress and by the evening of the first day were over the crest of the cliff or volcano lip that encircles the great plain of Kôr, and descending rapidly to a sheltered spot on the outer slope where our camp was to be set for the night.

Not very far from this place, as I think I have mentioned, stood, and I suppose still stands, a very curious pinnacle of rock, which, doubtless being of some harder sort, had remained when, hundreds of thousands or millions of years before, the surrounding lava had been washed or had corroded away. This rock pillar was perhaps fifty feet high and as smooth as though it had been worked by man; indeed, I remembered having remarked to Hans, or Umslopogaas—I forget which—when we passed it on our inward journey, that there was a column which no monkey could climb.

As we went by it for the second time, the sun had already disappeared behind the western cliff, but a fierce ray from its sinking orb, struck upon a storm-cloud that hung over us, and thence was reflected in a glow of angry light of which the focus or centre seemed to fall upon the summit of this strange and obelisk-like pinnacle of rock.

At the moment I was out of my litter and walking with Umslopogaas at the end of the line, to make sure that no one straggled in the oncoming darkness. When we had passed the column by some forty or fifty yards, something caused Umslopogaas to turn and look back. He uttered an exclamation which made me follow his example, with the result that I saw a very wonderful thing. For there on the point of the pillar, like St. Simeon Stylites on his famous column, glowing in the sunset rays as though she were on fire, stood Ayesha herself!

It was a strange and in a way a glorious sight, for poised thus between earth and heaven, she looked like some glowing angel rather than a woman, standing as she seemed to do upon the darkness; since the shadows, save for the faintest outline, had swallowed up the column that supported her. Moreover, in the intense, rich light that was focussed on her, we could see every detail of her form and face, for she was unveiled, and even her large and tender eyes which gazed upwards emptily (at this moment they seemed very tender), yes, and the little gold studs that glittered on her sandals and the shine of the snake girdle she wore about her waist.

We stared and stared till I said inconsequently,

"Learn, Umslopogaas, what a liar is that old Billali, who told me that She-who-commands had departed from Kôr to her own place."

"Perhaps this rock edge is her own place, if she be there at all, Macumazahn."

"If she be there," I answered angrily, for my nerves were at once thrilled and torn. "Speak not empty words, Umslopogaas, for where else can she be when we see her with our eyes?"

"Who am I that I should know the ways of witches who, like the winds, are able to go and come as they will? Can a woman run up a wall of rock like a lizard, Macumazahn?"

"Doubtless—" and I began some explanation which I have forgotten, when a passing cloud, or I know not what, cut off the light so that both the pinnacle and she who stood on it became invisible. A minute later it returned for a little while, and there was the point of the needle-shaped rock, but it was empty, as, save for the birds that rested on it, it had been since the beginning of the world.

Then Umslopogaas and I shook our heads and pursued our way in silence.

This was the last that I saw of the glorious Ayesha, if indeed I did see her and not her ghost. Yet it is true that for all the first part of the journey, till we were through the great swamp in fact, from time to time I was conscious, or imagined that I was conscious of her presence. Moreover, once others saw her, or someone who might have been her. It happened thus.

We were in the centre of the great swamp and the trained guides who were leading came to a place where the path forked and were uncertain which road to take. Finally they fixed on the right-hand path and were preparing to follow it together with those who bore the litter of Inez, by the side of which Hans was walking as usual.

At this moment, as Hans told me, the guides went down upon their faces and he saw standing in front of them a white-veiled form who pointed to the left-hand path, and then seemed to be lost in the mist. Without a word the guides rose and followed this left-hand path. Hans stopped the litter till I came up when he told me what had happened, while Inez also began to chatter in her childish fashion about a "White Lady."

I had the curiosity to walk a little way along the right-hand path which they were about to take. Only a few yards further on I found myself sinking in a floating quagmire, from which I extricated myself with much difficulty but just in time for as I discovered afterwards by probing with a pole, the water beneath the matted reeds was deep. That night I questioned the guides upon the subject, but without result, for they pretended to have seen nothing and not to understand what I meant. Of neither of these incidents have I any explanation to offer, except that once contracted, it is as difficult to be rid of the habit of hallucinations as of any other.

It is not necessary that I should give all the details of our long homeward journey. So I will only say that having dismissed our bearers and escorts when we reached higher ground beyond the horrible swamp, keeping one litter for Inez in which the Zulus carried her when she was tired, we accomplished it in complete safety and having crossed the Zambesi, at last one evening reached the house called Strathmuir.

Here we found the waggon and oxen quite safe and were welcomed rapturously by my Zulu driver and the voorlooper, who had made up their minds that we were dead and were thinking of trekking homewards. Here also Thomaso greeted us, though I think that, like the Zulus, he was astonished at our safe return and indeed not over-pleased to see us. I told him that Captain Robertson had been killed in a fight in which we had rescued his daughter from the cannibals who had carried her off (information which I cautioned him to keep to himself) but nothing else that I could help.

Also I warned the Zulus through Umslopogaas and Goroko, that no mention was to be made of our adventures, either then or afterwards, since if this were done the curse of the White Queen would fall on them and bring them to disaster and death. I added that the name of this queen and everything that was connected with her, or her doings, must be locked up in their own hearts. It must be like the name of dead kings, not to be spoken. Nor indeed did they ever speak it or tell the story of our search, because they were too much afraid both of Ayesha whom they believed to be the greatest of all witches, and of the axe of their captain, Umslopogaas.

Inez went to bed that night without seeming to recognise her old home, to all appearance just a mindless child as she had been ever since she awoke from her trance at Kôr. Next morning, however, Hans came to tell me that she was changed and that she wished to speak with me. I went, wondering, to find her in the sitting-room, dressed in European clothes which she had taken from where she kept them, and once more a reasoning woman.

"Mr. Quatermain," she said, "I suppose that I must have been ill, for the last thing I remember is going to sleep on the night after you started for the hippopotamus hunt. Where is my father? Did any harm come to him while he was hunting?"

"Alas!" I answered, lying boldly, for I feared lest the truth should take away her mind again, "it did. He was trampled upon by a hippopotamus bull, which charged him, and killed, and we were obliged to bury him where he died."

She bowed her head for a while and muttered some prayer for his soul, then looked at me keenly and said,

"I do not think you are telling me everything, Mr. Quatermain, but something seems to say that this is because it is not well that I should learn everything."

"No," I answered, "you have been ill and out of your mind for quite a long while; something gave you a shock. I think that you learned of your father's death, which you have now forgotten, and were overcome with the news. Please trust to me and believe that if I keep anything back from you, it is because I think it best to do so for the present."

"I trust and I believe," she answered. "Now please leave me, but tell me first where are those women and their children?"

"After your father died they went away," I replied, lying once more.

She looked at me again but made no comment.

Then I left her.

How much Inez ever learned of the true story of her adventures I do not know to this hour, though my opinion is that it was but little. To begin with, everyone, including Thomaso, was threatened with the direst consequences if he said a word to her on the subject; moreover in her way she was a wise woman, one who knew when it was best not to ask questions. She was aware that she had suffered from a fit of aberration or madness and that during this time her father had died and certain peculiar things had happened. There she was content to leave the business and she never again spoke to me upon the subject. Of this I was very glad, as how on earth could I have explained to her about Ayesha's prophecies as to her lapse into childishness and subsequent return to a normal state when she reached her home seeing that I did not understand them myself?

Once indeed she did inquire what had become of Janee to which I answered that she had died during her sickness. It was another lie, at any rate by implication, but I hold that there are occasions when it is righteous to lie. At least these particular falsehoods have never troubled my conscience.

Here I may as well finish the story of Inez, that is, as far as I can. As I have shown she was always a woman of melancholy and religious temperament, qualities that seemed to grow upon her after her return to health. Certainly the religion did, for continually she was engaged in prayer, a development with which heredity may have had something to do, since after he became a reformed character and grew unsettled in his mind, her father followed the same road.

On our return to civilisation, as it chanced, one of the first persons with whom she came in contact was a very earnest and excellent old priest of her own faith. The end of this intimacy was much what might have been expected. Very soon Inez determined to renounce the world, which I think never had any great attractions for her, and entered a sisterhood of an extremely strict Order in Natal, where, added to her many merits, her considerable possessions made her very welcome indeed.

Once in after years I saw her again when she expected before long to become the Mother-Superior of her convent. I found her very cheerful and she told me that her happiness was complete. Even then she did not ask me the true story of what had happened to her during that period when her mind was a blank. She said that she knew something had happened but that as she no longer felt any curiosity about earthly things, she did not wish to know the details. Again I rejoiced, for how could I tell the true tale and expect to be believed, even by the most confiding and simple-minded nun?

To return to more immediate events. When we had been at Strathmuir for a day or two and I thought that her mind was clear enough to judge of affairs, I told Inez that I must journey on to Natal, and asked her what she wished to do. Without a moment's hesitation she replied that she desired to come with me, as now that her father was dead nothing would induce her to continue to live at Strathmuir without friends, or indeed the consolations of religion.

Then she showed me a secret hiding-place cunningly devised in a sort of cellar under the sitting-room floor, where her father was accustomed to keep the spirits of which he consumed so great a quantity. In this hole beneath some bricks, we discovered a large sum in gold stored away, which Robertson had always told his daughter she would find there, in the event of anything happening to him. With the money were his will and securities, also certain mementos of his youth and some love-letters together with a prayer-book that his mother had given him.

These valuables, of which no one knew the existence except herself, we removed and then made our preparations for departure. They were simple; such articles of value as we could carry were packed into the waggon and the best of the cattle we drove with us. The place with the store and the rest of the stock were handed over to Thomaso on a half-profit agreement under arrangement that he should remit the share of Inez twice a year to a bank on the coast, where her father had an account. Whether or not he ever did this I am unable to say, but as no one wished to stop at Strathmuir, I could conceive no better plan because purchasers of property in that district did not exist.

As we trekked away one fine morning I asked Inez whether she was sorry to leave the place.

"No," she replied with energy, "my life there has been a hell and I never wish to see it again."

Now it was after this, on the northern borders of Zululand, that Zikali's Great Medicine, as Hans called it, really played its chief part, for without it I think that we should have been killed, every one of us. I do not propose to set out the business in detail; it is too long and intricate. Suffice it to say, therefore, that it had to do with the plots of Umslopogaas against Cetywayo, which had been betrayed by his wife Monazi and her lover Lousta, both of whom I have mentioned earlier in this record. The result was that a watch for him was kept on all the frontiers, because it was guessed that sooner or later he would return to Zululand; also it had become known that he was travelling in my company.

So it came about that when my approach was reported by spies, a company was gathered under the command of a man connected with the Royal House, and by it we were surrounded. Before attacking, however, this captain sent men to me with the message that with me the King had no quarrel, although I was travelling in doubtful company, and that if I would deliver over to him Umslopogaas, Chief of the People of the Axe, and his followers, I might go whither I wished unharmed, taking my goods with me. Otherwise we should be attacked at once and killed every one of us, since it was not desired that any witnesses should be left of what happened to Umslopogaas. Having delivered this ultimatum and declined any argument as to its terms, the messengers retired, saying that they would return for my answer within half an hour.

When they were out of hearing Umslopogaas, who had listened to their words in grim silence, turned and spoke in such fashion as might have been expected of him.

"Macumazahn," he said, "now I come to the end of an unlucky journey, though mayhap it is not so evil as it seems, since I who went out to seek the dead but to be filled by yonder White Witch with the meat of mocking shadows, am about to find the dead in the only way in which they can be found, namely by becoming of their number."

"It seems that this is the case with all of us, Umslopogaas."

"Not so, Macumazahn. That child of the King will give you safe-conduct. It is I and mine whose blood he seeks, as he has the right to do, since it is true that I would have raised rebellion against the King, I who wearied of my petty lot and knew that by blood his place was mine. In this quarrel you have no share, though you, whose heart is as white as your skin, are not minded to desert me. Moreover, even if you wished to fight, there is one in the waggon yonder whose life is not yours to give. The Lady Sad-Eyes is as a child in your arms and her you must bear to safety."

Now this argument was so unanswerable that I did not know what to say. So I only asked what he meant to do, as escape was impossible, seeing that we were surrounded on every side.

"Make a glorious end, Macumazahn," he said with a smile. "I will go out with those who cling to me, that is with all who remain of my men, since my fate must be theirs, and stand back to back on yonder mound and there wait till these dogs of the King come up against us. Watch a while, Macumazahn, and see how Umslopogaas, Bearer of the Axe, and the warriors of the Axe can fight and die."

Now I was silent for I knew not what to say. There we all stood silent, while minute by minute I watched the shadow creeping forward towards a mark that the head messenger had made with his spear upon the ground, for he had said that when it touched that mark he would return for his answer.

In this rather dreadful silence I heard a dry little cough, which I knew came from the throat of Hans, and to be his method of indicating that he had a remark to make.

"What is it?" I asked with irritation, for it was annoying to see him seated there on the ground fanning himself with the remains of a hat and staring vacantly at the sky.

"Nothing, Baas, or rather, only this, Baas: Those hyenas of Zulus are even more afraid of the Great Medicine than were the cannibals up north, since the maker of it is nearer to them, Baas. You remember, Baas, they knelt to it, as it were, when we were going out of Zululand."

"Well, what of it, now that we are going into Zululand?" I inquired sharply. "Do you want me to show it to them?"

"No, Baas. What is the use, seeing that they are ready to let you pass, also the Lady Sad-Eyes, and me and the cattle with the driver and voorlooper, which is better still, and all the other goods. So what have you to gain by showing them the medicine? But perchance if it were on the neck of Umslopogaas and he showed it to them and brought it to their minds that those who touch him who is in the shadow of Zikali's Great Medicine, or aught that is his, die within three moons in this way or in that—well, Baas, who knows?" and again he coughed drily and stared up at the sky.

I translated what Hans had said in Dutch to Umslopogaas, who remarked indifferently,

"This little yellow man is well named Light-in-Darkness; at least the plan can be tried—if it fails there is always time to die."

So thinking that this was an occasion on which I might properly do so, for the first time I took off the talisman which I had worn for so long, and Umslopogaas put it over his head and hid it beneath his blanket.

A little while later the messengers returned and this time the captain himself came with them, as he said to greet me, for I knew him slightly and once we had dealt together about some cattle. After a friendly chat he turned to the matter of Umslopogaas, explaining the case at some length. I said that I quite understood his position but that it was a very awkward thing to interfere with a man who was the actual wearer of the Great Medicine of Zikali itself. When the captain heard this his eyes almost started out of his head.

"The Great Medicine of the Opener-of-Roads!" he exclaimed. "Oh, now I understand why this Chief of the People of the Axe is unconquerable—such a wizard that no one is able to kill him."

"Yes," I replied, "and you remember, do you not, that he who offends the Great Medicine, or offers violence to him who wears it, dies horribly within three moons, he and his household and all those with him?"

"I have heard it," he said with a sickly smile.

"And now you are about to learn whether the tale is true," I added cheerfully.

Then he asked to see Umslopogaas alone.

I did not overhear their conversation, but the end of it was that Umslopogaas came and said in a loud voice so that no one could miss a single word, that as resistance was useless and he did not wish me, his friend, to be involved in any trouble, together with his men he had agreed to accompany this King's captain to the royal kraal where he had been guaranteed a fair trial as to certain false charges which had been brought against him. He added that the King's captain had sworn upon the Great Medicine of the Opener-of-Roads to give him safe conduct and attempt no mischief against him which, as was well known throughout the land, was an oath that could not be broken by anyone who wished to continue to look upon the sun.

I asked the captain if these things were so, also speaking in a loud voice. He replied, Yes, since his orders were to take Umslopogaas alive if he might. He was only to kill him if he would not come.

Afterwards, while pretending to give him certain articles out of the waggon, I had a few private words with Umslopogaas, who told me that the arrangement was that he should be allowed to escape at night with his people.

"Be sure of this, Macumazahn," he said, "that if I do not escape, neither will that captain, since I walk at his side and keep my axe, and at the first sign of treachery the axe will enter the house of that thick head of his and make friends with the brain inside.

"Macumazahn," he added, "we have made a strange journey together and seen such things as I did not think the world had to show. Also I have fought and killed Rezu in a mad battle of ghosts and men which alone was worth all the trouble of the journey. Now it has come to an end as everything must, and we part, but as I believe, not for always. I do not think that I shall die on this journey with the captain, though I do think that others will die at the end of it," he added grimly, a saying which at the time I did not understand.

"It comes into my heart, Macumazahn, that in yonder land of witches and wizards, the spirit of prophecy got caught in my moocha and crept into my bowels. Now that spirit tells me that we shall meet again in the after-years and stand together in a great fray which will be our last, as I believe that the White Witch said. Or perhaps the spirit lives in Zikali's Medicine which has gone down my throat and comes out of it in words. I cannot say, but I pray that it is a true spirit, since although you are white and I am black and you are small and I am big, and you are gentle and cunning, whereas I am fierce and as open as the blade of my own axe, yet I love you as well, Macumazahn, as though we were born of the same mother and had been brought up in the same kraal. Now that captain waits and grows doubtful of our talk, so farewell. I will return the Great Medicine to Zikali, if I live, and if I die he must send one of the ghosts that serve him, to fetch it from among my bones.

"Farewell to you also, Yellow Man," he went on to Hans, who had appeared, hovering about like a dog that is doubtful of its welcome; "well are you named Light-in-Darkness, and glad am I to have met you, who have learned from you how a snake moves and strikes, and how a jackal thinks and avoids the snare. Yes, farewell, for the spirit within me does not tell me that you and I shall meet again."

Then he lifted the great axe, and gave me a formal salute, naming me "Chief and Father, Great Chief and Father, from of old" (Baba! Koos y umcool! Koos y pagate!), thereby acknowledging my superiority over him, a thing that he had never done before, and as he did, so did Goroko and the other Zulus, adding to their salute many titles of praise. In another minute he had gone with the King's captain, to whose side I noted he clung lovingly, his long, thin fingers playing about the horn handle of the axe that was named Inkosikaas and Groan-maker.

"I am glad we have seen the last of him and his axe, Baas," remarked Hans, spitting reflectively. "It is very well to sleep in the same hut with a tame lion sometimes, but after you have done so for many moons, you begin to wonder when you will wake up at night to find him pulling the blankets off you and combing your hair with his claws. Yes, I am very glad that this half-tame lion is gone, since sometimes I have thought that I should be obliged to poison it that we might sleep in peace. You know he called me a snake, Baas, and poison is a snake's only spear. Shall I tell the boys to inspan the oxen, Baas? I think the further we get from that King's captain and his men, the more comfortably shall we travel, especially now when we no longer have the Great Medicine to protect us."

"You suggested giving it to him, Hans," I said.

"Yes, Baas, I had rather that Umslopogaas went away with the Great Medicine, than that you kept the Great Medicine and he stopped with us here. Never travel with a traitor, Baas, at any rate in the land of the king whom he wishes to kill. Kings are very selfish people, Baas, and do not like being killed, especially by someone who wants to sit upon their stool and to take the royal salute. No one gives the royal salute to a dead king, Baas, however great he was before he died, and no one thinks the worse of a king who was a traitor before he became a king."

CHAPTER XXV

ALLAN DELIVERS THE MESSAGE

Once more I sat in the Black Kloof face to face with old Zikali.

"So you have got back safely, Macumazahn," he said. "Well, I told you you would, did I not? As for what happened to you upon the journey, let it be, for now that I am old long stories tire me and I daresay that there is nothing wonderful about this one. Where is the charm I lent you? Give it back now that it has served its turn."

"I have not got it, Zikali. I passed it on to Umslopogaas of the Axe to save his life from the King's men."

"Oh! yes, so you did. I had forgotten. Here it is," and opening his robe of fur, he showed me the hideous little talisman hanging about his neck, then added, "Would you like a copy of it, Macumazahn, to keep as a memory? If so, I will carve one for you."

"No," I answered, "I should not. Has Umslopogaas been here?"

"Yes, he has been and gone again, which is one of the reasons why I do not wish to hear your tale a second time."

"Where to? The Town of the People of the Axe?"

"No, Macumazahn, he came thence, or so I understood, but thither he will return no more."

"Why not, Zikali?"

"Because after his fashion he made trouble there and left some dead behind him; one Lousta, I believe, whom he had appointed to sit on his stool as chief while he was away, and a woman called Monazi, who was his wife, or Lousta's wife, or the wife of both of them, I forget which. It is said that having heard stories of her—and the ears of jealousy are long, Macumazahn—he cut off this woman's head with a sweep of the axe and made Lousta fight him till he fell, which the fool did almost before he had lifted his shield. It served him right who should have made sure that Umslopogaas was dead before he wrapped himself in his blanket and took the woman to cook his porridge."

"Where has the Axe-bearer gone?" I asked without surprise, for this news did not astonish me.

"I neither know nor care, Macumazahn. To become a wanderer, I suppose. He will tell you the tale when you meet again in the after-days, as I understand he thinks that you will do.[*] Hearken! I have done with this lion's whelp, who is Chaka over again, but without Chaka's wit. Yes, he is just a fighting man with a long reach, a sure eye and the trick of handling an axe, and such are of little use to me who know too many of them. Thrice have I tried to make him till my garden, but each time he has broken the hoe, although the wage I promised him was a royal kaross and nothing less. So enough of Umslopogaas, the Woodpecker. Almost I wish that you had not lent him the charm, for then the King's men would have made an end of him, who knows too much and like some silly boaster, may shout out the truth when his axe is aloft and he is full of the beer of battle. For in battle he will live and in battle he will die, Macumazahn, as perhaps you may see one day."

[*] For the tale of this meeting see the book called "Allan Quatermain."—Editor.

"The fate of your friends does not trouble you over much, Opener-of-Roads," I said with sarcasm.

"Not at all, Macumazahn, because I have none. The only friends of the old are those whom they can turn to their own ends, and if these fail them they find others."

"I understand, Zikali, and know now what to expect from you."

He laughed in his strange way and answered,

"Aye, and it is good that you must expect, good in the future as in the past, for you, Macumazahn, who are brave in your own fashion, without being a fool like Umslopogaas, and, although you know it not, like some master-smith, forge my assegais out of the red ore I give you, tempering them in the blood of men, and yet keep your mind innocent and your hands clean. Friends like you are useful to such as I, Macumazahn, and must be well paid in those wares that please them."

The old wizard brooded for a space, while I reflected upon his amazing cynicism, which interested me in a way, for the extreme of unmorality is as fascinating to study as the extreme of virtue and often more so. Then jerking up his great head, he asked suddenly,

"What message had the White Queen for me?"

"She said that you troubled her too much at night in dreams, Zikali."

"Aye, but if I cease to do so, ever she desires to know the reason why, for I hear her asking me in the voices of the wind, or in the twittering of bats. After all, she is a woman, Macumazahn, and it must be dull sitting alone from year to year with naught to stay her appetite save the ashes of the past and dreams of the future, so dull that I wonder, having once meshed you in her web, how she found the heart to let you go before she had sucked out your life and spirit. I suppose that having made a mock of you and drained you dry, she was content to throw you aside like an empty gourd. Perchance, had she kept you at her side, you would have been a stone in her path in days to come. Perchance, Macumazahn, she waits for other travellers and would welcome them, or one of them alone, saying nothing of a certain Watcher-by-Night who has served her turn and vanished into the night.

"But what other message had the White Queen for the poor old savage witch-doctor whose talk wearies her so much in her haunted sleep?"

Then I told him of the picture that Ayesha had shown me in the water; the picture of a king dying in a hut and of two who watched his end.

Zikali listened intently to every word, then broke into a peal of his unholy laughter.

"Oho-ho!" he laughed, "so all goes well, though the road be long, since whatever this White One may have shown you in the fire of the heavens above, she could show you nothing but truth in the water of the earth below, for that is the law of our company of seers. You have worked well for me, Macumazahn, and you have had your fee, the fee of the vision of the dead which you desired above all mortal things."

"Aye," I answered indignantly, "a fee of bitter fruits whereof the juice burns and twists the mouth and the stones still stick fast within the gizzard. I tell you, Zikali, that she stuffed my heart with lies."

"I daresay, Macumazahn, I daresay, but they were very pretty lies, were they not? And after all I am sure that there was wisdom in them, as you will discover when you have thought them over for a score of years.

"Lies, lies, all is lies! But beyond the lie stands Truth, as the White Witch stands behind her veil. You drew the veil, Macumazahn, and saw that beneath which brought you to your knees. Why, it is a parable. Wander on through the Valley of Lies till at last it takes a turn, and, glittering in the sunshine, glittering like gold, you perceive the Mountain of everlasting Truth, sought of all men but found by few.

"Lies, lies, all is lies! Yet beyond I tell you, beauteous and eternal stands the Truth, Macumazahn. Oho-ho! Oho-ho! Fare you well, Watcher-by-Night, fare you well, Seeker after Truth. After the Night comes Dawn and after Death comes what—Macumazahn? Well, you will learn one day, for always the veil is lifted, at last, as the White Witch shewed you yonder, Macumazahn."

H. Rider Haggard – A Short Biography

Sir Henry Rider Haggard, KBE was born on June 22nd, 1856 at Bradenham in Norfolk, England.

More familiarly known as H. Rider Haggard, he was the eighth of ten children born to Sir William Meybohm Rider Haggard, a barrister (born, incidentally, in St Petersburg, Russia), and Ella Doveton, an author, poet and daughter of a merchant in the East India Trading Company.

Haggard was initially schooled at Garsington Rectory in Oxfordshire where he studied under the tutelage of Reverend H. J. Graham. His elder brothers, who seemed to find more favour with their father, graduated from various private schools whilst Haggard was sent to Ipswich Grammar School, saving his father a considerable sum in fees.

He failed his army entrance exam, and was therefore sent to a private crammer in London in preparation for the entrance exam to the British Foreign Office, which he appears never to have sat. However, it was during his two years in London that Haggard came into contact with a circle of people interested in the study of psychical phenomena and for which he too now developed a life-long interest together with a series of enduring friendships.

In 1875, Haggard's father used his family's connections to send him to Southern Africa to take up an unpaid position as assistant to the secretary to Sir Henry Bulwer, Lieutenant-Governor of the Colony of Natal. In 1876 he was transferred to the staff of Sir Theophilus Shepstone, Special Commissioner for the Transvaal. It was in this role that Haggard was present in Pretoria in April 1877 for the official announcement of the British annexation of the Boer Republic of the Transvaal. The official who had been nominated to read out the Proclamation lost his voice and Haggard was his replacement. It was a moment in history.

Haggard was to remain in the country for six years, during which time he served as Master of the High Court of the Transvaal and an adjutant of the Pretoria Horse.

It was here that he fell in love with Mary Elizabeth "Lilly" Jackson. He hoped to marry her once he obtained more certainty in his career path.

In 1878 he became Registrar of the High Court in the Transvaal and now the time seemed opportune to write to his father to tell him of his hope to marry. The reply from his father was uncompromising. He forbade it until his son had made a proper career for himself.

The following year, 1879, Lily married Frank Archer, a well-to-do banker.

Haggard returned briefly to England to marry a friend of his sister's, Marianna Louisa Margitson, a 21 year old, in 1880, and the couple travelled to Africa together. Haggard's years in Africa had proved, at least on a writing level, rich and inspirational for him, and while still in Natal he wrote two articles for The Gentleman's Magazine describing his experiences.

Moving back to England in (and accounts here differ as to whether it was 1881 or 1882) the couple settled in Ditchingham, Norfolk, Louisa's ancestral home. Later they moved to Kessingland and established connections with the church in Bungay, Suffolk. The marriage produced four children. A son named Jack (who tragically died at age 10 of measles) and three daughters, Angela, Dorothy and Lilias. (Lilias grew to become an author and her father's biographer.)

In England Law was to be the fulcrum of his career. However, although he studied, writing was growing in its appeal to him. His first book, Cetywayo and His White Neighbours, was an account and study of Britain's policies in South Africa.

From this point his career as a writer began to take substantial hold and with it a dramatic shift to fiction. Two years later he published his first fiction, Dawn followed in 1885 by arguably his most popular novel, King Solomon's Mines—detailing the life of the adventurer Allan Quatermain. This was followed the following year, 1886, by She: A History of Adventure, which introduced the female character Ayesha. Both characters, Quatermain and Ayesha, developed a series of books about their adventures.

The study of Law now fell away entirely. He appeared also to have a keen sense of his commercial appreciation. Rather than sell the copyright of his first best-seller, King Solomon's Mines, for a £100 fee he, instead, accepted a 10% royalty. This book is also generally accepted as the first of the Lost World writing genre.

Haggard obviously thought there were many further adventures to tell and it would be hard to find a publisher who would disagree given the start he had made. Sequels soon followed. Allan Quatermain continued his epic and swash-buckling adventures in Africa whilst the sequel to She entitled Ayesha played out her adventures in Tibet. Interestingly Haggard would later extend his characters adventures around the world with Eric Brighteyes, being the basis for an epic Viking romance.

The Haggard family lived at 69 Gunterstone Road in Hammersmith, London, from mid-1885 to mid-1888. It was here that he wrote his most famous works. His time in Africa had given him the experience and atmosphere as well as several observations and friendships of the people who would so influence his fictional characters. Chief among them were the larger-than-life adventurers Frederick Selous and Frederick Russell Burnham. Both were men of Empire and huge ambition as they helped uncover the great mineral wealth of Africa, as well as the ruins of ancient lost civilisations of the continent, such as Great Zimbabwe.

Three of Haggard's books, The Wizard (1896), Black Heart and White Heart; a Zulu Idyll (1896), and Elissa; the Doom of Zimbabwe (1898), are dedicated to Burnham's daughter Nada, the first white child born in Bulawayo; she had been named after Haggard's 1892 book Nada the Lily.

As is typical of the writing of the time his novels contain many of the stereotypes associated with colonialism, yet they also sympathise, to a degree, with the native populations. Africans often play heroic roles in the novels, although the protagonists are more often than not European. The time around the turn of the century was, after all, the great sprint to Empire by many European countries intent on gaining possessions of land, people and resources.

Three of Haggard's novels were written in collaboration with his friend Andrew Lang who shared his interest in the spiritual realm and paranormal phenomena and who was also a greatly admired editor.

Haggard's stories are still widely read today. Ayesha, the female protagonist of She, has been cited as a prototype by psychoanalysts such as Sigmund Freud (in The Interpretation of Dreams) and Carl Jung. Her epithet is, of course, "She Who Must Be Obeyed" and has for decades been used tongue-in-cheek to describe the presumed balance of influence between the sexes.

As a legacy it is easy to establish Haggard, and his pioneering work, as the author of the Lost World branch of writing and its influence of such other writers as Edgar Rice Burroughs, Robert E. Howard and Talbot Mundy. The Allan Quatermain character influenced many 'serials' in Hollywood during the 30s & 40s and can readily be seen as a template for Indiana Jones, the American archaeologist and explorer and huge box office film character.

Years later, when Haggard was a successful novelist, he was contacted by his former love, Lilly Archer, née Jackson. Lily had been deserted by her husband, who had embezzled funds and fled bankrupt to Africa. Haggard installed her and her sons in a house and saw to the children's education. Lilly eventually followed her husband to Africa, where he infected her with syphilis before dying of it himself. Lilly returned to England in late 1907, where Haggard again supported her until her death on April 22nd, 1909.

Haggard also wrote about agricultural and social reform, in part inspired by his experiences in Africa, but also based on what he saw in Europe. By the end of his life, he was adamantly opposed to Bolshevism, a position that he shared with his life-long friend Rudyard Kipling. The two had found friendship upon Kipling's arrival at London in 1889 largely on the strength of their shared opinions.

Haggard was extremely interested in the social affairs of the Country and eager to play a more active part in attempting reform. In 1895 he stood unsuccessfully for Parliament as a Conservative candidate for the Eastern division of Norfolk losing by 198 votes.

Also in 1895 he served on a government commission to examine Salvation Army labour colonies. This, and his heavy involvement in agriculture reform, led to him being a member of several further commissions on land use and related affairs, work that involved several trips to the Colonies and Dominions. This work, in part, helped lead to the passage of the 1909 Development Bill.

In 1911 he served on the Royal Commission examining coastal erosion.

He was an absorbed and dedicated writer of letters to The Times, nearly one hundred were published by them and the bibliography attached below reveals much in the range of subjects he wished to bring attention to.

He was made a Knight Bachelor in 1912 and a Knight Commander of the Order of the British Empire in 1919. Haggard was a member of several clubs including the Athenaeum, Savile, and Authors' clubs.

The district of Rider in British Columbia, Canada, was named in his honour.

Henry Rider Haggard died on May 14th, 1925 at the age of 68. His ashes were buried at Ditchingham Church. His papers are held at the Norfolk Record Office.

The first chapter of his book People of the Mist (1894) is credited with inspiring the 1912 motto of the Royal Air Force (formerly the Royal Flying Corps), Per ardua ad astra. "Through adversity to the stars" (or alternately "Through struggle to the stars") it is also used by other Commonwealth air forces such as the RAAF, RCAF, RNZAF, and the SAAF.

H. Rider Haggard – A Concise Bibliography

Novels
Dawn (1884) Published in three volumes
The Witch's Head (1884) Published in three volumes
King Solomon's Mines (1885) Allan Quatermain series
She: A History of Adventure (1886) Ayesha series
Allan Quatermain (1887) Allan Quatermain series
Jess (1887)
A Tale of Three Lions (1887) Allan Quatermain series
Maiwa's Revenge, or the War of the Little Hand (1888) Allan Quatermain series
Colonel Quaritch, VC (1889) Published in three volumes
Cleopatra (1889)
Beatrice (1890)
The World's Desire (1890) Co-written with Andrew Lang
Eric Brighteyes (1891)
Nada the Lily (1892)
An Heroic Effort (1893)
Montezuma's Daughter (1893)
The People of the Mist (1894)
Heart of the World (1895)
Joan Haste (1895)
The Wizard (1896)
Doctor Therne (1898)
Swallow: A Tale of the Great Trek (1899)
Lysbeth (1901)
Pearl Maiden (1903)
Stella Fregelius: A Tale of Three Destinies (1903)
The Brethren (1904)
Ayesha: The Return of She (1905) Ayesha series
The Way of the Spirit (1906)
Benita (1906)
Fair Margaret (1907)
The Ghost Kings(1908)
The Yellow God (1908)
The Lady of Blossholme (1909)
Morning Star (1910)
Queen Sheba's Ring (1910)

Red Eve (1911)
The Mahatma and the Hare (1911)
Marie (1912) Allan Quatermain series
Child of Storm (1913) Allan Quatermain series
The Wanderer's Necklace (1914)
The Holy Flower (1915) Allan Quatermain series
The Ivory Child (1916) Allan Quatermain series
Finished (1917) Allan Quatermain series]
Love Eternal (1918)
Moon of Israel (1918)
When the World Shook (1919)
The Ancient Allan (1920) Allan Quatermain series
She and Allan (1921) Allan Quatermain series / Ayesha series
The Virgin of the Sun (1922)
Wisdom's Daughter (1923) Ayesha series
Heu-Heu (1924) Allan Quatermain series]
Queen of the Dawn (1925)
The Treasure of the Lake (1926) Allan Quatermain series
Allan and the Ice-Gods (1927) Allan Quatermain series
Mary of Marion Isle (1929)
Belshazzar (1930)

Short Story Collections
Allan's Wife and Other Tales (1889)
Black Heart and White Heart: A Zulu Idyll (1900)
Smith and the Pharaohs (1920)

Publications in Periodicals and Newspapers
A Zulu War-Dance (July 1877) The Gentleman's Magazine
A Visit to the Chief (September 1877) The Gentleman's Magazine
Hydrophobia (letter) (3 November 1885) The Times
The Land Question (letter) (28 April 1886) The Times
About Fiction (February 1887) The Contemporary Review
Mr Rider Haggard and His Critics (letter) (27 April 1887) The Times
Our Position in Cyprus (July 1887) The Contemporary Review
American Copyright (letter) (11 October 1887) The Times
On Going Back (November 1887) Longman's Magazine
Delagoa Bay (letter) (17 December 1887) The Times
South African Policy (letter) (27 December 1887) The Times
Suggested Prologue to a Dramatised Version of She (March 1888) Longman's Magazine
Mr. Meeson's Will (18 June 1888) The Illustrated London News
The Wreck of the Copeland (18 August 1888) The Illustrated London News
Cleopatra (3 December 1888) The Illustrated London News
Hydrophobia and Muzzling (letter) (25 October 1889) The Times
The Annals of Natal (23 November 1889) The Saturday Review
Mummy at St Mary/Woolnoth's (letter) (25 December 1889) The Times

Mummies (letter) (27 December 1889) The Times
The Fate of Swaziland (January 1890) The New Review
In Memoriam (17 May 1890) Thompson's Seasons
American Copyright (letter) (5 June 1890) The Times
Mr Herbert Ward and Mr Stanley (10 November 1890) The Times
Nada the Lily (2 January 1892) The Illustrated London News
A New Argument Against Creation (19 December 1892) The Times
My First Book. Dawn. By H. Rider Haggard (April 1893) The Idler
The Tale of Isandlwana and Rorke's Drift (4 October 1893) The True Story Book
Lobengula (letter) (19 October 1893) The Times
The New Sentiment (letter) (6 November 1893) The Times
Wanted—Imagination   (25 December 1893) The Times
The Fate of Captain Patterson's Party (28 December 1893) The Times
The Three Volume Novel (letter) (27 July 1894) The Times
The Adventures of John Gladwyn Jebb (letter) (30 October 1894) The Times
Agriculture in Norfolk (letter) (30 October 1894) The Times
The Nelson Bazaar (letter) (16 February 1895) The Times
Everything is Peaceful (letter) (20 March 1895) The Times
Lord Kimberley in Norfolk (letter) (17 April 1895) The Times
The East Norfolk Election (letter) (23 July 1895) The Times
The East Norfolk Election (letter) (29 July 1895) The Times
Wilson's Last Fight (7 October 1895) The True Story Book
The Crisis in the Transvaal (letter) (2 January 1896) The Times
The Transvaal Crisis (letter) (13 January 1896) The Times
Jameson's Surrender (letter) (14 March 1896) The Times
The Rinderpest in South Africa (letter) (5 November 1896) The Times
Mr Rider Haggard and Dr Neufeld (letter) (9 January 1899) The Times
Shrinkage of Population in Agricultural Districts (letter) (9 May 1899) The Times
The South African Crisis—An Appeal (letter) (1 July 1899) The Times
Commandant-General Joubert and Mr H Rider Haggard (letter) (8 September 1899) The Times
Anglo-African Writers' Club (17 October 1899) The Times
The War (letter) (25 October 1899) The Times
Farming in 1899 (letter) (22 December 1899) The Times
Farming in 1899 (letter) (1 January 1900) The Times
Settlement of Soldiers in South Africa (letter) (5 May 1900) The Times
1881 and 1900 (letter) (2 October 1900) The Times
Farming in 1900 (letter) (1 January 1901) The Times
Central and Associated Chambers of Agriculture (letter) (6 November 1901) The Times
Small Holdings (letter) (8 November 1901) The Times
Rural England (letter) (4 February 1903) The Times
Mr Rider Haggard on Rural Depopulation (3 May 1903) The Times
Agricultural Distress (letter) (11 June 1903) The Times
The Motor Problem (letter) (24 June 1903) The Times
Fiscal Policy and Agriculture (letter) (16 December 1903) The Times
Telepathy Between a Human Being and a Dog (letter) (21 July 1904) The Times
Telepathy Between a Human Being and a Dog (letter) (9 August 1904) The Times
Mr Rider Haggard on Small Holdings (12 September 1904) The Times
Case L.1139 Dream (October 1904) Journal of the Society for Psychical Research

Mr Rider Haggard on Agriculture (22 October 1904) The Times
Mr Rider Haggard on Rural Housing (27 October 1904) The Times
The Deserted Village (letter) (25 August 1905) The Times
Decrease of Population and the Land (letter) (6 January 1906) The Times
Prevention of Cruelty to Children (3 February 1906) The Times
The New Land and Tenure Bill (letter) (12 March 1906) The Times
Garden City Association (17 March 1906) The Times
Mr H. Rider Haggard on the Zulus (19 May 1906) The Illustrated London News
To Be Proof against British Bullets: A Zulu Incantation (19 May 1906) The Illustrated London News
Housing of the Working Classes (26 June 1906) The Times
Mr Rider Haggard on Small Holdings (4 July 1906) The Times
The Unemployed and Waste City Lands (letter) (19 July 1906) The Times
Mr Rider Haggard on the Transvaal Constitution (7 August 1906) The Times
Vanishing East Anglia (1 September 1906) The Saturday Review
The Land Grabbing at Plaistow (5 September 1906) The Times
The Land Tenure Bill (22 November 1906) The Times
Publishers and the Public (letter) (19 February 1907) The Times
The Careless Children (2 March 1907) The Saturday Review
The Government and the Land (letter) (29 April 1907) The Times
Chambers of Agriculture (2 May 1907) The Times
The Government and the Land (letter) (8 May 1907) The Times
Miss Jebb on Small Holdings (15 June 1907) Country Life
Rural Housing and Sanitation Association (27 June 1907) The Times
St Thomas Hospital Medical School (28 June 1907) The Times
The Land Question (4 July 1907) The Times
A Plea for the Sitting Tennant (letter) (12 August 1907) The Times
A Literary Coincidence (letter) (19 October 1907) The Spectator
Town Planning Conference (26 October 1907) The Times
Dr Barnardo's Homes (16 November 1907) The Times
The Proposed Agricultural Party (5 December 1907) The Times
Mr Rider Haggard and Small Holdings (10 January 1908) The Times
Mr Haggard and Children's Legislation (13 March 1908) The Times
The Drink Trade and Common Sense (letter) (2 April 1908) The Times
The Zulus: The Finest Savage Race in the World (June 1908) The Pall Mall Magazine
Sparrows (letter) (18 August 1908) The Times
Sparrows, Rats and Humanity (letter) (5 September 1908) The Times
The Letters of Queen Victoria (letter) (26 November 1908) The Times
The Romance of the World's Greatest Rivers (December 1908) Travel Magazine
Afforestation. Mr Rider Haggard's View (1 March 1909) The Times
The Late Sir Marshal Clarke (letter) (13 April 1909) The Times
Mr Rider Haggard on Agriculture (27 November 1909) The Times
Mr Rider Haggard on South Africa (11 March 1910) The Times
Why? (letter) (25 April 1910) The Times
Mr Rider Haggard on Irish Agriculture (23 May 1910) The Times
Why Not? (letter) (12 July 1910) The Times
Mr Rider Haggard on Agriculture (16 September 1910) The Times
Mr Rider Haggard on Vermin (8 November 1910) The Times
Danish High Schools (21 December 1910) The Times

Sugar Beet Growing in Norfolk (6 March 1911) The Times
Rural Denmark (letter) (22 March 1911) The Times
Rural Denmark (letter) (3 April 1911) The Times
The Copyright Bill (letter) (6 June 1911) The Times
Mr Rider Haggard on Poverty. The Burden of Civilization (15 July 1911) The Times
Mr Rider Haggard and the Public Records (28 July 1911) The Times
The Farmers' Burden (1 December 1911) The Times
Egyptian Date Farm. The Financial Aspect (11 October 1912) The Times
Umslopogaas and Makokel. Sir H. Rider Haggard on Zulu Types (letter) (16 August 1913) The Times
The Death of Mark Haggard (letter) (10 October 1914) The Times
On the Land. Old Problems and New Ways. The War—and After. (15 March 1915) The Times
Soldiers as Settlers. After-War Problem for the Empire (20 August 1915) The Times
Raids by Air. Zeppelins and Zeppelins (letter) (22 October 1915) The Times
Women's Work on the Land. A Palliative in Hard Times (letter) (29 November 1915) The Times
Women on the Land. Town Girls' Unfitness for Farm Work (letter) (9 December 1915) The Times
Soldiers as Settlers. Sir Rider Haggard's Oversea Mission (2 February 1916) The Times
Soldiers as Settlers (letter) (7 February 1916) The Times
Soldier Settlers. The Future of Rural England (letter) (10 February 1916) The Times
Farewell Luncheon to Sir Rider Haggard (March 1916) United Empire
Soldier Settlers for the Empire. Offer from Victoria (18 April 1916) The Times
Sir R Haggard's Tour. Land for Ex-Service Men (22 July 1916) The Times
Sir H. Rider Haggard's Mission. Land for Ex-Soldiers (1 August 1916) The Times
Land for Ex-Soldiers. Outline of Sir R. Haggard's Report   (12 August 1916) The Times
Empire Land Settlement Deputation to the Secretary of State for the Colonies and the President of the
Board of Agriculture (September 1916) United Empire
Empire Land Settlement by Sir Rider Haggard (December 1916) United Empire
A Journey through Zululand by Sir H Rider Haggard (December 1916) The Windsor Magazine
Mr Wilson's Note. British Publicity (28 December 1916) The Times
Home Produce (letter) (22 February 1917) The Times
The Milk Supply (letter) (11 April 1917) The Times
Corn Production Bill. A National Measure (letter) (13 June 1917) The Times
A Protest and a Plea. Farmers and Meat (letter) (9 October 1917) The Times
Pig-Breeding. A Subject for Municipal Enterprise (letter) (22 February 1918) The Times
The German Colonies. Interests of the Dominions (letter) (5 November 1918) The Times
Light—More Light! (letter) (19 November 1918) The Times
A Great American. Tributes to the Late Mr Roosevelt (letter) (8 January 1919) The Times
Shut the Door (letter) (10 March 1919) The Times
Population and Housing. Emigration v Birth Control (25 March 1919) The Times
The Ex-Kaiser (letter) (11 April 1919) The Times
Empire Birth-Rate. Sir Rider Haggard on Emigration (17 April 1919) The Times
Ex-Service Men Abroad. Warnings from California (letter) (10 May 1919) The Times
Edith Cavell (letter) (16 May 1919) The Times
The Ex-Kaiser. Uncertainties of Trial (letter) (8 July 1919) The Times
Race Suicide Peril. Western Civilization Threatened (11 October 1919) The Times
The British Cinema. Production of Reputable Films (letter) (5 November 1919) The Times
Horrors on the Film. Limits of Publicity (letter) (19 November 1919) The Times
The British Museum (letter) (24 January 1920) The Times
Air Exploration and Empire (letter) (7 February 1920) The Times

The Liberty League. A Campaign Against Bolshevism (letter) (3 March 1920) The Times
Bolshevist Peril. Counter-Propaganda (4 March 1920) The Times
The Empire's Vacant Lands. Settlers and the Food Supply (14 April 1920) The Times
Films and Happy Endings. The Tyranny of a Convention (letter)   (21 April 1921) The Times
Land and its Burdens. Evil of Grinding Taxation (letter) (8 August 1921) The Times
Boy Emigrants (letter) (31 March 1922) The Times
Migration and Morals. Declining Birther Rate (7 April 1922) The Times
Labour Party's Programme. Confiscation and Class Hatred (letter) (28 October 1922) The Times
Efficient Denmark. Keeping the People on the Land (7 December 1922) The Times
The Egyptian Find. Tombs of Eighteenth Dynasty Queens (letter) (19 December 1922) The Times
King Tutankhamen. Reburial in Great Pyramid (letter) (13 February 1923) The Times
The Norfolk Dispute. A Truce while There is Time (letter) (3 April 1923) The Times
Rural Post and Telephone. Minister's Reply to Deputation (19 April 1923) The Times
Liberalism and Land Reform (letter) (1 May 1923) The Times
Small Holdings. Influence of Heredity (letter) (4 July 1923) The Times
Agricultural Parcel Post (26 July 1923) The Times
Country Houses for Sale. Empty East Anglian Mansions (letter) (14 June 1924) The Times
Plight of Agriculture (24 July 1924) The Times
Loans From the British Museum (letter) (30 July 1924) The Times
Zinovieff Letter. Mr MacDonald and a Political Plot (letter) (29 October 1924) The Times
Two Centuries of Publishing. Tributes to Messrs. Longmans (6 November 1924) The Times
Imagination and War (26 November 1924) The Times

Non-Fiction
Cetywayo and His White Neighbours (1882)
A Farmer's Year (1899)
The Last Boer War (1899)
A Winter Pilgrimage (1901)
Rural England (1902)
A Gardener's Year (1905)
The Poor and the Land (1905)
Regeneration (1910)
Rural Denmark (1911)
The Days of My Life (1926)

Film Adaptations

King Solomon's Mines
This novel has been adapted at least six times. The first version, King Solomon's Mines, directed by Robert Stevenson, premiered in 1937. The best known version premiered in 1950: King Solomon's Mines, directed by Compton Bennett and Andrew Marton, was followed in 1959 by a sequel, Watusi. In 1979 a low-budget version directed by Alvin Rakoff, King Solomon's Treasure, combined both King Solomon's Mines and Allan Quatermain in one story. The 1985 film King Solomon's Mines was a tongue-in-cheek parody of the story, with a 1987 sequel in the same vein, Allan Quatermain and the Lost City of Gold. Around the same time an Australian animated TV film came out, King Solomon's Mines. In 2008 a direct-to-video adaptation, Allan Quatermain and the Temple of Skulls, was released.

She
She has been adapted for the cinema at least ten times, and was one of the earliest films to be made, in 1899 as La Colonne de feu (The Pillar of Fire), by Georges Méliès. A 1911 version starred Marguerite Snow, a British-produced version appeared in 1916, and in 1917 Valeska Suratt appeared in a production for Fox which is lost. In 1925 a silent film of She, starring Betty Blythe, was produced with the active participation of Rider Haggard, who wrote the intertitles. This film combines elements from all the books in the series.

A decade later another cinematic version of the novels was released, featuring Helen Gahagan, Randolph Scott and Nigel Bruce. Unlike the book and the other films, this 1935 version was set in the Arctic, rather than Africa, and depicts the ancient civilisation of the story in an Art Deco style, with music by Max Steiner.

The 1965 film She was produced by Hammer Film Productions; it starred Ursula Andress as Ayesha and John Richardson as her reincarnated love, with Peter Cushing and Bernard Cribbins as other members of the expedition.

In 2001 another adaption was released direct-to-video with Ian Duncan as Leo Vincey, Ophélie Winter as Ayesha and Marie Bäumer as Roxane.

Dawn
The film Dawn was released in 1917, starring Hubert Carter and Annie Esmond.

Jess
This book was filmed in 1912, featuring Marguerite Snow, Florence La Badie and James Cruze, in 1914 with Constance Crawley and Arthur Maude, and in 1917 as Heart and Soul, starring Theda Bara in the title role.

Beatrice
The book was adapted into a 1921 Italian silent drama film called The Stronger Passion, directed by Herbert Brenon and starring Marie Doro and Sandro Salvini.

Swallow
The novel was adapted into a 1922 South African film.

Stella Fregelius
The book was adapted into a 1921 British film, Stella.

Moon of Israel
This novel was the basis of a script by Ladislaus Vajda, for film-director Michael Curtiz in his 1924 Austrian epic known as Die Sklavenkönigin (Queen of the Slaves).

www.ingramcontent.com/pod-product-compliance
Lightning Source LLC
Chambersburg PA
CBHW072057170626
46813CB00004B/1392